To the millions of women who are struggling to be caregivers, mothers,

coworkers, and spouses all at once—

and who left the workforce this past year in record numbers

(at four times the rate of men)—because women can do anything,

but they can't do everything

Praise for Chandler Baker

'Honest, timely and completely thrilling – I was so surprised
to find out who the murderer was!'
Reese Witherspoon

'Baker's caustic debut – about four women working in corporate
America who all have secrets about their new male boss – might just
make the strongest claim yet for the thriller of the #MeToo era'
Oprah Magazine

'Furious and relevant writing . . . I loved it so much'
Clare Mackintosh

'Slick, smart, fierce, it's *Big Little Lies* set against
attorneys and recast in the light of #MeToo.
Relevant, resonant and rage inducing'
Sarah Vaughan

'A barnstorming modern novel'
Evening Standard Magazine

'A fierce and funny #MeToo thriller set in the corporate world'
New York Times

'The best thrillers are those that leave us wondering if we're actually
reading fiction. Chandler Baker has given us that kind of book'
Christina Dalcher

'A witty and timely story that will make you cheer for sisterhood'
Liv Constantine

'This is a poolside treat. One of those novels you put down
reluctantly and long to get back to all day . . . A great read, brilliantly
written, in which class, betrayal and friendship take centre stage'
Daily Mail

'A clever whodunit that confronts what it's like to
be a working woman right now'
Good Housekeeping

'[Baker] captures keenly what it means to be a
modern woman in an old boys' world'
Entertainment Weekly

'*Whisper Network* manages to be provocative,
timely, and a ripping good read: A murder mystery
and a manifesto all rolled up into one'
Janelle Brown

ALSO BY CHANDLER BAKER

Whisper Network

THE
HUSBANDS

CHANDLER
BAKER

sphere

SPHERE

First published in the United States in 2021 by Flatiron, a division of Macmillan US
First published in Great Britain in 2021 by Sphere

13 5 7 9 10 8 6 4 2

A CIP catalogue record for this book
is available from the British Library.

Hardback ISBN 978-0-7515-7516-3
Trade Paperback ISBN 978-0-7515-7517-0

Printed and bound in the UK by Clays Ltd, Elcograf S.p.A.

Papers used by Sphere are from well-managed forests
and other responsible sources.

Sphere
An imprint of
Little, Brown Book Group
Carmelite House
50 Victoria Embankment
London EC4Y 0DZ

An Hachette UK Company
www.hachette.co.uk

www.littlebrown.co.uk

There are husbands everywhere. In suits, in polo shirts, in khakis and cargo shorts, flip-flops, square-toes, loafers, and sneakers, in baseball caps, with thinning hair, and sleeves rolled up, with tufts of chest hair at the neckline, with soft-mound bellies atop braided belts, in craft brewery T-shirts, with toenails in need of tending, short and tall, colorblind, with five o'clock shadows, and BABY ON BOARD stickers on their rear windshields, walking dogs with their ring fingers haloed in platinum, gold, silver, tungsten. There they are unemployed or making six figures, in three fantasy football leagues and two different text chains (meme after meme after meme), scratching their balls and applying aftershave, rifling for snacks in the pantry, watching internet porn, wearing towels around their waists and dripping water on the floor. They are better halves, partners in crime, high school sweethearts and complete assholes, roommates, deadbeats, and really great fathers.

Can you picture it? Excellent. Shall we continue?

Just a little further. You're getting sleepy now. Long breath out. That's it. Now try to *imagine*. Imagine a place, a special place, where the husbands are everywhere, yes, but instead of just putting the dishes in the sink when finished eating, they put them in the dishwasher, they carry up the items left on the stairs *and* put them away, they refill children's water glasses at 3:00 A.M. and lead sleepy toddlers back to their own beds, they write thank-you notes and dispose of the torn envelopes of read mail, they put their shoes away, they nail down plans and don't parent from the couch, they read school emails and listen to voice mails and make dinners and rinse out Keurig machines and remember to use sunflower seed butter and that gymnastics is on Tuesdays and that next week the nanny has off and that this week is a nephew's graduation. Do you have it? Very good. Now take a deep breath in, exhale. That's right. Deeper now. Just relax and imagine.

1

Nora is not in a fight with her husband.

She thinks about the phrasing conjured here: "*in* a fight." An idiosyncratic idiom dredged from her middle school years and with it a vision of long-sleeved Hollister T-shirts, chopsticks through buns, and *I'm-not-speaking-to-you-this-week*. She's thirty-five now, long past the stage of brushing her tricky curls into a cloud of frizz, but not so far that if she *were* in a fight this wouldn't be an appropriately moody, anxious, and adolescent way to describe it, especially given the number of times Hayden has asked "What's wrong?" and she has responded with "Nothing."

"Nothing" is what you say when to say "everything" would be ridiculous.

She's being a "drama queen"—that's the term for it. But only in her head, where it doesn't really count.

At a stoplight, they sit in their different silences, hers brooding, his oblivious. She's a passenger in her own SUV, Hayden the driver, as she prefers, even though, with the seat pushed way back to accommodate a thickset former rugby player, it jacks with her settings. Hayden has a bullish neck and a smattering of bald scars cut into his hairline from where he's had stitches. She finds them sexy even when she's pissed, which, as a reminder, she's not. Also, he's got a fading blue tattoo peeking out from the hair on his right forearm, and, more often than she cares to admit, she finds herself feeling proud, because she never would have guessed she'd have grown into the type of woman to marry a man with an arm tattoo.

"It's kinda far," he says, not meaning anything by it.

"It's not that far," by which she means: *Don't start with me yet.* "Look, it's on the left. Here. See?" She points out the windshield to the neighborhood's grand entrance, walls decked in hill country stone with the name DYNASTY RANCH spelled out in slanting cursive across its side. A fountain sprays a plume of water. It's, yes, a bit ostentatious, but there are worse things, aren't there?

Dynasty Ranch is an enclave community ten minutes outside of Austin's city limits, nestled into a land of self-serve frozen yogurt shops, movie theaters with enormous reclining seats, and chain Mexican food restaurants that all boast kids' playscapes. It's quite exclusive. Or at least that's what the tasteful home brochure had claimed when her secretary had dropped it into the mesh mail bin on her office desk. Really, they must have spent a fortune on advertising. Hayden grunts and steers into the left lane without using his blinker, a mistake which she hand-to-heart doesn't mention.

"We're only here to look," he says. "We have plenty of time."

Plenty of time, like the growing bulge of her stomach is a ticking time bomb, but Hayden, apparently, is happy to procrastinate for a little while before getting around to the tedious task of dismantling it. She thinks: Who in their right mind wouldn't want to neutralize the threat straight away, have time to spare on the back end, a margin of error, a cushion? While Hayden believes: It will get done.

Often, it doesn't.

He will take out the trash later. Do the dishes later. Clear the table later. She waits, she bides time, she goes with the flow, and her world goes kablooey. It's happened before. And before and before and before.

It *will* get done. But the part that he leaves out is that he'll have nothing to do with the doing. It's like he thinks their house, their toddler, their lives, are kept on track by magic. As though she is the family Rumpelstiltskin. He goes to bed and—voilà—*see, Nora? All taken care of! And, my god, woman, why are you so sweaty?*

She stews.

They follow the notice for the open house, sign staked into the ground on flimsy tongs. But the first actual home doesn't appear in Dynasty Ranch for nearly a half mile, which does seem like an awfully long way.

Vegetation is sparse. Where present, though, it's meticulously manicured, making things feel organized and stress free. When they come across a house—mansion, more like—what she imagines inside is a large, walk-in pantry with those clear plastic bins lined neatly on the shelves, the ones with vacuum-sealed tops and black chalk-pen labels denoting the type of fibrous cereal inside. That's the vibe of Dynasty Ranch on first glance.

They pass a man unloading groceries from the back of a Tahoe. He waves to them, the way that people do with passing boats.

Then—"What do you suppose happened there?" Hayden slows to a stop where on their right sit the scorched remains of a house. Black soot has been spat onto the grass and splashed up the rickety frame, but the feeling of black is all over, like Nora's looking into a hole. Yellow caution tape crisscrosses where a door would have been, and sunlight catches the shards of broken glass that have been left behind. "You think anyone was inside?" Hayden asks, pressing the button to roll down her window for a better view.

The house was probably lovely. She feels sorry for whoever lived there. And now all of it—photo albums, carefully selected furniture, artwork bought together on vacation—up in flames.

"I don't know." Nora flattens into her seat. "But we probably shouldn't *stare*."

Hayden leans into the steering wheel, staring. "Remind me to check the smoke alarms, will you?"

Nora's fingers tense at how easily her husband drops one more responsibility into her cup. *Remind him.*

She will, of course. Because she, in fact, does not want to die in a fire. But sometimes (meaning at all times, obviously) she feels as if there are no spare folds of her brain in which to cram the minutiae of their lives that she's been charged with tracking.

He eases off the brakes and the wheels begin to roll and the neighborhood resumes, as if nothing happened. A left turn and then another—stone, brick, freshly painted wood siding, each neat, picturesque, the American dream—and soon they've arrived.

2913 Majestic Grove sits on a generous corner lot. A Texas star is embossed into the smooth surface of its circle drive, a cast-iron door at its crest.

"First impressions?" Nora asks, putting on her let's-make-the-most-of-it voice.

"I don't know." Hayden climbs out of the car, puts his fists into the back of his hips, and stretches his crotch forward. "There's not much walkability."

"Where do we walk to now?" She comes around the hood of the car to meet him.

They bought their town house in the heart of Austin seven years earlier when Nora and Hayden had imagined a future strolling to brunch on South Congress, biking to work, and buying their produce from a local farmers' market. Nora had loved the cracks in the bright yellow walls, the uneven tiles, the stairs that creaked. What she never imagined was the number of times she would add "call a plumber" to her already lengthy to-do list, or the fact that her garage door wouldn't work for fourteen whole months because she had no idea what sort of person fixed garage doors, or the stark reality that after their daughter, Liv, was born, the two flights of switchback stairs would transform from charming feature into evil nemesis. All this before the accident. Before the idea of another baby in that house became wholly untenable.

"Yeah, but it's the *ability*." Hayden has kind eyes with happy bursts of wrinkles, the result of sun more than age, fanning out around the corners.

"Keep an open mind. Please," she implores. Nora has already run the math. The only way they're going to afford more space is if they make substantial sacrifices in the cool, hip location department. Given that she's never really been all that cool or hip, the decision feels relatively easy.

He takes her hand and squeezes. The fight they are not in, after all, is only in her head, and so anytime she wants she can choose to make up. Even now, for example.

On their way up the walk, a squirrel darts across their path and up into an oak tree. She watches it hunker in the branches, nose twitching. A woman in a trim blazer and a sleek, black ponytail greets them at the door. She is High Energy.

"Welcome, welcome. I'm Isla Wong." She foists a business card into Nora's hand. "Is this your first visit to Dynasty Ranch?"

According to her card, Isla is Travis County's number one selling agent, three years running! Is she really number one? If she is, then that is actually impressive. Something to be proud of. Well, she *is* proud of it. Obviously.

She leads them into the foyer, which echoes with the sound of her pointy-toed heels. Hayden arches his neck to peer up at the high ceilings.

"It is. Our first time," Nora answers. The house is even better than in the photographs, which almost never happens.

"Great, then let me tell you a little bit about our community. In Dynasty Ranch, we consider ourselves family-forward. We have a wonderful set of amenities for a very reasonable homeowners association cost. People are always surprised by all that we have to offer. We have a beautiful community pool and clubhouse, a sport court and—Hayden, do you golf?"

"Not well," he says with a chuckle. Nora doesn't think she's ever heard of a Joe Schmo who golfs well. She thinks that's why they like it so much, all equally terrible.

"I like to golf occasionally," she says, mainly because the question felt sexist directed only to Hayden and she's trying to do her part.

As for the house, it's a one-story ranch, an architectural term that, Nora has recently learned, has almost nothing to do with actual ranches. An open floor plan merges a spacious living room with a chef's kitchen. Nora can't help but linger on the oversized stainless-steel refrigerator with the extra bottom freezer space, can't resist fantasizing about an end to the avalanche of corndogs, tater tots, and steam bags of broccoli that fall on top of her every time she jiggers open her slender freezer door at home.

"There's a gorgeous golf course at the back of the neighborhood," Isla is saying. "Golf carts included. I hope you'll go see it on your way out. And Nora—may I ask what you do for a living?"

"I'm a lawyer"—she clears her throat—"and a mom." Should a Realtor be asking her what she *does* for a living? Nora is under the impression that to ask a person's profession in polite conversation is a bit of a faux pas nowadays.

Isla is probably trying to sort out whether she and Hayden can afford the place. Like a car salesman.

"Wow." Isla clasps her hands together. "What kind of law do you practice?"

"I'm a litigator. Personal injury, mostly. I work at Greenberg Schwall," says Nora.

Nora is a plaintiff's attorney, or, in more cynical circles, an "ambulance chaser." She'd always wanted—maybe as a "screw you" to her father, a philandering commercial defense lawyer—to make her path representing the little guy. Yes, as far as personal injury firms go, Greenberg Schwall is a bit "establishment," but it wasn't as if her goal had been to turn into one of those cheesy PI lawyers with billboards declaring themselves the "Texas Hammer" or the "Legal Eagle."

"I remember now." Isla touches her cheek with her gold-painted fingernail. "You're the one who went to Dartmouth. Isn't that right?"

Nora's taken aback. "Yes, but how would you—"

"The alumni network."

"You went to Dartmouth?" There's a small thrill. She hardly ever runs into East Coast grads here in Texas.

"God no, I'm not that book smart. I'm more of a *people* person. Targeted advertising. That's what I mean. I don't like to throw spaghetti at the wall. It's a waste of time." Isla beckons them farther into the home, trailing her hand over a set of built-in cabinets. "We have a very active networking group here as well that I think you might really benefit from. One of the small quirks of Dynasty Ranch is that there's an application and short vetting process conducted by the homeowners association. But honestly"—she drops to an exaggerated whisper—"I have a good feeling about you two."

So maybe the ad's claim of exclusivity wasn't all fluff.

"But I do have to show you this." Isla holds open an innovative, revolving door for them to pass through. "One of my favorite features. The dedicated playroom."

Without exaggeration, the very notion of a place for Liv's toys that is not inside her formal dining room takes Nora's breath away. She strides the perimeter of the room, Hayden following.

"I know it's a luxury, but it's so much easier to keep the home from being overrun by stuffed animals and LEGOs and plastic fruit. You get it."

And Nora does get it. The toys that multiply. Artwork that can't be tossed out. Stuffed animals and tents and miniature indoor trampolines. Contigo water bottles and sectioned-off plates and bento boxes spilling out of cabinets. With each year of Liv's life, their "cute" two-story house shrinks. And in six months a fourth family member will join, and it's like the Spangler family is part of *Alice in Wonderland* and can't stop eating the damn cake.

Next, there is the roomy master with his and hers closets and a stand-alone bathtub, a backyard already fitted with a swing set, then back to the kitchen, where Nora peeks into the walk-in pantry and recalls what it's like to fall in love.

"Remember when we used to crash these things?" Hayden murmurs in her ear. Sundays used to look different.

"What questions do you have for me?" asks Isla.

Hayden looks to Nora. She used to like that, the way he defers to her, always waiting for her to take the lead. It seemed so modern of him.

"I do like that there's a little gym already built in." Hayden pushes his hands into his pockets. "That'd be a nice plus for me."

Nora imagines herself getting "in shape," doing those Beachbody at-home workouts all the preschool moms are going on about. She could be a suburban mom, drink wine in a Yeti tumbler, that sort of thing.

"Why are the current owners leaving?" she asks.

"Wife got a fancy new job. They're moving to Princeton, New Jersey." Isla opens a folder and thumbs through a few loose-leaf sheets. She hands Hayden a glossy pamphlet in the same style as the brochure she received earlier. A group of middle-aged men play pickup basketball on the cover.

"You said 'we' earlier," Nora says. "Was that a figure of speech or—"

"Oh! I live down the way on White Mare, second house on the left. We've been here five years now. It's been a real game changer."

A game changer. Well then.

Nora's phone trills from inside her purse. "Sorry." She digs it out. "Probably our daughter's grandparents. They've got her for the afternoon."

It's not. It's the office, calling on a Sunday. She clicks the button on the side of her phone and lets it go to voice mail. But within seconds, she has a push notification from Outlook. She tilts the screen to read.

Nora, call me on my office line ASAP.

She feels her internal pressure valve turn. "Duty calls." Her smile is tight.

"I get it." Isla raises a palm like: *preach*. "Never off the clock really. If you don't mind, please sign the guestbook on the way out. Full transparency, we're fielding inquiries on this property, but let's just say I have a vested interest in making sure that this house goes to a nice family." She winks. "So don't hesitate to reach out if you have any other questions."

Nora hastily scrawls her name on an empty line, noting that they are the seventh visitors of the day. "One thing." She sets down the pen. "Do you know what happened to that house a couple blocks back?"

"Terrible house fire. Something with the electrical maybe. But don't worry. We took extra precautions and had this house preinspected with special attention to the wiring. Everything came back perfectly clean."

"That's good to hear." Hayden touches Nora's waist. "Thanks again."

"Hope you have a great, productive day" is the last thing Nora catches before stepping back out into the day's Crock-Pot heat.

⁘

Having retrieved four-year-old Liv from the in-laws, Nora spends her afternoon on the phone with Gary, a senior partner at Greenberg Schwall. The reason for Gary's frantic email turns out to be his computer, which isn't connecting to the color printer. Naturally, he thought to call Nora, given that his secretary doesn't work on Sundays. Nora uses the directory available to all attorneys at the firm, including Gary, to call the

IT hotline, then waits for a team member to call her back. During this time, she makes two separate snacks for Liv, one nutritious, one not, dumps unfolded laundry onto the kitchen table, and digs out a sticker book from a crammed craft drawer that she still needs to make time to clean out. When IT calls back, she conferences in Gary because she knows he'll be annoyed if he feels she pawned him off on support staff.

"Mommy, watch this. I can do a *trick*!" Liv tugs on her dress. Nora tries to watch as her daughter attempts, rather unsuccessfully, to stand like a flamingo. According to Nora's rough calculations, 80 percent of her parenting life is spent "watching this" while the other 20 is spent chasing Liv through the house with a brush and a hair tie begging her daughter to "please, sit still." At least it's cardio.

"Nora, are you there?" Gary's gruff on the other end.

"I'm right here, Gary. Make sure you don't have CAPS LOCK on, okay?" It's a testament to how taken care of Gary is that he doesn't consider her comment utterly condescending. "Is the light on the left side of your keyboard green?"

Gary grunts. He makes no effort to mask his frustration, which is aimed not at the computer or himself for not knowing how to use it, but at Nora and at Bruce from IT. Nora, however, is accustomed to weathering the partner's tantrums and takes it no more personally than she does her toddler's.

Meanwhile, the other half of her brain wanders, wondering where Hayden has gone. She untwists the lid of an applesauce pouch and hands it to Liv. She checks her in-box. It has begun to fill up, as it does every Sunday evening, clients and other lawyers hoping to get their requests to the front of the line come Monday. She checks the clock. Maybe an early bedtime for Liv and she can get a head start on the week's work. She's up for partner this year. She does good work. She writes persuasive legal arguments. People like her. But Nora isn't what's known as a "rainmaker." Instead, she's earned her keep by servicing the clients of the established senior partners who already have lengthy client lists. Like Gary.

Not that she hadn't planned on cultivating her own client list. Once. It's just that she reached the point in her career at which she could responsibly begin to take on her own clients at the same time she became a mother, and this convergence had so often precluded her attendance at happy hours, lawyer luncheons, and in-person continuing legal education courses that she'd all but given up. She focused on her strengths. She's content to be the brains behind the spectacle. She's reasonably sure that she has a deep-seated phobia of public speaking anyway, so it's probably for the best. She does the research, writes impressive briefs, pieces together compelling arguments, and leaves it to others to stand up in court and sell her words. Everyone knows how vital her work is. Or at least that's what she tells herself.

The call ends. Her in-box has grown again. She feels the mounting stress like an itch beneath her fingernails.

"Hayden!" she shouts, barely clinging to a note of self-control. "Hayden!" She leans deep into the two syllables. She can't help it. Her husband appears from the garage, tilting his head to remove his AirPods. "Where were you?" She sounds like a detective trying to intimidate a suspect into providing his alibi. She hates herself a little for it.

"Sorry." He pours himself a glass of water, and a stream of it drips onto the front of the refrigerator where it will leave marks on the stainless steel and a puddle on the floor. "I was just working out. I had my headphones in. Did you need me?" He takes in her face. "What's wrong?"

"What's wrong? I'm trying to do my *job* with a toddler hanging on me while you're off in la-la land." This to say nothing of the fact that she is also three months pregnant.

It hasn't escaped her notice that she managed to arrive at partnership eligibility, a year typically marked as being one of the hardest in a young lawyer's life, knocked up.

"Come on." He gives a rueful shake of his head. "Don't be like that. I didn't know. You should have come to get me. I would have been happy to help."

"I didn't know where you were." She takes a stack of opened mail and pushes it into a drawer so that she won't see it.

"I was just in the garage."

"Well, don't be," she says, turning away.

"Geez. Someone's in a mood."

She grabs a broom from the pantry and begins sweeping up the crumbs from Liv's snack. She doesn't know whether she is doing this to make a point or because the crumbs are actually bothering her. It's so hard to tell sometimes. "I'm not in a mood. I just need to work."

"Don't you think it's kind of ridiculous that they expect you to work weekends?" He watches her sweep. She isn't illustrating a point to anyone.

"They don't." She relinquishes the broom. "I just have to, Hayden. You go to work and you get to, you know, *work*. Honestly, I can't remember the last time that happened for me. I'm always dropping off Liv at school or taking off to bring her to a doctor's appointment or skipping out to buy a birthday present for one of her friends, and don't get me started on what happens when she's sick. An entire eight hours of doing my actual, paying job? That would be, like, amazing. The reason I have to work on weekends is because I have to make those hours up sometime."

Nora realizes that she could choose to gripe about Gary here and instead chooses to gripe about Hayden. There's something wrong with her. She's going to ruin her marriage if she keeps it up.

"Okay." He takes a deep breath. "Tell me what you want from me."

"I just need time." Nora sounds like a broken record. Time, time, time, she's always stressed about time. She once heard that you can choose to worry about time or you can choose to worry about money, but the good news is, you get to pick.

"We'll figure it out," says Hayden. "We'll hire more help. It'll be okay." Nora nods, but even as he says "we" she hears "you." And isn't this always his magical fix for everything? Hire more help! As if "hiring help" is as simple as ordering pizza.

He holds his arms out and she allows herself to be nuzzled into his broad chest, which smells of fabric softener and deodorant.

Her rib cage convulses. Her throat goes soupy. The volume of what lies ahead just this week threatens to drown her before she's even started swimming. And really she does *not* want to wreck her marriage.

He stretches her out to arm's length. "*I* will help out more." He lowers his chin so that his pale blue eyes are staring directly into hers. "I'll pack lunches. I'll . . . clean up Liv's room. I'll do drop-offs every day."

Gratitude rises like freshly baked bread inside of her and she is thinking, *Yes, yes, please, let's do that.*

And yet, somewhere in the back of her mind, she listens for the needling sense of déjà vu, the memory that perhaps she's heard this all before. Fool me once, that's to be expected. Fool me twice, that's love.

"Deal?" He grins crookedly, stretching out his calloused hand for her to take.

She is a believer. She has to be. For this man is the same one who forgave her for the worst thing she's ever done.

www.lexingtonpost.com

Necessity Is the Mother of Innovation

BY LEONARD CASEY

"As moms enter the workforce in record numbers, women have employed creative problem-solving to make the most of their time."

_____

Read Comments

_____

BexyFord

If by "creative" the author means working (why yes I am counting child-rearing + my paying job) seventeen-hour days then—as he puts it—problem solved! SO glad that's settled.

StronglikeMom20

LMAO, pretty sure this author thinks he wrote a feel-good piece when all this makes me want to do is sob into my leftover spaghetti. Secretly change into exercise clothes behind office doors to sneak in a quick "mat workout" in order to save the time it'd take to go to the gym? Buy wearable breast pumps to express milk while on-the-go? Bring a laptop to work through hair appointments? Excuse me while I take that mat and go nap under my desk, thanks.

Jonathan SC

Interesting that there weren't any men interviewed. Women like to act as though they are the only ones who struggle with work-life balance. Like it's their cross to bear. When, in fact, most of the men I know are shouldering 50 percent of all household responsibilities. I guess maybe it's just not new for them or it's not as trendy to talk about. But articles like these devalue the role of men at home. I would expect a more objective eye from the editorial staff here.

Neesi

Anyone else read this and think: Hold up, maybe dudes should be making 80 cents on every one of our dollars instead?

2

Nora groaned when she saw the calendar reminder for the Women's Leadership Initiative pop up just after striking SEND on her fifth email of the morning. She thought about calling in sick, but she did that two months ago and can't pull that stunt again.

The brainchild of the firm's executive committee, the Initiative is a series of monthly meetings that started a year ago. Attendance is mandatory for female associates and maybe, if anyone were paying attention, that might be a tipoff that the women at Greenberg Schwall aren't actually so keen on being initiated. Like a menstrual cycle, it has become a pain that Nora must endure with clockwork regularity.

At noon, eight women sit around a conference room table reading the emails that stack up in their Outlook accounts while they're stuck in this second-rate conference room in what feels like time-out: *Stay in there and think about how to break that glass ceiling!*

Beside her, a first-year associate opens the box lunch that's been provided by the firm from one of the local sandwich shops and inventories the usual soggy sandwich, off-brand chips, hard cookie, and paper-wrapped pickle with a disappointment Nora knows all too well. Another minute of excruciating silence and Barbara Tims at last knocks on the conference table to get everyone's attention.

"Shall we get started?" Barbara is a senior member of the executive committee. Her face is loose-jowled and colorless, framed by a female-politician haircut and clip-on earrings. Five years ago, Barbara's toast at the firm's thirty-fifth anniversary party included a "fun" anecdote about that time she took only a weekend off following her C-section. Through the grapevine, Nora's heard that Barbara tracks the amount of time the female associates take off for their honeymoons. Nora took seven days, two of them falling over a weekend, and this apparently was on the very cusp of acceptability.

"Today," Barbara announces, "we're talking about learning to embrace direct language." Barbara wraps her fingers into fists. "As women, we're programmed from a young age to couch our opinions, needs, and even facts in qualifiers." She reads with forced feeling from a handout in front of her. "We say we 'think' when really we 'know.' We use 'probably' when we mean 'definitely.' Even worse, we sit back and say nothing at all."

As a matter of fact, Nora would very much prefer to sit back and say nothing at all here. It doesn't seem fair, all the office men at their desks, billing hours and crossing things off their to-do lists.

Barbara asks them to go around the table and say two things they're good at without downplaying. Tia, the only other senior associate, says she is good at putting clients at ease and is formidable at negotiations during mediation. She says it just like that. *Formidable.* Maybe Tia doesn't have a problem with confidence after all.

When it's Nora's turn, she tells the group that she's a fast, efficient worker and that she's good at drafting colorful court motions that manage to be persuasive and not completely boring. This even gets a smile out of Barbara and gives Nora a small flush of pride, not that she'd admit to it.

Barbara crosses her ankle over her knee, splayed like a man, her slacks opening wide and exposing the bottom of her shin. "Let me pose this to the group. If a woman doesn't ask for a raise and a company doesn't volunteer one, whose fault is that?"

The first-year beside Nora finishes chewing and raises her hand. "The woman's," she answers, no qualifiers. "The company isn't required to be altruistic and it isn't a mind reader. A company is a business. Women have to take more responsibility."

Nora glances at the girl's ring finger: vacant. Sorry, but what does this first-year know about responsibility? Apparently nothing, seeing as how she wants more of it.

Nora's phone rings. She slides it into her lap to check the caller ID, an unknown local number, which she declines.

"Exactly." Barbara punctuates with pinched fingers in the same way one might throw a dart or puncture the air from a balloon. "*We* are the best stewards of our own careers. *Us.*"

Nora's phone vibrates with a text message:

> Hello, Nora! It's Isla Wong, the Realtor from yesterday's open house in Dynasty Ranch. Would you mind giving me a call back at your convenience?

Actually, Nora had been thinking about the house. Before she'd fallen asleep, she'd started a pro-con list on a scrap of paper in her nightstand. Pros: Space, one story, backyard, new, price per square foot. Cons: commute, complicity in urban sprawl, lack of charm. She's going to have to be methodical about it if she's going to motivate Hayden, who she can already tell has set himself up as a speed bump: *Not so fast, missy.*

Barbara finishes the seminar with an exercise that requires the women at the table to guess whether a man or a woman said certain lines of dialogue during a negotiation. The women at the table get all the answers right.

As she's packing up her lunch and trudging over to the too-small trash can, Nora's phone buzzes again. The same text chain as before.

> I have something I'd like to discuss.

Nora waits until she's ensconced in her office with its messy desk, undecorated walls, and towers of file crates before phoning back the telephone number.

"Nora, hi! So glad I caught you," Isla greets her.

"I'm afraid we're not ready to make an offer on the house." Nora heads her off. "We're still thinking. We haven't been looking long and my husband—"

"Oh gosh, this isn't about the house, no. Sorry." Isla sounds genuinely apologetic. "No, it's about a *legal* matter." She enunciates the word *legal* like it deserves special care. "A wrongful death case. You did say you do personal injury work, didn't you? I hope I don't have you mixed up."

For a moment, Nora feels a touch competitive. Mixed her up with whom, she'd like to know. Another buyer?

"No, no." Nora gives a little shake of her head, replacing her preconceived notions with the realization that she might have managed to network without trying to network at all. She should tell the Women's Leadership Initiative. "I mean, yes. I do."

"I thought so." There's a satisfied smack to her confirmation. "Listen, I thought I might connect you with a couple of my neighbors who have been searching for an attorney with your credentials. Would you mind?"

"Neighbors, you said?"

"Yes, but don't worry about that. If nothing comes of it, honestly, I know these ladies and they're always happy to add strong women to their network."

Nora is familiar with this phrase. *I'm looking to connect with other women, I place a premium on networking with other women like you, strong women, strong women, strong women,* and occasionally, when people are feeling cheeky, *nasty women*. Not that Nora is a skeptic, not really, but the phrasing has begun to signal something else: *This woman wants something from me.*

Nora checks her calendar, checkered with conference calls, draft deadlines, and reminders to herself that only she can decipher. But she can't think of a polite way to turn down the request. *Never burn professional bridges.* Hadn't that been one of Barbara's takeaways from an earlier Initiative meeting? "Okay," she says. "I'd be happy to meet with them." She's not making any promises.

Except by the time the call ends, she has promised one thing: to return to Dynasty Ranch tomorrow afternoon, four o'clock.

❖

"In two-hundred-and-fifty feet, turn left on Bluebonnet Parkway."

"In two-hundred-and-fifty feet, turn left on Bluebonnet Parkway."

"In two-hundred-and-fifty—"

Nora shoves her finger into the red END button on her phone, and finally the overly polite British voice falls silent.

The lights on the dash of Nora's SUV have gone berserk. It feels like they're yelling at her: *Your tire is flat!*

So that's happened.

Up until this point, the GPS Lady had projected two more minutes before her arrival at Dynasty Ranch. She'd been very *smug* about it, too.

But even then, Nora had been running late, which seems like the theme of the day. Hayden had an early meeting in the office and so school drop-off had fallen on Nora after all. She hadn't even received a celebratory bagel or some such when, with monk-like self-control, she'd managed not to say everything that popped into her head the moment Hayden told her that actually, sorry, but no, he wouldn't be able to do any of the things today that he'd promised her just *two* days ago he

| 21 |

would, and also, dear, would that be perfectly all right? A question, as if there were multiple acceptable answers.

No, honey, not okay. Can't do it. You're going to have to figure this one out.

Imagine!

She parks her car on the shoulder of a not particularly busy road and gets out to survey the damage.

She knows *nothing* about cars. It's one of the more pathetically unfeminist things about her. But what she can sort out is that there's a giant fucking nail sticking out of the black rubber and that her tire's not supposed to look quite that *floppy*.

She tries to remember the last time she'd renewed her AAA membership. This year or last? She can't find the card in her wallet, but she can find three expired credit cards and an old gum wrapper in case those might come in handy.

She wriggles her arms out of her work blazer and rests it on the hood. The Texas weather has made its leap from winter straight into summer. This is the twenty-first century. She should be able to figure *this* out, for Christ's sake. A tire store won't work. She's too far into pancake territory to make it there. She could call Hayden, but he'd gone on and on about his busy day. So she'll have to call a tow truck instead. That means waiting for an hour at least.

And this is the problem with being stretched so thin. She's constantly on the verge of disaster. She feels it now, coming for her. A landslide over her lungs. Call in the National Guard. She's heard the saying: I didn't know whether to scream or laugh. Nora knows exactly which she wants to do.

Because she still wants to get back to the office in time to finish Gary's draft motion and to review a diligence project and to order groceries in time for delivery tomorrow and—

She turns at the sound of an approaching engine. It belongs to a silver Volvo. She side-eyes the man behind the steering wheel as he parks directly behind her. He looks like a normal middle-aged father, which is to say that he doesn't look like someone who's going to kill her and chop her body up into tiny pieces, but that's what they'd said about Ted Bundy, too.

"Need a hand?" The man in the Volvo gets out of his car. It occurs to her too late that pregnant women are always the ones getting murdered. Though she doesn't look very pregnant, does she?

She considers waving him off, telling him that help is on the way when it's not.

"My tire's flat," she calls out. But Ted Bundy definitely didn't have a Volvo. And besides, she's desperate. "I ran over a nail. Pretty sure it's a goner."

The man is slender with an impressive head full of graying blond hair that flops down to nearly chin length. He bends at the waist and pats her tire. "I can put on the spare for you. At least get you home."

"You could do that? Really?"

He smiles at her. A beat. "Of course. I'm always happy to help."

"That's amazing." She thinks better of hugging him. "And out of curiosity, how long would something like that take?"

"I should be able to get you back on the road in, oh, about thirty minutes."

She'd been hoping for fifteen but tries not to let her disappointment show. "That'd be fantastic. Thank you. Thank you so much."

The man gets straight to work. No small talk. There's a hiccup when the spare isn't located beneath the trunk board, but is instead below the car's undercarriage. He has to lie on his back in the dirt.

There are nice people, Nora thinks with a little too much surprise. Maybe this is how it is in the suburbs. Maybe she's been unfairly prejudiced.

The man—it's too late to ask his name—looks up and wipes sweat from his forehead, leaving behind a streak of dirt. "Could you give me the time?" he asks.

She taps her screen. "Almost four o'clock."

A string of cars passes by, whipping hot air into their faces.

"Four?" he says.

She nods. "Is that a problem?" A niggle of fear that she's about to be abandoned with her SUV still dangling above ground like that.

"No." He grunts, tightening more quickly now. "It's just—my wife. She's expecting me."

"Oh. Do you two have big plans?" She's going to feel terrible if she is the random idiot who screws up their date night.

His cheeks pinch as he exerts force on the wrench again. "I need to do the grocery shopping and pick up the dry cleaning in time to fold the laundry." He speaks fast, a touch of nerves creeping in.

"Right," she answers, slowly, watching him. He's going to throw his back out if he's not careful. "Got it. But, you know, I'm sure she'll understand."

He crawls to his feet. "That ought to do it." This time, he checks his own phone. Immediately, he starts back toward his car.

"Please." She follows after. "Let me give you some money."

He throws the tools into his trunk. "I really have to get going. It's important."

"Important," she repeats, sounding it out. Maybe there's more to the story. "Well, at least let me put in a good word with your wife. I could give her a call or—"

"No, no." He's behind the steering wheel already. "That's not necessary. Glad I could help. Take care now."

"Right. Okay then. I guess I'll just—"

The Volvo peels away, kicking up a cloud of dust. She considers jotting down his license plate, but doesn't know what she'd do with it exactly. Hunt him down and send him an aggressive fruit basket?

And so, instead, she gets back into her own car and continues down the road to Dynasty Ranch.

3

Nora climbs the stone steps to a house not unlike the other large-scale homes in the neighborhood, but with a more inviting and lived-in quality to it. Ivy grows on front porch columns. Geraniums tumble out of pots. Wind chimes ring softly from a shade tree beside a hummingbird feeder.

She presses the doorbell—Nora always has a piece of Scotch tape over her own, right beneath a bleeding Post-it message that reads SHHHH! DON'T WAKE THE BABY! Liv's four now.

The door crackles open, breaking the weather seal, and, on the other side, there stands a wiry man with snow-white hair. "I might have the wrong house," says Nora, fishing to pull up the address she was given. "I'm looking for Cornelia White?"

"You must be Nora." He nods once. He has the regal air of a greyhound. "Please! Come in, come in. I'm Asher White, Cornelia's husband."

When she steps across the threshold she spots a flood of discarded items cluttering the hallway behind him. An absolute volcano of a mess. "I'm sorry," she says, tugging her shirt away from where it's sticking to her stomach. "I've caught you in the middle of something."

Asher glances back, wiping his hands on his trousers. "The innards of the hall closet. You've caught me mid–Marie Kondo."

Nora fumbles to stick her sunglasses into an oversize purse. She can tell she's exuding frazzled energy, has it seeping out of her pores. "Is it sparking joy?"

"Don't you just love an organized closet?" Asher answers earnestly. "It makes life so much easier. I can breathe." He inhales with the gusto of someone taking in a fine wine.

"I do actually, but it's a rare delicacy in my home."

"I understand. You're probably just like my Cornelia. She works so hard. I won't keep you. Cornelia's in the study. Down to the end and take a left." He gestures politely toward the back of the house but seems eager to return to organizing.

"Will do," she says. "Thanks." Nora takes in the oversize furniture, particularly the mirrors, leaning precariously against walls and on antique buffets. On one wall, she pauses to glance at a series of photographs. Two happy teenagers in matching graduation robes smile from separate frames. In another a family photograph featuring three children—two girls and a boy—on a ski trip.

When she hooks left, Nora hears impassioned voices. She hesitates outside, unsure of what to do.

A woman: "I'm having trouble letting go."

A different woman: "Of what?"

"Of everything," says the first, under genuine distress.

Seconds stretch out. A chair creaks. Then the second woman returns. "Lucy, wanting to have it all and needing to do it all are two very different things. We've been over this."

"I know. I know. I'm just so used to doing. You know, stuff around the house, stuff for the kids, stuff for Ed. When I'm not I sometimes feel guilty. Relieved, sure, but . . . guilty."

"Ah. That's very interesting," says the woman who is not Lucy. "Why do you think that is?"

"I don't know. It doesn't make any sense."

Nora knows she shouldn't eavesdrop, but she doesn't feel like she can interrupt *now*.

"I think I have an idea," says the second woman. "I believe you've come to value yourself based on your ability to perform. Maybe you even place value on the martyrdom of performance. Ed, let me ask you a question. What do you value about your wife?"

A third person in the room. Ed. Nora's riveted. She has no idea what Hayden would say if he were asked that. Not one clue.

"Lucy works so hard." Ed has a bit of a higher voice, like a tenor.

"Of course she does, Ed, thank you for acknowledging that, but we're looking for something deeper here."

There's a rustle of fabric. "Lucy has a great laugh," Ed tries again. "She's a huge comfort to our children. She makes our time special at home. She's my best friend. She's extremely sexy."

It's completely involuntary, the sound that Nora makes. A cross between a cough and a pure expulsion of air. Not loud, but.

She hears a sudden clicking noise from the interior room and then everything stops. "Hello?" the woman who had been asking questions calls out.

Nora squinches—caught. She taps on the doorframe and steps out of the hallway. "Hi, it's me. Nora Spangler?" As she enters the room the first thing she notices is that no one's here except for one woman behind a desk. She wears a crisp button-down untucked over a pair of slim black jeans. Nora pegs her as early fifties, chic, with shoulder-length hair that she's allowing to go gray at its own pace. "I didn't want to interrupt."

"You're not. I was just finishing up these session notes." She points with a gold pen down at a file folder that she's been writing in. "Do you mind if I finish my thought and then—I'm sure Thea will be over any minute and we can—it'll only take a second."

"Of course." Nora clings to her purse strap and tries to make herself unobtrusive, busy in the way that makes clear she's perfectly capable of occupying herself. A clock ticks in the background—a *real* one. She never hears those anymore. *Tick, tock, tick, tock.* It makes her restless. She circles the room, keeping a polite distance from everything.

An undergraduate degree from Berkeley, followed by a master's, and an MD from Stanford, each framed and proudly mounted. A number of certificates for various courses completed, each signed by a Dr. Neha Vita, also adorn the wall. On the shelf nearby there's a photograph of a younger Cornelia in a white lab coat accepting a certificate while shaking hands with a female doctor with unkempt black hair. Awards, clear monolith sculptures with DR. CORNELIA WHITE inscribed, occupy the same real estate. *40 Psychiatrists Under 40. Trailblazers.* A grand prix of $100,000 toward cutting edge research in the field of cognitive behavioral therapy and family development. Nora frowns, impressed.

She peruses the spines of books stuffed in the case. She enjoys looking at the sorts of books other people keep. It's the only socially acceptable form of snooping.

I Know How She Does It; *The Fifth Trimester: The Working Mom's Guide to Sanity*; *Overwhelmed*; *Stretched Too Thin: How Working Moms Can Lose the Guilt.*

Well, they certainly have a theme.

Nora pulls a title from the trove of self-help books. *Burnout: The Secret to Unlocking the Stress Cycle.* She flips to a random chapter that covers the top thirteen mistakes made by couples and how to fix them.

"There. All set. Thanks for waiting," says Cornelia.

Nora closes the book with a pop. "Browsing." A slight flush rises to her cheeks. "Um, do these contain the secret then?" Three children, advanced degrees, enough career accomplishments to wallpaper a room.

"Those books?" Cornelia laughs. "God, no. A complete waste of time."

"That's . . . too bad."

Cornelia softens. "Do you know the problem with those books? Not just *those* books, but the entire industry that supports them?" Nora shakes her head. "It's that they're only read by women. And because they're only read by women, they're only *aimed* at women."

It takes a moment for this to sink in and then Nora lets out a harsh one-note laugh herself. "Sounds about right."

"Knock, knock." Another woman, who quickly introduces herself as Thea Jenkins, enters the room. *Dr.* Thea Jenkins, Cornelia corrects, which is met by an eye roll from Thea.

Dr. Thea Jenkins wears tailored hospital scrubs and pink sparkly Crocs. Her hair is sectioned off into neat cornrows and she sports gold eye shadow with cat eyeliner drawn on with surgical precision—fitting, since Thea, it turns out, is actually a neurosurgeon.

"Sit, sit." Cornelia beckons. "We don't want to waste any of your precious time." There's no sarcasm here. Cornelia seems to genuinely believe Nora's time to be limited or perhaps just expensive. The three women choose seats. Just then there are the sounds of pounding footsteps overhead and Nora is startled into a flinch. Her eyes flit up to the ceiling. Cornelia's follow. "My youngest daughter getting home. They're so *clompy* at sixteen." She pulls her attention back level and Nora is only a beat or two behind. "Anyway, as I was saying, I don't know how much Isla told you, but about a month ago, there was a terrible house fire in the neighborhood."

Nora straightens. "Yes! I saw it actually. It looked like they lost everything."

Now, as she says it, she remembers what Isla had said on the phone call. A wrongful *death* suit. And everything takes on a new meaning.

Thea brushes lint from her scrubs. "One of our dear friends' husbands was killed in the fire. Richard March." The corners of her mouth turn down and she glances away.

"And your friend?" Nora asks.

"Penny." Thea nods, eyes still trained out the window. "She was with us at the time. I had just opened a brand-new neurosurgery wing at Austin Health and was hosting a benefit to raise money that night. Penny came to support me. She and Richard were generous donors to our research."

"But he didn't come to the benefit?" She's asking out of curiosity more than anything else.

Thea's frown deepens. "He came down with something last minute. A migraine, I guess. He had to bow out. By the time we got home the house had been gutted and Richard was dead."

Cornelia pinches the bridge of her nose and takes a breath. "Sorry, it's still fresh."

Nora hesitates. She's unclear of her role here, what is being asked of her. She poses the question anyway. "And the neighbors? None of them noticed and called nine-one-one?"

Thea shrugs, but not like she doesn't care, more like her shoulders are heavy. "Many of our neighbors were at the benefit. But to answer your question, yes, one of them did. Alexis Foster-Ross. She had to leave the gala early to relieve a babysitter. But by then it was too late. The firefighters couldn't control the burn, and they, unfortunately, weren't alerted to the fact that Richard was in the home."

"I—I can't even imagine." Nor does she want to try. But just for a flash—a single blink—that day, that terrible day, punches her eyelids. Blood, bone, everything coming undone. The aftermath of the accident is this: She can *always* imagine the worst happening. It's keeping herself from imagining that's the problem. "Did they have children—Penny and Richard?" As if the tragedy isn't already large enough.

"Two," says Cornelia, recovering now. "But the youngest—Julia—she's a sophomore in college. She's gone back to campus. Everyone agreed it was for the best. We're trying to manage things for Penny without her having to get too down in the weeds, at least not more than she needs to." Cornelia looks to Thea.

Nora wonders who would do this for her if Hayden died. She *has* friends. Unfortunately, these days they feel more like the "long-lost" variety. She knows—she *knows*—she's supposed to make time for herself. She should get her nails done and have wine night and attend book club, but nobody has told her *when* precisely she's supposed to do those things, and besides, it's not as if anyone is inviting her anymore. She does still have her childhood best friend, Andi Ogsby, but since Andi became a quasi-professional expat their schedules rarely line up.

Thea hums low. "Hiring a lawyer was Penny's idea. She's already been through so much that if it were up to us, she'd wait until things settle down. But there's no telling her right now. She's hell-bent on holding someone's feet to the fire for Richard's death."

Nora nods. "So she wants to sue. The home manufacturer or the electric or gas company or the contractor, that kind of thing. Whoever is responsible for Richard's death."

Cornelia's bracelets jangle as she talks. "Truly, it's not about the money. Not for her anyway, though she does need to be thinking—"

"—financially," concludes Thea. She's not wrong. There could be significant money at stake. A nice house in the suburbs. A family man. Gone. It should count for something.

"Exactly. And she's so vulnerable right now. We don't want anyone taking advantage of her in her current state. That's why we've taken it upon ourselves to help her find the right lawyer."

Thea finds Cornelia's hand in the space between their chairs. Nora registers the squeeze, the way these two accomplished women sit side by side in this thick part of life. "It's hard to think about those things during a time like this," Thea says. "But she has to be smart. If she's going to press forward, we want it done right. We don't want her to be left—I don't know how to say this, but—"

"Empty-handed," Cornelia concludes. "So would you? Would you take the case?"

Nora's gaze travels between the two pairs of expectant eyes trained on her. "Me?"

"The last thing we want is some old cueball with a pocket square." Thea gives a dry laugh.

Nora sits back. Of course, she'd expected the meeting to be about a potential case. Maybe a request for free legal advice. People are always asking her for free legal advice. She even thought she might get a lead for a potential client. But she hadn't expected it to be so personal, so close to home—literally. "I'm flattered." And she is. She likes them straightaway. They seem both hypersuccessful and completely normal. Nothing like fucking Barbara from work.

And yet. "My husband and I looked at a house in the neighborhood. It's—well, it's not out of the running." Nora puts an apology into her voice. "Quite the opposite, I'm hoping."

"Great." Cornelia smiles. "I'm glad to hear it."

"What I mean is, I don't think I can take the case. It would be strange if I'm considering moving in just down the street."

Nora has seen so few houses that check her boxes. *A low-inventory season*, she'd read in the real estate section of the local paper. She liked the Majestic Grove house. No, she loved it. She wanted to make babies with that house. Or at the very least move there with her own.

"Strange how?" Cornelia tilts her head and Nora can imagine her listening carefully to one of her patients.

"We'd be neighbors." *Friends* is what she almost says before realizing how it'd sound.

"So?" Thea says it the same way she would say "duh."

"I'm not sure I'd feel *comfortable* representing someone in a situation where the personal and professional boundaries could so easily blur. Wrongful death cases in particular, they can get very . . . personal.

My job would be to attach a numerical value to your friend's husband's life."

Wrongful death suits are an ugly business. For starters, if she were to take on the case, it would be her job to decide who or what was responsible for the fire. That would involve opening up an investigation, poking her nose around all sorts of places it didn't belong. Under the best scenario, she'd discover a smoking gun, something to suggest that someone hadn't done their job right, preferably someone like a home manufacturer with deep pockets. And after that comes the really dirty bits, the bits where an attorney must ask: How long would the victim have lived otherwise? How much money would he have made? How educated was he? How much did he love his children? How many friends did he have? How much did he suffer when he died? How happy was his marriage?

For her troubles, Nora could take home upward of 40 percent of however much the jury decides the answer to those questions is worth.

Cornelia nods. "I see. Though it could be beneficial. Did Isla mention the application process for the homeowners association? She did? I thought so."

"Often potential members seek out a sponsor," says Thea, "someone who already lives in the neighborhood. Part of our focus on networking here. Working with Penny could give us a chance to get to know you."

"Two birds, one stone, that kind of thing." Cornelia smiles warmly.

A sponsor. Nora hadn't counted on that. "I . . . don't know." She stumbles. "I mean I could recommend you to another lawyer, be sure that you're in great hands." It's not that the temptation isn't there. She thinks back to Sunday afternoon, helping Gary with his printer problems. This could be hers. Beholden to no one. Still. She's chosen her path. And this would be not only more responsibility, but a distraction. Potentially a messy one at that.

"It's your decision, of course," Thea says. "But you should at least meet Penny. Everyone loves Penny."

And Nora thinks: *Yes, of course, because, really, what could possibly be the harm in that?*

⊞

Nora knocks tentatively on the door to Cornelia's pool house, where this Penny woman is staying. She'd expected to be chaperoned or at least introduced, but instead she's been thrust out on the errand alone.

Through the glass she can see a woman cocooned in a nest of blankets on a leather sofa. She looks up from her book, unknots her legs, then thinks better of it and beckons Nora in while folding herself back into the cushions.

"So you're the lawyer tasked with explaining the legalese to me then?" she asks, dog-earing the page and tepeeing it over one thigh. "I suggest slowly."

Penny is rosy with soft cheeks and chestnut hair. She's at least ten years older than Nora, but she sits cross-legged, thick-thighed and ample-bosomed, on the couch like a teenager. The book splayed over her leg is *The Invention of Wings* by an author that Nora thinks she's heard of before, but doesn't say so.

Nora has always considered herself a reader until recently when a hairdresser asked what books she'd enjoyed lately and—*my god*—she hadn't finished a book in over a year. Alarmed, Nora had rush-ordered the latest Oprah's Book Club pick, but now it languishes on her nightstand, making her feel guilty.

"Nora," she confirms. "It's nice to meet you." Nora gingerly takes a seat in a stuffed armchair. "Not exactly." It's harder than it should be to say no, face-to-face like this. Probably Cornelia and Thea knew that it would be. But really. There are plenty of lawyers who can take the case. Penny will be fine. "I'm very sorry for your loss. I—it's"—Nora searches—"devastating."

Penny offers a smile, as if she feels bad about putting Nora in this position. "Hard to know what to say. I get it. Actually." She brightens. "I keep trying to think of the whole thing as a letter one of my readers would write to me. Dear Penny, I lost my husband in a tragic house fire. Now, everyone treats me with kid gloves, like I might break if they mention that my husband is dead, like somehow if nobody mentions it, I might not notice." She bobs her head back and forth, considering. "As though my husband might be a word on the tip of my tongue or a train of thought I've lost, and after a second or two of scratching my head, I will turn and say, oh well, no matter, I can't remember, that's that. But . . . it's not remembering that's the problem. I'm not trying to forget. I'm trying to make sense of it. Was it my fault somehow?" She weighs with her palms facing up, a scale. "Did I do something? Is the universe random; is it preordained? *I* thought I had it all under control. What the hell happened? Sincerely, Baffled."

"You're a writer?" Nora guesses.

Pink rises to the surface of Penny's skin. "Yeah. Oh, sorry, thought you knew that part. Probably think I'm loony. Anyway, I was. An advice columnist, if you can believe it. A Penny for Your Thoughts. Don't worry, I'm not going to ask if you've ever heard of it. I hate when people ask *me* that question. You're a writer? Oh, anything I've *heard* of? Fuck you, how am I supposed to know? And why are *you* the measure of success? Like, if you've heard of me then I'm a real writer, I guess? Not *you*, you. Just—well, you know." She rolls her eyes, takes a sip from a mug with the tag of a tea bag hanging out.

"Wait," Nora says, surprising herself. "You're not the same Penny that was in the *Times*, are you?" What Nora doesn't say is that in her awkward, forced family visits to her father's house, when she was technically an adult but barely, he would insist they all sit around and read the paper on Sundays, like they were in a 1950s sitcom. He was always an asshole about those kinds of things. And Nora, for her part, would dig around for Penny for Your Thoughts, hoard it for herself, trying not to let her tears blot the pages as she sipped her oversugared coffee, experiencing what she now recognizes as catharsis.

She'd heard that the column had been turned into a book. She recalls thinking that she should buy it, but she never got around to it.

"Well." Penny scoffs, but at herself. "Admittedly, I haven't written in months. I guess if I had maybe I'd know how to respond to myself." She has a nice laugh, round, no sharp edges to it.

"There need to be Pennies for the Pennies of the world, I guess."

"Right? There should be more of us." She snaps her fingers. "A support group! These days the world is filled with people writing deep thoughts in a caption below a picture of a fucking sunset and that's supposed to be enough for us to get by."

Nora wishes she'd brought something to sip on, too. The conversation seems to call for it.

"You're thinking about what you would ask me, aren't you?" Penny says. "I know the look. It's okay. Everyone does it."

Was she? If she'd been thinking of anything, it hadn't been specific. Just the usual low-frequency buzz of her life. Lots of little nothings. Molehills into mountains.

"So." Penny nestles into the sofa seat, getting comfortable. "What would it be? Come on. Out with it."

Nora scratches her temple. "Oh. I don't know."

"Are you married?" Penny asks. Nora offers a half grin, an acknowledgment that, sure, there's more to be mined underneath this ground. "Are you a mother?" This, too, she confirms, but she can't wrap a question around either of them. She's married, not divorced. Her husband loves her. Her daughter is healthy. *Don't cry for me, Argentina*, and so forth.

Penny narrows her eyes, gives a slow, wise nod. "Okay, so something else. Professional. Should you . . . ah. Should you take on my case?" At this Nora glances sharply, because she has already decided she won't, but of course she hasn't relayed that to Penny.

Penny lifts her thin brows. She's not glamorous the way that Nora thought a writer—an author—like Penny might be.

"You have the answer for that?"

"Let's see." Penny stuffs her chin into her palm, resting her elbow on her free knee. Nora experiences a small flutter of anticipation. Penny March is going to give her advice. *The* Penny March. It's such an unexpected, delightful turn to the day's events. She's looking forward to telling Hayden, *You'll never believe who I met.* "If I were writing to you about that, I might say something about . . . about *Knowing*." Nora can sense that the word is capitalized. "Knowing which opportunities are the right opportunities to take. I could say it's a little like falling in love. I would tell you about my college boyfriend. He was a trip. Performed at being the nice guy, the sensitive guy. He wasn't either of those, mind you. I'd probably write about the abortion I had when he got me pregnant. How that wasn't the right opportunity for motherhood, not for me." Penny looks up at the ceiling as she composes out loud. Confessions were always one of Penny's hallmarks. She never just gave advice. She got down from the pulpit and waded into the mud. She made herself human, and it was always beautiful. "Then I could tell you how I fell in love with Richard at exactly the wrong time. Journalism school. We were both so ambitious, like racehorses huffing at the gates. That was the wrong time, right opportunity. One's more important than the other, see. I would tell you timing is really just a matter of volume and capacity. Neither are finite. If the ship is so full it's sinking, you might think to yourself, I can't possibly add one more thing to the deck. But what if the thing is the one that could save you? A giant telescope that will show you in which direction there's land, for instance. Then, I would tell you to throw something or someone overboard. Make room! But if all the added thing will do is sink your ship into the ocean that much faster, turn it away. We need every fucking breath on this earth." She takes a deep inhale and levels her gaze at Nora. "How's that? It's a rough draft, I know."

A patch of goose bumps rises along the back of her arm. She rubs it and deflects. "You said you haven't written in months. Why?"

"Has she gotten to you, too?" Penny asks.

"Who?"

"Cornelia." She crosses her arms, reminding Nora again of a teenager. "She keeps telling me it isn't healthy. She's trying to therapize me, thera*prist* me? Not a word. Anyhow. Says I *owe* it to myself. Just like that. *Owe.*" Penny enunciates, tries to sound fancy. "Well. It so happens that I *am* myself and I checked. Balance paid in full. Receipt printed. All good. So, yeah, I mean I think I'd know. Really, I love Cornelia, I do. She can't help that she's a shrink any more than you can help that you're a lawyer, no offense. My squirrelly little artist brain drives her bonkers. I know that. I can't help it. What were we talking about? Oh, right, whether you should take my case." She turns grave. It's like she's had a hidden trapdoor in her all along, throughout this entire conversation, and the laughter has just fallen out of her in one go. "I need a lawyer, a good one. Richard deserves that much. And if my friends believe you're the ticket, I'm inclined to believe them." Her eyes search. "So. What would you do?"

"I—" She's trying to say that she won't do anything, but that's not what Penny asked. She said what *would* you do. Nora clears her throat. "I would start by investigating what started the fire and once I did, I'd move to determining *who* is responsible for the what. And then I would make that who pay for what happened to your husband so that everyone would know to never let this happen again."

The moment lingers as Nora reminds herself sternly that she really must stop agreeing to things just because she feels bad. She's thirty-five for god's sake. And still, Nora's the first one to break, though she swears it's only because she doesn't want to sound harsh. Not after Penny's beautiful bit of advice. She'll call tomorrow after she's appeared to mull the proposal a bit more.

"I'll think about it," she says. Which feels like all she ever does, her body soggy with the thoughts that seep down into her muscle tissue and arm flab when her mind gets too, too full.

www.facebook.com

Central Tx Moms Group

1. No screenshots

2. Play nicely

3. No blocking admins

4. No solicitations or promotions

5. Posts here are to be considered opinions only, not legal advice

Anonymous Poster

Admin * 5 hours

Recently I've been super busy at work. I started a new branch of an existing brokerage firm and the low interest rates right now have made our business go crazy (in a good way). I haven't been getting much sleep because of all the extra work and I can't turn my brain off at night. I feel like there's so much to remember. Last night I got weepy, which isn't like me, but, hey, it happens. Today, though, my hubby seemed really annoyed and so I finally asked him what was wrong. He told me he didn't sign up for this. He said he feels like he's being held prisoner by my work and that I'm not spending enough time with our two daughters right now, who are six and eight. He said he'd actually prefer that I make less money and be more available. Really I'm just in a busy season. I don't think this is forever. But we did move to a new city for my job. And he works more traditional hours. I love my job and don't really want to make a change professionally. How can I make things better at home?

> **Noelle Russell**
>
> This makes me sad. We all have busy times in our careers. Growing times, I like to think of them as. In a marriage you should be able to count on your partner to step up during those times. You need support! Ask for it.

> **Rosa Falcon**
>
> Hold up. Why are you being charged with making things better at home again? This sounds like his problem, not yours.

Liz Wenzel

It doesn't sound like you're willing to compromise on much of anything. Don't you think his needs matter, too? Notice how in the movies the workaholic guy is always the jerk? That applies to women as well. I mean, you're his wife. You have to meet him halfway.

Imani Brown

You wouldn't be having this conversation if HIS job were the priority right now. Just saying.

Cornelia White

Oh, honey. This is so common at the age and stage you are in right now. Hang in there. I have to ask: Have you tried couples therapy?

4

Back home, the sound of a television wafts down from upstairs. Liv's backpack is on the floor along with her socks, which aren't even tucked into her shoes. Nora finds one pink Velcro sneaker hiding beneath the ottoman. She has no idea where the other one has landed, but knows it will drive her nuts tomorrow morning when they're running late to school. In the kitchen, she runs a wet paper towel over streaky countertops and peeks in Liv's solar system lunch box. Her nose wrinkles. She presses her sleeve to her nostrils and dumps out the slimy turkey and smashed raspberries and the half-eaten applesauce. The sight makes her pregnant stomach curdle until she's successfully pushed the mess down the drain and run the disposal.

She feels her blood pressure rising and wills it not to. She walks upstairs still in her high heels, wondering how she can be so eager to see her family, her favorite faces in the entire world, and yet also feel a horror movie–level of dread: *Don't go in there!* She can't even say that these warring emotions are in equal measure. It's more like they overlap. A perfect Venn diagram: The things she loves and those that drive her to madness are the exact same.

Hayden watches the news while Liv scribbles with a marker on a notepad.

"Is it smart to let our four-year-old draw with marker on the carpet?" Nora keeps her voice light, an honest question, but inwardly she cringes. She might have started with *hello* or *how was your day*, might have kissed him on the forehead like a good wife.

"They're washable." Hayden peers down his nose at Liv as though he has the whole situation firmly under his grasp.

"Yeah." Nora kneels and starts gently capping the markers, praying that Liv won't notice and throw a fit. "But who is going to wash the carpet?"

Hayden sighs. "How was your day? How are you feeling?"

"Fine." She sits back on her heels. "My boobs are killing me. I'm bloated. I feel vaguely sick but not too sick."

After Liv, Nora wasn't sure she wanted another child. There was already so little Nora to go around that she hadn't been able to imagine dividing herself up for another baby.

It's not like that, a friend had once told her. *You don't split your love in half when you have another kid, your heart grows to twice its size.* Which sounded lovely, if suspiciously like the end of *The Grinch*. Still, she couldn't make sense of it. Would the length of her days double alongside the size of her heart? Would she now get forty-eight hours rather than twenty-four?

So far no one has promised her that.

At some point, though, Nora had to make a decision, another baby or not, and so she did it.

"Mommy." Liv has abandoned the markers in favor of her Little People camper. "Next year I'm going to be a Giraffe and Giraffes get to sing 'Shepherd Shuffle' in the Christmas pageant. Did you know that?" She bangs the squatty, plastic people around on their pretend bunk beds.

Liv's favorite topic of conversation is her school, Trinity Fields. The subjects covered can range from what her teacher ate for lunch, which classmates are out of town, what is happening on Friday, and Spanish. Lately, though, "next year" has taken on an almost mythic quality. This year, Liv is a Monkey, next year a Giraffe. Liv feels more Giraffe-y than Monkey-ish, apparently.

After a few more minutes of playtime, Nora claps her hands and tells them, "Come on, up, up, up." And Hayden shuts off the TV and the wheels are set in motion. The sprint to the day's finish, when the house will go quiet and they can all breathe until morning, begins. "Dinner and bath. Let's go."

But there's nothing in the refrigerator, and so Hayden orders Uber Eats from his phone and they dine on mediocre Indian food half an hour later than normal. And this is how the Spangler family will go broke, one $3.99 delivery fee plus $5 driver tip at a time.

Liv whines. The evening stretches. The finish line moves.

"Did you order Liv new shoes yet?" Hayden asks.

"Not yet. It's on my list." She taps her temple.

"Okay, but we should probably, you know, prioritize this. We can't have Liv taking off her shoes every day at school. It's becoming a problem."

She experiences a tremor of agitation. "Feel free," she tells him, trying hard to remind him that she isn't the only one with a credit card in this family.

"But . . . I don't know Liv's shoe size."

Nora sighs. "I'll do it tonight, okay?" She resists the urge to scold her husband by noting that someone with a master's degree like himself might be able to work out how to locate one of the many pairs of their daughter's shoes littered around the house and check the inside for its size.

But everything's fine. Everything is normal. They're back on track. Just a little further to go. She should have taken off her bra when she got home, but now she chooses not to because it will be all the sweeter as a reward.

When it's time for bed, Liv won't agree to walk up the stairs. She goes limp and lies on the floor. "I'm too tired, Mommy. My legs stopped working."

Nora's pencil skirt is half-unzipped in the back. She's oily and needs a shower. "They do work, Liv." A vague sense of worry passes through Nora, given how often Liv pulls this routine. What if there *is* something wrong with Liv's legs? What if she *should* take her to the pediatrician? *When* can she take her to the pediatrician?

"Yes, but I'm hungry," protests Liv.

"You just ate."

Or at least she'd sat and pushed her food around for a few minutes before sliding from her chair and then crawling back onto it and then sliding back down it again, over and over and over.

"Can I have a snack?" Liv rolls onto her back and uses her entire palm to wipe a single strand of hair from her forehead. She has, in truth, the sweetest little hands, still delightfully plump at the wrists. Nora sometimes has to resist the urge to nibble them.

"Liv, no. It's bedtime."

"But I'm thirsty," Liv tries again. "I'm *starving* for thirsty."

"Starving means that you're hungry, honey."

At this, Liv rolls onto her belly, flattening her cheek to the hardwood floor that Nora hasn't Swiffered in well over a week. "Yes, I'm *starving* for *thirsty*, Mommy."

Nora stretches out her back and looks around. Where has Hayden gone to now? She swears he really is like the incredible disappearing man. They don't exactly live in a mansion and yet he's able to—*poof!*—vanish. Usually to the bathroom. He gets an inordinate amount of privacy on the toilet compared to Nora, who is almost always accompanied by Liv.

"There's a water bottle by your bed." Nora holds out her hand to Liv, but Liv is over it, over the whole evening, so at least they have that in common. There's probably some parenting trick that Nora is missing here. Or rather, this situation has probably unfolded precisely because Nora doesn't know any parenting tricks. Like, if only she'd been more consistent when Liv was three, done more time-outs or maybe fewer, or created a fucking star chart, then Liv wouldn't do this, whatever *this* is.

"That bottle is old. Yuck."

"I'll refill it." Nora gives up and scoops Liv from the ground, cradling her like a giant baby, her shirt scrunched up to show her round toddler belly. "Hayden? *Hayden?* Can you *please* help here?" Nora begins lumbering up the stairs, weighed down by her deceptively heavy daughter.

"What?" Hayden emerges at the top of the banister—when did he even *go* up there? She shoots him a look. "Okay, all you had to do was ask. The tone, Nora. Watch the tone."

She feels like a teakettle, seething through her teeth. "I turned my back for a second and then you weren't there." She thumps Liv down on the floor of her bathroom and fumbles for her toothbrush.

"Oh, come on. Don't act like I don't help you. I'm so sick of that."

"Help me? *Help* me?" Alarm bells sound in Nora's head. If she was shrill before, her pitch is piercing now. And the voice in her head goes, *stop it, stop it, stop it,* but her mouth doesn't give a fuck. "Excuse me, but why is it helping *me* exactly? How is unloading a lunch box, rinsing it, and putting it in the dishwasher helping *me?* Did I have rolled turkey, string cheese, and raspberries today? Not that I can recall. So, please, explain, because I hear this all the time. Why *is* helping around the house only considered helping *me?*" She avoids her reflection in the mirror.

He runs a hand down his face. "You know what I mean." Nora brushes Liv's teeth without taking her eyes off Hayden. "You're getting all worked up over semantics. I'm not opposing counsel, Nora. The point is I help. You act like I don't, but I do."

"Hay-den. I packed her lunch, got her dressed, took her to school, got a flat tire—"

"That's my fault, too?"

"—worked a full day, just like you, came home to a mess, unpacked her lunch—"

Nora tries to wrangle Liv onto the toilet.

"Enough with the scoreboard. Do you hear yourself?"

She does. That's the worst part. And she has never felt less sexy.

"I swear, you might as well just write it all down. A column for you, a column for me. Would that make you happy?"

It's a trick question. She's considered it. More than considered it, really. A couple months ago she started taking notes on her phone, but the thought of waving it in his face sounded so incredibly bitchy that she deleted everything and now she wishes she hadn't.

Instead, she sometimes stands at the kitchen sink, fantasizing about what would happen if she died. She doesn't want to die, but she would certainly *kill* to see the look on his face when he realized how much work she does at home.

Nora's voice is calm now. "I don't need a scoreboard to tell me that I'm winning by a landslide. Pretty sure I can just look at the field of play and see that I'm kicking your ass."

In perfect kismet, she reaches down to wipe her daughter's.

He turns away, thumping the bathroom counter, and just like that, he's disappeared again and it's her fault. If only she hadn't lost her temper she wouldn't be doing this alone.

Liv wriggles off the potty and starts to cry. "Liv! I swear!" Nora shouts, but the anger in her shreds. She kneels and helps Liv into her Pull-Ups and then leads her by her sweet little hand into her room and shuts the door.

The two of them lie over the covers on Liv's big-girl bed.

"I love you," Nora tells her, trying to breathe.

"I love you one hundred and seventy-eighty one hundred dollars," her daughter replies, with wide, wondrous eyes. Hayden's eyes, soft blue.

"I'm sorry for yelling," Nora tells her.

"You were frustrated and angry," she says, naming the emotions the way they've taught her.

Nora reaches for the books stacked at the side of the bed, but Liv's eyes are already closing, the corners of her mouth twitching. Nora lies still, staring up at the ceiling as a tear slides down her temple and onto the pillow. Her body shudders. *Oh god, quit it, will you? Hayden's not leaving you. He's not having an affair.*

But the tears squeeze out anyway.

It's mortifying actually, arguing about whether her husband takes too long in the bathroom at bedtime. Their problems are all so utterly mundane. Before she got married, she worried whether they could handle things like an affair or cancer. And now she wonders whether her reaction would be any stronger and more furious if her husband were sleeping with another woman than if he asked her again where they kept the extra paper towel rolls.

She stays as long as she needs to stay, listening to Liv breathe, before finally moving to pull the blanket over her daughter's body, over a smattering of red, shiny scars, over evidence of the way the smooth, toddler skin had been sliced apart and stitched back together, where metal pins drilled bone into bone, over everything that Nora tries daily not to notice, but tonight can't help but see.

"I'm sorry," Hayden says. "I'm trying."

Nora is tucked into their bed, her laptop propped over their old quilt.

She's pulled her unruly curls into a messy knot on the top of her head and used a brand-less wipe to clean the day off her face and neck. The seams of an oversize blue T-shirt hang limply off her shoulders. "I know," she says.

He comes to sit on the end of the bed and puts a palm over the mound of her feet. "Do you?"

Her mouth quirks. "I do."

He lowers his head and mashes the heel of his hand into one eye socket. "We both have a lot on our plates."

Some of us more than others. Her internal monologue is so miserly, never granting him an inch. She hates this about herself, wishes she could lobotomize whatever piece inside her skull she needs to in order to make it stop.

"This is what happens when two people have full-time jobs and a family," he's saying. "And a life."

She keeps her face passive, but there's a needle-and-thread pull in her stomach.

Because who said anything about a *life*? Not Nora, who definitely doesn't feel like she has much of one. Men fought wars for the right to life, liberty, and the pursuit of happiness. Rights so fundamental that men agreed it would be better to *die* rather than have those rights taken away.

But Nora isn't at liberty to ditch her responsibilities. At home. At work. Anywhere on Planet Earth. Because guess what? She is the safety net. She is the government bailout. She's the default setting. And so how can she pursue happiness when there are full Diaper Genies to empty, school loans to help pay down, and seven preschool teacher planning days a year?

"I was just angry and frustrated," she quotes her four-year-old.

"I know," he says, quoting Nora, and she clamps down on the urge to repeat his *do you?* back to him. Because before it even started, the conversation was a loop, a trap. *This is the song that never ends and it goes on and on, my friend.*

She hates the invisible barrier that thickens between them like scar tissue after these arguments. Because Hayden really is her best friend in the whole world. On car rides, they make up games. (Say: *I enjoy long walks on the beach at sunset*, but say it like you're Barack Obama. Now in a British accent. Now Irish.) She laughs till she pees a little, something that never happened before Liv, by the way. Or they get a babysitter so they can walk five miles at dusk, getting drinks and street food along the way, talking about high school and college and first loves. They go on epic searches for the best coffee in foreign cities. They take turns reading Stephen King novels out loud in bed.

She hates that it's up to her to make things normal again because she's the one with the list of grievances. And so she has to start by making conversation, has to drop that scrolling record of all the things she wants to say, all the reasons she knows she's right.

"I was in Dynasty Ranch today," she tries, thinking how she must add metaphorical baking soda to her voice to make it lighter. She reminds herself that it feels like this at first. *Fake.*

"That place where we went to see the house?" He squeezes her foot, which is sore from being stuffed into high heels all day long. It feels nice.

"Yeah." She scoots her back deeper into the pillow. "I got a call about another home there, the one we saw that had burned down. A man died, and his widow is Penny March. She's this best-selling writer. I used to read her work." She finds herself getting into it, enjoying having something interesting to tell him, something that doesn't involve Liv. "She wrote this really—I don't know—like *touching* stuff. Actually. Here. Listen to this." A tab is open on Nora's screen, a preview of Penny's book. "'Dear Penny. My husband has stopped trying at work. He makes casual remarks about how his manager has issued warnings about his performance, but he seems unconcerned with striving to meet those goals. I'm worried he may lose his job and that will put me in a tight spot, since I'm going to night school at the same time as I'm maintaining my normal nine-to-five. What do I do?'" Nora glances at her husband. "And then Penny writes . . . she says, 'When I was twenty, my college boyfriend got very sick. He had a fever so I went to the store and got him ibuprofen to bring his temperature down. He had diarrhea, so I got him Imodium. I was trying to nurse each of his symptoms and it helped, but not really. It turned out he had sepsis, which—'" Nora sees Hayden tug his phone out of the pocket of his shorts and peek at the screen, just for a second. "Well, it's long but you get the point."

"So . . . she gives relationship advice."

"I mean, not *just* relationship advice." Hadn't that been obvious? "She's kind of a big deal. Actually, the other women I met were pretty impressive, too. A neurosurgeon and a psychiatrist. Or maybe a psychologist. I never know the difference." She laughs. "There must be something in the water there. I told them we're seriously considering the house and—"

"I don't know about *seriously*." Hayden pushes himself off the mattress and pads into their adjoining bathroom, where he runs the faucet and sticks his toothbrush underneath it.

"Well I am." Nora leans forward to keep him in view. "It's the best place we've seen by far. I love it actually." She'd been pleased when he'd actually read the brochure that Isla gave him. Nora had thumbed through it, too. She'd been a tad put off by how many pictures there were of middle-aged men clinking beer glasses and laughing in golf carts. But the sports court, community clubhouse, and swimming pool had been nice. And meeting Thea and Cornelia today had eased her concerns.

"Yeah." He shrugs, starting to brush. "But, I don't know. I mean, I'm just saying that maybe we could do better."

"Hayden."

Nora begins every day scouring Redfin and Zillow for houses. "It checks all of our boxes and it's in our budget. Anyway, there's not any guarantee that we'd get it. It's a little, like, competitive I guess. There's an application process. Some potential buyers even get sponsors—or I think that's what she called it."

"So, like a sorority?"

"No, not like a sorority." It wasn't, was it? Nora's never been in one.

"You told me to keep an open mind so that's all I'm saying." Minty white foam gathers in the corners of his mouth. His words are muffled. He spits into the sink. "So? No big deal. We both just promise to keep an open mind."

"Okay." She sits back and stares at the wall on the other side of the room. Sherwin-Williams Repose Gray—she'd painted it two years ago. "Yes, sure, fine." Nora takes one more look at the excerpt on her screen and closes the laptop, tucking it beneath her nightstand.

She waits until Hayden finishes getting ready for bed and climbs in next to her. They lean together and kiss the way they do every night.

"Love you," he says.

"Love you," she echoes, and she truly does love him, loves him with her whole heart, wants to strangle him with her love, wants to love him until he's dead sometimes.

5

Nora lies in bed trying to quiet the monologue that has been running through her head for the last three hours. It had started out innocently enough—had she remembered to hit SEND on that email to Gary about the Ramirez case? A minute later—she can't forget to send the book fair order form with Liv tomorrow, it's the last day. Oh shit, there's no way she's going to remember that, shit, shit, shit, should she get out of bed and do it now?

No.

Relax. Breathe. *Peace.*

But. The more she tries to stamp out the thoughts the more they flare up. Nora is six months late scheduling her annual teeth cleaning. She's behind on her time entry at work. It's professional assistants' day next week and she hasn't scheduled a flower delivery. Friday is Moms and Muffins at Liv's school, and so it goes.

Nora becomes aware of what her face is doing. Her eyes are pinched shut, mouth pursed tight. Certainly no mystery as to why she has wrinkles in her midthirties. She wills her features to flatten, coaxes her mind to erase. But each time, after only a few minutes, she'll realize that her face has contorted into the exact same expression she had that one time she attempted a Reformer Pilates class.

Shut up, she yells at herself so angrily she nearly wants to cry. She rolls onto her back.

The older she gets the more common these sleepless jags become. She's developed a near phobia of them, and for good reason, because once one takes root there's no telling how long it will last, screwing her up for days, turning her into a zombie.

At 2:00 A.M., she can no longer lie still with the restlessness crawling around inside her legs, and so she gives in and gets up. She rummages through the medicine cabinet for the bottle of melatonin, knocking it into her hand—empty. But next to it is an amber container, the word AMBIEN neatly typed above her late mother's name. She eyes it hungrily. And with self-loathing.

Four pills rattle around the bottom. She holds up the container and swirls them around the rim. Just one and she could sleep through the night.

God how her body aches for sleep.

A few weeks ago at an obstetrician's appointment that Hayden had to miss, she'd asked her doctor as casually as she could whether taking the drug might harm her unborn baby and had been told matter-of-factly that because of a lack of studies, there was no evidence it would, but it'd still be best to avoid unless circumstances turned dire.

It hadn't been like she was planning to take it.

Nora doesn't take Ambien. Not anymore.

Gently, reluctantly, she returns it to its spot in the back of the medicine cabinet and checks the time again, realizing it's morning in Berlin.

On the couch, Nora FaceTimes Andi, who answers straightaway.

"Isn't it four o'clock over there?" Andi spoons milky cereal into her mouth, slurping through the gap between her front teeth. She's slouched in a small but sunny breakfast room.

Nora's best friend is slender with a short retro haircut and an impressive collection of overalls for a woman her age. She's an artist—a painter. Nora had always known she was good; she likes to say that she discovered her, which turned out to be important, given that Andi's own parents spent three decades trying to convince Andi that she was *not* a painter. She'd had a far easier time getting them to accept that she was gay.

"Two thirty," says Nora. "I can't sleep."

"Ah. Great. Then I can have a cup of coffee with you." A mug comes in frame and she takes a sip. "I was going to call you tomorrow, by the way."

"What for?" asks Nora, tucking herself farther into the corner of her living room sofa and pulling a throw over her knees.

"Your mother's birthday. It's on my calendar."

Nora can't believe she's nearly forgotten this, too.

She'd taken her mother's side in the divorce and never looked back. During her parents' ill-fated marriage, her mother had dedicated herself to homemaking. She was homeroom mom. She did charity work. She kept the house organized. She walked the family dog. She helped Nora and her brother, Tom, with homework around the kitchen table. She organized Trivial Pursuit nights and family vacations. Nora was all of thirteen when her parents divorced, fourteen when she learned that her dad had left her mother for his paralegal, Mrs. Frick. After that, everything was different for her mother, who hadn't worked in more than twenty years. She cobbled together odd jobs, working as a substitute preschool teacher, a hostess at a fancy restaurant, a receptionist at a law firm, where she'd first seeded her obsession with Nora becoming an attorney. *No one can ever take a law degree away from you*, her mother had told her. *You will always have something to fall back on. That's what matters.*

"She'd be really proud of you," says Andi, looking straight at her through the camera. Ever since Nora's mother passed eight years ago,

Andi has taken over the job of earnest back-patter and head cheerleader for Nora.

Nora drops her cheek into her palm. "She may get to tell me in person, seeing as how my job's trying to kill me." Tonight is a warning sign. The next few months are going to be an uphill struggle that will hopefully end in her being voted partner. She'll plan a vacation then. Somewhere tropical.

"Hayden's helping out, though, right?" Andi stirs a small spoon in her coffee.

"Yeah. He is." She sighs. "What was it like when you were with Martha?" Martha and Andi broke up last year, after being together for five. Nora had assumed they'd get married. But Andi's taking it well.

Andi tucks her knee underneath her chin. "Martha was a mess. She never cleaned up the dishes. But, you know." She points with her spoon. "It wasn't because she thought I should do it for her. It wasn't like that. Mess just didn't *bother* her."

"Right."

"I don't know," Andi continues. "I guess my brother is my closest frame of reference and, well, it's not like he's ever raised his hand to host Thanksgiving, if you know what I mean."

Nora does. It's the same reason why she and Tom hardly ever speak. When her mother had gotten sick there'd been little discussion about whose life was going to be upended. Nora called the home health-care nurses. She arranged to have groceries delivered. She set up maids to clean. She visited more often. She sent gifts with both her and Tom's names signed to them. Tom hadn't married yet. He believed—still does—that he'd done his part when he'd written the checks to pay for half of it. But the caregiving, that had mostly been Nora, all the way up until the terrible end.

At the funeral, her mother's friends had fussed over her, saying how lucky her mother was to have a daughter to care for her, and Nora didn't really understand it because didn't Tom have a mother, too?

"I'm sorry," says Andi. "But I've got to run. I'm going to be late for work. Kisses." Andi's lips take over the screen as she leans into the camera and gives it a loud smooch. "Love you."

Nora yawns and rubs her eyes. "To death," she tells her friend.

But when the call ends, she finds that she's not actually ready to return to bed.

Of all the things that had been relentlessly scrolling through her mind, she only has energy for one.

Her phone screen glows blue in the dark. She draws her elbows in and thumb-taps at the keyboard. "Fire Dynasty Ranch Richard March." Guilt corkscrews through her stomach in the moment of lag time that she spends waiting for the results to load.

A cold breeze ruffles the back of her neck. Probably just the AC vent. But by instinct, she looks up into the curtain of darkness around her. When she and Andi were teenagers, they'd once spotted a Peeping Tom leering outside of Andi's TV room. Nora still remembers his deep-set eyes and the crook of his nose pushing toward her. The shock to her heart. Andi yelled at him to fuck off and said that it was probably just some neighbor, as if that made it any better. But Nora's never quite gotten over it.

Even now, she imagines her face lit up, someone watching her from outside the window. The shutters are split open, a miniature version of herself reflecting back.

It's nothing. Just the night doing what night does.

A full page of hits pulls her attention in. She chooses the most relevant, a local news article, which she reads while pushing her knuckles into her front teeth.

Local man burned alive, autopsy reports.

Aren't people supposed to die of, like, smoke inhalation first? That at least sounds less barbaric.

She reads on with sick fascination, the way she reads about serial killers. She knows she shouldn't, and yet.

The victim's body was found lying in the home's kitchen. Apparently his limbs had become shrunken and deformed, the result of something that's called a "pugilistic stance."

"Pugilistic," she whispers into the dark, and she can't help looking it up in a medical dictionary. She learns that it's a condition caused when high temperatures cause muscles to shorten and stiffen, warping arms into a "boxer-like appearance."

The cause of Richard's death was listed as thermal injuries, his body so badly charred that they had to make a formal identification based on his dental records. It sounds bad, much worse than Cornelia and Thea had described, to say nothing of Penny, who must be completely traumatized. Her poor husband.

Nora skims a few of the later articles, rooting around for more gruesome details.

Time passes. She lets her screen darken. Her thoughts grow muddier despite her efforts to sift through them, which is probably for the best because she's already overthinking the decision she's all but made not to take the case.

She unspools. Everything will feel smaller in the morning.

Or it will feel the same.

It doesn't matter. The morning will get here either way.

6

ary calls Nora into his office at 10:00 A.M.

"Nora, good, you're here." As though he's surprised she's managed to make it into the office by midmorning. "I've invited Barbara to join us so that we can chat through a few quick issues. Do you mind?"

Nora is nearly certain that if she doesn't mind now, she will by the end of this conversation.

Barbara sits on the edge of one of the guest chairs, her knees pressed together. On her lap, a slim folder. A panorama view of the Four Seasons and Town Lake fans out in the floor-to-ceiling windows behind her back.

"Not at all." Nora takes the extra seat, trying to remember that she's not "in trouble." It's not middle school. Not that she'd ever been in trouble in middle school.

And yet. She tries to mask her efforts to take a deep breath. It doesn't help that her brain is still foggy from the night before. She needs more sleep. And probably more vegetables, if she's being honest.

Gary's stuffed leather chair squeaks as he leans back, steepling his fingers. Wispy strips of white hair bridge the expanse of aging scalp. He's probably looked like a middle-aged partner since he was two years old. "The executive committee met about the rising class of partner candidates yesterday afternoon." Nora now gives up on taking deep breaths and decides to hold all of it in, her lungs swelling. The firm won't vote on new partners for another two months, at the end of the fiscal year. "We're meeting with each of you to go over expectations and make sure we're all on the same page."

Nora calms considerably. "It feels like yesterday that I started at the firm." She smiles. She always smiles in these types of meetings. She's exceedingly pleasant at work.

"Barbara, you want to start us off?" he asks.

"I'd be happy to." The Austin legal community is filled with Barbaras and Garys, who serve as a sort of Custer's Last Stand against the city's tech takeover and its accompanying wave of Warby Parker, vape pens, office casual, and increasingly permanent flexible work-from-home arrangements. "Nora, now nothing is set in stone, but the executive committee raised a few concerns about your track record here at the firm."

The back of Nora's neck prickles. "Concerns like?"

"First of all, your billable hours." Barbara opens her folder, referencing.

"My hours have been on target, I thought." Nora feels light-headed. It's as though everything in Gary's office is getting farther away—the thin carpet, the dusty Oriental rug brought in by his wife, his daughter's wedding photo, framed atop the antique president desk.

Barbara pushes her frameless glasses back onto the ridge of her nose. "When we consider new partners, we take a bird's-eye view. We look at all of your years here."

"Okay." Nora fights a frown like she would a yawn.

"Your billable hours have fallen below the threshold in certain years, as I'm sure you're aware. For the birth of your daughter, for instance."

"I took maternity leave," Nora answers, slowly, not wanting her voice to waver. But her internal meter whizzes.

"Absolutely," says Barbara. "Twelve weeks paid out of the office. Which we *fully* support."

Fully is a strong word.

"But the hours." Nora cocks her head, trying to compute. "You're saying what exactly? That you expected me to make those hours up?"

Like they were a missed test at school.

"Not entirely," Gary tells her. "Anyway, we shouldn't get too bogged down here. There were other years. The years straddling . . . the years straddling the accident, Nora."

Her flinch is visible. More like a spasm. He may as well have fired a gunshot straight into the glass behind her.

"I—I took the time allotted from the Family Medical Leave Act." Her words rake the insides of her throat. "Not even the whole time." She has the insane urge to laugh too loud with her nostrils pulling up, a hyena bray.

"Which guarantees you a job at your same level upon return." There's a false gentleness to his tone.

Barbara clears her throat. "If I can jump in here. Nora, I'm a mom. I get it. I do. But you're not the only parent up for partnership this year."

This is true, but barely. The only other woman in Nora's class doesn't have children, and the three others are dads, and while Nora knows it'd be wrong to shout out how different that is from being a mother, she wants to all the same.

"I *know* you," Barbara continues. "You don't want special treatment. You don't want to make partner and have the conversations behind closed doors be that you made it only because you're a woman." She gives a casual roll of her eyes like the two of them are absorbed in some good old-fashioned girl talk.

"Who would say that?" Nora sputters, despite knowing that there are plenty of men in the firm—no, in this room—who already mutter sentiments along these lines and not even particularly quietly. *A bad time to be a white man,* they say. *Affirmative action, out of control.* And Nora pretends not to hear.

That aside, Nora knows the generation of lawyers before her think that associates have gone soft, that they don't want to work hard. In fact, she frequently hears Barbaras and Garys droning on about how many hours they billed back in their day.

And Nora wants to scream at them in the break room, *"Things were different!"* They billed for spending the night at the print shop, waiting for closing documents to be spat out and manually compiled. They billed the hours they slept on a plane traveling to in-person meetings. They counted the time spent driving to any number of legal libraries for archaic case law research that has now gone completely online, all while chitchatting on the road. Chitchat is now obsolete.

In contrast, for every six-minute increment of their time billed, Nora and her peers sit hunched over computers. Meetings happen on-screen. She takes calls on the evening commute. Her email chimes just before bedtime. The volume of work she can handle in a day has more than doubled since Gary was a young attorney, and yet somehow Nora's work ethic is the butt of every senior partner's joke. *Millennials,* as a punchline, stands on its own.

It's at this exact moment that the forgotten lime-size human swimming inside her uterus asserts its presence with a swell of clammy nausea. She clamps her mouth shut. And so they probably think she agrees with them.

"We need to set the right precedent here," Barbara says. "We want the best outcome for you. That's why we're being up-front. If all goes according to plan, you'll be an owner in this firm, too, and you'll be glad that someone drew the line."

Will she? Could she possibly be glad? Looking at Barbara, she prays that she won't be.

"Maybe it'd be different if you had your own clients," says Gary.

⊡

"But—"

She looks up from her hands sharply. "What if I did?" she spits out, surprising even herself.

"Did what?" Gary lets the chair swing him upright.

"Have my own clients."

"Well." He shrugs, the question he's considering still hypothetical.

Her heart beats faster. "I have a lead on a wrongful death case," she says, straightening. "A strong one. It's in a suburb nearby. There was a fire. The father of the family died. I think it could lead to more work, even. It's a good neighborhood. A lot of professionals, well connected. It could be a real watering hole." Nora's gaining steam. "I had considered not taking it, Gary, because I know how much help you need with your own caseload, but if you think I should—"

"That sounds promising." Barbara folds her hands in her lap, no longer looking at the folder. She probably thinks she's such an inspiration. Women's Leadership Initiative, following in her footsteps.

"I . . . don't know." Gary's chin tunnels into his throat.

Barbara lifts her eyebrows. "This certainly sounds like a solution to me. I'm sure you can continue to help out Gary. Nora, you need the hours, and I know the executive committee would be thrilled. Assuming that you think it's a winner."

Nora glances between them. "I do," she says, when, in truth, she has no idea.

Barbara dusts her hands together. "Great." She flips closed the folder. "Then I think this has been a very productive meeting, don't you?" They rise together, Barbara and Nora, Nora wondering what she's just agreed to.

She has always been good with promises. She doesn't tell confidences when she's asked not to. She never forgets an IOU. When she vowed to love Hayden no matter what, till death do they part, she meant it. So when Barbara says, "Promise to keep me updated?" Nora promises that, yes, she will.

⊞

The first thing Nora does when she returns to her office is order lunch— chicken noodle and a crusty baguette—to settle her stomach. Her hand is still trembling as she tries to eat her soup, and she spills a spoonful onto her gray pencil skirt.

She gives herself time that she doesn't have to recover from the meeting, to stop hearing Gary's words—*the accident, the accident, the accident*—ringing in her ears.

Once it subsides, she picks up her cell. "Cornelia? Hi, it's Nora Spangler."

"Nora! I wasn't sure if we'd hear from you again."

"A nice surprise, I hope." Though Cornelia hadn't actually sounded all that surprised. "I realized I left without getting Penny's number, so I'm hoping you can relay the message for me. Can you tell her that I'd be happy to represent her in her case? If she still wants me to, that is." Nora bites her lower lip and stares up at the ceiling. She would hate to have to go back to Gary with the news that actually Penny March had obtained alternative legal representation. "If you can give her my number and ask her to call then I can send over an engagement letter and all the necessary formalities."

"I can tell you right now she's going to be so grateful. She really liked you, you know."

It's probably a little bit sad that the idea of another woman liking her gives Nora such a thrill, but she says, "Likewise." And tries not to sound too eager.

"So," Cornelia says. "I guess we'll be seeing more of you then. Have you considered the house any further?"

"I . . . think my husband might be second-guessing it."

"Ah." There's a pause, and Nora worries the line's gone dead. Then— "You know, I just had an idea. How about the two of you come over for a dinner party at my house? We can give him the soft sell. We're very persuasive."

"A dinner party?" Nora repeats.

"My husband, Asher, is a great cook. He doesn't even need to measure. Can you believe that? I always have to measure. So. How about it? Will you come?"

Nora's poor nails. She's perpetually gnawing them off right as they start to look like they don't belong to an anxious third grader.

"I'll talk to Hayden," she says. "We'll check our calendars."

"Absolutely, looking forward to it," Cornelia replies.

And Nora feels it, the train leaving the station, the ship unmooring, the racehorse out of the gates. It's all been set in motion.

That night, Hayden doesn't make it home until after Liv has been fed and put to bed, but he does bring her a bouquet of pink and pearl buttercups. Hayden's good about flowers. She often gets them for no reason, and she knows that should make her feel very, very lucky, because there are plenty of men who think romance is sex on a Tuesday with their socks on, so.

"Not a total asshole, am I?" he teases, kissing her on the temple. (He's not.)

His lips are warm and she closes her eyes and leans into them, exhausted from the day. The worry that she won't sleep well again tonight is seeping in as she gets closer to bedtime.

"You know, you don't give me enough credit." Hayden takes his shoes off in the laundry room while she removes a vase from the cabinet, fills it with water, and snips the ends off the stems.

Nora cuts him a look that she hopes conveys the same sharpness as a vasectomy scalpel. He lifts his palm. "I do more around here than any of my friends do around their houses."

"Good thing I didn't marry them, then."

But she considers. The other day when she'd met Cornelia's husband, Asher, and he'd been voluntarily cleaning out a closet, she'd been quite tempted to come home to Hayden and rub his nose in it. But then she'd found herself thinking of it in reverse. What if Hayden came home and was like, "I walked in and Bob's wife was just giving him a blow job like she does every Wednesday." That wouldn't go over well.

But this is different. This is so very different, isn't it? Their household isn't a dick.

She lets him roll his eyes at her. She probably deserves it at least a little. She knows that she's bad with apologies and that she is rarely, if ever, the one to initiate them.

"Thank you." She displays the flowers on their countertop, fussing over the arrangement. "And I never said you were an asshole."

"Oh, I think it was implied." His delivery makes her smile. And she wonders, *Would I be funny, too? If I weren't always so damn overwhelmed?* Nora wants to sigh at herself, because even her internal questions are nagging.

She shoves him gently and before she knows it they're having sex. The good kind. And she is feeling so grateful that she still likes having sex with her husband and that he is not, in fact, an asshole and that everything is mostly, mostly fine.

Two orgasms later, she rolls onto her side and rests her hand on the wiry hair of his chest. "You know," she says. "We've actually been invited to a dinner party."

Modern Dads Do Three Times More Housework
Than Their Fathers

By Karen Pilmore

"In the wake of the #MeToo movement, men are raising their hands to share at least one area where they have clearly shown improvement: domestic life."

———————

Read Comments

———————

Francesca Beso

I don't mean to be harsh but what it boils down to for me is this: No matter WHAT a man does it won't be equal to my contribution to the family. Sorry. My husband whines at me that he takes the trash out and helps clean up and cooks a couple times a week. Look. I carried our babies for nine months each. I wrecked my body, I spent two years trying to get the baby weight off, each time. My nipples are a hot mess and I pee when I laugh. I didn't sleep a full night for six years straight and you're out here trying to be like: I carry a bag of garbage twelve feet every other day? STFU.

MILF212

@FrancescaBeso Yasssss. My partner thinks I got off "easy" because I had a planned C-section so I didn't have to go through labor pains, like labor pains are the reason women are so salty. I was literally sawed open and then had to hobble around for a month whenever I wanted to change a diaper, which guess what? I did. I fed my son sometimes twelve feedings a day even when I had mastitis—twice. I feel like my partner should have to do everything childcare related for a full year and then we'll talk.

JaniceT

@FrancescaBeso 100%. Probably nothing my husband could do could compare but it's like he's not even trying

Remy Stein

@JaniceT @FrancesaBeso Bad news: my kids are adopted and I still feel this way. My husband and I made the decision to adopt together and I figured we'd be on more level playing ground. None of that BS my friends get that the baby just wants his mommy. But I swear my husband has a supernatural ability to tune out our kids' cries. If I didn't keep a schedule of when they needed bottles, I have no idea when he'd remember they had to be fed. He's happy to do it. But little initiative.

WkingMum

Time for some elementary school math. 3 x 0 = 0. Hell, 100 x 0 = 0

Matt Lang

@WkingMom Zero?? Why the hell would any man want to do anything for you when you don't appreciate any of his hard work? You women want more help but then when men ACTUALLY step up, you criticize the way they do it, you micromanage. It's exhausting. We give up. So congratulations. You bring the situation on yourselves.

WkingMom

@MattLang But show me the lie.

7

---

ora must start at the beginning, at Richard and Penny's house.
Ground zero. And so, the following afternoon, she lets her car
crawl to a stop and unbuckles her seat belt before climbing onto
the stretch of sidewalk in front of it.

She's seen burned houses before, witnessed the way a fire can render
a family's lovingly constructed existence into a pile of strewn garbage,
but she hasn't seen any as thoroughly destroyed as the former March
home.

She'd spent the morning reading through the police and insurance
reports, but there's no replacement for legwork. She pulls a pair of ten-
nis shoes out of her trunk.

The ravaged carcass of the house rises from a black mound in the
ground. Nora pushes her knuckles into her hips and stares up at the
standing doorframe, the slope of a truncated roof, naked without its
shingles, the handful of matchsticks that suggest rooms existed inside.
The smell of ash still permeates the air, like the soggy remains of a camp-
fire. She thinks: *I signed up for this.*

The mosquitoes are out, sucking at her ankles and wrists, giving her
the willies.

She pauses in the threshold where a spot has been cleared of ash and debris. There, spray painted in orange letters, are the words BURN BABY BURN.

She presses her mouth closed. Who would have written that? And she wonders whether it was foolish to come alone.

Despite the heat, she shivers. The house is doing something to her. Setting her teeth on edge. Because beyond the empty spot left behind lies green grass, mailboxes with tin flags raised, dogs barking from fenced yards, fresh mulch. A safe neighborhood.

And so she turns her attention back to the vandalized ruins she's come to excavate. There's a crumpled beer can on the ground, but no other signs of squatters. "Hello?" she says it once and then feels silly. She can see straight through the house, nowhere to hide.

But on the remains of the fireplace there's another message scrawled in the same neon orange: DEATH TO DRONES.

The existence of the messages turns her anxious, which she imagines was more or less the author's intent. *Un-clutch your pearls, Nora*, she tells herself. *It's only graffiti.*

She sidesteps the fireplace and pulls out her cell phone, snapping pictures as she pecks through the wreckage. From her cross-body bag, she retrieves the survey print that she'd asked her secretary to pull from the property tax records, taking note of where the living room used to be, the master bedroom, the upstairs media center and office, the garage that feeds into the laundry room. She pauses there. There's a scent that's out of place. She sniffs. It smells nice. Like pine maybe. And lemon. Like her mother's old furniture polish. Like—Nora feels a wave of sadness and blames her crazy pregnancy nose for it. Hayden's always teasing her about this nine-month superpower, the way she complains about the trash can's odor when it's not even close to full or how she can tell what he's eaten for lunch. And here, the whiff of perfumed air, like a phantom of the life lived here. It's disorienting because when she looks around all she can see is how everything went so terribly wrong.

She finally ends up in the kitchen, where Richard's body had been found.

She kneels close to the ground, trying to envision the kitchen as it was. A charred refrigerator tilts on its side. Granite countertops, powdered with gray residue, are half-buried in dirt. She reads through her notes and attempts to reconstruct in her mind what must have happened.

Working backward, she knows that Richard died of severe burns. The question then is: How did it happen? *Why* did it happen?

Nora digs through the layers of dust, leaves, and other detritus until her nails scrape foundation. The floors must have been hardwood or else they'd likely still be intact. From her vantage point, she sits back and observes. She'll need to confirm whether the fireplace was gas or wood burning. Either way, it's one of the top causes for home fires. But Richard died in the kitchen. Or rather Richard finished dying in the kitchen. She shouldn't jump to conclusions. But it would seem to make the most sense for the fire to have started there. She looks up to see the stains left by black smoke on the beams.

Okay, so if she allows herself to believe that the fire started here, why wouldn't Richard make a run for it? She sees at least two, maybe even three, possible exit points, but Richard caught on fire and—what—stayed put?

Nora marks off the spot where Richard's body was found and lies down, faceup, staring at the swath of sky where a roof should be.

It hardly makes sense. Unless he was injured, unless he was incapacitated, unless he was trapped, unless there was the presence of some intervening force that she's missing. None of the reports mention one. And with the current state of the scene—burned and still dissolving under the elements seeing as what the flames didn't consume, the firefighters' hoses ruined—there won't be much evidence.

Her breathing slows. She allows herself to think like a lawyer, to analyze.

But outside the house's decaying borders, there is a *beep-beep* and then, "Hello? Hell-o-o? Is someone here?" A woman's voice.

Nora bolts upright and scrambles desperately to brush ash and god-knows-what-else from her back, hair, and ass. "Hi," she calls back. "Hi, it's me—*shit*—Nora Spangler. Sorry. Oh." She stumbles in the rubble and fragments.

A wave of dizziness yanks her sideways and she stumbles just as a woman in clear-rimmed glasses with caramel hair, stylishly colored in ombre waves, pokes her head through the gnarled doorframe.

"Who?" she asks.

Nora swallows down nausea. She shouldn't have gotten up so fast. "Nora. Spangler. I'm a lawyer working on—" She waves at the house. "All this."

"Oh, *ri-ight*, Cornelia mentioned you. I didn't realize you'd officially come on board. Alexis Foster-Ross," says the woman, extending a hand. The name pulls a mental trigger. Nora takes the woman's hand, but in doing so has to remove her palm from her forehead, which she realizes too late she's been clutching. Her vision tips and blurs.

"I'm head of the HOA here in Dynasty Ranch. Are you okay? You look . . . well, I don't have a frame of reference, so I apologize if I'm catching you on your very best day, but you look, well, you don't look great. Are you always this pale?"

"Oh," is all Nora musters, and then she sinks down, bending her knees to lower her center of gravity to the ground. Within seconds, equilibrium returns. "I'm pregnant. I must have gotten up too fast."

Nora has once again gone most of the day without remembering that she's expecting. She does feel bad about that, as though her baby is already getting saddled with "second kid syndrome." She could hardly think of anything else with Liv: *you're pregnant, you're pregnant, you're pregnant.* The words beat like a drum inside her.

Things are different now.

Nora rubs at the debris still stuck in her rowdy hair while Alexis circles her. "You know you're not supposed to lie on your back when pregnant," she says. Then—"Wow, I have no idea why I just said that. I'm not in the business of telling pregnant ladies what they should and shouldn't do. Lie on your back, don't lie on your back, eat handfuls of deli meat. Live and let live. Honestly. Here." She holds out her hand again and this time Nora uses it to pull herself up. "Come on, I live right down the street. Probably could do with a glass of water. And some air-conditioning." She fans herself. "You really are looking a little—what did my mother used to call it?—peaked. How far along are you?"

"Thirteen weeks."

"Ah. Mazel tov. First one?"

"Second."

"I just had a baby. Well, five months ago. Does that still count? And I've got another son, too. He's eight."

"I shouldn't impose." But even as she protests, Nora sees the opportunity. If Alexis is head of the Dynasty Ranch homeowners association then this could be the perfect opportunity to ask questions about the case. Not to mention parse out this application process she's heard about. "But—if it's not too much trouble," she adds just in time.

Honestly, she could use a restroom. She could *always* use a restroom these days, one of the many more joys of pregnancy.

Within a minute, Alexis ushers her into an icy blue Prius with a new-car smell and Jay-Z on the speakers. She's around forty. Not just a regular mom, but a cool mom.

Nora, on the other hand, is more of a regular mom, which is fine. She's never gotten the hang of casual dressing, always wearing too much plaid, like it's some kind of weird preschool mom uniform that she decided looked good three years ago and bought way too much of. Nora looks better dressed up. Her aesthetic is more universally flattering wrap dresses and tailored pencil skirts, which is why the trend toward work-from-home positions secretly terrifies her.

Alexis's house truly is down the street. They pull into a three-car garage. (Space, space, so much space.) "Your house is beautiful," Nora says as they exit the mudroom.

"Thanks, we love it here. I met Isla Wong at a charity luncheon six years ago. The luncheon was so dull, but by the end of it Isla had completely sold me on the place. We hadn't even planned on moving."

In the half-bath downstairs, Nora splashes water on her face and pats her cheeks dry with a scented hand towel before returning to meet Alexis, who is waiting with Brita-filtered water in a glass.

"Better?" asks Alexis. "Sorry, don't mean to rush you, but I have to log in to a team meeting in thirty minutes."

Nora tries to mask her surprise. "What do you do?"

"I'm the CEO of a tech startup in town. We're setting up a gig economy for service provider professionals. Like you, as a matter of fact. Lawyers, accountants, doctors even. We're like the Uber of people with advanced degrees. I'm a coder by trade. And now this." She smiles warmly. "We should connect. How long have you been practicing law?" Alexis turns and pulls a bag of baby carrots from the Sub-Zero fridge.

"Nine years. That's part of why I'm here, actually. I'm up for partner this year and I need to really prove myself."

"Brutal." Alexis holds out the bag of carrots for Nora to take one. Nora shakes her head without thinking. "One of my girlfriends is a partner at one of those big New York firms, but at a satellite office in Philly. Her skin literally got gray. Not that your skin is gray. It's not. I promise."

"There's still time." Nora lets half of her mouth curl up as she wraps her hand around the cool glass again.

"You went to good schools?" Alexis asks, with genuine curiosity.

Nora shrugs, surprised and disarmed by the turn of conversation.

"In my opinion. UT for law school. Before that I was at Dartmouth," she says, realizing that it's probably important that Alexis likes her.

"Grades?"

"Top twenty-five percent."

Alexis nods, like Nora has passed a quiz. "And you have a kid, you said?"

"A toddler. She's four."

"*And* you're expecting." Alexis clucks her tongue. "Wow. Big year. I'm so proud of you." Her forehead wrinkles. "Is that weird to say? That I'm proud of you? Do I sound like your grandma?"

After that Nora can't speak for a moment because of the absolutely absurd clog of emotion in her throat. Most days it feels like she's falling behind on so many fronts that no one could possibly be anything but vaguely disappointed in her. She manages a perfunctory "thanks" and changes the subject. Looking over her shoulder, back toward the front door, she asks, "Do you happen to have any idea who might have graffitied the March house?"

"Was there graffiti?" Alexis crunches into another carrot. "I didn't notice. Nothing serious I hope."

Nora hadn't thought it could be missed.

BURN BABY BURN.

"It sounded a little ominous, maybe," says Nora. "Probably nothing, though, you're right."

"We're a very low-crime neighborhood, no big shock there. We don't have any prowlers lurking about." She turns her hands into claws, looks nothing like a *prowler*. "If that's what you're thinking. People would notice. It's possible that a few teens from one of the other high schools could have heard about the house I guess. Something like that."

Alexis checks her watch and Nora knows her time is dwindling.

"Look," Nora says, deciding to drop the graffiti line of questioning, at least for now. These things happen. Alexis is right. "Feel free to say no. But, given that you're the head of the HOA, I'm looking for records, community plans mainly, areas where there might be exposed power lines, uncovered grills, dry brush, nearby campsites, backyard firepits, those kinds of things." She must first play process of elimination. "Are these something—"

Before Alexis can reply, they both turn at the sound of voices entering through the garage. A boy with a European soccer haircut bounds inside in socked feet and a jersey.

He gives Alexis a side hug and looks shyly at Nora, who waves. She's never been great with other people's kids. In fact, two months after Liv's birth, Hayden had joked with Nora's father that he hadn't been sure whether she'd take to motherhood, and her own father had laughed heartily as though this was some joke they'd all been in on. *Nora Spangler: known child hater.*

At the time, she'd been strangely pleased that she'd proven everyone so wrong that they could easily laugh about it. She loved Liv. It turned her heart inside out. But then, a little over a year later, there was the accident, and she wondered if anyone would laugh off such a remark now.

"Cruz, this is Ms. Spangler." Alexis squeezes her son's shoulder and the boy offers a closed-mouth smile in return. "She's an *attorney.*" She stresses Nora's profession in a way that makes Nora blush. "My youngest is in daycare. And this . . ." Alexis cranes her neck as in walks a man with dry cleaning flung over his back and groceries in the other hand. And not just any man, the Good Samaritan. The man who'd changed her tire. "This is Max. My husband."

"Oh my god, hi!" Nora waves and flattens her palm to her forehead like *what a coincidence.* "We actually—"

Max gives her a vanilla smile, guillotining the end of her sentence. "Hello. Nice to meet you."

Nora falters. "Hi—"

"Still a few more groceries in the car," he says. "Sorry, I'm behind schedule. I'll just be a moment. Please excuse me."

Alexis beams at Max with genuine affection and plants a kiss on his cheek as he passes.

Nora looks down as she takes a sip from her glass. *What was that?* Is it possible he doesn't recognize her? It's definitely him, isn't it?

A few moments later, he organizes the produce in the fridge, a pleasantly open expression on his face, then heads to the laundry room. Nora hears the clank of the dryer door opening.

Groceries. Dry cleaning. Laundry. That's *exactly* what he'd said. And here he is a week later, same routine.

Alexis flashes a smile, not smugly the way that Nora might have if Hayden were caught helping, just regular. "Where were we?"

Nora blinks several times. "Oh, right. The . . . the community plans." Max reappears carrying a load of laundry from the dryer. "If you have access," says Nora, trying to regain her footing while her brain careens— Should she say something again? She mentally weighs the options. Either, one, he doesn't recognize her, in which case he won't think she's rude, or, two, there's a compelling reason he wants to pretend they've never met. Her mother always warned her that she shouldn't presume to understand what goes on behind closed doors. She decides she better not risk it. "It'd save me a lot of time," Nora finishes.

"And we all know how valuable that is." A nonanswer. Alexis eyes the clock on the microwave. "Speaking of time, it's gotten away from us. I need to prep for my meeting. Let me drive you back to your car."

"It's only a block. I'm feeling much better, thanks. I can walk." Alexis looks unconvinced. Does Nora really look that awful? And here this woman had a baby five months ago and she doesn't even look tired. "I need to get my steps in." She taps the Apple Watch on her wrist. Every woman she knows is always trying to get her steps in, so who could guess that Nora isn't one of them?

"I'll walk out with you, then."

Nora feels a pang at having to leave this clean, organized space, with high ceilings and an actual backyard that isn't in desperate need of mowing. "Your family is great," Nora says, still unsettled by the interaction with Max but determined not to show it. "Does Max—What does Max do? Does he work outside the home?"

"He's a civil engineer. Brainy type." Alexis shakes her head but not in annoyance, more in bewilderment. CEO of a tech company sounds plenty brainy to Nora.

They exchange numbers, and Alexis opens the garage to let Nora out. "Thank you so much, Alexis." And it's then that the name finally fits into its slot. "You were . . ." Nora pauses. ". . . the person who called nine-one-one, weren't you?"

Alexis sucks air through her teeth. "I was. It was a nightmare. Honestly, I still haven't wrapped my head around it."

"Did you see anything? I mean you must have, or else you wouldn't have picked up the phone."

"There was a glow. When I pulled into the neighborhood just before I turned onto my street. It was so strange. Eerie, kind of. It was night so I couldn't see smoke, but I smelled it and I just knew something was wrong. I drove up a little ways further and by then the fire had already eaten into the house pretty good, and the sky was—yeah—glowing."

"Which side of the house?" Nora asks.

"Both I think." She squints one eye shut, thinking. "I don't know. The one closest to me would have been the east side. Definitely there. I didn't hear sirens so I called it in, but I never—it didn't cross my mind that—that Richard . . ."

There's a lot dangling at the end of that sentence.

"I'm sorry," Nora says, feeling embarrassed at how ineffectual two words can seem to be in this sort of situation. "But I'd like to at least see if anyone nearby has footage from a doorbell camera. Everyone's got those in our neighborhood. Do you think you could make an introduction for me?"

"No need. We don't allow any security cameras that save to a cloud device. That one's my fault. Occupational hazard of being in the tech industry, I'm afraid. I'm a privacy nut."

"Oh, well, I guess that makes sense." Though naturally Nora had been hoping for better news. "Okay then." Nora is moving to leave when Alexis stops her.

"If you have any questions about the neighborhood on a personal level, though, I'm your gal."

News travels fast here. On the whole, she supposes she's flattered to be the talk of the town. "Fingers crossed anyway." Alexis demonstrates. "I met with a woman yesterday who was interested in Majestic, too, a—what was she—some kind of project manager I think? Anyway, you know, we don't have a lawyer yet."

Despite her sudden spike of envy, Nora starts to laugh, only to realize that Alexis has already disappeared inside, the door closing behind her with a soft click. They don't have a lawyer yet? That was a joke. Surely. But then again, in her short time, she has met a psychologist, a neurosurgeon, a Realtor, and a tech CEO.

8

— — —

ave, hi, did you get the pictures I sent through?" Back at the
office, Nora rolls into her desk chair and kicks off her high heels.
The curly cord of her outmoded firm phone stretches with her as
she rummages through the mess of papers, looking for a pen.

Dave Champley is her investigative fire expert. She thinks of Dave
using a possessive pronoun on purpose. Every law firm has a Rolodex of
experts on retainer, and Greenberg Schwall is no exception.

Before becoming a lawyer, Nora might have thought that the word
expert implied some level of objectivity, an ability to interpret the facts
the right way, but instead she's learned it means the ability to explain
the facts in a convincing way, and that those are two very different things.
It's about making sure her expert appears the most expert.

"Just loaded them up and was figuring you'd call. Now tell me what
we've got here." He has a slow, soothing drawl. Dave is a former firefighter
with a natural country-boy charm that juries love because he seems like
the type of guy who knows what a carburetor is and yet can still say "I
love you" to his children.

"Wrongful death case in the suburbs. Father died. Origin of the fire
remains unknown."

"Looks like Hell went and paid a visit. Not much left."

Nora locates a pen, and as she listens, she idly practices her signature on a pad of paper. "It's the worst I've seen."

He grunts. "Larger the fire, longer it burns, harder it is to figure out what started the whole mess. Guess that's where we come in. Gotta find someone to blame. When did they release the scene?"

"About a week after." She checks her in-box, finds two new emails since the last time she refreshed her phone while waiting for the elevator. *Confirming receipt*, she replies quickly to Gary.

"Okay, so that right there tells us something," Dave says. "Now there was a fatality so I'd expect that to add a few days. But longer than that? They weren't sure right off the bat what caused this bad boy. Maybe there was some lingering doubt about whether or not it was an accident. Maybe they never really got sure. They're just reading the circumstances and trying to avoid opening a new case file. A lot of cutbacks in the departments. A scene like this? Compromised, destroyed, time-consuming. It's a lemon."

"For us?"

"Depends. Maybe. Maybe not. Look at this fourth picture you sent me." Nora opens up the email from her sent folder. She clicks through pictures of the house frame, peeled of its skin and left raw and unbandaged, until she arrives at the fourth photograph, a picture of where the kitchen met the laundry room. "This is what's known as a V-pattern," he says. "It's faint on account of the damage, but I'd bet my son-in-law that's what it is."

Nora leans her nose toward the screen. "How much do you like your son-in-law?"

"I've got three, but I'll bet my favorite one. How about that?"

Nora zooms in on what looks like a spray of diminished soot across the refrigerator front and part of the adjacent wall, or what's left of it. "Okay, so say it is a—a V-pattern."

"Some people believe it's a sign of possible arson." *Arson.* Not the word she wanted to hear. It's a quiet neighborhood. Alexis had even said there was hardly any crime.

"I . . ." She chooses her words carefully. "I don't like the word *possible*, Dave. Juries don't like the word *possible*. It's possible that I will win the lottery tomorrow. See? That word renders the rest of my sentence all but meaningless. Are you 'some people' or not?"

"Not really."

She exhales.

"It's pretty much junk science." Probably for the best that Dave can't see her look when he says "pretty much." "Trying to read fire patterns is like trying to read tea leaves. I'm just telling you what I'm seeing and how other people might interpret it."

Nora's job is to figure out who or what caused the fire and make sure that they're held responsible. She will literally make them pay. Companies shiver at the sight of a plaintiff's firm like Greenberg Schwall on the docket. This is what she loves about her job: just the existence of personal injury lawyers makes corporations want to do their jobs *better*. And so, by "other people," Dave of course means one of the likely candidates—manufacturer, builder, contractor, all of the above—to sue. They just have to figure out which one and then convince them that the death of Richard March is their fault. But arson, arson changes the game entirely. Arson raises the question: What did I get myself into? If only she weren't the one to have to answer that.

"The truth is," Dave goes on, "only ten percent of arsonists are ever caught. Arson is one of the most costly crimes in our country, but prosecutors are more than happy to let insurance companies foot the bill for it because it's a royal pain in the rear end to prove."

"And now it's a royal pain in my rear end."

"Don't shoot the messenger," he says. "Look, nine out of ten times with arson it's the property owners that did it, for the insurance money."

"Penny?" The incredulity is clear in her question mark intonation. She'd gotten a fair read on Penny and believed her. Nora's bullshit radar hadn't exactly been blip-blipping.

"And don't forget about the husband."

"I'll keep that in mind, thanks," she says with a dollop of sarcasm that poor Dave hasn't ordered.

"I'll do a walk-through later this week, collect samples and so forth. Should take a few weeks to get results back. But we'll see where we stand."

"I'll see what else I can dig up that might be useful." Nora thanks him, glad to have at least one person on her side. She is hanging up the phone when an appointment reminder pops onto her screen.

OB-GYN Appt. @ 11:00 AM.

That's in fifteen minutes. It slipped her mind completely.

It's too late to cancel without getting charged for the appointment, and besides, she'd still have to reschedule. Are these appointments completely necessary? There are an awful lot of them. She's only thirty-five. She's healthy. Her baby is probably doing peachy in there and doesn't like to be poked and prodded any more than she does. She wonders: *Would a midwife require fewer appointments?* She should investigate.

In the end, she's only ten minutes late to the appointment, but the nurse—Jamie—gives her a withering look all the same. *Oh, please,* Nora rails internally, *as if I haven't been stuck in your waiting room for over an hour a time or two.*

"So, are you ready to find out the baby's gender today?" asks Jamie. She can't be more than twenty-three and speaks in the same tone to Hayden and Nora that she probably uses to coo at infants in the hospital nursery.

"We're going to have a gender-reveal party," says Hayden. "So just an envelope with the answer inside." He puts his arm around Nora.

"Yeah." She works to muster some excitement. She's doesn't really *want* a gender-reveal party. She's already tried to wriggle out of it by telling Hayden that she thought the whole idea might be a bit—she didn't know—*offensive* to the concept of gender fluidity, which is a thing good parents care about these days.

But he'd looked so sad. It was her fault—she'd been the one to go and marry an extrovert. And he'd really wanted to have one with Liv, only Nora had never gotten around to planning it. And anyway, he promised, promised, promised, that they weren't those kinds of parents. The party would reveal the sex, and he solemnly swore with the most adorable level of earnestness that after that the baby could be a boy, a girl, or whatever it liked in between. So there went her reasoning and now it looked like Nora would be putting on a party because marriage is compromise. She thinks.

"Wonderful, we'll just take a few vitals and—" Nora stretches out her arm and Nurse Jamie straps a blood pressure cuff to it. She stands, listening to a vein at the crux of Nora's arm through her stethoscope, watching numbers on-screen that are meaningless to Nora. "Right." She strips away the Velcro. "I'll just be one minute. Let me get Dr. Perez to see you."

Hayden pats Nora on the leg.

"Do you think she means a literal minute or a figurative one?" The white paper rolled across the exam table crinkles when she shifts her weight. Nora finds that people rarely talk about time as precisely as they ought to.

"Patience, young Jedi."

She studies the birth announcement cards pinned proudly to a corkboard in the room. Then she gives in. She hops off the exam table and rummages through her purse for her iPhone.

At that moment, the door to the room opens, thumping her in the backside, and she stumbles forward. "Yikes!" Dr. Perez shuffles in, an O of surprise on his own face. "Sorry about that."

"Sorry," Nora parrots while trying to wrap the paper gown over her bare ass. "So sorry."

Pink-faced, she returns to sit up on the table like a good patient. Hayden holds out his hand and she forks over her phone before she can check it.

Dr. Perez drops down onto a rolling stool and scoots closer to her. "Nora, your blood pressure is higher than it should be, and I'm going to be honest, it worries me."

Her eyes dart between Dr. Perez and Hayden. "I'm sure it's nothing," she tells them both. She knows that people are always saying how there is nothing more important than a person's health, but the fact remains that she can think of at least five more pressing matters right this instant. "I've never had high blood pressure before."

Nora forces better posture, wanting to look healthy. She'd chosen Dr. Perez precisely because she'd wanted an older doctor, someone who had delivered more babies than he could count, not just because she valued his experience but also because she knew he wouldn't freak out about things like having a daily cup of coffee (or two). It's always been a comfort. Until now.

Nora's fingers tense and puncture the examination paper. "I haven't eaten much today. I had a cup of coffee. I'm probably just, you know, stressed."

"Exactly," the doctor says.

Hayden rubs her back and leans in to press his nose into her hair while Nora stares at the array of posters for different types of IUDs, a gallery of women smiling about the metal prongs shoved up their cervixes.

"Everything is going to be fine. We're going to monitor you very closely."

"I'll have to come here more, you mean?"

Dr. Perez clutches his heart. "I'm stung."

"I didn't mean—" *Ask about the baby*, she tells herself. That's what everyone in the room is waiting for her to do.

And she does care. She really, truly does. But she swears the baby is *fine*. She once read that fetuses are like tiny, adorable vampires. They siphon off every bit of nutrient they need if they must. Nothing left for Mommy, too bad.

"I'm kidding." Dr. Perez scratches behind his ear. "I understand it's inconvenient. But jokes aside, high blood pressure isn't something to be trifled with. You can risk low birth weight, a lack of nutrients crossing the placenta, heart disease, kidney disease, not to mention the risks to your own health."

"So what am I supposed to do? Eat less red meat?"

"Sure, but most importantly, put your feet up more, take time to relax, slack off a bit at work. Doctor's orders." He winks, like she's a kid and he's just given her permission to sneak her jammy little hand into the candy dish.

"I'm always telling you you're working way too hard, Nora," Hayden butts in. "You're *pregnant*."

Why is it automatically work's fault? Dr. Perez had clearly named *three* components and yet the only one Hayden heard was work.

"It's kind of an important year for me."

That's the frustrating part about being pregnant. Everyone treats her like she has a HANDLE WITH CARE sticker slapped across the back of her maternity leggings. It's like how at the airport, when she traveled while pregnant, at least five people would offer to help her stow her belongings in the overhead bin. But now when she travels with Liv and could actually use a hand? Oh! *Now* it's crickets. So, she wants to tell them, it's like that, but with her career.

"I understand," says Dr. Perez, who, she is sure—beg his pardon—doesn't understand. In fact, she would love to hear a time when either

Dr. Perez or Hayden's careers have been affected in the slightest by having children. Go ahead, she'll wait. "But think about what's important at the end of the day," he's saying, "the health of the baby. Now, why don't you lie back and let's find out what kind of baby we're having, shall we?"

9

D espite the bad news about Nora's blood pressure, or perhaps
rather because her husband hoped to compensate for it, Nora
and Hayden arrived at Dynasty Ranch that evening in good spirits: the thrill of a night off from the usual routine, of putting on nice
clothes and spritzing hair, of a well-curated Spotify playlist on the way
over and the weight of a bottle of wine in hand. *Sex is great, but have
you tried actually getting to do your hair? Sex is great, but have you ever
hired a babysitter?*

"On our best behavior," Nora warned. "We need to make a good
impression, you know." And Hayden feigned offense.

The lights in Cornelia's dining room are dim, making all the night's
attendees lose ten years of age simply by stepping foot inside. The house
smells freshly cleaned and Nora feels like she's in a dinner party from a
movie. Sparkling crystal. Fine china. Free-flowing wine. Glittering conversation. Or that's how the script would read. And somehow Nora has
found herself in the center of it all.

Except not exactly the center, only just left of it. She and Hayden
have been seated across from Thea and her husband, Roman, a corporate and securities lawyer at Boston & Browridge. Next, Cornelia and
Asher, and, though Nora has already met Asher, she's just now learned
that he is a dentist, a first-rate cook, and originally from Portland, the

one in Maine, not Oregon. They are followed by Alexis and Max and, at the head of the table, Penny. Forks clatter over their first course of Bibb lettuce, apple, and blue cheese.

"So." Cornelia smooths a napkin over her lap. "Tell us. How'd you two meet?"

Nora looks to Hayden out of habit but answers first. "Online," she says.

Cornelia winks, tipping her glass to them. "I like your honesty."

"Honesty?" Alexis huffs. "Don't treat it like it's some dirty little secret, Cornelia. Is there even still a stigma around online dating?"

Cornelia gives a lazy hand wave. "I'm old. You're probably right, but what I mean is—well, it's not always the best story, is it? All this internet dating business?"

Hayden reaches under the table and squeezes Nora's knee. "Actually," he says. "We do have a bit of a story." His eyes ask her for permission, which she grants. Happily. He's so much better at telling it. Nora always races through like whoever's listening is being put through a painful orthodontic procedure and she's really sorry, but she just has to get through this one little bit, she'll make it quick, she promises. "Nora and I had been exchanging messages for a week or so, back and forth. We'd finally pinned down a time for our first date. Just coffee, you know, in case she was a total weirdo."

"*Me?* You're the one who listed dry nonfiction accounts of natural disasters as your favorite book genre."

"I stand by that," he says, seriously. "As I was saying, a few days earlier I was out with a group of guys and I saw her across the bar on another date. With . . . another guy she'd met online." Hayden raises a finger. "I know this because I went over to eavesdrop on every word that she said. Naturally."

"Nora Spangler." Tonight Thea's hair has been loosed from its braids into an Afro. "I would not have pegged you as a player."

Nora shrugs as if to say: *So what?* "It's a game of odds, that's all."

"So," says Hayden. "I recognized her from her picture. She looked the exact same. Beautiful, of course." He puts his arm around her and all the women at the table go soft around the eyes. "And I was watching her and I could just tell she was a good person. You know how you just know? I *knew.* I was so jealous. Jealous and I hadn't even met her yet. And I was all at once struck with this crushing fear that she was going to have a great date with this other man and that she would cancel ours and that I'd never get my shot and—"

"Wait, wait, wait," Penny jumps in from the other side of the table. "*Were* you having a great date, though?"

"Oh god, no." Nora's eyes widen. "I still vividly remember that he had said something to me like, women talk about other people and men talk about ideas."

"*No!*" Thea and Alexis react in unison.

Nora nods with her eyebrows up, like, *thank you, you get it.* "When I went to the bar for another drink, Hayden was waiting for me. The first thing he said to me was, 'I didn't realize until this instant that, at first blush, I might seem like a stalker.' It was the fact that he said 'blush' that made me like him."

"*Blush*? I thought it was my tattoo."

It's in the ensuing laughter that her eyes meet Max's and her own laughter falters. He's smiling, shoulders bobbing with the requisite amusement. But his stare. *His stare.* Like a nail tracing the knobs of her spine.

She takes a sip of her water as an excuse to look away and as soon as she does, she feels silly. Yes, there is still the strangeness of the tire incident, but Max is being perfectly lovely. They . . . all are.

"So?" Cornelia snaps her out of it.

"Oh." Nora blots her lips with her napkin. "Uh, I ditched my date and Hayden ditched his friends and we met up at the bar next door and closed the place down."

"By the time our official first date rolled around," says Hayden, "it was actually like our third or fourth."

Nora watches as a viscous drop of Hayden's red wine spills out onto his cream cloth napkin. She's suddenly keenly aware of how much they've been dominating the conversation.

"Roman." She sets her sights on Thea's husband. "You went to law school here in town? We must know some of the same people."

"I don't keep in touch with anyone from law school," he says without a fleck of regret.

"Nora doesn't either really," Hayden adds. She furrows her brow. "What? You don't. Do you?"

Nora inhales. "There's so little time."

"Exactly," agrees Roman. "On Sundays, I do the meal prepping, and our daughters' violin lessons are on Tuesdays, and on Wednesdays I like to spend the early evenings putting away the clean clothes and sorting through the kids' backpacks. Then there's Thursdays and—"

"See? I'd be completely lost without my Roman. He is an angel on earth, isn't he, though?" Thea squeezes his cheek between her thumb and pointer finger and kisses him.

"Sometimes what they say really is true," says Cornelia. "Happy wife, happy life."

Hayden clears his throat. "Good for you, man. Nice to see we all have these modern marriages these days." Is it Nora's imagination or is her husband actually making his voice deeper? "Nothing like my parents growing up."

Asher rises to collect the group's salad plates.

The wrinkles around Cornelia's eyes deepen. "Oh? What do you mean?"

"That things are equal now. Fifty-fifty partnerships, each doing half the housework and child-rearing and all that." He runs his hand over his fuzzy head. "I can't imagine not being involved with Liv. I mean, I doubt my dad ever gave me a bath or anything like that. Crazy to think about now, isn't it?"

Nora makes a noise. She wishes she could snatch it back the moment that it flies from whatever deep nesting place inside her body.

Hayden does a slow, bemused turn in her direction. *"Yes?"*

Nora's neck goes hot. "I—well—the numbers may be doctored a little," she says. "Fudged?" To her credit, she does sound as if she's teasing. All in good fun.

Hayden scoffs good-naturedly. "Oh, come on. Back me up here, guys." He gestures to the other husbands sitting round the table, and Nora can think back to years past when she's had similar conversations at similar parties. Men are from Mars, women are from Venus. That sort of thing. Each side ganging up on the other, again, totally kidding, but also completely not. (Women: *I swear I have to tell him the same thing five times before it sinks in!* Men: *She always chooses the most inconvenient times to tell me something important—when I'm trying to get out the door for work, when I just started reading an article on my phone, when I'm trying to fall asleep!*)

Asher comes around with their entrées—seared scallops with brown butter and lemon sauce on a bed of warm risotto. Nora's mouth waters as she picks up her fork.

"Alexis works so hard," Max replies to Hayden, and she can see the wheels turning in her husband's mind as he tries to sort out whether or not Max is joking.

Asher rejoins the table with a satisfied grin. "There's a great website that you should check out, Hayden. It's called Coming Clean. It gives all of these fantastic tips on organization and housekeeping. I live by it." He pierces his fork through the meat of a scallop and pops it into his mouth.

"I'll . . . look into it," says Hayden, a bit sarcastically for Nora's taste.

"Me, too," Roman agrees. "I follow Dirty Little Secrets. Her posts on running a household, they changed my life." He presses his fist to his chest. "Did I tell you, Max, that I just ordered that new label maker you recommended?"

"The Brother P-touch?" Max leans into view.

"I'm excited."

"I'm sorry, there are websites about this stuff?" Hayden scratches the plate as he cuts his food. "And people actually read them?"

Honestly, could he try not to be such a sore thumb about it? It would be best to *fit in*. She figures the dinner party invite is a good sign, but nothing's guaranteed about the house on Majestic Grove she still has her heart set on, Hayden be damned. And she has every intention of getting her way.

Roman sets down his fork. "Dirty Little Secrets has two million Instagram followers."

"I had no idea."

Nora kicks his ankle beneath the table and when she does, the remaining bit of buttery scallop drops onto his slacks.

"Shoot," he says, pushing back and wiping. There's an obvious grease stain right near his crotch. Nora winces and Hayden gives *her* a dirty look.

"I have an excellent remedy for that," pipes in Max. "Lestoil. I've tried everything and that is the one thing that takes stains right out. It still contains pine oil, but it's a lot more potent than your typical Pine-Sol, so I like to buy it straight. Do you have any you could lend, Asher?"

"I've always been told to try a bit of baking soda and Tide, but I don't find it to be a perfect solution. That's good to know."

"Hayden, you can just order it on Amazon," says Max. "It's like magic."

"Thanks," Hayden says, slowly, eyeing the men.

"Penny." Roman leans in, trying to include her in the conversation. "What about you, do you have a favorite stain remover?"

Penny shoots back the last of her glass of wine. "We've always just used Shout pens, I'm afraid. You know," says Penny suddenly, lifting the bottle to refill. "I think I'll excuse myself to get some air. Don't hold anything up on my account." She shoves away from the table, pinning her draping cardigan down with one hand. She offers Nora an apologetic smile.

There's a long pause until the door to the outside patio chimes.

"Maybe a bit too heavy on the couples talk." Alexis bites her lip. "I feel bad now."

"She'll be okay. It's just going to take time," says Thea.

"She loved Richard so much." Alexis drinks her wine.

The conversation moves slowly away and they soon discuss the research Thea's doing at the new neurology center. "We're doing something really cutting edge." She speaks with such excitement. "What we're trying to do is bridge the gap between psychology and neurology. A patient goes in and sees a psychiatrist for depression, for instance," she explains. "Studies show that the medications prescribed along with talk therapy change the makeup of the brain, but only temporarily, only so long as treatment continues. You constantly hear about patients with depression and anxiety going off their meds. They don't feel right. They hate the side effects. It's a big problem. Recovery becomes a cycle. There's no endgame for those patients. We want to find a way to solidify the changes to the neural pathways created through the efforts of our colleagues in psychiatry. We hope to make them permanent. Nobody's ever done that before."

"Make them permanent how?" Hayden's on his third glass of wine and he's finished half of the chocolate tart on his plate. Penny has yet to return. Nora worries.

"Surgical intervention," says Thea.

"You mean like brain surgery?" Hayden sounds appropriately impressed.

"Exactly." She points at him with her knife.

Nora yearns for her own glass of wine.

Still, she's happy enough to be a part of the easy run of conversation, the edges of which have been smoothed by a good meal and a nice vintage. "You're a psychologist," says Nora to Cornelia. "What do you think of Thea's work?"

Cornelia crushes her chin into her palm. "I'm one of Thea's biggest advocates. I think the work she's doing is so important in the world and could have hundreds of real-life applications. I'm like a proud mama bear."

"About all of us really." Alexis tips her head to Cornelia's shoulder, and Cornelia lovingly pats her hair.

"I do like to keep tabs," she says. "Actually I think you'd be really impressed by what some of our residents here are doing."

"My next-door neighbor Donna Hedges was just elected to the state senate." Thea reaches for the decanter on the table. "And Martha, over near you, Alexis, she's the school district superintendent."

Alexis is clearly getting sappier as the minutes—and ounces—pass. "Oh, you *have* to meet her. She has this heart for disadvantaged children, reducing class sizes, instituting teacher merit pay."

"And Devi." Cornelia traces her finger around a crystal rim. "She has a higher success rate in the pediatric oncology unit than any doctor in the whole country."

"And they all live *here*?" Nora asks. Here, in Dynasty Ranch. Which is lovely, yes, but not one of the more traditionally prestigious neighborhoods. It has none of the old-money cachet of a Tarrytown nor the hipster nouveau riche status of the east side.

"It's a nice place to live," says Thea, raising her glass before downing the final swig. The women cheer that.

With Nora's plate scraped clean of every ounce of chocolate she could spoon into her mouth without embarrassing herself, the dishes are cleared and Nora takes her chance to slip out onto the patio, where she finds Penny, swirling the final quarter of her own wineglass and staring out into the blue glow of the swimming pool.

"Oh god, did I miss the whole thing? I lost track of the time."

Nora pulls up a patio chair to sit beside her. "What have you been doing?"

"Sitting, thinking. I'm really good at that. One of my best skills, really. Being in my own head. Though it's not always a good thing, I don't think."

Nora, too, stares out at the pool, mesmerized by the calm water, wrestling with the urge to dip her toes in. "At least you're always entertained."

"Ha. I doubt you're struggling for entertainment. I remember that time of my life, when my kids were little. Well, I recall the feeling of it anyway. It's all a bit of a blur. I'm a little like, was I drunk the whole time? Everyone kept telling me: You're going to miss this." She wags her finger and acts stern. "Let them be little. Slow down or you'll blink and they'll be in college."

"That wasn't true?" Nora asks.

"It was. But it wasn't helpful. Advice should be helpful. That's the whole point of it. Like I bet when your mother says, you really should make your child eat her vegetables, you're not thinking, gee, Mom, thanks, never thought of that one."

"My mother's dead." It slips out. She wonders when the reality of the fact that her mother is no longer a reality will sink in.

"Oh." Penny reaches over and slides her fingers across Nora's forearm. "I'm so sorry. Did she get to meet your daughter?"

"No, actually." Her voice, for a moment, husky.

"That's hard." Penny retrieves her hand. "I hate thinking about what Richard will miss. I'd really looked forward to being a grandparent with him, if you can believe it. Know we're still a ways off. But.

Seeing him walk Julia down the aisle. Going on a fiftieth-anniversary cruise. I had a writing teacher once who told me that a story always begins with a 'what if,' but I keep thinking how my 'what ifs' don't begin anything. It's over. Richard's gone. The end. Maybe you feel a bit of that, too."

"At least I got to say goodbye." It feels natural, this need to cede ground to Penny's grief, which is fresher. Hers, though she hates to admit it, has grown stale over the years.

"I don't know if that makes it any easier. But—yeah." They lapse into silence and, for a while, it's nice.

Nora keeps her voice low. "Penny, do you remember anything, anything you might have overlooked earlier?"

She's been trying to construct a timeline of the night of the fire. At 6:45 P.M., Cornelia and Asher picked up Penny at her house after Richard knocked off sick with a migraine. They arrived at the hospital's grand dome, which had been transformed for the purpose of the night's evening benefitting the new neurosurgery wing. Twenty-two residents from Dynasty Ranch were in attendance, and Thea gave a short speech at approximately 8:45 P.M. One person said that by dessert Penny seemed quite drunk and was audibly slurring her words, but no one else could confirm this. Alexis placed her emergency call just before 9:50 P.M. Parking tickets show Asher leaving, presumably with Penny, at 10:20. A collection of times, places, players. And still the story is gap-toothed and incomplete. What happened to Richard and why?

Penny waits, and for a moment, Nora isn't sure that she's heard her, thinks that perhaps she's gone too far into her own thoughts. But then she squints, her cheek buttoning. "He'd become sort of . . . preoccupied with the house."

"What do you mean?"

"Obsessed, I guess you could say. I came home one day and he'd taken apart the stove. Just unscrewed it and laid it all around the kitchen. He thought something was wrong with it, but then he couldn't figure out what it was. There were several weeks like that and then whatever had been bothering him stopped. It was a relief. For a while. But it returned eventually."

"When?"

"Right before. Before the house burned down. He dug up the floor-boards in the laundry room."

"Did you tell the police this?" Now. She could be on to something. A problem with the house. Followed by a fire. And it had driven Richard mad, which surely meant he'd complained to someone, somewhere, she just needed to find out to whom. An ignored problem is even more compelling to a jury than a regular one.

"I mentioned something to that effect. I told them that Richard be-lieved there was something that was defective. At the time Richard was going on about it, I was in the middle of drafting a book. I was trying to avoid his . . . his chaos. I didn't mean to be selfish, but writing can seem that way. A selfish endeavor, I mean." She twists the rings on her finger, one after another, avoiding eye contact. "I just wish I knew what happened that night."

"I know," Nora says. "That's why I'm going to do everything I can to find out."

Hayden and Nora spill out onto the driveway amid a barrage of *that-was-so-fun, we-should-do-it-again-sometime, so-glad-you-could-make-it, thank-you-for-having-us*. And then they are shoulder to shoulder, walking down the drive to the sound of crickets, and above them actual stars poke holes in the clear night sky.

"That's it. Hand over the keys, mister." Nora digs around in the front pocket of Hayden's pants.

"Hm." He smells like garlic and alcohol. "That's nice. Think you can move a little to the left?" His nose grazes her hair.

She tosses the keys in her open palm, grinning. "What are you, fifteen?"

They both move for their respective car doors. He snorts, dropping into the seat beside her. "Fifteen! I didn't get any action when I was fifteen!" He looks at her with lazy eyes, buzzed, but not, like, shit-faced. Definitely not that. "Did *you*?"

Nora swallows the canary. Well.

"Nora!" He shoves her arm gently as she starts the ignition. The headlights flash on and the cabin light fades.

"Liv's going to be fifteen someday." The buckling of her seat belt is all the punctuation she needs.

"There goes my libido, thanks." Hayden props his elbow up by the window.

"What'd you think?" Nora asks before the car's even in drive. She always looks forward to unpacking a social event with Hayden. *Did you see how . . . ? Can you believe . . . ? Did you hear . . . ?*

"I didn't get to talk to Penny much." Hayden rests his head against the side window. "Which is too bad, I know how much you like her, but Cornelia and Thea were *surprisingly* interesting. I mean, you know how women are, they usually only talk about people, not ideas." He turns his hand into a talking puppet: *blah blah blah.* Then he gives her a tired wink.

"Okay, comedy workshop. How about the menfolk?" She's never once been to a party and been more interested in what the men were talking about, and that's not just because she doesn't like sports.

He pulls a face. "Seriously? I couldn't stand them. All they did was talk about their wives; how hard their wives worked; I just love my wife." He runs his tongue across the bottom of his teeth like he's tasted something bad.

"So? What's wrong with that?"

"I don't know, don't you think that's a little fucking weird?"

She tightens her grip around the steering wheel, driving slowly through the empty neighborhood streets. "You don't have to curse."

"They all need to grow a pair of balls, if you ask me."

"I'm sorry I did ask." She registers only in the periphery as they pass the burned remains of the March home.

"What? Do you not want me to be honest?"

"Of course I want you to be *honest*. I just want you to *honestly* have a different opinion, preferably one that's not so misogynistic."

"Please. It's not like I want you to fawn all over me either."

Heat rises up her throat. This is not smart. She shouldn't be having this conversation after Hayden's been drinking. It's like driving without working brakes.

"Hayden." If she were a different type of woman, this might sound like a warning growl, but she always is disappointed to find that, in these moments, she tends to share more in common with a small, yappy dog. "You take your socks off in the living room for me to pick up." An insincere laugh.

He gawks at her. "What does that mean?"

"It means: What's the difference?"

"Oh, here we go again." He presses his fist into the roof of the car. "Okay, so *that's* what you're looking for in a partner? Back there? Good to know."

"What, like they look so miserable? They're happy. They're *nice*," she says. And honestly, for all she does for her husband would it have *killed* him to muster an ounce of genuine interest? After all, Nora certainly planned to look up the organization accounts that Roman and Asher had suggested, but that's not really the point, is it?

"It's like you can't turn it off," he mumbles.

She glares at him. Feels his words scoop her out, the anger welling up to fill the empty space like water.

"Nora!" His eyes widen. "Watch out! Nor—"

Her head snaps forward and her right foot mashes hard into the brake. She feels the tires skin the road. The golden ray of headlight cutting through nothing. Hair. Skin. Eyes that shine back.

The car grinds to a stop with a shudder and Nora's heartbeat reverberates throughout her entire body. She and Hayden both stare, open-mouthed, at the teenage girl standing in the center of the road, motionless.

Nora raises a trembling hand apologetically, like she's just cut in before her turn at a four-way stop rather than nearly killed someone.

The girl's skin is alabaster in the high beams. Her long legs protrude from a barely there sundress, fully visible bra straps indenting her shoulders, her feet shoved into sneakers and high-kneed athletic socks.

The girl remains frozen.

"Do you think she's okay?" Nora whispers.

"I mean. We didn't touch her." Hayden sits forward, chest pulling at the seat belt. "Can she see us?"

Nora fiddles with the switches in her car, which she's never fully mastered, until the headlights lower in intensity. "What's she doing? Is she going to move?"

"Just give her a second," Hayden murmurs. "Maybe she's in shock."

Nora waits, still keeping her foot firmly planted on the brake. "She doesn't look like she's in shock, though."

Strands of the girl's long blond hair catch the light as they float in the nighttime breeze. And still she doesn't move. Her presence is like a challenge.

"Go around her." Hayden reaches to place his hand on the steering wheel, twisting it toward him.

"She's not cattle in the road," Nora hisses.

But he has a point. Slowly, Nora does ease off the brake. The girl stays put. Nora's hands are slimy as she lowers the window. She curves around, giving the girl a wide berth. "Are you all right? Do you need help?" Nora asks in her best mom voice.

The girl's head turns. One side of her mouth curls as she raises her hand and holds out, for Nora's review, a middle finger.

Nora expels air in one big huff and she presses down on the gas. *Bitch*, she thinks. The bitter taste of annoyance at having been mocked by a teen makes her feel something like shame. Worry calcifying into something stern and adult.

The sweetly acrid scent of cigarette smoke floats high on the breeze.

"Look at this place." Hayden leans his head back on the rest as soon as there's distance. "What the hell do teens have to be so rebellious about in a place like this? School of hard knocks, is she?"

A peal of laughter rings through the open window. Nora looks up into the rearview and finds the road empty. Beside it the disembodied pinpricks of cigarette butts bob and hover. And the words of one of her mother's favorite old adages comes harkening back to her out of the darkly shadowed ether: *Where there's smoke . . .*

Studies Show: Moms Need More "Me" Time

BY WESLEY DAVIS

"A lack of alone time may cause a mental health crisis for mothers. Researchers suggest that moms should view self-care as a necessity, not a luxury."

Read Comments

JennaBrix1212

Hi, guys, I think you need to publish a correction. The byline should read, "Captain Obvious." Keep up the good work!

MotherMayI

I feel like my husband thinks I get plenty of "me time" because he lumps a lot of things under there that I personally wouldn't. For instance, I had a baby nine months ago and am still hanging on to fifteen pounds of pregnancy weight. And now my desire to have time to exercise is considered an indulgence. Personally, I think my husband and I both put this extra weight on me when I agreed to carry our child for the better part of a year, so he owes me the time and space that I need to get it off. I actually don't like exercise. So it's super annoying when I'm treated like time to exercise is the greatest gift he could ever give me.

Hannah Lane

@MotherMayI I actually like working out, but I rarely can get away long enough to take an actual exercise class. I swear, I give my husband opportunities to nap or smoke weed on the porch and then when I ask for thirty minutes to knock out an in-home workout, I spend the entire time doing push-ups with a kid on my back and squats with another one hugging my crotch. When I yell for my husband he's all: "I tried, they want to be with you!"

WillWork4Cupcakes67

Anyone else feel like their husband is just waiting to clock out the second he's no longer "in charge" of the kids? I think his understanding of the situation is that I'm supposed to take care of the kids every minute except the sixty- to ninety-odd minutes he's agreed to grant me my "me time," which let's face it, is usually time I spend catching up on work. The second I'm back he shoves them at me and that's that.

Bina Sutker

Exercise or sleep or read or attend book club or use the bathroom alone or shop online or go to the dentist: a real Sophie's Choice.

Kelley Elena

The thing we have to realize is that men are going to get their alone time one way or another. They're going to take it. So women should too. Here's what I've started to do: ignore the sighs, the annoyed glances, the feeling that I am putting my husband out by taking time out. Because trust me, when it's the other way around, he has no problem ignoring my annoyance. That's on him and I am not going to take that bullshit on anymore. Men know how to be selfish and we have to force ourselves to be.

10

've sent you a house. Have you gotten it?" Nora calls Andi on her
morning commute.

"How much was the postage on that?" Andi's just gotten off of
work at the café. Nora greets the joke with dead air. "Fine, hold on,
pulling up my email." They wait while she loads Isla Wong's web page
for the listing on Majestic Grove. "Oh . . . it's *nice*. I like it. *Very* pretty.
God"—Nora can hear the mouse clicks—"I will murder you if you have
a walk-in closet. That is not fair."

"Okay, so *you* think it's nice, right?"

"One hundred percent. Plenty of room for sofas I can crash on."

"Do you think you could put in a good word about it to Hayden,
then?"

Nora has always understood that when a couple gets married, there
will be his friends and her friends and those lines rarely, if ever, melt away.
But Andi became an "us" friend almost instantly. When Andi lived in
the States, Hayden pushed to meet up with her almost as frequently as
Nora did, and he's already been leading the charge on a trip to Berlin.

"To Hayden? Why? What doesn't he like about it?"

"I swear, it's the stupidest reasons." Nora drives very responsibly,
hands at ten and two, the complete opposite of Andi. "I met this group

of women there and they're very—well, they're very accomplished. And they all have perfect marriages. It's amazing, really. And I like them a lot, but Hayden's a skeptic. Thinks it's some weird sorority thing and that the husbands need to grow a pair of balls. That's a direct quote."

"Okay . . ." There's rustling on the other end of the line. The squeak of bedsprings.

"Why do you say 'okay' like that?"

"He has to be picking up on something. Hayden's a good guy."

"I never said he wasn't."

"What I mean is, he's not threatened by accomplished women. He married *you*."

"True." Nora moves to the far right; her exit is coming up as she nears downtown.

"So, you never know what goes on behind closed doors," Andi says.

"I know that, too."

"And the grass isn't always greener."

"Are you following some American-idiom-a-day calendar over there?"

"Shit," Andi says. "Is it happening? Am I finally turning into a basic bitch? I did order a caramel macchiato today. It was delicious." Nora can hear her friend's grin, and it makes her homesick even though *she's* the one at home.

"Will you say something to him?" Nora asks again.

"I don't think it's a good idea to go meddling in other people's marriages."

"I'm not other people. I'm your best friend."

A friendship with her husband is all well and good, but when push comes to shove, Andi's supposed to take Nora's side. It's understood.

"And I'd like to *keep* it that way."

"I'm pulling into work," says Nora. "But please. He doesn't always know what's good for him." There's a note of desperation with which Nora isn't wholly comfortable. But after the dinner party, she's feeling that the pressure is on. The case. The house. Is she in or is she out? "Remember when he used to want to wear all those newsboy hats and you talked him out of it?"

Andi sighs. "Okay. I'll email him or something and only if it can come up naturally, okay?"

"Okay," Nora agrees. "Love you."

And Andi completes their ritual—"To death."

❖

Nora has spent a solid hour and a half deep inside the zone. It's a rare phenomenon that occurs near the end of a day on which there's enough pressing work to instigate her body's adrenal responses—her chest is tight, her pupils turn to pinpoints, her mind snaps awake—a stopping point is tantalizingly within reach. If she can just buckle down, if she can maintain uninterrupted focus for long enough, she could leave the office and not have to open her computer tonight.

An alarm goes off on Nora's phone. The message on-screen—

Take ten deep, soothing breaths

—is Hayden's handiwork. She shuts it off and returns to the paragraph she was reading, but finds that she can't shake the guilt. It's like she's broken a rule. A dumb rule, but still, one that's been written down. *Do not pass go, do not collect two hundred dollars. . . .*

Oh, fine, she thinks, resigned, tossing her pen down like a petulant child and shutting her eyes tight.

One Mississippi . . . Deep breath in.

Two Mississippi . . . Deep breath out.

Ten? Really, Hayden, TEN breaths? This is going to take for-fucking-ever. She leans back in her chair. It's that attitude that's gotten her into this mess. And if she's not careful, she'll wind up on bed rest, doctor's orders, and then won't that be a pickle?

"Hello." Nora jumps at the sound of a voice coming through her speakerphone. She'd forgotten that she's been on hold with an appliance customer service hotline. "This is Suzy and I'll be happy to assist you today."

"Hi, hi, yes." Nora pulls the speaker closer. She's spent the better part of an hour making her way up the chain of command at the appliance hotline and she has finally—hopefully—reached Suzy, a manager. "I'm calling about a customer service call that was placed a few months ago by Richard March. I'm his attorney and we're following up regarding a complaint that was made."

"Yes, Ms. Spangler, my team lead filled me in. I've got the case notes in front of me. What can I do for you?"

Nora shows a total of seven calls having been made by Richard to the customer service help line at the appliance company that made not only the stove Richard had taken apart, but also the washing machine, the oven, and the refrigerator. It's as good a start as any.

"Could you tell me what specific complaint was made by Mr. March?" Nora crosses her fingers.

"There are a number of calls logged from that number." She sounds wary, like a woman who's used to dealing with angry customers all day. "But . . ." Her breath hisses through the speaker. "They all seem to say the same thing, more or less. The summary of the complaints all read: clicking noise."

"A clicking noise?"

Suzy the Manager reads: "Customer complains of a clicking noise coming from an indeterminate place, maybe in the kitchen. Customer is frustrated that the clicking noise persists; a repairman was called out to the house previously, but no clicking noise could be heard and so no further action was taken. Customer says that clicking noise persists on and off at unpredictable times of day."

"How did your agents respond?"

"We sent two different repairmen out on two separate occasions. No problem was found with the appliances. Neither heard a clicking noise."

"It could have come and gone."

"Of course. That's why we offered to replace them."

"Replace them? Replace what?"

"All three appliances—the stove, washer, and refrigerator. Free of charge."

"Wow, that's—"

"My customer service agent who fielded his last call, she was insistent that the man—Richard—he sounded pretty distraught. She really believed that he was being genuine. That there must have been some clicking noise. She wrote here in her notes, 'Customer says he is being driven insane.'"

"But appliances in the March house, they weren't new. I checked. They're the same ones originally installed. An older model." Nora's computer switches over to the screen saver mode, a picture of a European mountain town that she will probably never visit.

"We tried to arrange a time for delivery. I show that we attempted to contact the customer on three separate occasions, leaving voice mails each time, but he never returned our calls."

"And when was this?"

"The week of March twelfth." Suzy the Manager is good at her job.

"I guess that makes sense. By that time," Nora says, "Richard was dead."

***

After Nora hangs up, the last notes from the customer service call are still ringing in her ears when she senses someone approaching her office.

"Knock, knock." Gary pokes his head in. Nora doesn't miss his look of distaste at the papers and accordion files strewn around her office. "Nora, it's all hands on deck tonight," he says. "Discovery response deadline has come up for one of Schwall's clients, and it's first thing tomorrow morning." Nora glances at the time on her computer screen. Just after five. "I'm divvying up the assignments. My secretary will send over the ground rules and accompanying files." She curses in her head, but perhaps a bit of it shows on her face because Gary asks, "Is that a problem?"

Nora understands that Gary isn't actually interested in her response. The question is completely rhetorical and, in fact, Gary is already turning his back to her when she spits out, "It's just that I have to get my daughter," wishing she could spontaneously decompose straight into the carpet. *RIP.*

"You're married, aren't you?" He rocks onto his heels to address her without committing to returning his full attention.

Nora takes a breath in through her nose. "He's . . . he has a client dinner tonight, I think. I'll try him—" She reaches for the landline phone.

"Ask your nanny to stay late then." It's clear from his tone that Gary doesn't think *he* should be the one problem-solving this issue. What's worse is that it's not as if Nora disagrees. But what's she supposed to do? A small part of her had been hoping he would tell her, *that's okay, Spangler, we can handle this one without you,* when instead he will probably ride the elevator back up to his office and lament with one of the other white-haired senior partners about how this is the problem with hiring women. "You do have a nanny, don't you?" he asks, incredulously.

She nods, silently. She can feel herself sinking, the dappled light of the surface getting farther and farther away.

Her babysitter isn't an option. She has a class tonight and Nora is one tardy away from her quitting, but she knows better than to try to explain this to Gary.

"I'll figure something out," she says.

Alone, she rings Hayden. "What's up?" he answers. She can hear clinking glasses and laughter in the background.

"Gary needs me to stay late tonight."

"What?" he shouts into the phone, and she holds it away from her ear.

"I have to stay late," she enunciates. The last thing she's going to do is shout her personal business for the entire hall of her law firm to hear.

"Okay, call Brittany. I'm sure she's willing to stay." Unlike her job, his as a software salesman actually lends itself toward something called "human interaction."

"No. Brittany *isn't* willing to stay, Hayden. She's got class." How doesn't he know this by now?

"Well, I don't know what to tell you. I mean. Try one of our sitters. You've got some in your phone, don't you?"

"There's no way I can find a sitter in time. Can you make it home? I know you've got that client dinner, but you're not the only salesman there, right? Can't someone cover for you?"

"Come on. I can't skip out on work, Nora. I'm sorry. I wish I could help. Really, you know I do. But—hey—what?—oh yeah, hey, we're paying our tab and heading over to the restaurant. I've got to run. Text me how it goes."

Nora stares at a dead phone, listening to the dial tone playing through the handset before she bangs it into the cradle. Twice. For good measure. She mouths a very naughty, not safe for work, word.

"Okay now, that doesn't look good." Cameron Drummer leans his shoulder on her doorframe, hand resting casually in the pocket of his wool slacks. He grins at her, lips spreading wide to show a white lump of chewing gum between his molars.

"Now's not a great time. I'm a little busy having a mental breakdown." He's the only person in the office to whom she can talk that way.

Cameron joined Greenberg Schwall two years ago following a mostly amicable divorce from his then-wife, Eleanor, who'd recently made partner at his then-firm, Dannon, Morris & Zeller. Cameron graduated a year after Nora, meaning that he won't be up for partner until the following summer, if he's lucky. From what Nora has heard, Eleanor didn't even insist that he leave Dannon Morris, but when the position came open at Greenberg, he jumped ship to start over, and Nora, for one, is grateful.

It doesn't hurt that Cameron is—*what's the technical term? Oh, right*—a stone-cold fox. The man is an easy six foot four inches, a former University of Texas wide receiver who chose the law over owning a local car dealership (poor decision), and if Nora can judge based on the fact that he married Eleanor, a smart woman a few years older than him (yes, Nora stalked her firm profile, so sue her), as opposed to a twenty-three-year-old he met on Sixth Street, not a total Neanderthal.

"Uh, yeah, anyone walking by in the hall can clearly see that." He walks in and snaps the door closed behind him. This gesture alone sets him apart. He's one of the few men in the office who hasn't bought into the #MeToo backlash bullshit that's managed to turn every female attorney into the bogeyman. *Watch out! Don't go in there! Run for your life before she has the chance to ruin it with a bogus sexual harassment claim!*

Nora drops her forehead to her desk, willfully ignoring the sad buildup of breakfast bar crumbs between the glass topper and wood.

He drops down into the guest chair across from her. "So I see the Gary Fairy already paid you a visit."

"Hayden's out. Babysitter's out. Somebody needs to get Liv and—"

"You're the somebody." He rubs his palms over his thighs. "Got it. What can I do? What do you need?" He crosses his legs and sits back, appraising her.

"A parachute would be nice." She sits up. "A safety net. You know what? *No.*" Nora snaps her fingers. "I need a wife. You've had one. Any advice?" She slumps. "Sorry, that was probably insensitive."

Cameron tilts his chair onto its back legs. Men in the office are always doing this and it never fails to cause Nora considerable anxiety. Aren't they worried they're going to topple over?

"Let's see. Advanced degree. High-paying job. Decent bone structure." She rolls her eyes and he smirks. "I'd say you should be able to snag one pretty easily. Oh, *shoot*, but the mom-mobile. Afraid that's going to work against you."

Nora had made fun of Cameron relentlessly when he'd traded in his Tahoe for a red Porsche Panamera, especially given the toddler car seat strapped in the back. And for the record, it's not even like Nora drives an actual minivan, though Cameron says this is only a technicality, given that her SUV has three rows and a terrible turning radius.

"Ignore me." She pinches the bridge of her nose, trying to think. "I'm fine." Her dream of a night free from her laptop has gone up in smoke. She's not fine, but the words have become a verbal tic. Women may be mocked for saying "like" too much, but in Nora's humble opinion, it's "fine" that's the problem.

I'm fine. It's fine. No worries, totally fine. Sorry, fine, fine, fine. Fine, thanks.

"You know what?" Cameron lets the front legs of the chair fall back down with a *thunk*. "Fuck it. I'll do it."

"Do what?" she says, scrolling through the contacts in her phone, hoping to stumble across a forgotten babysitter. The mom version of a little black book—fewer dick pics, just as many unreturned texts.

"Your chunk of the assignment. Whatever Gary gives you. I'll do it," he says.

"No." She glares at him.

"I'll be stuck late anyway. And, besides, Eleanor has Zara this week. What's a few more hours? There's free coffee here."

"But—"

Cameron sticks his fingers in his ears. "La-la-la-la, can't hear you. La-la-la-la, get out of here before I change my mind. La-la-la."

Nora hesitates, debating whether she can possibly let Cameron do this colossal favor for her, debating whether she should laugh or cry with relief.

"Scram." He jabs his finger at the door. *"Now."*

Without logging out of her computer, Nora grabs her purse and charges for the door.

⊞

That night, after Liv is in bed and before Hayden has returned home, Nora does open her computer. She navigates to her remote desktop and logs on to her Outlook account. She replies to an existing email thread with Cameron by attaching a GIF. It's an image of Snow White being rescued by the prince. The caption reads "You're my hero."

Not more than three minutes later, Cameron's reply shows up in bold: *Ding dong feminism is dead.*

Yes, and so? Comes the answer in her head.

Because, frankly, part of her wants to murder feminism herself. Somebody, please, hand her the knife, and Nora will be happy to stab that saucy bitch straight in the back. The traitor!

From the minute Liv was born, Nora has fretted needlessly about the messaging of princess movies. *You don't need rescuing, darling. You'll be perfectly capable of saving yourself.* That's what good mothers say, isn't it? Ones that are paying attention to think pieces and message boards and who don't just tell little girls that they're pretty, right? In return for not eating the evil apple of misogyny (*Has she heard: She doesn't have to MARRY a CEO, she can BE the CEO!*), little girls are now promised adventure and freedom and meaningless sex in their twenties. And all across the land, the magical kingdom will be populated not by princesses but by *queens* straightening one another's crowns. So be it decreed on Instagram.

But as exhaustion seeps into her bones, Nora wants to scream: "Look around! Not only will you be getting to save yourself, you'll be getting to do literally everything else yourself, too!" Brava! What a win for womankind.

If only Nora could have a glass of wine, but, of course, she can't, given that she's also tasked with growing human life. Details . . .

All she's saying is that it had felt a little bit *good* to be rescued today, to allow herself to be rescued. That's all. And that maybe, just maybe, if women had known that the only math involved in the equation of getting fancy new jobs would be addition at best and multiplication at worst, they might not have been so eager to cast off Prince Charming, who, by the way, was apparently quite happy to be like, *cool, you've got this now*? And saunter off to read his iPhone on the toilet for an hour, happily ever after.

Nora begins to type up a response when there's a noise in the backyard and her heart jump-starts. Only a single light is on in the house. Outside, the darkness is complete. Once again, her reflection in the window stares back at her. Once again, her skin crawls.

She sits still, sure that she's imagined it. And then. A swish from the other side. Out there.

The night seems close. Has she locked the door? She can't remember. *You're being ridiculous,* she tells herself, the way she always does when she's home alone.

It doesn't work. She hears it again. Someone there.

Hayden? she texts.

No response.

The knob twists. Not locked, not locked. It cracks.

"Nora?" A whisper.

And in the end, there's nothing to be afraid of. It's only her husband.

11

Nora had woken sometime in the middle of the night to scrawl a note to herself, one that had felt important enough to warrant rummaging in her nightstand for a pen and a scrap from an unused journal, but now as she reads, *Assume nothing*, in the indentions left from a pen nearly out of ink, she hasn't the slightest clue what about it had seemed so profound. Still horizontal in bed, she unlocks her phone, and the last browser page already open is a list of search results: mental health warning signs. The last thing she'd read before falling asleep.

She remembers now: She'd been thinking of Richard March.

Customer says he is being driven insane. That word—*insane*—had stuck out to her, wriggling its way underneath her skin. And here she had researched it and strung together a list of symptoms. Confused thinking. Excessive fear, worry, or anxiety. Social withdrawal. Delusions or hallucinations, including seeing or . . . hearing things.

She'll have to review Richard's medical history in more detail. And is this really what she meant when she wrote, *Assume nothing*? Assume not even that she was dealing with two rational—or even lucid— human beings with the Marches? She very much hopes that line of thinking won't come into play. But now that she's thought it, she can't *un*-think it. Not until she's found a more compelling lead with which to replace it. That's how her brain works. That's why she's good at her job.

Fortunately, at least, Nora won't have to wait long, given that she's already on her way to Dynasty Ranch right this very moment.

※

"Hello?" Nora calls. "Anyone home?" Rather than stand another five minutes in the steam room heat, Nora tries the door to Alexis's house when no one answers. They'd said five o'clock to collect the community plans Alexis had managed to track down, and Nora has to be home by no later than six. From the foyer, she hears running water, shuffles, people sounds. "I let myself in," she says, feeling small and self-conscious.

And then she hears a voice—"We're up here!"—from a distant corner.

Nora peers up to the second-floor walkway, her hand on the polished wood of the banister.

"Come on up!" Alexis hollers the way that Nora does to Liv or Hayden when she doesn't want to walk herself all the way back up or back down. And so Nora obeys, ascending, unsure who the "we" is that she'll find.

The stairway opens up into a flex space—or that's what a Realtor like Isla Wong might call it. The Foster-Rosses seem to be using it quite flexibly indeed as a casual-TV-watching/free-weight-storing/pool-playing playroom. On either side, halls jut off, creating a master plan community's version of a Robert Frost poem. Nora chooses the one on the left, following the sound of running water. On her way, she passes a little boy's nursery, adorable woodland creatures adorning the walls, an empty crib and abandoned glider. A piece of her stirs.

It's been ages since Hayden disassembled the crib, years since she nursed Liv to sleep, her daughter's eyelashes soft across the mound of cheek, lips tuliped around her mother's nipple. She runs her hand across the small lump formed just below her belly button and thinks: *It all feels so precious; it all feels so terrifying.*

But either way, she will be there soon enough, and so she draws toward a thundering faucet and pokes her head into the open bathroom.

"Oh, sorry." Nora sees now that the person kneeling down beside the tub where a small baby slaps at water in a Skip Hop Moby Smart Sling (oh, how she wishes her brain were reserved for more important things) isn't Alexis.

The woman turns, and when she does she's not a woman at all, but a girl. A teenage girl with long legs and blond hair reaching to her elbows. The girl smiles at her kindly, and Nora wonders how can it be that this girl, *this* girl, is the same one that stood in the center of the road like a demon threatening Nora and Hayden? But it is. And though *threatening* may be a strong word, she had definitely been out of line, that was for sure.

"They're in Alexis's room," the girl says, keeping her hands wrist-deep in the tub as she gently scoops water onto the baby. Nora looks for signs that the girl recognizes her. Maybe not. Then again, maybe. "Down the other hall."

"Thanks," is all Nora can say because what else could she? *You're in big trouble, young lady?* Or, *in my day kids respected their elders?* Exactly—no. Nora doesn't have a choice but to walk away with her proverbial tail between her legs.

She's relieved then to find Alexis and Cornelia in the master bathroom with a full inventory of Sephora spread out over the vanity. Cornelia perches on the edge of the bathtub with a beaded glass of white wine while she watches Alexis dab a gold dusting of eye shadow at the creases.

"Going somewhere special?" Nora asks, making her entrance. The bathroom smells like shampoo, the remnants of fog lingering on the mirror's edges.

"Date night with Max." Alexis leans her hips into the countertop and twists her mouth to the side to apply bronzer under the cheekbone. "He made reservations at that new sushi place on Lamar. Cornelia's weighing in on outfit options."

Nora's glad to see the two of them again. It feels like it's becoming routine, which is as nice as it is unexpected. Like this is a group of women with whom she could really fit in.

"That's so great that you and Max are able to get out and do that," Nora says, and means it. "Hayden would love more date nights."

But, for her, there's often the matter of pinning down a sitter and making reservations at a restaurant and getting up early with Liv the following day, and though she hates to admit it, on any given day her life feels like Jenga—adding any one of those items to it would topple her over. It might be easier to offer Liv and Hayden each a shoulder or a meaty thighbone, a piece of her flesh, and let them cannibalize her. Go to town. *There, there, loves, have some of me, just don't ask for seconds.*

"Oh, I'm sure you and Hayden do, too. You guys seemed so sweet together at dinner." Cornelia sips her wine.

Had they? thinks Nora. That's reassuring. "Thanks, I mean—we do our own things," she hastens to add. "He got me flowers last week." It's embarrassing how good it feels to brag on Hayden like this, and she suddenly has the urge to text him and thank him again for the flowers.

Alexis lets out a low whistle. "I can't remember the last time Max bought me flowers. My fault, I guess. I'm not really a *flowers* kind of girl anyway. I think my love language is unloading the dishwasher. How's that for sexy?"

Nora grunts. "I'd jump into bed for that."

"Oh god." Alexis unsheathes a cylinder of lipstick. "Believe me, I do."

And for a moment, Nora imagines a beautiful world in which folding laundry is foreplay.

Alexis studies her in the mirror. "Sorry, I've got you all hot and bothered now."

"Anyway," Nora says pointedly. "I wanted to ask you, who's that girl in the bathroom with—with your son?"

"You met Francine?" says Cornelia. "That's my youngest. She'll be seventeen this summer. Makes me feel old."

Alexis colors her lips a deep berry shade and smacks them together. "She's the best babysitter. We're so lucky to have her."

Nora struggles with how much to say. "I think I saw her when we were leaving your dinner party."

Cornelia shrugs. "You might have."

But something else is occurring to Nora. "Does Francine babysit for you often?" she asks.

Cornelia is the one who answers. "She likes to make the extra cash."

Nora nods. "The night that Richard died, though, Alexis came home early to relieve a babysitter." She visually confirms with Alexis now. "That wasn't—I mean, was Francine babysitting that night?"

Cornelia rises and goes to more closely examine her own reflection, correcting a slight smudge of lipstick. "She fell asleep on the couch after the boys were in bed. She feels awful."

"Right," says Nora. "I . . . can imagine."

Alexis balances on one foot as she wobbles to slip on a pair of studded heels. "You're here for the community plans. Let me just grab them for you." She tugs the heel up on the left side and hops.

"Alexis, do you mind if I run to the restroom quickly?"

"There's one attached to the guest room before you reach the nursery. Help yourself."

"Thanks."

Alexis trots down the stairs while poking an earring through her lobe just as Nora cuts away toward the guest room. It's well appointed, the bathroom painted a soothing shade of moss green. If Francine was the babysitter in question on that fateful night, why hadn't they just said so? Why refer to her as 'a babysitter'? Surely, that didn't feel natural.

Nora's finishing up, washing her hands and exiting when she hears Francine's voice, low but urgent in the nursery next door. She might not have registered it, but the word that catches her attention is *fuck*. "Shut the fuck up," Francine says, and Nora at first thinks, with alarm, that she's talking to the baby. She misses some syllables in between, but she hears fairly distinctly a few more: "no," "I told you," and "nobody knows you were here—you shouldn't—" are among them. "I don't know, I heard she's asking around about Penny's. I'll find—it's fine. Relax." With a prickle, Nora senses that the "she" in question is *her*.

She pauses at the threshold of the nursery where Francine has just finished diapering the baby. Francine turns, tucking her phone into her back pocket.

"Sorry, just had to take a call. My math tutor."

The lie is so obvious it's infuriating.

"Right," Nora says slowly in a way that makes clear that although Alexis and Cornelia may not see Francine for who she is, Nora does. But Francine simply shrugs and puts the baby on her hip, bobbing him up and down until he grins and grabs a fistful of her shirt to cram into his tiny mouth.

The doorbell rings below and she hears the *click-click-click* of Alexis's high heels. "Are you coming down?" Cornelia waits for Nora at the top of the stairs.

Nora twists her wedding ring. "Yes," she says, turning slowly from Francine. "I'm coming." She's considering whether it's advisable to discreetly tell Alexis what she heard Francine muttering into the phone when the front door is opened, and instantly, they're met with the unmistakable sound of sobbing.

"Lucy?" Alexis ushers a woman inside. Cornelia hurries down to meet them with Nora lagging awkwardly in the background. "Lucy, what's wrong? Come, sit down. Please. Oh, honey. It's okay."

Lucy is a petite woman, no more than five feet tall with bird wrists and a sinewy neck. Alexis curls her arm around Lucy's shoulders and guides her to sit on the sofa, where their hips are pressed together. Lucy sniffles loudly, though she's calmed considerably in Cornelia's and Alexis's presence.

Cornelia sits on the plush ottoman across from the two of them, taking a more clinical posture. "What happened, Lucy?"

Lucy presses her knuckle into the tip of her nose. "It's Ed." His name comes out high-pitched. Like she can't bear it. Whether it's Cornelia's demeanor or the mention of Lucy's husband's name that elicits it, Nora can't say, but suddenly she recalls the recording she'd overheard in Cornelia's office—the couples counseling session—and is struck with a certainty that this must be the same "sexy" Lucy.

Nora doesn't know if she should offer to grab tissues, but even if she could, she's having a difficult time pulling her stare away from the bruise that's darkening along Lucy's cheekbone. Red fingerprints are beginning to rise on the meat of her arm, surfacing out of thin air, as though she's been wrestling a ghost.

"Shhh . . . shhhh . . ." Alexis rubs Lucy's shoulders gently. "You're okay now. Everything is okay. Nora?" She looks over the couch to where Nora is hovering, unsure of what to do with her hands. "Can you get a bag of peas from the freezer, please?"

"Peas. Yes," Nora says with too much enthusiasm, given that a woman has quite obviously been attacked by her spouse. But she's grateful to have a task.

Cornelia leans forward and takes Lucy's spindly little hands in hers. "Did you say something, did you do something that triggered him?"

Nora stops rummaging through the freezer to listen. Is that what you're supposed to say to a domestic abuse victim? It doesn't sound right, though Nora is far from an expert in the subject.

Lucy whimpers again. "I don't think so. Maybe. I—Do you think I could have?"

"I'm sure you didn't," Alexis coos. *There you go, Alexis, good for you.* Nora locates a bag of peas and closes the Sub-Zero.

"No, of course not." Cornelia gives Lucy's fingers a gentle shake. "This is not your problem. I only mean that it's helpful to understand the root causes."

Nora already knows the root cause: *Lucy's husband is an asshole.* There, she's solved it! "Here." She hands the peas over to Alexis, who presses them to the side of Lucy's face. "Tissues?" she asks, wanting to feel part of the team, the solution, the group effort, whatever *this* is.

"That'd be great." Alexis's voice is soft.

As Nora carries over the box from the kitchen desk, she hears Lucy ask, in a small voice, "Is this normal?"

It's a good thing that no one is looking at Nora's face when the word *normal* pops out of poor Lucy's mouth.

"No." Cornelia jumps in with fervor this time. "This is not what happens. You have to know that. Things will get better. Everything will be fine. *We* are here for you. Okay?"

Lucy's lower lip looks unsteady but she nods, bravely.

Alexis checks her watch. "Max will be home any minute." She pets Lucy's hair down her back. That must be nice.

Cornelia stands. "I'll take her back to my place. Call Thea. Tell her to meet us there. We might need her. Nora, I'm so sorry, but I really should go. We'll connect soon."

"Of course. Please." Nora shoos her. "Go."

With one more apologetic glance back, Cornelia guides Lucy the same way as Alexis had done, arm around her shoulders, as if she's actually supporting the weight of the woman beside her.

"I just didn't expect it to be this way," Lucy is saying when the door snaps shut behind them.

"Do you think we should call the police?" Nora asks.

Alexis plops down on the chair at her kitchen desk. "Cornelia will handle it. She's in really good hands."

Nora presses her lips together. She can't argue that. "She's lucky to have you two."

"Thank you for saying that. I—Lucy just moved in the house next door three or four months ago. She's so great. She deserves so much, you know?" Nora detects a quake of genuine emotion beneath the surface and finds that it's contagious for all the very wrong reasons. Like: Lucy Whatever-Her-Name is a battered woman, that much is absolutely obvious, so obvious that nobody needs to express it out loud. And therefore what Nora is experiencing is definitely not (because it clearly cannot be) envy. And yet.

And yet.

It's all right to notice how nice it is to have good friends to rally around you in a time of need. New friends at that. It's probably perfectly okay to see—what's it called—the silver lining. So that's what Nora sees. And who can blame her? Because Nora is also experiencing a time of need. Around the clock, 24/7—she needs time and money and support and patience, and it's occurring to her that perhaps what she needs most of all is friends.

"Anyway, you should meet her on a better day." Alexis's smile is small. "Now where were we? Oh yes, that's right." She opens the drawer in front of her and pulls out a manila file folder labeled with Magic Marker. "The community plans."

Nora doesn't stay much longer, ten minutes tops, during which she manages to casually pass off a collective invitation to her impending gender-reveal party, no pressure.

"And don't forget your phone," Alexis chimes. "I noticed you'd left it upstairs." Nora takes it, surprised and grateful, because she's never *not* aware of the whereabouts of her cell phone, the same way that she's never not aware that she has an arm or toes. She takes it as a sign—maybe there's hope for her after all.

Nora spots Roman on the drive out, walking a small, fluffy dog. "I'm really happy to run into you," she says, rolling down her window. The dog's behind wiggles up at her while, for his part, Roman's still dressed neatly in his work clothes.

He smiles broadly. "Welcome to the neighborhood."

"Oh, thanks, but no. Just running an errand. On behalf of Penny. Actually, that's why I'm happy I've bumped into you. I hope you don't mind, but I've been meaning to get a man's perspective," she says, conspiratorially. "I'm still in the process of gathering information and I'm curious if you might tell me what Richard March was *like*."

"Richard?" He blinks at her.

"Yes, Richard." She waits, the question mark writ large on her face. "You know, like how was his relationship with Penny? Just generally speaking. What was he like with the other husbands when you were watching football or drinking beers or—I don't know—whatever other manly things husbands get up to." Gosh that was so reductive, Nora wonders if she ought to apologize. For the most part, though she has become more aware of her language, she'd also be lying if she said a few "man ups" hadn't slipped when trying to keep Liv from whining, and she'd be lying, too, if she claimed she was particularly bothered by them.

"I hadn't spent much time with Richard recently."

"Really. Why's that?" Nora hangs her elbow out of the driver's-side door, her foot pressing firmly on the brake. She hopes she hasn't put Roman too much on the spot. She only thought . . . well—

"We didn't share many of the same interests," he says, and she tries not to show her frustration. But isn't this just the way of things? So often getting Hayden to tell her about his day is like pulling teeth and then three weeks later she comes to find out he had lunch with his college roommate who he hasn't spoken to in ten years and somehow that didn't bear repeating. She'll never understand men.

"That's interesting." She attempts to tease it out of him. "So you grew apart?"

Roman looks down the quiet street, as if it's somewhere he'd prefer to be. She notices that his fingers clench more tightly around the leash despite the little dog sitting, tail wagging, by his feet. "Yes. Apart."

"In what way do you mean?"

"Pardon?" Roman asks.

"You said you didn't share the same interests. How did they come to differ?"

"My priority is being there for my family," he says, only not as if he's bragging. "I think it's important to make sure I'm around to ensure their needs are met first. I enjoy helping things to run smoothly around our home."

"And Richard?"

A small shake of his head. "I don't want to speak badly about Richard. But it was harder for him lately. I guess we didn't have much to talk about by the end."

"I see. And the other husbands?"

"I think they felt the same. I'm sorry." And he does look it. "But I have dinner in the oven and I really—"

"Oh, yes, please," she says, pulling her elbow back in through the window. "Didn't mean to keep you." But when she rolls up the window and lets her foot off the brake, she sees that Roman doesn't walk back in the direction of his house, but continues on.

Assume nothing. Her own sloppy handwriting on the note returns to her. Not even, for instance, that everyone is telling the truth.

12

T he sheet of paper on which Nora would find the next step in her investigation sat buried in a pile of unread documents on her desk for the better part of a week, as so many things do. On it, she'd been surprised to recognize a name—Jenkins.

And she'd thought to herself: *Jenkins*. As in *that* Jenkins?

Because typed on a medical bill for Richard March was "Jenkins, T." for "neurology services rendered" and billed to the Marches' insurance plan just a few months before he died.

Now this was something. Something that she'd been tempted to shove back underneath the pile of papers, but something nonetheless. In truth, she could shove all she wanted, but these things had a way of surfacing, usually when an insurance company and its trusty defense lawyers got involved.

So Nora bucks up. Better she face the music now than in front of a twelve-person jury.

"Let me at least show you around first." Thea dons her white lab coat like many of the other doctors who have passed by, but as usual, it's her makeup—a shimmery bright pink shadow and a perfectly applied cat eye—that sets her apart. Thea's proud of the hospital wing. There are two CT scan machines, a stereotaxic impactor, an MRI, and an EEG recording system, all of which Nora assumes she should be impressed by.

Thea scans the badge that is attached to a retractable cord on her lab coat and a door clicks open for them. Through the door, they come upon the model of a human head, a sort of cap fitting over its plaster scalp, like one of the caps her mother used to buy at the convenience store to highlight her hair by poking the plastic with a metal tool and pulling strands of it through.

"Brain-machine interface," says Thea when she spots Nora looking. There's a buckle that snaps under its chin, similar to the one on a bicycle helmet. The skull-shaped portion has a number of holes with sensors stuck in. "It helps to create neural pathways. Neural pathways are causal relationships forged in the brain. When you practice a good habit, like waking early, for example, you've created a new neural pathway. Same with bad habits, like cracking your knuckles. Those are neural pathways you might want to *un*do. Stroke victims, for instance, they might lose the function of a limb, and it's because of an interrupted neural pathway, a lost connection that needs to be bypassed. We can do that by using brain-controlled functional electrical stimulation to regain volitional control."

Nora finds much of the explanation has flown over her head: Maybe she has one of those interrupted neural pathways. Science always makes her feel like a dimwit. But she makes an encouraging noise as they continue to walk and talk through the next corridor, where closed doors line either side. It's quiet here, not like an ordinary hospital wing with its hustle and bustle. They enter a small, whitewashed room filled with computer screens and backlit X-rays. "This is Trevor." Thea waves at another doctor in a lab coat. He's younger, clean-cut, with something inexplicably northeastern and Ivy League about him. "And that's Trevor's brain." She points to one of the images pinned to a screen. "It's just a point of comparison," Thea explains as they pass through. But Nora looks back at the black-and-white shapes, pooled in inscrutable masses.

They arrive at last in Thea's office. Like Cornelia's study, there are a good number of degrees decorating the wall and plenty else to be proud of on the bookshelves. A glance and Nora can see what she might have already guessed. Thea has been recognized in magazines, validated by her peers, and rewarded professionally. All things that Nora would like for herself, come to think of it.

Thea slides on a pair of retro, square reading glasses.

On a backlit board more images of brains hang. The dark gray masses each sit within the white halo of a human skull. On some there are arrows, pointing this way or that, at darker hollows and rivulets running through the spongy core. She finds herself reading them like a Rorschach test. (*That looks like a butterfly. There, a banana. That bit looks like a smiley face.*) Which is to say that she can decipher absolutely no meaning in their depictions, doesn't know whether the brains are healthy or sick, smart or dumb, happy or depressed. But what she can make out, typed neatly at the bottom, are names. *Wong. Badgley. Ross. Akins. March.*

"March," Nora reads out loud. "Is that Richard? Because that's actually why I'm here." She moves in for a closer look.

"Ah. I'm just lucky to have friends that are okay volunteering to be my lab rats."

"Volunteering? For what?"

"These are just pictures. I like to have as many data points as I can. I sort of collect them."

"But you actually *treated* Richard." From her purse, Nora extracts the insurance claim. "It says that you treated Richard here just over a month before he died." The line item is cursory. Date of treatment. Supervising physician. Description.

Thea applies a layer of tinted ChapStick and leans back in her ergonomic chair.

"It's important," Nora continues. "Given the state of the body, the autopsy couldn't reveal much. You're a neurologist. If Richard came to see you about—I don't know—a brain tumor that would have shortened his life span or even something else, something that could hint at an underlying medical condition that might have rendered him uncon-scious or even dead before the fire—say, an aneurysm—then we need to know that now. Before the defense brings it up."

"Because of how he died, you mean." The laugh to which Nora's be-come accustomed has gone out of Thea's eyes.

"He burned alive. If it bothers me, it'll bother a jury. The defense could say that it wasn't the home builder's negligence, but Richard's own health that's responsible for his death." That is, if they don't try to argue arson first. Still, Nora must head off each possible counterargument to the best of her ability. "I want Penny to be taken care of," says Nora, care-fully.

Thea blows out her cheeks and passes the insurance claim back to Nora. "It was nothing like that. Richard didn't die of an aneurysm or any other neurological condition. At least nothing I was aware of, any-way."

"You're sure?"

"Absolutely sure."

"Then why did Richard see you? There must have been something."

Thea swivels her chair to look out the window, a view of a busy park-ing lot on a hot day. "He was considering participating in a study." In-stinctively, Nora's fingers run along the base of her own skull. "He wasn't a candidate. And while he was in, I prescribed him a very basic medi-cation for some migraine pain he was having—Sumatriptan—you can look it up, children can have it, it's nothing. Really."

"That's . . . good to hear." Nora shifts. One of the strangest parts about being a personal injury lawyer is how the job necessitates asking many uncomfortable, but necessary, questions. So much so that Nora will often think that she's immune to the awkwardness only to find a weak spot, such as now. "One more thing," she says. "If someone were, say, hear-ing things, would you be able to tell by looking at their brain scan?"

"Someone?"

"If a patient were hearing things that nobody else was hearing, could you tell? Would you know that something's wrong?"

"Like schizophrenia? There would probably be abnormalities in the corpus callosum, yes."

"So you would have known."

"Not all perceptual disorders like what you're describing are neurological conditions. Some are only psychological, and that would be more Cornelia's purview."

"Thanks," says Nora. "That's very helpful." But as she frees herself from the labyrinth of hospital walls, a new possibility opens up before her. What if Thea's right? What if there was nothing wrong with Richard? What if the appliance company was right, too? What if there was nothing wrong with the house? What if Richard made it all up? What if what Penny told her holds true, that a story always begins with a "what if"? And now it's up to Nora to figure out how that story ends.

13

On Saturdays, the hallways of Greenberg Schwall are quiet, but not dead. Nora clocks the telltale motion-sensor lights of occupied offices on the way in, glad that today hers is among them. At least somebody is bound to notice. If somehow she managed to make weekend trips into the office a more regular occurrence, she might have a fighting chance.

Nora blames paternity leave, if anyone would like to know. Or rather, the lack of it, which is exactly what makes maternity leave such a scam. It's genius, really, as far as total rackets go, and since she's such a big person she's willing to give credit where credit's due.

Here's how it happens: A company magnanimously grants, say, twelve weeks of time off to the mother for the birth of her baby. How wonderful, how grand! Nora was quite excited to spend twelve weeks in her PJs streaming Netflix while nursing her adorable newborn. Yes, sleep had been sparse, but she could sleep when Liv slept. Days passed in a blur during which Nora, who was not someone who'd ever once forgotten a meal, would look up to realize it was after noon and she hadn't managed breakfast. She'd go days without showering. She relished the quick scramble to put on a stitch of makeup and change herself and Liv into fresh clothes before Hayden returned from work just after five.

What amazed her most was how time simply stopped during those three months. The world survived without her. She got nothing more done than keeping her baby alive, and that, as it turned out, was precisely enough. Everyone thought she was a great mommy. She read Chronicles of a Babywise Mom on her phone, got Liv on a schedule, sleep-trained, pumped extra breast milk, kept Liv company during tummy time.

And then, just as quickly as it began, it was over.

Your first day back at work will be hard, people warned her, and it was, but not insufferably so. Only when time began to tick again in Nora's world did she realize it had never truly stopped in Hayden's.

She'd assumed the reorganization of their responsibilities would take place organically. But with Nora still breast-feeding, it didn't make sense to wake him in the middle of the night, even though they both had work the next morning. And, of course, if she was up already, she might as well also be the one to change the diaper and rock Liv back to sleep and get up first the next morning, too. No point in both grown-ups being tired. And then there was the matter of Liv's feeding and sleep schedule, which Nora had designed and executed and which now, for some reason, when translated for Hayden, seemed to be in a language he could never independently comprehend. To speak nothing of the packing of the diaper bag, a skill—if it could even be called as much—that Nora had been able to intuit by adding up the number of hours Liv would be away from the house and then solving for the number of diapers needed through simple division. While Nora had graduated maternity leave with an advanced degree in her baby's care, Hayden felt underqualified and therefore didn't apply for the job.

The cement dried on the division of their domestic responsibilities before Nora even knew it had been poured.

And now, four years later, sitting at her desk, a second maternity leave brewing in her belly, she finds that while she appreciates the fact that Hayden would never be dense enough to call watching his own daughter on a Saturday "babysitting," she still feels her absence from home life more than she'd like.

Nora's been converting her incomprehensible notes into fleshed-out client narratives to be included on invoices for forty-five minutes when the first text from Hayden buzzes her phone.

> Liv won't go potty.

Nora sighs, drums her fingers on the screen, considers, but types her reply right away.

> That's ok, try again later.

Liv's potty boycott is a near daily occurrence, not headline news.

This evening is the baby's gender-reveal party, and the threat of all that time already spoken for freaks Nora out. She *has* to be productive.

> She needs to go. She's being stubborn.

Hayden returns with equal punctuality.

> We can't leave the house until she goes potty.

> Then offer her a treat if she goes. Let her use your phone.

Not her best parenting advice—give her what she wants! Bribe her!—but, if anything, motherhood has turned her into a far less principled person. She often thinks now of idealistic young people, fervent, unyielding, and wants to tell them, *Sure, but have you tried having a child?*

I tried.

I don't know. I'm not there.

She replies and then turns her screen facedown, out of sight. He can figure this out. Teenagers have babies for Christ's sake. So Hayden Spangler can certainly handle a well-mannered four-year-old. *Everyone just relax,* she tells herself, like her mind is engaged in some kind of high-stakes hostage negotiation: *Put down your phones.*

Nora sets her mind to regaining focus on her work, despite a gnawing resentment that her flow has been broken so soon after she found it. But after pressing PLAY on a white noise playlist on Spotify, Nora's fingers tap more quickly at the keyboard. She powers through one more day for the client pro formas, then two, and then a full week.

She is stretching her wrists when Cameron pops into her office. He looks new to her in a Patagonia tee and gray sneakers.

"Where you think you're going to wind up this month?" He throws away the question about her expected monthly hours like he doesn't care about the answer. She feels a quiver of disappointment pass across her lips—*oh no, not you, too, Cameron.* The last thing this firm needs is another cutthroat associate.

"Just over two hundred hours if I'm lucky." She's still in the process of tallying it.

He grins. "Think we have different definitions of 'luck,' you and me. That sounds about as lucky as a root canal."

"It would be a lot more fun with a bit of nitrous oxide."

"Figure out who you're going to nail on that fire case?" Nora had told Cameron the whole story of how she'd caught Gary off guard by agreeing to take on Penny's lawsuit, and he now maintains a vested interest in her ability to "show him what's up"—his words.

"I wish. I'm looking, but I'm not seeing an obvious culprit."

"Just remember every investigator has a blind spot. Make sure you check yours." His eyes track down to her desk and he cocks his head. "Hey, is that you?" He points. "You're ringing off the hook."

It's true. Her vibrating phone, which she's been dutifully ignoring, is traveling across the slick surface of her desk. She turns it over just as it stops. Six missed texts from Hayden plus a call.

"You've got to be kidding me."

"Everything okay?" asks Cameron.

"Yes." She inserts her thumbnail between her two front teeth. "No. Dammit." Nora presses her thumb into the wrinkling space between her eyebrows. She once read that it's a technique for preventing wrinkles. A better one might be less stress.

"Swearing in mixed company. Well, I never." He dons an exaggerated southern accent, and Nora knows she's meant to pick up the bit, but she's too distracted by the thumbnail icon of a video that pops up in the text chain with Hayden. No sooner has it loaded than Hayden's number is calling her again.

She motions for Cameron to hold on.

"Hello?" she answers, angling her office chair away to hide the annoyance on her face.

"Did you see it?" Hayden's voice is taut. She knows that voice. It's the one he gets in bumper-to-bumper traffic.

"See what?"

"The video I just sent to you. I'm losing my mind, Nora. Liv is throwing a tantrum."

"You . . . sent a video to me . . . of Liv . . . throwing a tantrum?" The heat in her body spikes.

"Because, *Nora,* it's not a normal run-of-the-mill tantrum. It's an epic tantrum. I don't know what the hell to do. I'm so frustrated. I'm in the bathroom trying to calm down. She's gone exorcist."

"And so you thought the best thing to do was to video her. On your phone."

Out of the corner of her eye, she sees the looming figure of Cameron. She'd almost forgotten he was there.

"So you could see what I'm talking about. Something's wrong." He matches her contempt. She hates this part of when they argue. It feels like someone taking a pair of rusty scissors to the stitches that hold in each of their worst instincts. "It's not normal."

"Actually, yeah, Hayden, it is normal. She's four. Tantrums definitely fall into *normal* four-year-old behavior."

"That's what I'm telling you. It's not a normal tantrum. Watch the video."

"I'm not going to do that." Nora is hunched over, her fingertip squashed in one ear even though there's no background noise. "I'm hanging up," she says. Her heart pounds. One more second and she worries she may spontaneously combust. She thumbs the red button and sets down the phone, feeling like a teenager who's hung up on her boyfriend.

She spins around to face Cameron.

"Sorry, what were we talking about?" Her eyes burn.

"Are . . . you sure you're okay?" He draws out the word, as if it's spelled with twice as many letters.

"I'm fine. Stuff coming up at home. I should get back." Nora is already shoveling folders and notepads into her purse, hands trembling.

"Hey, hey, hey." Cameron stoops so that he can look her in the eyes. "Slow down. That purse never did anything to you."

She lets the purse straps go limp, deflating. "You're right. I'm sorry. You have a daughter and you're never . . . like this." She motions at herself, at everything.

He grunts. "Yeah, well, that's because I'm not trying to wind up on the *Today* show."

"The *Today* show?"

"Yeah, viral video of a black dad combing his daughter's hair like, *Wooooow, he can comb hair?*" He lets his voice go up a couple octaves and Nora almost laughs. "We've got to interview that guy!"

"I'd be impressed. Hayden can't comb *my* daughter's hair."

"Yeah, well, that's because *you're* combing your daughter's hair. If he had to, if you took yourself out of the equation, I bet he'd figure it out. Now I can box braid, fishtail, zigzag part"—he counts the hairstyles off on his fingers—"you name it, that shit is what they *invented* YouTube for. You got your hands on the steering wheel, though. So, you know, he's the lazy traveler." She answers him with a blank stare. "The *lazy traveler.* It's a theory about couples. Two people are traveling together, and no matter what their two individual personality types might be, one person will start *doing*, right? That person starts figuring out which way to the metro, what the day's itinerary is, how to exchange currency, all that stuff, and the other one, they sit back." He laces his fingers behind his head and leans back to demonstrate, chest puffed out. "Because it's being done for them. They don't pay attention to which way they're going. In fact, they probably wouldn't even be able to find the nearest metro station if they were plopped alone right back on the same spot they started from. They're along for the ride. Because they can be. They become the lazy traveler."

"I see. So you're saying it's my fault."

Is he right? What if Hayden, finding no other option, no net, no parachute, would gladly step up to the proverbial plate and *do* his 50 percent of domestic chores if only she could relinquish her death grip on her extra thirty? What if she is an enabler? (What if the call really is coming from inside the house?)

"I mean, I'm not *not* saying it's your fault."

She hesitates. She tries to fight the irresistible sensation that she *needs* to be home managing things.

"Stay." He holds her gaze like she's a dog in training. "He will be fine.

Liv will be fine. It might not go exactly how you want it to, might not be done exactly the way you'd do it, but it'll be fine. I promise."

Meanwhile, a message from Hayden springs on screen.

> I'm just saying. I'm not judging, but do you really think this morning was the best morning to go to the office?

"I have to go," she says, because resistance is futile.

He looks disappointed in her but not surprised.

Another text—

> I'm trying to get the house ready for guests tonight. And I need to go to the grocery store.

She chews the inside of her cheek, tasting blood almost right away.

> Then do it.

Hayden's inability to watch Liv and do any other task simultaneously is a source of raw frustration for Nora. It's as if he honestly believes that every time Nora does the dishes or folds laundry, she doesn't have a four-year-old clinging to her leg. She thinks it would feel good to scream. But instead she bottles it up like a sneeze.

"When you were married to Eleanor," she says slowly, "what type of traveler were you?"

He tucks his lower lip up, dimpling his chin. "Lazy," he says. "I was definitely lazy."

The house hasn't burned to the ground by the time Nora returns home. And her daughter isn't confined to a straitjacket. Nora enters through the garage to find Liv at her miniature table and chair, coloring a picture of Elsa. Sound the alarm. This kid is clearly out of control.

"Hi," she says to Hayden when she sees him puttering around the pantry. Most of her anger leached out on the drive over, and she has no desire to restock it, not today. Today's supposed to be Fun.

In the end, Nora stays home with Liv to clean the house while Hayden makes a grocery run alone, returning an hour later with wine, beer, chips, and dips. They move around each other like magnets with opposing force fields.

Hayden dumps a bag of ice into a cooler. "You know," he says, "a certain expat emailed me a link to a 'great new house' she'd recently come across. Completely by chance."

"Oh?" Nora asks, innocently. "That sounds interesting."

"Very. And the strangest thing was, it just so happened to be the exact same one we'd visited for that open house." He's teasing her, and she's both grateful and jealous because she never understands how he manages to let go of a tense situation so quickly. "What are the odds?"

"So," she concedes. "Maybe we're not master criminals after all."

"I thought it was very smooth. And Andi did raise a few good points."

"She did?"

"A couple." He transfers beers into the ice chest. "Enough room for friends to visit, for instance. Lower property taxes."

"Not to mention your wife likes it." She sets out the wineglasses.

"All I'm saying is that it's a conversation."

"A conversation."

"Yes," he says, "a conversation."

"Okay, good. Then you can start by making *conversation* with Cornelia, Alexis, and Penny, seeing as how they're coming tonight."

14

Nora's in-laws—whose names are literally Mary and Joseph—arrive to the party ten minutes early, bearing the white frosted cake. "I was dying to paw into it on the way over," confesses Mary, setting it down on top of the dryer in the laundry room. "I kept wanting to peek to see if I could tell whether there was blue or pink on the inside." The nurse's office called in the results to the bakery, and Nora was delighted when Mary offered to pick it up before the party. "Joseph says I have no self-control. And I told him I never claimed otherwise."

Mary joins Nora in the kitchen and pulls up a barstool while Nora pours her a glass of champagne without asking. Mary is round-faced, with a ruddy complexion like Hayden's. Hayden takes after her, his features translating far better to a man's face than to her own. Not that Mary seems to have ever minded.

"So." Mary takes a sip of the champagne. "Have you told work about the baby?"

Nearby, Hayden grabs beers for himself and Joseph and joins them.

"Not officially." Nora pulls out a bowl for the salsa and pours it from the jar.

Mary widens her eyes, surprised. "Hayden's told work. Haven't you, honey?" He nods, crunching into a tortilla chip. "He's too excited to keep that kind of news in."

The doorbell rings. "Well, fortunately for Hayden," Nora says lightly, moving to answer it, "nobody thinks he can't do his job because his wife's pregnant and he's got a baby on the way. As for me, I still have the partnership vote to worry about."

Cornelia and Alexis wait on the porch, a welcome exit from the turn of conversation with Mary. "Come in, come in." She ushers them. "What happened to Penny? I thought she was coming."

As Nora busies herself with taking their purses, she clocks a fleeting look passing between the two women, and it's like hearing a couple speak in a foreign language. There's something to pick up in the tone, sure, but she can't translate it without having the proper background education. "She needed to have a rest," Alexis says. "Didn't want to ruin your evening."

"I'm sure she wouldn't have." Nora tries not to sound too disappointed.

"And who is this lovely lady?" Cornelia crouches down to where Liv has appeared, half hiding behind a wall, sporting a pink and blue dress selected by Nora for the occasion. Nora may not have much of a desire to splurge on her own clothes, but when it comes to Liv's she finds it hard to resist.

"There's cake," Liv announces with authority.

"Why do you think I'm here?" Cornelia winks.

The door chimes again. Nora turns, torn. She wonders what Hayden has gotten himself up to and why all the hosting duties have suddenly fallen on her.

"Liv." Cornelia stands and offers Nora's daughter her hand. "Your mommy's told me a lot about your stuffed animals and I've been really looking forward to meeting them. Do you think you could introduce us? I'm hoping to meet a soft dog. You don't happen to have one, do you?"

"Thank you," Nora says to both of them before retrieving two of her neighbors from the front porch, a couple, the husband whom Hayden sometimes plays video games with online and the wife who is a bit dull.

Soon enough, Nora is taking drink orders and showing guests to the bathroom and sweating. Four more warm bodies pile in.

"Are you doing all right?" Alexis clasps her elbow as she swoops by. "You look flustered. Can I help?"

Nora looks around a tad bleary-eyed. Actually, everyone seems well sorted at the moment, drinks in hand, munching cheese and crackers. She takes a deep breath. "No, no, you're fine, thanks, really. I should slow down anyway." She's self-conscious about how cramped and disorderly her home looks compared to Alexis's. "I've been meaning to ask you," Nora says. "You mentioned an application process for the HOA. Is that something that I'd need to do before we made an offer or is that after?"

Alexis's eyebrows hiccup upward. "The HOA? You're sure?"

"Not one hundred percent, but—" She's watching Liv play happily on the floor with Cornelia. Andi's always been good with her, too.

"We do want to count on a certain level of community involvement," Alexis muses. "Speaking of, any updates on Richard and Penny's case?"

Nora experiences a small amount of whiplash at the change in subject. "I'm working hard on it." Though not as hard as she should be, maybe. Most recently, she'd been sorting through the Marches' financial records, but she hasn't found anything out of the ordinary. Certainly nothing to suggest Richard March was on the brink of collapse. "I have a few promising leads and—"

"I would have thought it'd be pretty open-and-shut. But I'm not a lawyer." Alexis manages to make the comment sound genuinely curious rather than judgmental, but it does make Nora question whether the case was, in fact, intended as a conditional precedent for everything else. "Would be good to get that squared away sooner rather than later." She smiles.

"And the application . . . ?"

"Never hurts to get a jump-start on these things. But, honestly, I wasn't under the impression that Hayden—" Together, their eyes land on him, leaning on the counter and not sweating at all.

"No, he's really interested," she says too loudly. "He was just saying so before the party. Actually, I know he was looking forward to seeing you two, let me just"—if she can only show them they are Dynasty Ranch material—"one second."

"Hayden?" Her husband is easy to find, exactly where she'd left him at the start, as if all her running around has happened in a time warp. Here, she hasn't missed a beat.

"Things are so different now," her mother-in-law is saying, her cheeks rosy after only half a glass of budget champagne. "When I was your age men hardly changed diapers. There were still dads who didn't venture into the delivery room! Men of your generation, they want to be so involved. It's so much more hands-on. A nice change. Something to be proud of."

Hayden looks pleased to have Nora join in. She attempts to signal that she means to extract him from the conversation, but instead he says, "Dr. Perez wants Nora to slow down at work."

"That's not exactly what he said," says Nora, unable to resist. "He wants me to slow down." Why doesn't anyone understand that these are two distinct things?

"Oh god." Mary puts down her champagne glass. Joseph, for his part, is scrolling through Yahoo articles on his phone. "Is everything okay? Is the baby all right?"

Hayden puts his arm around Nora. "Yes, baby is fine. Nora's blood pressure is a bit on the high side. But we can still course correct." Again with the "we." Is Nora insane or was there a decided *lack* of concern for her blood pressure this morning when Hayden was texting videos of Liv throwing a tantrum while she was trying to work?

"Oh, Nora darling." Mary's drooping eyelids swoop up, concerned. Nora glances around the small group milling in her kitchen, wishing to plot an escape from this conversation. "You have to take care of yourself. I always tell Hayden you work too hard."

It's true, Mary does always tell Hayden that. But the thing is, the comment never seems to be made out of concern for Nora. Of all the times not to be able to drink.

"It's a big year all around, I guess," Nora manages through gritted teeth. "Hayden?"

"What?" He plays with her ponytail.

"Nothing is more important than your *health*," Mary continues. "Take it from an old lady. You won't look back and wish you'd spent more hours in the office." She taps her ringed fingers on the granite countertop for emphasis. "I can be around more," offers Mary. "You know, help out extra."

"Really, Mom? That'd be fantastic. Wouldn't it, Nor?"

Nora's facial expression freezes on her face and she says in a pleasantly chipper voice that sounds nothing like her, "Hold on, I think I forgot to put something in the oven."

Like her head, for example.

Nora weaves through her chatting acquaintances, making her way to the refrigerator, where she already knows there is nothing that needs putting in the oven, but the chilly air cools her cheeks and she stands for a moment pretending to look for party supplies.

Hayden's hand finds the small of her back. "Everything okay with you?" he asks. "You need to sit down?"

She spins, closing the refrigerator door, and she feels the expression of rage splatter across her face before she remembers where she is. "No, Hayden. Not okay." She marches stiffly past him and closes herself in the laundry room, where she proceeds to pace. Then, because she needs a justification for hiding here, she takes the cake out of the cake box and organizes the plates and the forks.

She wishes Hayden wouldn't follow her in here, but of course he does because that's what good husbands do. They don't let their pregnant wives stew.

They try. They *care*. Hayden is a good husband.

"What did I do?" he asks.

Her back is to him, her hands splayed across the top of the washing machine, letting her head droop so that she can stretch her neck.

She feels herself start to form the word, *nothing*, but stops her tongue from looping its way around the familiar vowels and consonants.

"You know I don't ask for much," she says, a quiver audible in her sentence.

Behind her Hayden huffs. "Nora, please, can't we keep whatever *this* is to the issue at hand and not make it some big, general, sweeping argument?"

She tenses. "This *is* the issue at hand."

He always does this, convinces her that it's only fair to talk about a specific instance, turning her argument small and contextless.

"Okay." He accentuates his resignation, making his lack of buy-in painstakingly obvious, so that she would get it even if she were a complete idiot. "What? What were you going to say?"

She speaks slowly, overenunciating each word like she always does when she's angry. It's too much, but she can't stop. "I needed a few hours at the office today to get things done. I do so much work that is completely invisible to you and I needed a fraction of it back so that I could stop feeling like I'm completely drowning."

"Okay, well, my mother offered to help more. So problem solved."

"I don't want your mom to help. I did not have babies with your mother. I want *you*."

Nora still doesn't turn to look at him. The electric charge between them is enough for her to know exactly where he stands.

"I'm so sick of you acting like I'm this terrible guy, Nora. Have some perspective. I'm not out getting drunk or going out to the bars. I'm not carousing with women. Look, I'm not saying I want to be, I'm just saying—"

"Did you really just give yourself extra *credit* for that? Can you imagine a mother saying, 'Look at me! I'm a great mom. I'm not even getting drunk and going out to the bars! I'm not cheating on you!' Honestly? Can you?"

"You know, maybe if it's stressing you out this much to try to make partner, then it's not worth it."

She shuts her eyes. "Not worth it to who?"

"To you. To us."

Her fingers curl in. "Of course that's what you think. Of course that's what you let your mother think. And you know why?" She can't tell if she's breathing anymore. "It's because if *I* have to work a little harder at the office then it means that maybe *you* have to work a little harder at home and you don't like that. I'm asking for a couple months!" she squeaks. "So that I can do what I need to do to finally get what I have already worked so *effing* hard for, but I can't even get a morning. A single, measly morning!"

Nora hears the slap of Hayden's palm on denim. "You are out of control. So unfair. I know you're pregnant, but are you even listening to Dr.—"

Nora emits a strangled cry of frustration in the same instant that her fist crushes down into the cake. It hardly makes a sound. Her chest heaves up and down.

"What the *hell*?" Oh, she can hear the victory in Hayden's voice. The game is keeping your cool the longest, and she has lost it.

Vanilla icing and cake crumbs coat the side of Nora's hand from the second knuckle up to her wrist. The laundry room goes dead silent. She excavates her fist from the smashed cake. Her husband's eyes are wide, staring at her as though an alien has taken over his wife's body. And that feels as plausible as virtually any other explanation because nothing feels real. Her ears ring as she turns her arm and licks the side of her finger, noticing now the color of the cake's guts.

"Um, excuse me," says Alexis awkwardly, frozen there, the door cracked open. "So sorry to interrupt. Liv's been wanting to know if she can have another juice box."

"I guess we're having a boy." Hayden's voice is monotone as he stalks out the door, past Cornelia and Alexis, the entire moment as ruined as the stupid cake.

⊞

The frosting is bitter in Nora's mouth. Alexis slips into the laundry room, followed closely by Cornelia.

"Jesus, Nora." Alexis examines what's left. "What did Hayden do to make you so mad that you'd harm a perfectly innocent cake?"

"It's nothing." She quickly shakes her head. Humiliation flames on the surface of her face. "Nothing specific anyway. Honestly." Nora can never clearly articulate what the problem is with her marriage, at least not without making Hayden sound like a complete deadbeat or her like a total bitch.

"So a classic case of wife rage then," Cornelia diagnoses.

"Wife rage?" Nora repeats, though the words already feel familiar.

"Oh yeah." Cornelia nods like she's seen a dozen cases just like it. "Mom rage, wife rage, all the various rages that are indigenous to the female species."

Rage. That word hasn't felt like it belonged to her. Rage is violent, unruly, out of control, gut-churning, *masculine.*

But when she tries it on, she finds that it does fit. Nora is indeed enraged.

"I just get so frustrated sometimes," she says, finding that, having been caught blue-handed, as it were, she has no choice but to be truthful. "I'm doing so much. And I know I'm not perfect. I do. But I'm tired of trying to nag my way to an equal partnership. I feel like all I ever hear is that the key to a happy marriage is communication. I'm communicating my ass off. And it's *kill*-ing us. Then there's all of you. With your amazing careers and families and you guys make it look so damn easy." She wipes the rest of the icing off on her dress, not even caring. "I'm sure you think we're a train wreck."

"Do you want to leave Hayden?" Cornelia asks gently.

Nora's head jerks up. "I'm *pregnant,*" she says. But then, more softly— "And, no. I love Hayden." Because this is the heart of the matter. There's no one else she would rather be with. Not in a million, trillion years. She loves him down to her toes. It's just . . .

Cornelia stares at her a long while. She seems to decide against something and then reassess it. She opens her mouth to speak but thinks better of that, too.

"What?" Nora says when she can't bear it.

"Have you considered couples therapy?" she asks.

In response, Nora's face falls. She already knows how it would go with Hayden. Poorly. And besides, Nora's not exactly the therapy type either. She tried. After the accident. But she'd never stuck around long enough to tell anyone, not even a therapist, the truth.

"Not just any couples therapy," Alexis assures her. "Couples therapy with *Cornelia.*"

As if that addition doesn't make the suggestion even worse. "No offense, but wouldn't that be a little strange?" Nora's face screws up.

Alexis blows out through her cheeks. "You would think, but we've all done it."

Wait. "What do you mean?" asks Nora.

"We've all let Cornelia help us through couples therapy. She's a genius."

"Stop. You're making me blush." Cornelia looks way too chic to be leaning her elbow on Nora's Maytag dryer.

"You and Max were in couples therapy?"

"Please. Max and I were at each other's *throats* until we saw Cornelia. I actually broke a crown, grinding my teeth. He made me so mad sometimes. Cornelia changed our entire dynamic. It's like we have a new marriage."

Nora feels that she's getting somewhere. They're telling her that they've experienced marital discord, just like she has. The only difference is that they're saying it can be fixed.

"I don't want to spark a new argument with him." Which is what she pictures in couples therapy, and Nora doesn't like conflict. Although Hayden would probably disagree. His favorite phrase is: "I don't want to argue." Like she loves it. Like if she were writing out a dating profile she would list "arguing" first under her list of hobbies.

"Well, something to think about." Cornelia rubs Nora's back the way her mother used to do, and it occurs to Nora that this is a conversation she wouldn't have been able to have with Andi without her trying—at least somewhat—to see Hayden's point of view. "I truly believe that anything can be salvaged. Except," she says, "for that cake."

With that, Alexis scoops up a handful of icing and smears it straight across her chest. "God," she says. "I'm so clumsy." She takes another fistful. "I'm so sorry, but I think I accidentally dropped your cake."

Top Posts

BOOKS FOR SALE!

21 new comments added by your neighbors

Sophia Raymond * 1 day ago
Hi neighbors, I've got five big boxes of boys' books in great condition that I'm looking to sell. $10 per box (a steal!) First come, first served.

_____

See previous comments

_____

Julie Kaneski
What exactly do you mean by "boy" books?

Harvey Cavner
Oh god, here it comes. Cue the Social Justice Warriors.

Nonie Ramirez
Sophia, I'm saying this out of love, but you need to think about what you mean by "boy books." The idea that boys won't read about "girly stuff" is damaging both to boys and girls. The fact that "girly" things are considered embarrassing or less than for young boys to consume contributes to a stigma that also makes boys that become men uninterested in "women's work." Think: doing dishes, folding laundry, volunteering as a classroom parent. Not consciously, but baked in.

Kathleen Jacobs
My girls love to read about trucks, trains, pirates, and *Star Wars*. This categorization feels so outdated.

Lori Lake
But I'm inclined to agree with Nonie. Let girls have My Little Ponies and rainbows and unicorns and princesses and pretty dresses and fairies. But let's stop acting like those things are any less interesting and cool than

trucks and trains just because they are things that our girls are into. I think it's the messaging that traditionally "girly" things are (a) inherently girly and (b) not badass that is the real problem.

Melinda

I'll take 3 boxes for $25.

15

***

Nora might have expected the gender-reveal party to be a total disaster after her laundry room tantrum, but of course, it wasn't, due, naturally, to their willingness as a couple to lie through their teeth. Hayden, having little choice in the matter, agreed to go along with the story of Alexis dropping the cake and everyone in attendance consoled them merrily. Then everyone toasted their son and made a show of eating the ruined cake for good luck and the whole thing was a smashing—pun intended—success. Until the last guest left and the two of them were left stranded alone together.

Hayden comes down the stairs from putting Liv to bed just as Nora finishes stuffing the last trash bag. "Anything I can help with?" he asks like a little boy who has been taught how to clear his plate after dinner—but automatically and without joy because he knows that's the rule.

So that's that. Her husband is terrified of her. No, it's worse, her husband—*what?*—obeys her. He is obligated to play Good Husband. In fact, maybe he needs his own chore reward chart to hang right next to Liv's in the pantry.

There's an ache of tenderness throbbing behind her ribs. They shouldn't *be* here.

They sit down on the couch and she tucks her feet underneath his thigh to warm her toes.

Hayden relaxes, but not all the way.

"I love you," she says.

Hayden's eyes get happy. He has great happy eyes. She wants them to stay like that always. She thinks about what she'd be willing to do to keep them happy, how much of herself she'd sacrifice, how much she would shoulder.

Only that's exactly what she's been doing, isn't it? That's been her whole plan of attack. She can try to do all the things, but then what will *her* eyes say? They won't be happy, that's for sure. And Hayden *wants* her to be happy. Nora knows this into the cuticles of her nails, into the roots of her hair.

At least for now.

Because some days she thinks: *How does this man still love me?* Often when she looks in the mirror she half expects to see a crypt keeper with a Target credit card and a phone full of thirty-nine sent text messages that say,

> Reminder!

and

> Please acknowledge that you are picking up our daughter today!

and

> Hello! Why are you not responding?!

Hayden probably never feels like a crypt keeper. The fact is that he's never unhappy unless she's unhappy first and that makes her feel very unhappy! That (!) is the Circle of Life, Simba.

She's been thinking about how to begin and has decided on this: "Hayden, what do you think about trying couples therapy?" Because "can we talk" sounds serious and ominous and she's generally trying to avoid sounding too "-ous" about anything at the moment.

"Really?" She catches him wince.

"It's for me, mainly." She hurries to put him at ease. "Honestly. I need to communicate better or . . . differently, I think. I don't know. I just thought, you know, it might help. We've been married awhile now. A brushup couldn't hurt."

He rubs his brow bone. "You'd be surprised. I have a low pain threshold." She feels like she might cry. She doesn't want this to be another conversation where Nora cries. "Oh, come on," he says. "I'm kidding. I'm kidding!"

She draws a deep breath, willing the tears to absorb back into her eyelids. "So you'll go?" she asks. Does she sound desperate? If she does, she supposes it's only because, well, she is.

"I'm not a caveman. I can talk about my *feelings*," he teases.

This is the trouble with Hayden's breed of guy. Eighty percent of the women she knows have downloaded Dad Version 2.0. They give baths and drive kids to school and read books at night and feed bottles and they feel fucking *great* about it because their dads didn't do any of that shit, and besides, they can still always point to one or two guys in their high school friend group who post long rants on Facebook about Hillary Clinton.

All the while they're flaunting feminist terminology. Even the *Bachelor* is saying things like, "I'm looking for an equal partner in a marriage, someone to really *challenge* me," and Nora is thinking, just like Hayden did, *really?* Because how can any of them know that they're in it for fifty-fifty if they don't even know what 100 percent looks like? It's elementary math.

So when Nora leans down and kisses her husband's head and says,

"Yes, honey, you're very evolved," she's only being partially facetious. He is evolved, just not far enough.

As she brushes her teeth and ties her hair up in a topknot so that she can wash her face—water splashing the sink—she has hope.

Cornelia's a genius. Alexis had said so, and look at her marriage. Everyone has their issues. Nora knows that. But she suspects she'd happily trade hers for theirs.

Things might change. Hayden might change. Is that really all she wants? Someone to tell her husband that the only reasonable thing for him to do *is* to change?

That's probably not even how therapy works. She's not going to be able to march Hayden in to see Cornelia like she's the school principal— *Here, straighten him out.* No, they're going to be expected to talk about their Issues. And she's afraid, she realizes too late, to uncover how he feels about her, how he thinks about that day, that day when she learned how life can be completely and utterly irreversible in only the blink of an eye.

16

—

"Have you two tried couples therapy before?" Cornelia's office is uncluttered. The sleek, modern chairs on which they're seated have no cushions and yet are surprisingly comfortable. Nora finds herself preoccupied with how anyone could work at a desk with no drawers.

Nora fidgets. "Um, let's see . . ." she says. "Once or twice, maybe? Not really I guess. Just, you know, in the beginning, when we were newlyweds. We might have gone then, after a big fight or something. To try to learn how to hash it out. We didn't keep up with it."

"Didn't seem necessary." Hayden's voice is thoughtful, gentle. "Normal stuff. Regular relationship growing pains, I guess. We sorted it out." He reaches across and gives Nora's hand a squeeze, as though one of them is getting ready to be wheeled back in for surgery, though they haven't yet been told which one.

Remarkably, there had been an opening in Cornelia's calendar that same week, which had given Nora the feeling of stepping onto one of those moving sidewalks at the airport only to find that it was going much faster than she'd expected.

"That's great to hear." Cornelia beams from behind the desk. "You might find these sessions a bit different from your previous ones. For the better, I think, but hey, I'm biased. Anyway, it's best to know that going in. My therapy sessions are an immersive experience, disorienting even. Some of the techniques you may find . . . well, you may find them unconventional."

Immersive. Disorienting. She makes it sound like they're going on one of those simulation rides at Disney World.

Hayden shifts his weight. "How so?"

Cornelia rests her arms, elbows straight out, on the flat surface. "I've found results are best when clients go in fresh, no preconceived notions. A movie is more enjoyable if you haven't read the synopsis first, isn't it? Think of it like that. Okay, okay, I'm sorry, Hayden, I see that you're a thinking man who likes to gather a bit of info before jumping in with two feet, fair enough. Here's the thing." She leans closer to them. "I'd like you to consider: Most therapists, they ask you to do the work." She says this like she's telling them a delicious secret. Something she shouldn't. "You talk, I listen. That sort of thing. You have the breakthrough." She lifts a finger like: *ah-ha!* "Not here. I want to do the heavy lifting *for* you. Will you let me do that? Allow me to do the breaking? I promise it's less painful this way. But that's for another day, another session." Beside Nora, her husband nods. Really, what else is there to *do* in these situations? It's like when she's handed a liability waiver. *Do you mind risking death and dismemberment for both you and your child while visiting this indoor trampoline park? Are you aware that treating your ingrown toenail may result in hair loss, blood loss, a heart attack, and permanent lung damage? Is it perfectly fine with you if you fall off the boat during this whitewater rafting trip, suffer a severe head wound, and absolutely no one tries to save you? Fantastic! Let's proceed.*

"First, some ground rules." Cornelia delivers this as if it's very good news. "Every session will be recorded for quality control purposes, but I assure you that the confidentiality of everything you say and do here will be fully protected by the law as well as by me. That goes for communications either one of you have with me separately, too. If Nora tells me something as her therapist, Hayden, I cannot tell you, and vice versa. I'm sure you understand. Next, and perhaps most important, a session can't be stopped in the middle. Go to the bathroom before we begin. Leave cell phones in the cubby outside. I require your full attention. Oh wow, your faces. You both look nervous. I've frightened you. I'm sorry. This is mostly just legalese. I don't need to tell you that, of course, Nora. The important thing to keep in mind, maybe the only thing to keep in mind, is: I want to help. Truly, I do. I have dedicated my life to helping couples exactly like yourselves avoid divorce at all costs."

Hayden jerks back. "We never said anything about splitting up. Who said anything about splitting up?"

"Of course. My mistake. All good, and now that the housekeeping is out of the way, the last thing I'll need is your consent to the treatment. Please speak loudly and clearly so that the recording can pick it up. Hayden, want to go first?" Cornelia asks.

"Nora, we're good with this, right?"

If she were being honest she would say that couples therapy has always seemed pointless. It's a contest, really, to see who can win the therapist's endorsement. *Vote for me, I never raise my voice, I have a PhD in compromise. I am oh-so-reasonable.* And the stakes are high because whoever wins gets to go home and say, "Even the therapist agrees!" and neither spouse can argue, because that advice just cost $250, not covered by insurance.

The end result is that everyone in couples therapy is making a herculean effort to hide his or her crazy. It's like going to the doctor with the flu and when he asks what's wrong, you say, "Nothing, nothing at all," and still expect to leave with a Tamiflu prescription.

So, yes, Nora wants to sigh and call the whole thing off, but it had been her idea and she can't be rude and they have a problem and maybe, just maybe, they should at least *try* to fix it.

She nods. Once. That's all he needs.

"Okay, yes, uh, Hayden here, I consent."

Nora improves her posture. "Me, too." She looks at her husband. Her sweet, sweet husband, who is a really good husband, but could really be better. "I consent, too."

Nora is thinking with a clearer head posttherapy, which she might very well chalk up to a placebo effect, but where would be the fun in that? She's decided that she must get down to brass tacks when it comes to the March case. No more excuses. No more beating around the bush. Alexis made it clear enough at the gender-reveal party that they expect results, and if there's a question as to whether Nora is the sort of woman who can deliver them, she intends to answer it.

There's a methodology to casework that appeals to her otherwise messy brain, and yet something about this case in particular strains to defy neat categorization. That evening after their first session with Cornelia, Nora finds herself with a restless energy, as though trying to scratch an itch between her shoulder blades despite her arms being an inch too short. Finding no other outlet for it, she composes a text message to Penny.

> What do you think about me coming by after my daughter goes to bed? I'd like to give you an update and discuss a few loose ends.

The response is swift and, thankfully, affirmative. Ever since she got married, Nora's life has never fallen into place, not exactly, but she has, through the same force and willpower that saw her through fifteen hours of labor, been able to wrestle it there. For the first time in a long time, she wants to be equal to the task again. The question, then, of

Richard March's death is one of geometry. To solve the equation, she must be sure that she's coming at the problem from the right angle.

⬚

The night is darker even just a few miles outside the city center. For Nora it's one of the less appealing things about the suburbs. It hasn't escaped her attention that the scariest news stories always seem to begin *"In a quiet neighborhood,"* and although she understands that the reason they make the news at all is because of their rarity, coupled with a not inconsequential dose of systemic racism, the dollhouse rows and glass box windows of Dynasty Ranch do invite a frightening temptation to shatter the peaceful veneer of innocence.

When Nora sees movement in what is left of the March house, she's convinced her eyes are playing tricks. She slows and rolls down her window. Smoke rides on the breeze. And it isn't from a fire. Instead, it's the cloying, chemical odor of cigarettes, followed by—she thinks—the catch of voices. Nora unclicks her seat belt and climbs out carefully, pussyfooting her way through the wreckage in the dark. Stupid. Determined. Or maybe both.

"You have a hard time staying away from this place, don't you, Francine?" The girl sits with her back to the blistered fireplace, elbows on her knees, in an oversize Rolling Stones T-shirt. A bottle of vodka sits open close by. Beside her, a teenage boy stands up in that protective, shoulders-cocked, chest-puffed sort of way that teen boys try on for size. *That won't be necessary*, she wants to tell him as her eyes skirt the scene.

"We're the neighborhood watch. Gotta keep an eye on things." Francine uses two fingers to gesture: *I'm watching you.*

Nora turns her phone to flashlight mode, and the beam of light crosses over a small mound of cigarette butts feet away from where Francine sits.

"I'm Nora," she says to the boy. "We haven't met." He has the baby face of the nicest member of a boy band but clearly has been trying to make up for it with time spent at the gym. It's working. She imagines that he's prompted more than a few girls to doodle his initials in notebooks over the years.

Francine's voice is a knife cutting across any possible connection. "You don't have to tell her anything," she says before he can answer. "She's not a cop. I mean, you're not, are you?"

"No," Nora says, and the boy visibly relaxes. "I'm a lawyer."

He swivels to Francine, lifting his eyebrows. Something passes between the two.

"Well, I'm just a friend of Francine's," he says. Two friends—no, *just* friends—hanging out in a burned-down house, now what could spark concerns about that? Someone was going to have to sedate Nora when Liv got to be this age.

"Nice to meet you." Nora uses her best grown-up tone.

Even at sixteen, she doesn't believe that she would have bummed around a place where someone had *died* recently. It's disrespectful, which is a thought that, if Nora's being honest, doesn't just sound grown-up, it sounds old. "Okay then, Francine, as neighborhood watch, I have a few questions for you. For starters: Did you see anything unusual on the night this house burned down?" She's speaking only to Francine, who sucks the end of her cigarette, either bored or pretending to be—it's so hard to tell at this age.

"I was off-duty that night."

"You tagged the house with the 'burn baby burn' message."

"I told you not to do that," the boy mutters.

"Yeah, well, I love disco infernos." Francine grinds her cigarette butt into what's left of the fireplace ledge.

"You were at Alexis's house babysitting at the time of the fire."

"Oh, look at that. An alibi," Francine says.

The boy's watching the two of them like a spectator in a game of Ping-Pong.

"I never said anything about an alibi." Winged bugs dart in and out of the light cast by Francine's own cell phone. "So you never left Alexis's house that night?"

"That wouldn't be very responsible of me. Would it?" Francine swats a mosquito on her leg.

"You didn't hear anything. You didn't smell anything. You didn't notice anyone in the neighborhood who didn't belong."

"Francy." The boy opens his mouth and hesitates.

She glances up at him sharply. "I fell asleep on the couch."

He twists his fingers over the back of his neck.

"That's what you told your mother," Nora says.

"It was a school night." Something in Francine's demeanor shifts, and she says this last bit under her breath and without the previous hints of bravado. She unscrews the top of the vodka and takes a swig. The burn of alcohol shows on her face.

Nora softens her own tone. "I'm just trying to help figure out what happened that night, what went wrong. If—if there's something you're not saying—"

The boy sits down beside Francine and quickly stands back up. He can't decide which he prefers. It's obvious who's in charge here and it's not him.

"Why would I tell you?" Francine asks.

Nora wonders if it's having Cornelia as a mother that causes the girl to ask so many questions. What does having a therapist parent do to a kid? If Francine is any indication, it's not all sunshine and rainbows.

"Because it's my job. Because I've been hired—"

"I mean, you're one of *them*," Francine overenunciates.

"One of who?"

"My mother's friends."

"No. Not exactly," Nora says, defensively, as though Francine's just accused her of still watching *My Little Pony*—which she does, incidentally, but with Liv. "Not yet," she corrects without knowing whether or not it's true.

"Does she know you're here?"

"Who?"

"My *mother.*"

"I could ask you two the same question." Nora glances between Francine and her "friend," doubting very much that the two had been sitting together singing "Kumbaya" before she'd showed up.

"We should go." The boy lowers his voice. He's trying and failing to cover up the fact that he's quit making eye contact.

Nora and Francine linger a moment longer, sizing one another up. Nora tries to sort through what her role here is, attempts to calculate which would be worse, to tell Cornelia and Asher or not to. "You're going to find yourself in real trouble, you know, if you don't quit with this whole wannabe rebel schtick." She gestures toward the alcohol and to everything else.

But still. Nora retreats first. She's glad to be out, to step foot into clean air.

The reply comes just as she's almost free of the house. Francine's voice, high and clear in the night air: "Girls can be anything we set our minds to."

Penny insists that she's a night owl even though she's already in her pajamas when Nora knocks on the door to the pool house. Nora's kept her waiting.

"Please." Penny posts up on the couch. "I just think I've been through enough without adding pants with an unforgiving waistband to the mix." She wears a classic button-down pajama set in a playful watermelon print.

Nora takes her own seat in the armchair and begins pulling out her notebooks and a thin manila file folder. "I don't know what happened to Richard," she says, straight off the bat. "Not yet."

"Oh." Penny's posture wilts ever so slightly. "All right then." She adjusts. "Do I look that eager?"

Nora's lips disappear into a straight line. She plans to detail her conversation with the appliance manufacturer and her review of the community plans as well as to ask a few gentle questions about details of Richard's mental health history that may not have found their way into official medical records, but instead, she finds herself folding her hands on top of the folder. "What do you know about Cornelia's daughter, Francine?"

The girl had all but put up a wall with a sign that read KEEP OUT, and the way Nora sees it, there are at least two possible scenarios—either Francine saw something that night and doesn't want to say, in which case, why, or she's trying to cover for her own whereabouts. Either way, it had been impossible to miss the silent negotiation and goal tending taking place between Francine and her mystery friend, and it doesn't sit well with Nora. Left unscratched, it's bound to itch.

Penny's face pinches inward. "A lot, I guess. She's my goddaughter. What do you want to know?"

"Your goddaughter? I didn't realize." There's a lot that Nora has left to learn about this place.

"Not officially official. Cornelia's not, like, Catholic or anything, and I didn't know her at the time of Francine's baptism, but yes. Since she was around seven years old. It was nice. Especially after Julia and Shae went off to college."

"You must be close then." Nora treads carefully. This line of inquiry is already thorny enough. She's not even entirely convinced of what she's getting at. Only that maybe if she keeps fumbling around in the dark long enough, she'll touch on something useful.

Penny uses the one-syllable *ha* in lieu of genuine laughter. "She's a teenager. We haven't spoken in a while."

"How long?"

Penny squeezes one eye shut, calculating. "A few months at least. I don't know the exact date."

"So that would have been before Richard died."

"Yes."

"What happened?" Nora worries she may be pushing her luck. "There's got to be some reason for the rift, doesn't there?" She's interested in knowing what makes Francine tick.

"Oh, she thinks I'm a tattletale." Penny picks at a stray thread on the sofa cushion piping. "I'm paraphrasing, but that's the gist. It all seems sort of ridiculous now, given everything else. Francine had this boyfriend." At this, Nora perks. "*Devin.* He was her first, like, *real* relationship, I think. Very cute. I mean, I'm old but I have eyeballs. And Francine really liked him. No, loved him, apparently. Look, I sound so condescending. She loved him. Teenage love is real love, I'm an asshole. But they were kind of volatile. Honestly, I think they were just working out their feelings, learning how to be *in* a relationship. That's a skill in itself. But they fought a lot and Cornelia thought it was affecting Francine's ability to focus on her own goals and whatnot so she suggested they try couples therapy."

"*Couples therapy?*" Nora's look is disbelieving. "With Cornelia? But they're so *young.*" She imagines trying to drag one of *her* high school boyfriends to couples therapy. Not in a million years.

"Cornelia's really excited about the research. It's a pet project of hers. She says that early intervention—in teens or even before—may lead to better results. You know, like behavioral changes in adults. I'm not good with the science-y words, don't ask me, but I do think the root of it makes sense. I mean, look at me, I'm already so set in my ways."

"Sure, but what sixteen-year-old boy in their right mind would agree to it?"

"I know. I was giving hand jobs in the school parking lot at that age, but Francine's generation is a whole different species. They're so in touch with their feelings and with their causes. Half the time, their idea of fun is a hundred-thousand-signature petition. Or at least that's what they project. Most of it's horseshit, I'm sure. Young people are still young people, come on."

"So you're saying he did it." Nora's a tiny bit impressed. Devin. Did the boy she'd seen look like a Devin?

"Until Francine broke up with him."

"Ah." So maybe not.

"Or that's what she told Cornelia," Penny continues, gaining momentum with the story. "I had to drop by Cornelia's in the middle of the afternoon one day and let's just say I caught Francy and Devin in a compromising position." She drops her head into her hands. "I was mortified. Francine was supposed to be in school. Naturally, she begged me not to tell her mother, but I had to. Cornelia had rules."

"How did Cornelia react?"

"Not. Well. She didn't like the fact that they'd been sneaking around behind her back. What mother does? She said that this alone revealed Devin was a *toxic* personality. And that either they could continue therapy with her until Cornelia felt comfortable with the dynamic of their relationship or she wouldn't be allowed to see him. Francine blamed me. I tried to sit down and have a chat with Francy, but she's *so* headstrong. Cornelia thinks naive is more like it. I thought she'd at least be able to work it out with me. But she wasn't ready, and then the fire and it's all been put on the back burner, pardon the turn of phrase."

Nora considers her short interactions with Francine thus far. Maybe Devin is still in the picture after all. With Nora as their witness. Should she tell? She hates to prove Francine right. *One of them*, Francine had called her with such a healthy amount of derision, and now Nora understands. But why should any of this keep the girl from saying what she believed to have happened the night Penny's house had burned to the ground? Could she really stay that mad at her god-mother?

So no, it doesn't complete the picture. Not at all. "But," she says. "Cornelia can't really keep her from seeing Devin, can she? I mean, she can't truly control what she does."

Penny's expression captures something dubious. "If you believe that, then perhaps you don't know Cornelia very well."

17

That night, Nora had gone to bed, but not to sleep. It seemed that just like in her marriage, she could never leave well enough alone. What Nora had now was another thread: Francine, a girl who had it out for Penny. And Nora strongly suspected, given the way Cornelia and Thea had attempted to quietly tuck away the identity of Alexis's babysitter, this thought had occurred not just to her.

How could Nora decide which loose string she ought to follow?

For hours, the bottle of her mother's Ambien beckoned to her from the back of the medicine cabinet, promising a precious few hours of oblivion. But she resisted.

Now, in the light of morning, she regrets that willpower.

She tries to trace liner onto her puffy lids with the aid of the too-small visor mirror in her car. "Green means go, Mommy." Liv pushes her toes into the passenger seat. "Please, Mommy. I don't want to be late. The Monkeys are making lemonade today."

There's a honk behind her and Nora gives a little start, lurching her foot onto the gas. The liner tip flips up, leaving a black mark exactly where it doesn't belong. On the way into the preschool parking lot, she tries to scrub it off with saliva, but it winds up looking like she slept in her makeup overnight.

Actually she did. She'd once read a celebrity magazine interview—

someone with amazing skin, pick one—and the celebrity had said, quite authoritatively, that skin ages an extra month for every night a woman sleeps in her makeup. By these calculations, Nora's face must be nearing sixty, but then, she's pretty sure it's only sixty in Jennifer Lopez years, not in the years of a regular person. In which case, that's really not so bad.

She checks her email the moment her car is in park. If faced with the choice between losing her cellulite and kicking her compulsive email checking, she'd choose the latter nine times out of ten. But for once, she's glad, because there's a message from school. The subject line reads: Reminder: Teacher Meet-and-Greet THIS Friday!!

She opens it:

Dear Parents,

If you have enrolled your child for next year, you will have received a list of your child's classmates and teacher last week. This year, we're giving parents an opportunity to meet with their child's fall teacher to learn more about expectations and new skills to work on as we near the end of this term and cruise into summer. Come ready with all of your questions. This is a parents-only event. Childcare will be available in the Creative Movements Room.

Love and Peace,
TFCP Staff

Nora turns in her seat to her daughter. "Liv, did you get any papers in your backpack?"

"No."

"Are you sure? Nothing that Ms. Tara handed out that maybe you forgot to bring home?"

"*No.* Mommy, you need to put on your listening ears."

Nora unfastens her seat belt and checks the clock. At the classroom drop-off, she asks the same question of Ms. Tara, who says she can't recall if there had been a paper for Liv, but she thinks maybe not, though there could have been, and, on second thought, she can't really remember.

So, Nora traipses up the stairs and over to the administration building to get a copy of the missing form. She's actually been looking forward to learning who Liv's KinderBridge teacher would be because, unlike past years, this year she'd gotten her act together. She'd done her research and had put in a teacher request!

She'd carefully picked Ms. Sandra because she's been teaching at the school the most consecutive years—twenty-four—and is, by all accounts, the absolute best, and Nora has relished the fact that she's now the sort of mom who knows this type of thing. To seal the deal, she'd even managed a donation of a hundred dollars to the Christmas Festival. The Spangler Family is a gold-level sponsor. *Yippee.*

Nora will get it all squared away and then she'll be off. She bellies up to the wraparound vestibule in the admin office that's been decorated with dozens of scribbly drawings and paper plates stuck with googly eyes and pipe cleaners. She'd forgotten all about pipe cleaners, which had, for whatever reason, seemed an important part of her childhood.

"Hi." She's greeted by the young woman seated behind the desk. Should a preschool administrator have so many arm tattoos? She guesses that these days everyone has arm tattoos.

"My daughter lost her teacher-assignment sheet for next year and I was wondering if I could get a copy. So sorry."

"Who's your daughter again?"

"Olivia Spangler," answers Nora, though she'd thought the woman should know this.

She scoots over to the computer and types. A mom wearing funky printed leggings and carrying two boxes of doughnuts passes through on her way to the two-year-old classrooms. The woman at the computer looking up Olivia's name glances up. "Oh, are those for Jake's birthday? How sweet!"

Nora's stung. She pretends to study one of the flyers left sitting out.

"Hmmmm . . ." The woman leans into the screen. "Let me just check one thing." She gets up and disappears into the back office.

Nora gets the email impulse just before remembering that parents are supposed to put cell phones *away* on school grounds. She shoves it into the pocket of her slacks.

That's how bad her in-box addiction is, by the way. Her phone in her purse gives her separation anxiety.

"Nora?" The tattooed administrator returns holding a thin manila folder. "I don't show that Liv is registered for next year."

"She's registered." Nora pushes the flyer off to the side.

"We're not showing any paperwork submitted for her. Are you sure you weren't planning to send her straight to kindergarten?"

This is ridiculous. *Nobody* sends her kid straight to kindergarten anymore. It's holding kids *back* that's all the rage.

"No." Nora shakes her head. "Absolutely not. Liv's staying for KinderBridge. Ms. Tara recommended it."

The woman—whose name Nora probably should remember—looks apologetic. "The thing is, registration was due a couple months ago."

"Right, that's when I turned it in."

"Along with a check."

"Which I also submitted."

There's a glimmer of hope in the woman. "Great, that'll help. Can you look at your bank account and see when the check was cashed?"

Flustered, Nora agrees. Her fingers fumble for her phone. She pulls up the app for her online banking and sifts through the last few months of checks written. There aren't many, given that basically no one wants checks anymore except preschools and her housekeeper. Her mouth is dry as she scrolls back and forth, back and forth on the tiny screen, certain she could locate it if she were just at her computer. "I'm . . . not seeing it, but I know I turned it in. You must have lost it." Nora registers the look of disappointment reflected back at her. "I don't mean you," she corrects quickly. "I mean someone. *Someone* must have lost it. Never mind, it doesn't matter. I'll write another check. I'll fill out the form again." She digs around in her purse.

"The KinderBridge classes are completely full."

Nora's face freezes. "They can't be."

"They are."

"But you can squeeze another student in. She already goes here. Liv is small, too." She demonstrates with her hand lower than her waist. "Small for her age, which is exactly why she needs this extra year before she goes off to elementary."

Her chest is tight. Hayden. What will Hayden say when he finds out that Nora has dropped the ball on Liv's registration? A cloying desperation seizes her, and she begins frantically rummaging in her purse again. Perhaps a donation. A big one. Straight to platinum, baby.

The woman uses a preschool teacher voice on Nora. "I would make an exception if I could, but the state sets the required teacher-student ratios and the classes are full."

"Full," Nora repeats, dully.

"But I'd be happy to recommend some other great schools in the area."

No! Nora wants to scream. *This* is Liv's school. She *loves* this school, and Liv doesn't love every little thing. She's picky. Like, really, *really* picky. And she's *going* to be a Giraffe next year and sing the "Shepherd Shuffle" and—

A calendar notification buzzes. Discovery documents on one of Gary's cases have just come in.

Nora takes a deep, shaky breath. She hasn't a clue what else to do.

"I'm going to get to the bottom of this. I—well, I'll be in touch. Just—thank you!" The tone of her voice shifts awkwardly as she tries to make an about-face into an extra-friendly mom, a mom that Trinity Fields definitely wants to have around for another year, a mom that gets really good teacher-appreciation gifts, not last-minute ones, and volunteers for the Scholastic Book Fair. That kind of mom. "Thank you *so* much for all of your help! Talk soon!"

Nora leaves the preschool stunned. Of course, it's 100 percent clear that this can't be happening. Liv must go to Trinity Fields Christian Preschool next year, but Nora's stomach churns all the same.

The sun accosts her as she hurries past lingering mothers in the school parking lot, mothers who most likely all have kids registered for school next year.

Back at the office, Nora ignores Gary's discovery documents and instead shuts her door and begins bulldozing through the embarrassing buildup of detritus piled on her desk. *American Bar Journal* magazines, campaign flyers, updated phone lists—none of which she's ever even considered reading—litter the surface. She dumps them unceremoniously into the trash. Next up are the legal pads, the scribbled notes, the old pay stubs, and dry cleaner receipts.

She's just starting to feel good about being able to see the surface of her desk when she spots it. The smoking gun in the form of the Trinity Fields letterhead. Nora collapses into her desk chair and barely avoids emitting a primal scream of frustration.

Too much.

That's what it feels like: *too much.*

All of it. Every damn thing.

And what genius thought it'd be wise to add another baby to the mix?

Really, she'd love to blame this all on Hayden, but she'd never asked him to fill out the registration in the first place. He probably doesn't even know registrations were due. And it's not just this. She can think of a long list of ways in which she is bad at the job of Mother. If there were Yelp for Motherhood, she'd have loads of One-Stars.

Though there'd surely be quite a lot of nice reviews, too. She does make a big deal out of birthdays, for example, and she always attends the classroom parties. When Liv is sick, she gets up and it doesn't even bother her, plus she can make milkshakes in the blender, which truly are the best remedies for a sore throat. She listens to kid music in the car, and she makes a very sincere effort to watch her language. So, yeah, not all bad, she attempts to soothe herself.

But it's still morning and already the day has the makings of an absolutely spectacular disaster.

Nora sits still while Cornelia fastens straps around her upper chest and stomach.

"Women tend to breathe through their chest," Cornelia explains, moving to secure a blood pressure band around Nora's arm. "While men are belly breathers."

Hayden shoots her a comical look from across the sofa as he is equipped with the requisite cords and skin sensors, and it's clear from the way that he's sitting that he thinks he's not allowed to move. Poor thing probably itches.

Cornelia sticks a last sensor to the tip of Nora's ring finger. "There, comfortable enough?" Cornelia breezes back to her desk chair.

Actually, it seems a bit excessive, is what Nora wants to say, but she says yes, the teacher's pet inside her coming out in full force. Welcome to couples therapy, session two. She'd strongly suspected (correctly, it seems) that their first one had intentionally been a softball designed to ease them into a false sense of security.

Cornelia clicks something on the laptop facing her. Hayden and

Nora each have keyboards with USB cables connected to her computer port alongside the wires from their respective breathing apparatus. Nora doesn't have the faintest idea how any of it works.

"Now," Cornelia says, intertwining her fingers and resting them on the stainless steel desk in front of her. "The therapeutic journey on which the two of you have agreed to embark is based on an offshoot of PACT, short for Psychobiological Approach to Couples Therapy. This discipline has been spun off and further perfected by one of my most esteemed mentors, Dr. Neha Vita. Today's focus is on the bonds of partnership where we'll be taking a bird's-eye view of the strength of your marriage. I know, it sounds heavy, but no need to be nervous. This is a polygraph test, colloquially known as a lie detector. It's simple."

Shit, Nora thinks, suddenly panicky. Because she has absolutely no intention of telling Hayden what's happened with Liv's preschool until well after she has a workable solution in sight. Probably not a tactic that'd be endorsed here in couples therapy, especially not with a *lie* detector strapped to her, but Nora has her reasons.

Anyway, it's not like she *enjoys* lying. Honestly, it's exhausting. But lies get such a bad rap. If Nora lies, it's only because it's the truth that would give the false impression. On the surface, though, she knows, her screwups loom so much larger than his because hers affect Liv.

Cornelia checks her screen. "Are you okay, Nora?"

"I'm fine," says Nora. "Just anxious to get going."

"Right. So that's all there is to it. I will read you a series of yes-or-no questions and you will type *Y* for yes or *N* for no." Cornelia sits back in her chair, balancing her gold pen between her fingers. It makes a satisfying click as the inky point unsheathes. "Let's dive right in, shall we? First question: Have you ever lied for your partner?"

There's a pause. Nora glances over to Hayden's face. His tongue is poking out from between his teeth.

Y, she types, and hits ENTER. Her eyes meet Hayden's and he pulls a face and she barely holds in a laugh. Cornelia's attention moves between the two of them and Nora thinks, *Good, let her see that we're in love. We are not every messed-up couple that walks through this door. It's just this one thing. . . .*

"Have you ever lied to your partner to avoid conflict?" Cornelia asks.

The muscles in Nora's forehead flick to center. She hesitates, not wanting to answer the question with its own lie, but also isn't it more important to get to the spirit of the question? It's not as though Nora's cheated on Hayden or spends too much on their credit cards. She doesn't want to give Cornelia any ideas.

N, she types, and holds her breath.

Cornelia jots down a note and clicks her pen twice. "Very good, Hayden," she says.

Wait, what? What did he say?

Cornelia moves her chair into the desk and when she does, she knocks it, and a pyramid-shaped paperweight tumbles off the other end, closest to Hayden.

"I'm so sorry. Hayden, would you mind grabbing that for me?"

He stoops and returns the paperweight to its position with a smile.

"Such a gentleman," she gushes. Her pen clicks in and out, in and out. It's starting to get on Nora's nerves.

Cornelia resets. "Inside of the confines of your marriage, do you consider failing to omit a substantive detail to be lying?"

Nora flushes at the new question, realizing that she's now backed herself into a fairly tight corner. *N*, she types. Better to be consistent than a flake. And even if she wanted to, she hasn't had the chance to talk to Hayden about the Trinity Fields registration, so that shouldn't count. Should it?

"Excellent work." Cornelia's voice is warm, encouraging. But even though she doesn't say his name this time, it's clear that Cornelia is directing the compliment to Hayden.

Nora's mouth twitches at the sound of the pen top again. Cornelia scribbles. What is Nora doing wrong? *Relax, it's not a contest.*

Except that it is, and somehow Hayden of all people is winning. There's a fullness to the tops of his cheeks like he's holding in a smile. He *knows*.

"Do you resent your spouse?" Cornelia asks.

Y, Nora answers swiftly, hits ENTER, and glances up. This is why we're here. *She* is the one with the issue with *him*.

Click-click-click. "Hayden, so sorry, would you mind reaching over and closing those blinds? I'm getting a face full of sun over here."

"Sure, no problem." He obliges, reaching over, careful not to pull on the wires, and tugs at the cord.

"So much better." Cornelia beams. "Very, very much appreciated."

Nora's fingers hover at the keyboard with a touch of impatience.

"If you came into a large sum of cash, would you share it with your spouse?"

Y, Nora answers.

Again, Cornelia praises Hayden, and Nora experiences the long-buried feeling of finishing a test too early and wondering whether she received the same paper as everyone else.

Cornelia clicks the gold pen, once, twice, three times before asking the next question: "Think of the worst thing you've ever done in your life. Does your spouse know what it is?"

Nora swallows. *Y*. One tap. A pause. She deletes the letter.

N.

"If you could go back in time and marry your spouse again, would you still choose him or her?"

She tries to meet eyes with Hayden, but he's watching Cornelia with an intensity that surprises her. Not in a bad way. After all, she wants her husband to buy in. Nora does want this to work. *Y,* she types. Definitely *Y.*

"If your spouse committed murder, would you cover for him or her?"

My god. What kind of question is that? How did murder enter the equation? She's tempted to raise her hand and say, "Excuse me, Cornelia, but I think we can actually skip the killing people part of the curriculum. I'm really just looking for him to, you know, put away Liv's clothes without being asked. That kind of thing. Run-of-the-mill married people stuff."

But Cornelia had started the session off by reminding them: The program should not be interrupted under any circumstances. Even bathroom breaks are out of the question. And Nora wants to follow the rules. So she keeps her mouth shut and types out her answer.

18

---

missed your birthday." Nora's squarely in the middle of reading a history of Steele Heritage, the Marches' home manufacturer, when this thought sends her scrambling to her calendar.

"I was wondering how long it'd take you to notice," Andi answers gamely.

"You might have put me out of my misery. Three whole days." Nora hates that the old adage "out of sight, out of mind" does seem to bear at least a passing resemblance to her relationship with Andi. But it simply can't be helped.

"I think you've broken a record."

"I am *so* sorry." Nora has terrible posture behind her desk. "You should see me. I'm groveling." She's not.

"Hm. Well. I ate an obscene amount of cake. Pornographic really. Rated triple-X."

"Thanks for that mental image."

"Anyway," Andi says. "What's got you so preoccupied that you can't remember your best friend's birthday?"

Nora stretches her neck out. Her eyes itch. "I've got this case and it's driving me a bit bonkers."

"What sort of case?" To Andi, the idea of a traditional nine-to-five has always been exotic.

"A fire." Nora's eyes skirt over the assortment of accordion folders she's methodically ticking her way through as part of Penny's case. "It killed a man. Actually the husband of one of the women whom I've gotten to know in Dynasty Ranch, that neighborhood with the house I love? Hayden's on to us by the way."

"Isn't that hitting a little too close to home? Pardon the pun."

"I hope not," says Nora, starting to feel distracted by the gravitational pull of work. "Richard, the husband, he was burned alive in the fire. It was terrible."

"Burned alive? That really happened? It sounds so, I don't know, *pagan*, I guess. A human sacrifice. Like, what's it called? A wicker man? Christ. I mean, sorry. Look who's a heathen now. What'd Hayden say about the house, by the way?"

Nora sighs. "It's an open conversation."

"That's progress."

"We're in couples therapy, actually," she adds, because she doesn't think it's something she ought to feel ashamed about. Lots of couples need help. If anything, it's quite mature of them.

"What for?"

"Cornelia suggested it. She thought we could really benefit. She's a genius. Apparently." Though out of Nora's mouth it sounds sillier than when Alexis had said it.

"That's one of these neighborhood biddies, I take it?" At which Nora feels a tiny smolder of annoyance. "You sound a little—I don't know—*evangelistic* about this whole thing. You do know, she's not an actual genius, right?"

"How do you know?"

"I don't. Obviously. I just, I don't want you to feel desperate for their approval or anything. You're an equal, Nor. You don't have to try to fit in." There she goes, trying to mother her.

"I know," Nora says, but what she really wants Andi to do is shut up. Nora should have never brought it up in the first place.

"So, are your periods all synced up?" Andi teases.

Nora cracks a smile. "Hey now, I think it's nice to want to get to know your neighbors." Nobody tells you how far you will go, as an adult, just to make the types of friends for whom you don't have to clean up before they come over.

"Yeah, what's the saying? Keep your friends close and your enemies—"

There's a hiccupping pause in their connection, and Nora removes the cell phone from her ear to see that Alexis is calling. She ignores the little skip-rope jump in her heart, certain that Andi wouldn't approve.

"Andi—" she interrupts. "I'm sorry, but another call's coming in. I have to run. Love you." But before Andi can complete the final two words of their ritual, Nora's clicked over to the waiting call.

"Nora, I was calling to see if you'd like to join us for yoga this evening."

"Yoga? Where?"

"We do it every week. This time it's at Cornelia's. We have an instructor and everything. Manika. She'll make your body feel like cooked spaghetti."

"Every week? Really?" Nora asks incredulously. Also, she's never exactly aspired to noodledom. But.

"Don't sound so surprised. It's an hour, Nora," Alexis cajoles. "Not a two-week vacation to Puerta Vallarta." Though in Nora's life, one would be no more likely to occur than the other. "Look at you. You're wound so tight. Thank god you met us when you did."

If Hayden had said the same thing, she would have heard it as "uptight." But coming from Alexis, it actually does come off as good-natured, which is how Hayden always says he intends it.

"So, will you?" She can hear Alexis typing in the background, probably doing exactly what Nora herself is doing. Certainly Nora's no busier than the CEO of a startup, is she?

She chews the inside of her cheek, too hard as usual, enough so that it will bother her for days and she'll accidentally and painfully dig her teeth into it whenever she eats. Alexis is right about that; she is uptight.

"Nora? Are you still there? Did I lose you?"

"Sorry. I'm only thinking. I mean, I guess I could ask Brittany to stay late today. She doesn't have class. And I'd considered swinging by soon to return the documents you gave me." Now that her secretary has made copies and created electronic files of the community plans.

So yes, it's decided. Nora will attend yoga. It's only after she's hung up with Alexis that she realizes she should have asked whether the class is suitable for beginners.

❖

Asher opens the door holding a silver tray. "Nora, it's such a pleasure to see you again. Can I interest you in a juice? Carrot-apple-ginger. I just made them. My own personal blend."

"Are you serious?" Nora, in never-used-for-yoga yoga pants and a sweat-wicking top, plucks one of the cold glasses from the tray. He's included gold-leafed cocktail napkins. She takes a sip. The juice is fresh and scrumptious. She licks her lips, hoping she's not left with an orange mustache. "You made this?" She eyes the juice more closely.

He guides her through the house and its imposing antique mirrors. "I like to make sure Cornelia gets her vegetables. She works so hard."

She works so hard. Of course, Cornelia must, so why is it that Nora's caught off guard? Asher *should* be proud. Bravo.

"The ladies are in here." He hovers outside a closed room. "There's already a towel and mat set up for you. The instructor, Manika, is very good. Enjoy your hour." He takes her empty juice glass before propping open the door for her.

Right. So, that was nice.

And then—*I mean, it was nice . . . wasn't it?*

She steps into the darkened room, where aromatherapy candles flicker around the perimeter. She can make out the shadowy outlines of Thea, Cornelia, Alexis, and Penny, sitting straight-backed and cross-legged on their respective mats.

"Welcome." Manika, a long-necked woman at the front of the room, waves her in with graceful undulations of both arms. "Please join us for opening meditation."

The temperature is balmy as Nora removes her shoes and takes a seat at the back of the unoccupied mat. She looks around nervously, but each of the women sits with her eyes closed, the backs of her hands pressed to her knees. Nora matches their position and squeezes her eyes shut.

For the first several minutes, her heart thunders so loudly she's sure it must be bothering the others. She can't slow her pulse. Her mind is filled with the same annoyed inner monologue that she can't help subjecting herself to during a massage. *Enjoy this, Nora! Are you enjoying it? If so, then excuse me, but why does it feel like your fingers are warped into claws? That's not right. You're doing it wrong. Wrong, wrong, wrong, Nora!*

Not exactly helping matters, is it?

She'd hoped that a bit of deep breathing might help her stop thinking about what she's going to do about Liv's school and how she's going to explain it to Hayden. Not so. She is very *much* thinking about it. Maybe more.

Fine, be that way. Maybe the whole secret to being Zen is to give up on being Zen. And slowly, unexpectedly, Nora's mind does, in fact, ease. She begins to feel the spaces between her breaths.

She meets the eyes of Alexis, who offers her a tranquil smile before turning into Warrior pose. The rest of the time passes fluidly. Nora can feel the soreness creeping into her muscles as she folds herself into Child's pose, but it's the good kind of soreness. The kind that reminds her she has a body and that it's for more than lifting a child into a car seat.

"Namaste." Manika presses her hands to her heart as the hour ends and quietly makes her departure out of Cornelia's studio.

"So glad you could make it." Cornelia bends down and grasps Nora's hand once everyone has stirred from their yoga stupor. The five women spill out into the hall, and Nora has the feeling of being born into air-conditioning, blinking and disoriented.

"That was wonderful." She finds herself saying this to Thea and means it, mostly. Thea wears a hot pink top with neon yellow pants that accentuate her hips.

"Warm towel?" Asher appears and offers them each a steaming towel and a cup of herbal tea. Nora dabs the towel on her neck and behind her ears.

The women collapse in the front sitting room, loose limbed and with teacups balanced in their laps. Cornelia wears a contented smile while Thea rolls her neck, indulging in a long exhalation.

"I hate yoga," says Penny.

"You do not," Alexis says confidently.

"I do so."

"Then why do you come every week?" Alexis drinks from her tea. "No one's holding a gun to your head."

"I don't want to be left out, do I? You might all share *secrets* without me."

Nora likes the idea that by being here she's been selected to be privy to those secrets, even if they are only hypothetical ones.

"What about you, Nora?" Penny sets her teacup down on the coffee table, running her tongue over her teeth with a sour expression. "Are *you* a yogi?"

"Hardly." Nora laughs. "My mind goes on a loop. Today it was about my daughter's preschool." She edits out any mention of her other preoccupations—Francine, Richard, the appliance company, Dave's pending results—not wanting to rock anyone's Nirvana quite so soon. "Over and over and over," she says. "Highly annoying, as you can imagine. And by the time I manage to stop it, the class is over."

"Exactly." Penny points at her, as if to get all the women to see.

"Where does Liv attend preschool?" Thea asks, blowing onto her own tea.

"Trinity Fields," Nora answers automatically. "Or, she did. Wild about it. That is, until I neglected to turn in her registration on time. Or at all, for that matter."

"That sounds bad." Alexis grimaces.

Nora chugs the remains of her tea, as if willing it to be something much stronger than Calming Chamomile. "Bingo," she says.

There's a small flutter in Nora's stomach and she presses her palm to the soft area on the side and below her belly button. The baby announces himself. Perhaps not for the first time. She really should pay more attention to him.

"Excuse me," she says. "I'm just going to run to the ladies' room. Carry on." The bottom of Nora's cup makes a delicate clinking sound when set back against its china saucer. She doesn't think she's set eyes on her own china since her wedding day.

After she's washed up and used the French soap, Nora fully intends to rejoin the group until she notices a reflection in one of the large antique mirrors mounted such that it makes visible a portion of the front sitting room, and in it, Francine. Nora hesitates, but slowly finds herself drawn away from the other women, pulled closer to the mirror image of an oblivious Francine White.

As she creeps forward, her hand slides over the gentle curl of a slick mahogany railing at the foot of the staircase. She listens to the women's voices, out of view, and can't make out any of their words.

A long Persian rug dampens the sound of her footsteps. As she approaches, she hears the murmur of Francine's voice. "Daddy," she says. "Stop, you don't have to do that."

Once closer, Nora gets a clearer picture. Asher busies himself, bent over a coffee table with a paper towel.

"It's clean. It looks good." Francine's long blond hair is a curtain over her back. There's the sound of a dull *ker-thunk* on a plush carpet. "Here," Francine says softly. "Let me get that." She stoops and comes up with a small porcelain cat, returning it to its original position on the coffee table. Francine puts her hand on her father's shoulder and leans to press a kiss to his cheek. "Love you, Daddy," she says.

A noise from behind Nora below startles her. A gust of laughter blowing in from down the hall, but when she brings her attention back to Francine, she sees that their eyes have met in the mirror. Francine's expression clouds over and Nora feels the embarrassment of her own intrusion and quickly retreats back in the direction from which she'd come. She returns to the group, pink-cheeked and jittery.

"Nora." Alexis tilts her head. "We were just talking about you."

"Good things, I hope." She tucks a strand of hair behind one ear and reclaims her teacup.

"I just received your application for the HOA and, good news, we already have a volunteer to sponsor you and Hayden."

"We do?" Nora glances at Penny, who fidgets.

Thea raises her hand.

"Thank you." Nora doesn't know what else to say.

"Great." Alexis clasps her hands. "Then I guess now all that's left is for you to make an official offer."

19

Nearly a week later, Hayden grins as he takes a beer from the refrigerator. "So," he says. "Might as well say it. I think I got an A plus in therapy today."

Nora pours olive oil into a hot skillet. She's making Hayden's favorite meal, pan-fried pork chops, a decision she'd made that morning back when she believed her husband might need a pick-me-up after their third round of couples counseling.

But Nora had once again misjudged the situation. Cornelia continues to love Hayden. *Hayden, that's so interesting. Hayden, I'm really inspired by your honesty. Hayden, that's not always a given with the men that come through my door.* Today, she and Hayden were asked to sit back-to-back in a modern podlike chair that gave her the sensation of having blinders on. And the fact that Cornelia stood in front of him instead of her for nearly the entire session made her feel as if she was being punished. It kicked her competitive spirit into high gear.

They were each asked to share a traumatizing experience that happened to them before the age of ten. Nora described losing her parents at an amusement park, eliciting very few follow-up questions from Cornelia, while Hayden described having been bucked off a horse named Lola and breaking his femur. She thought: *Well, he'd never thought it interesting enough to bring up before.* And this, too, annoyed her. But here Cornelia was eating up the details with a silver sp—not spoon, but gold pen, more like. *What did the bone-splintering feel like? How did it sound? Take me into the pain.*

Now Nora wishes for carbs. And chocolate, preferably. Both in large quantities.

But instead, she places the conciliatory pork chops in the pan and goes to check on Liv in the living room. Hayden follows.

"Maybe next time you'll let me borrow your notes." She makes sure to look happy for him—not to be a sore loser. Cornelia *had* warned them that it wouldn't be like *normal* couples therapy. Still, she'd expected maybe a bit more scolding. Of Hayden, naturally.

"Depends what you're willing to do for them," Hayden says, giving a light spank to the sweatpants that she'd pulled on not five minutes after walking through the door.

The truth is that Nora likes her husband when he's a bit of a pig. Contrary to popular belief, she doesn't want to castrate him and wear his testicles on a necklace or anything.

Liv sits on the rug, holding a hot pink plastic phone. She has a very serious expression for a four-year-old. "What are you doing?" Nora kneels down beside her.

"Working," says Liv without looking up. "Hold on. This is my job."

"Oh my." Hayden chuckles. "What do you do for work?"

Liv looks up at him, her brow still creased. "Computer."

"You do *computer*? That does sound very important," he says. "I bet you make a load of money doing that."

"A *load*," she agrees, then shrugs. "I have to finish this. It's important."

"Well," Nora says, "let's make dinner a firm deadline. Have it on my desk by then?"

Liv's beautiful blond curls fall down over her ears. She is an absolute boss lady. "Mommy. I'm just busy. *Busy* is how God made me."

Amen, thinks Nora.

Hayden sinks onto the couch and keys into the talking heads screaming at one another on TV. A couple of minutes pass before Nora sits up sharply. "Do you smell that?" She sniffs the air, smelling smoke. *Smoke.* "Oh god." She scrambles to her feet. Remembering.

In the kitchen, a flicker of flame leaps from the pan. Her eyes widen.

"Where do we keep the fire extinguisher?" she yells, opening up the cabinets under the sink where she finds nothing but sponges, Clorox wipes, and an empty bottle of Windex. "Hayden!"

The smoke alarm blares in a persistent, earsplitting beep. She rushes for the pantry, fumbles with her disorganized shelves, fingering the array of boxes until she finds the baking soda.

The flame has climbed higher.

Now Liv is in the kitchen, too, and Hayden is holding her back by the chest.

Nora shakes the box of baking soda onto the fire. The flame licks the white, milky part of her forearm and she jerks away. Hayden pushes Liv back, using his dad voice to command her to stay put. Don't move. He bellows. He grabs the drawer full of dish towels and shoves them over the top of the fire. The flame jumps onto one of her favorite holiday towels—a hand-painted Santa Claus given to her by her mother. The edges curl into black and Hayden yelps, tossing that one in the sink and throwing on the tap until—pat, pat, pat—and the rest of the fire goes out.

Along the ceiling crawls a cloud of black. The dish towels are ruined.

Liv covers her ears. The bleat of the smoke alarm won't quit. Nora runs her arm beneath the faucet. She slurps in air as the cold water hits her skin.

While Hayden opens the door and waves out the smoke and tries to cancel the alarm with a broomstick, Nora watches as an angry red splotch spreads out on her arm. Parts of her skin have already begun to blister.

She slurps air through her gritted teeth. It feels like the universe is sending her a warning, doesn't it? To solve the case.

It's not as if she's not trying. But cases, they don't get any easier to solve the more time that passes. More often than not the opposite holds true. And what Nora's losing, what she's always, always losing, is time.

⊞

That night Nora dreams she sets fire to her house. The hardwood floors, the unwashed sheets, the pile of towels in the laundry room, the messy closets, they all burn. She wakes up sweating hot, surprised to find light flooding through the shutters. Nora's collarbone is slick; her chest heaves and then, suddenly, panic sets into her lungs like a virus.

Were Hayden and Liv inside the house?

She can't remember. Her mind searches. Blind. Fear.

Another beat until her brain catches up. She breathes their names and leans her head onto the comforter between splayed knees. Up until now, her worst dreams have always involved Liv's accident.

Nora retracts at the sound of Hayden entering their bedroom. "I made eggs," her husband says.

She raises her head to see him extending a plate full of them to place in her lap.

She has no appetite. "Where's Liv?"

"Eating breakfast."

She picks up the fork and stabs at the gummy whites. "Thanks." Her voice carries the morning rasp. She's still trying to shake free of the dream, but it's got her in a death grip.

"No sweat." He has a conspiratorial smile, like he's debating pouncing on Nora the way he used to on mornings before Liv. "Just don't get used to it."

When he disappears, she fumbles for her phone, always the first thing she does when she opens her eyes. Her fingers navigate to her in-box on autopilot where an unread email waits for her at the top with its subject line cast in bold. She reads it once, twice, three times before her eyes manage to focus and her brain can scrabble to translate the letters, but there they are in black and white.

The Truth about Dynasty Ranch

20

Under ordinary circumstances, Nora wouldn't look twice at the woman now seated across from her at the coffee shop, the one with blunt bangs and a T-shirt with that ever-popular Etsy style of calligraphy, *Mom. Wife. Boss.* written vertically down her chest. To an outsider, Nora and Sylvia Lamb probably look like two mommy friends passing time while the kids are in school, which makes the reality of their meeting all the more grim.

"Thanks for meeting," Nora says, though it's clear Sylvia had been the one to engineer it. Upon arrival, Nora already knows that Sylvia is from a small town outside of College Station where she was top of her class at A&M then onward to Columbia Business School, after which she did a brief stint in New York arranging financing for off-Broadway musicals prior to returning here to marry and have children. None of this is at all obvious on first glance.

"I've been trying to get someone to listen to me about Dynasty Ranch for weeks." Sylvia takes a sip of her tea and flinches. Too hot. "First let me say, I liked Penny. I have no ill will toward her, really, I don't," she's speaking rapid-fire, like she's a bottle of fizzy water shaken up, the cap now removed. "You would think—anyway, I read everything about what happened to her. I feel terrible. She doesn't deserve any of it. I read

every article I could find. I set a Google alert and everything and that's
how your name popped up."

Nora takes a deep breath in an effort to lead by example. "I'm sorry,
I don't follow. You'll have to fill me in. Why would there be ill will?"

Nora curls her hands around the base of her coffee. It really is scald-
ing. It's as though these coffee places have learned nothing from that time
McDonald's got sued for boiling an old lady's legs. Yes, personal injury
attorneys like Nora had gotten a bad reputation from the case, but importantly, in her opinion, the lawyers had been right—the coffee *was*
dangerously hot.

"Because of the discrimination." As if this was obvious.

"Who discriminated against whom?" Nora tries to strike a tone that
is neutral and nonjudgmental.

"The HOA." Sylvia's volume rises and Nora flinches visibly. The
space has an urban warehouse vibe and the concrete floors do have a ten-
dency to make voices echo. "They didn't want to sell a house to a stay-
at-home mom."

"You wanted to buy a home in Dynasty Ranch?"

"I was under contract. 2913 Majestic Grove." Nora goes still. "I loved
that house. I pictured my kids growing up there, you know?" She does.
"Then right before we closed, the seller unilaterally terminated the contract. Poof! Gone."

Nora swallows. "How could they do that?"

"Have you taken a look at the deeds?"

Nora has little patience for the game she now finds herself playing,
but she also finds she has little choice. And so, she asks warily, "For
what?"

If there's one thing that's becoming obvious it's that Sylvia has been
champing at the bit, waiting for someone to hear her side of a story, and
Nora has just inadvertently offered her an ear.

"For the houses in Dynasty Ranch. When we made the offer, my Realtor had pointed out this one strange little clause. Anyone might overlook it. A restrictive covenant, she called it. Do you know what that is? Of course you do, you're a lawyer." Nora rifles through her memory of her Property Law class as a 1L. A restrictive covenant is a condition passed down to each new owner of the house that keeps the owner of the property from using the home in certain ways. Like, a property owner in a residential area can't set up a business in his home or can't build a fence over six feet high. That kind of thing. "Every house in Dynasty Ranch has a restriction written into the deed stating that the HOA has final approval over any new buyer."

Nora blows slowly over the top of her own cup of black coffee. She can easily check the documents to confirm, but there are all sorts of ancient artifacts written into home deeds. Nora had been warned about the HOA admissions process, and what's interesting to her is hearing how it plays out.

"*I* thought," Sylvia continues, "maybe the seller had decided not to sell at all, but then not more than two weeks later the house was back on the market. For only five thousand dollars more. I mean, come on. It's not that they didn't want to sell it. They didn't want to sell it to me."

Nora scoots her chair in an inch. Everyone has their own version of the truth. Nora knows that better than anyone. "But why would that be?" she indulges Sylvia. If the seller had another offer waiting in the wings, then sure, spring for the better deal, ethics be damned. But instead it seems the seller had simply started over, relisted the house for no apparent reason. Why take the chance?

Sylvia leans forward. "Up until a couple months ago, I was a wealth manager at one of the big banks. I did very well, but the job was stressful, and anyway, my kids are young—six and eight. I wanted to be around more. That was always the plan. We live in Westlake. Property taxes are insane. So, my husband and I decided that we'd move somewhere more affordable and I could quit my job and do the stay-at-home mom thing for a while. As soon as our offer was accepted, I put in my two weeks' notice. Right before closing, I happened to mention to Penny that I'd left my wealth management role. We'd become close." And this—this is the first thing Sylvia tells her that catches Nora off guard. "I'd really gotten to know the women there. A few days later, the contract fell through. They returned my earnest money, but that wasn't really the point."

"I'm not sure I follow." Nora is still stuck on how Sylvia had said she'd gotten close to the women. So what? Nora isn't in an exclusive relationship with Penny or Cornelia or Alexis or Thea, and even if she were, they'd clearly broken up with Sylvia.

It's not middle school.

"They didn't want to sell a house to a stay-at-home mom," says Sylvia. "They only want high-powered *career* ladies." The fact that Nora thinks this is a ridiculous accusation must show up on her face because Sylvia laughs. "Don't tell me you haven't noticed everyone's résumé. In fact—" She appraises Nora. "—I'm sure they love you. *You* they would actually let buy a house there." Nora wishes they were having this conversation elsewhere, preferably someplace where she could wear sunglasses. "Oh. *Oh.* Wait. Wow." Sylvia gives her an I-told-you-so smile, and Nora feels her face redden. "You're considering it? They've recruited you, haven't they?"

"I went to an open house." Her words come out smooth.

"Isla Wong? I thought so. She's in charge of their recruitment."

"She's a Realtor."

Sylvia scoffs. "This is why I called the local news." She slaps the table. Too loudly. The students at one of the community tables notice, even with their noise-canceling headphones on. "It's discrimination. Absolute blatant discrimination."

"And that's why you contacted the news. Because you believed they wouldn't let you buy a home because you . . . don't work." Honestly, Nora wants to laugh. Sylvia sounds like one of those crazed, middle-of-the-night conspiracy theorists. She could use a hobby.

Sylvia's caramel eyes snap to attention. "Obviously. I thought the threat of one of those segments where they expose, like, poor commercial behavior would get the HOA to stand down. And, after I saw *that* wasn't going to happen, then I just wanted them exposed, period. But I never could get anyone to call me back."

"I understand your point of view," says Nora, eager to prevent this fact-finding mission from becoming one long bitch session. She could see that Sylvia would very much like to poison the well. "But I don't see what any of this has to do with the fire that killed Richard March, which is what *I've* been hired to investigate."

"I'm telling you all this as a courtesy. I just thought you might want to know what all you're getting mixed up in before it's too late."

Nora stands to leave and Sylvia stops her. "Just tell me," she says. "Have you made an offer on that house yet?"

"No," Nora says. "Not yet."

Sylvia narrows her eyes. Nora can't decide if she's pretty. Maybe if she weren't so mad. "But you will. Well. Don't quit your day job, as they say. I'm sure you've already seen the roster."

Nora can't help herself. "What roster?"

Sylvia's tone when she answers is gloating. "The one that shows the list of women they've collected."

Nora pushes her chair in. She tells herself that this has been a colossal waste of time. She tells herself that Sylvia hasn't gotten to her.

"You know," she says to Sylvia, evenly, "I do have to ask myself, if it's such a terrible place to get mixed up in, why are you trying so hard to stir the pot?"

www.powertenmag.com

The Problem Isn't That Women Aren't Being Promoted, They're Not Working

By Jessica Padma

"Many top-tier companies are eager to promote women into leadership roles, but complain that the ranks of midcareer women are so thin that it gives a false impression of sexism in the workplace."

_____

Read Comments

_____

Kristen O'Brien

I left my job at forty-five years old. Honestly, I did get the impression I was being groomed to take on more responsibility at work and that was exciting. But also, I couldn't compute how I was going to handle more responsibility. I was already at max capacity. So I left. Part of me wishes I stuck it out. It's been ten years and I know if I went back, I'd be starting so far down the ladder and having to repeat my steps. And anyway, I really am happy. I love the time I've gotten to spend with my family. It's a blessing.

TwinMommy

I felt guilty. And no, it wasn't "mom guilt" like everyone thinks. I felt like I wasn't being fair to my work colleagues. I worried they were all working so much harder than me or that I was being cut some kind of slack because I was a mom. I had a great boss and I truly believe he wanted me to succeed. But I just got tired of feeling bad about not giving my career and my coworkers my all.

Vicki Sanchez

I didn't leave the workforce but I did switch from partnership track at my law firm to take on a cush job as a counselor in the career services office at my alma mater. I make a third of the money, but I get good benefits, summers off, and my hours are strictly nine to five.

A Housewife

It's sad that women today feel so overwhelmed. They have way too much to do. I think of all the great contributions that women could be making to science, academia, politics, art, you name it, but they can't because they're making ham sandwiches.

Tammy Zang

The messed-up part is that you don't even have to be a mother to get hit with the "motherhood penalty." Everyone just assumes that you have an interest in bearing children. If you say you don't, they figure you're lying or you just haven't started to feel your biological clock tick yet.

BoyMom32

My husband and I talked about it and during this period of our lives in which our kids need full-time childcare, we can't justify the cost of me working. I'd barely be making more than it'd take to keep them in daycare. I do plan on jumping back in when they're older, though.

Christina Paxton

I saw such a need for stay-at-home moms. I tried to be involved in my kids' education and extracurriculars while I was working, but I saw how much the SAHMs were doing. Without them, I didn't feel like we'd ever raise money for new playground turf, or organize decent field trips, or argue with the principal about outdated rules, or have soccer jerseys. I'm lucky. My husband makes enough money, so I decided to join them. They need help. And for the record, I really do think working moms get that. Emphasis on the *moms*. I swear if I read one more click-bait article about Mommy Wars, well, I'm going to scream. I mean, have you ever heard of "Daddy Wars"? Hmmm, why do you think that is?

21

Nora leaves a voice mail for Alexis. Say what she likes about Sylvia, but the conversation left her with more questions than answers. The truth about Dynasty Ranch? Nora's doubtful, but that doesn't mean someone's not covering something. It'd be nice to find out who before stepping on a landmine either professionally or personally.

At least Andi has texted with good news:

> Surprise! I'm taking a last-minute trip stateside to visit my mom and I booked a 4-hour layover in Austin on Sunday. Can't wait to see you xx

Otherwise, the day has proceeded to become a very Monday Monday. She tried calling new schools for Liv; all the good programs are full. She forgot her lunch. She felt queasy until three o'clock. If she could just get through the week, she'd told herself this morning when she had opened up her Outlook calendar to find a checkerboard of appointments, action items, and work deadlines. But through it, she wonders, *to where?*

Every time she thinks she can't possibly get any more buried in the daily grind than she already is, the universe proves her wrong. It's the only constant. And yet, she pretends that this period of Liv's activities and her own nose-to-the-grindstone is nothing more than a blip on the radar, something she has to get through.

It's a version of one of her absolute favorite fairy tales, the myth of the "normal week." It's a well-loved bedtime story, the one she tells herself to relax. Next week, things will get back to normal. There won't be a holiday from school, or Liv won't be sick, or work will have calmed down, Nora will have recovered from her cold, Hayden's brother won't be in town, her cleaning lady won't be coming. That's the funny thing, though. The normal week never gets here and so there's nothing really *normal* about it.

But she likes the idea.

At 5:06 P.M., Gary spots her in the hallway, making her way back from the ladies' room. "Nora," he bellows from too far away. "Can we catch up quickly about those discovery documents?"

Nora's stomach tightens. She reminds herself that there is nothing NSFW about the fact that she has a child who needs to be picked up and that despite her previous interaction with Gary, she can admit that this is a thing she does still need to do. "I'm just heading out to get Liv."

"It will only take a minute," he assures her. "I'm going to be in late tomorrow and need to make sure we circle up now."

She considers clueing him in to the invention of the telephone.

"Sure." She does, in truth, have some time to spare, even if she'd allotted it to stop in the grocery store sans toddler in tow.

Gary takes more than a minute of her time. He takes minutes in fistfuls. He eats her minutes for dinner and then asks for seconds. She walks him through her findings on the discovery review and patiently answers his questions before he skips over to a different case altogether and progresses to a story about a judge he knew down in Lubbock. And even though the story itself is neither long nor unpleasant, the pressure of all those lost seconds builds in the back of her neck and she thinks of Dr. Perez and she finally wrenches the words out of her throat. "I'm sorry, Gary, but I do have to go get Liv."

His first reaction is gracious—"Oh gosh, I'm so sorry, I totally forgot." He checks his watch and furrows his eyebrows, which have wiry, white hairs sticking out in odd directions. "I . . . say this as your mentor, so you can be fully prepared. But, you know, there are times when work is going to interfere with—with life. The more responsibility you take on at the firm, the more you have to be prepared for that. It's manageable, of course. We take work-life balance seriously here. A lot of attorneys are attracted to this firm specifically for that reason. But just something to be aware of going forward."

Which attorneys are attracted to the firm for that reason? She would love to know.

How often do you go to the grocery store, Gary? When is the 100-Day Celebration at your kids' schools, Gary? How many class parties did you volunteer to organize this year, Gary? When was the last time you waited at home for the handyman to show up or swept the crumbs from underneath the kitchen table or put away your wife's laundry, Gary?

Because the crazy thing is that Gary thinks the two of them have the same job and that he's just better at it. In reality, Nora does do the same job, but manages it in two-thirds the time while maintaining an entire other career as a wife and a mom and—*yeah*—she does it in dresses without pockets.

And the most horrible, insidious thing is: She gets how he reached that conclusion. She understands that he has no idea what she's up against, what running a household even looks like. She knows, too, that Gary's perception of a thirty-six-year-old Nora Spangler is dictated by his sixty-year-old wife, who probably never considered *not* matching his socks for him.

"Understood," she says. "I do have a great setup at home. Laptop docking station, a big monitor, a scanner, really it's very efficient."

"That's great to hear. Although sometimes there's no replacing time working face-to-face." He smiles gently. "Have a great night."

Back in her car, Nora tries to shake the exchange. The key is not to let herself take it on. She is not a paper towel. She will not absorb it. Gary won't even remember that they had the conversation by morning. *Let it go.*

Incidentally, this is the very same refrain she finds herself listening to for the umpteenth time with Liv buckled tight in the backseat, finally on their way to the grocery store.

Elsa belts out: *Let it go, let it gooooooo.*

At last they fumble out of the car and Nora looks desperately around for the carts that come in the shape of cars with steering wheels. There are never enough to go around.

"Can you ride in the cart, Liv?" she asks.

"No, I want to help push, Mommy."

"Please?"

"No, ma'am. I'm going to *push.*"

There's no sense in arguing. Or maybe there is and Nora's too lazy. Liv's hands stretch up to the cart handle and in order to help steer the cart, Nora must straddle her daughter's feet so that they can push together. Slow going.

Before they even reach the produce section, Liv needs a snack because *hungry* is apparently how God made her today (this, according to Liv), and so they set off to find something suitable, finally agreeing to open a carton of Goldfish. With Liv satisfied, Nora stashes the box to pay for at checkout.

Now Liv no longer wants to walk, but she doesn't want to sit either. She wants to be *carried.* It takes much coaxing to convince her that she should walk like a big girl, and Nora is already resigning herself to picking up only the bare necessities. She'll have to make a second trip this week and she's mentally calculating when she can make that happen.

"Nora! Oh my god, how are you?" A cart pushed by Emily Cohen trundles up the aisle toward her. Nora switches on a smile.

"Hi, Emily. It's been forever." Thirteen years since Nora saw Emily at their five-year high school reunion.

Emily is wearing a baby in a carrier across her chest. Her blond hair is pulled into a high ponytail.

Liv slides down and takes Nora's hand, watching.

"What are you up to these days?"

"I'm still a lawyer at the same law firm downtown."

"Good for you. I left consulting when my firstborn, Rex, was two. It just became unbearable. I don't know how you do it, but I give you all the credit. This is Mabel. She's six months." Emily turns to model the plump little girl in the carrier, cheeks squished into her mother's breasts, a soft pink headband bow peeking out. "And who is this?"

Emily kneels down to Liv's level. Liv squeezes Nora's leg but she does wave by scrunching her fingers.

"This is Liv." Nora feels the familiar swell of pride she gets whenever she has the chance to introduce someone new to her daughter. It used to bother her when her own mother did this, back when Nora first became old enough to understand that "Why don't you run a quick brush through your hair?" or "Just stay until the Petersons get here for dinner" were thinly veiled pretexts for wanting to parade Nora about. But Nora *gets* it now. "She's four."

"And a half." Liv's little voice croaks.

Emily claps her hands together and presses them to her mouth. "She's the sweetest, oh my goodness, looks just like you. Oh." Emily stretches out a finger, reflexively, stopping short of touching Liv's face. "Did you fall? Did you get a boo-boo?" She frowns a mom frown, the practiced empathy of someone who has applied countless Paw Patrol Band-Aids. Nora's heart climbs her rib cage like a ladder.

Liv shakes her head and Emily looks to Nora.

Nora clears her throat to push her heart down. "A couple years ago. Not recently."

Nora hardly ever notices the bright, red scar across Liv's right eye or the one that runs from her chin down her jaw. She's so used to them. She wasn't always. For months afterward, Nora couldn't look at Liv without experiencing physical, throbbing pain. She'd been so sure they'd go away. Give it a couple weeks, then a couple months. The plastic surgeon promised the more Liv grew, the less noticeable they'd become. And Nora hangs her sanity on that some days.

Emily pushes on her knee to stand. "We've had our fair share of hospital visits. Rex broke his arm last year," Emily says, and Nora understands the hidden meaning: *It can happen to anyone.*

But it couldn't. It could only happen to her. Not *to* her, even, but because of her.

"She hasn't eaten dinner yet. Ticking time bomb. We should get going." Nora's tone is artificially breezy.

Emily gives a pained smile. "Same. Hope to bump into you soon!"

Nora scoops Liv up and holds her on her hip as she chases down Pull-Ups and school snacks and checks out at the cash register. She forgets to ask the cashier if he has stickers for Liv and she feels bad when Liv reminds her once she's already snapped back into her car seat and it's too late.

Don't blame yourself.

The words take shape in her mind as she rounds her way to the driver's seat. Sometimes she'd like to know where this voice comes from. It's not her own. It's not Hayden's. It's not even her mother's. It's a collection, she supposes. A peanut gallery. Her mother often liked to recite facts with the authoritative preface of "They say." "They say a glass of red wine for dinner is good for you." "They say kids have too much homework these days." "They say you should breast-feed until one."

Who is "they," Mother? The Today *show?* But anyhow, the voice inside Nora's head is exactly like that, disembodied, poorly researched, a know-it-all.

They say, *don't blame yourself.* But the biggest secret, the one that no one has ever guessed, is that for as many moments as she's spent blaming herself for what happened, there are an equal number in which she doesn't—she blames Hayden.

"Mommy, I'm thirsty." Liv squirms and whines in the backseat as they pull out of the parking lot. She should have gotten her those stickers. "I want milk."

And that's when Nora realizes she forgot the fucking milk.

22

Hayden waits for her in the lobby of Cornelia's office where he stands up to model his sweatpants and ratty T-shirt. "Was the 'wear gym attire' a joke?" he asks.

Cornelia had sent an email along with the appointment reminder, telling them to come ready for physical exertion, and Nora had been tempted to pretend that she hadn't seen it. One exercise session felt like more than enough for one month, thank you very much.

She hugs her husband. His T-shirt is soft from a couple decades' worth of washes. "No, I just need to slip into the bathroom to change." She pawns her laptop bag off on him and, in a couple of minutes, returns wearing the same knock-off Lululemon outfit she'd worn to yoga. "Better?"

"Maybe we're doing trust exercises." Hayden pushes the button on the elevator.

"It's not summer camp." Though it's not such a bad guess.

She's looking forward to the session. She imagines that this time she'll be invited to talk about what's been on her mind, about how being in charge both at home and at work is dragging her down, making her crazy. Since Cornelia will be there to witness, Hayden will hear her this time. He won't get all defensive. *Oh, honey*, she might say, *because I'm completely overwhelmed, you see, I didn't enroll our daughter in school, so would you mind problem-solving us out of that one?* Yes, she's still holding on to a few secrets, but overall, she's ready.

When they arrive, though, Cornelia ushers them into a separate room where two treadmills sit side by side.

"Cornelia," Nora says, "I'm really out of shape."

"Don't even worry about it. We're going to try to do a bit of active meditation before the session. Now, Hayden, since you're in great shape—really, look at that physique, those *pectorals*—we'll want to make things a bit more challenging for you for best results, so we'll use something called E-Stim," Cornelia continues. "That's the hip lingo for electric muscle stimulation. It's a perfectly safe method used in all sorts of contexts. Runners use it, occupational therapists, many gyms are even starting to offer it as a way to burn extra calories."

"Will it hurt?" he asks, taking her direction to climb aboard the SS Treadmill.

"Not one bit." Cornelia takes her gold pen out of her front pocket and clicks the top to jot down a few quick notes.

Nora straddles her own treadmill's conveyor belt. She'd rather take an algebra test than do an activity that might force her to shower and blow-dry her hair an extra time this week. Few men will ever fully understand the curse of blow-drying and the need to strategically plan—or altogether avoid—one's workouts around it.

Soon, Cornelia has finished setting Hayden up with electrode sensors on his abdomen, calves, and chest. *This had all better be worth it,* Nora thinks.

She wants their marriage, wants a partnership with her husband, and if it takes trying something a little off the beaten path, then there's no real harm in that. Maybe she can think of it like a chiropractor or an acupuncturist? If it works for her, all the better.

"Put these on." Cornelia hands them each a pair of noise-canceling headphones and Nora fits them over her ears. The treadmills are started up and both she and Hayden take off at a brisk walking pace.

Within a minute, a country song comes on in her headphones and she's actually relieved it's not meditation music. "I just wish you were a better man," the woman croons. She looks to Cornelia, who winks back. Nora likes the little joke. Nice not to take everything so seriously. It's marriage, for crying out loud, not cancer.

She glances then at Hayden, who has a pleasantly bewildered look on his face. She wonders what song is playing in *his* headphones. She could probably think of a few options that would be less than flattering for her. *Your wife's a nag.* Name that tune!

She does notice that Hayden's sweating pretty heavily, even though he's not going much faster than she is. It begins with dark circles that creep out from under his arms, but by the end of the first mile he has a damp spot seeping into a triangle around the neck of his T-shirt. He doesn't seem bothered. It's nice, actually. Getting some exercise during the day. *Yes, Nora, what a breakthrough! Moving your body makes you feel better. You are the first person to discover this; a hot take.*

But there's something about seeing a message on one too many as-pirational Instagram accounts that makes her want to hit IGNORE. She looks at these women who meal plan and remember to use makeup primer and do yoga poses at sunset, who count macros and write posi-tive affirmations on their mirrors and complete their outfits with hats, and thinks—why even bother when she's had clothes on the floor of her closet for the past six months?

The song plays on repeat and by the third time, the joke's worn thin. She's going to have this tune stuck in her head for the entire day. But, in the nick of time, Cornelia cuts them off and both she and Hayden are permitted to remove their headphones.

Cornelia sits leaned back in a rolling chair, her legs crossed. She clicks her pen twice, checking her watch and making a note, beckoning them to join her in two folding chairs that have already been set up. "There, didn't that feel good?" She saves her most benevolent smile for Hayden. "Now that you're all warmed up, let's get down to the nitty-gritty. Shall we?"

Nora adjusts her weight. *Let the games begin.*

"Nora, why don't you start us off. We are going to dive right into one of the toughest questions. That's where the meat is. In an earlier session, you answered yes to the question of whether you resent your spouse. So go ahead, tell me. Why do you resent Hayden?"

A flush of heat rises to Nora's cheeks. She wishes there was a better word than *resentment.*

"Okay." Nora fills her lungs. "Well, sometimes I feel—" She remembers hearing once that therapists like when people start their sentences with "I feel." "I *feel* that, although Hayden is a great dad and does help—I'm not saying he doesn't help at all, I think it's important not to speak in absolutes. He always thinks I'm trying to say he does nothing. Oh, well, okay, sorry about that, I just did it. I don't mean *always*. But what I'm saying is that he doesn't, you know, help *enough*. Comparatively speaking."

"And I feel like she's keeping a scoreboard." Apparently Hayden has heard of the "I feel" trick, too. "But that she has a really bad memory for all the things that I do. I change the oil in her car. I clean the garage. I mow."

"But those are at-your-leisure activities." Nora makes sure that when she says this it doesn't come out as a whine.

"What's that supposed to mean?"

"It means that you do them when you feel like it. They aren't part of our daily grind, you know? Like if I don't get Liv dressed for school and do the dishes and pack her lunch box and do her hair and make sure she has clean laundry, the rest of the day literally can't go on." It's the relentless rhythm of these circadian tasks that makes Nora feel like the wood peg in one of Liv's play sets, being knocked down by a rubber mallet a centimeter at a time. "And then it's not like I don't have the at-your-leisure activities, too. I make doctor's appointments and sign up for dance classes, that sort of thing. But I have those on top of the day-to-day ones."

Before Hayden can draw his bow and fire back, Cornelia holds up her hand to silence him. She sits back, pensively, tapping the bottom of the pen on her knee. "Nora, tell me what you need Hayden to do so that you can feel like he's pulling his weight."

For all the relentless internal monologue playing in her head through-out the day, this is the part where Nora struggles. It seems she can never articulate what precisely would make things better. "So you want me to pack lunches," Hayden will say. "I'll pack lunches then."

And she'll stammer, "Yes, I want you to pack lunches. But I don't want you *only* to pack lunches." And he'll tell her to be specific, which sounds reasonable, but then she'll say she can't. It's not like that.

She just knows that as soon as she tells him "pack lunches" and "or-der Liv new socks" then that's it. That's all he'll do. And he'll feel good about it. He'll feel accomplished. And if there's one thing that Nora can't stand it's the idea of Hayden feeling accomplished for doing an eighth of her job.

"I guess the main thing is . . . I want him to know what needs do-ing. Just like I do." She pauses, waits for either Cornelia or Hayden to say: So you want him to read your mind? But neither do. "I guess I don't understand what's so hard about that."

"Tell me more."

"Like, I overheard a mom at preschool talking to her friend at one of the school parties once and she said, *Are you directing your husband, are you asking him to do things, because if you're not then maybe it's your fault, not his, because you always just do it.* She really said that. Nobody directs me. That's what I want. I want him to know that Beckett's birthday party is Saturday and that we need to pick up a present at Target before then or, better yet, order one from Amazon, rather than have him ask me, 'What do we have going on this weekend?' I want him to know when picture day is at school and be the one to think to schedule Liv's well-child visits at her pediatrician. All these tasks that I have to remember. It's exhausting. I don't want to always be the delegator. Because the delegator still needs to keep track of all the things that need to be delegated. I don't feel like equals when it comes to household tasks. I don't want to tell him to do the dishes. I hate telling him to do the dishes. More often than not if I have to tell him to do the dishes, I'll just do them myself. I want him to see his domain as larger than what he does now. It's more than washing the car and killing ant beds every few weeks. Those things need to get done, too, and I appreciate that he mostly does them, but that's a small fraction of the whole picture." Nora shuts her mouth abruptly and folds her hands in her lap. "Sorry, I got carried away there."

Cornelia appraises her. "No, I think it's important."

"I don't know." Nora's not looking at Hayden. "I— Hayden's smart. I know he's smart and I think that's the thing that bugs me. He's just as capable as I am of doing any of these things, of holding them in his head. So, why doesn't he?" She mumbles the last part, embarrassed. She's asked for too much. She's missing something critical. She's not being fair. Hayden *is* better than so many men. She's grateful for that. She should be grateful. Shouldn't she?

Cornelia turns to Hayden now. Her thumb toys with the end of her pen. "Hayden," she says, voice clear, assertive. "I want you to watch me for a moment. Good. Now I want you to feel your muscles. Are they relaxed? I bet you're exhausted. That was a tough turn you just took on the treadmill, wasn't it? Good. Yes, now, let's let a good, pleasant, contented feeling settle in. Do you have it? Great. Hayden, you hear your wife, don't you?" He nods. "Now, what would it be like if you kept track of what needs to go on to run a household?" He stares. "What about if you kept a calendar of events relevant to your household? Might that be nice? And, while we're at it, just think, what if we considered the possibility of you buying birthday presents and scheduling doctor appointments and doing dishes and packing lunches and sticking to bedtime routines, all things of that ilk, how about it?"

"Yes." He swallows. "I will."

"And you could be happy about that?" Cornelia cocks her head as she looks at him, like he's an abstract painting in a museum.

Nora chews the gnarled cuticle on the edge of her thumb before realizing what she's doing and tucks her hand under the warmth of her thigh. What is Hayden's angle? She expects he's decided that Cornelia's methodology is a bunch of mumbo jumbo and so the best thing he can do is to roll over and play dead. Nora wants to sink her head down into her hands, but that would be rude and Nora's most terrified of being rude.

"Yes, of course. I want to help," Hayden says.

He could at least pretend.

"Right, that's good to hear." She flips her notebook closed. "So I feel like we've made progress. But let's schedule a follow-up appointment, let's say, for one week from now? And we'll see where there are areas for improvement." She rubs her palms along the fabric of her pants and sits straighter.

Nora's eyes bounce between her husband and her therapist. "But, wait. Don't you need to ask Hayden?" she says.

"Ask Hayden what?"

Nora hesitates, but she's sure that the session shouldn't be quite so lopsided. Hayden was skeptical to begin with and had made more than a couple remarks about how a female therapist was bound to take Nora's point of view. She doesn't want him to be right. "What he resents."

Cornelia presses her index finger to her lips for a beat. She frowns. "Okay, then. Sure, if you insist. Hayden, what is it that you resent about Nora?"

Hayden stares right through her and says the very thing he swears he's never held against her, exposing an entire three years of their married life as a lie, a sham. And in return, she'd told herself another one: *He doesn't blame me.* And it's like the boards holding up their marriage have been wet and rotting for years since.

In that moment, she knows with lightning-bolt certainty why she needed to hear his answer.

She's ready.

Ready to explain the truth, ready to face exactly what happened that day, even if the result strips the temporary patch off of the flotation device on which their relationship's been bobbing, even if it sinks them. She's going to tell.

"The accident."

23

The following morning, as Nora hops down the hallway, trying to slip on her heels without sitting down, Hayden reveals that he "washed Liv's blue dress."

"You did?" She checks to make sure she's remembered to put on deodorant. "Why?"

He rummages through their junk drawers looking for god-knows-what. "It's picture day."

"Shit," she says, then checking to make sure Liv hasn't heard her. "You're right. I *hate* picture day." Most years, Nora remembers it only upon arriving to school to find a sea of little girls with their hair down, bows clipped in, and sporting an array of smocked dresses. Nora routinely finds her place among the forgetful mothers, the ones who roll their eyes at themselves as their own children march through the doors in well-worn shorts and mismatched tees. Flash-forward to a week later when Nora will feel like an asshole if she doesn't purchase a twenty-dollar wallet-size photo to commemorate this "very special year." "How did *you* know about picture day?"

"I saw it on the school calendar and made a mental note," he says, locating a folded bill in the drawer, no doubt still unpaid.

"Right. Of course you did," she says, sarcastically, then sees her husband's expression and regrets it instantly. "Oh, you're serious."

"Why would I be joking?" She assumes this is a rhetorical question. "Anyway," he forges on, "I thought I'd take Liv to buy new shoes tonight. I'll pick up dinner for us on our way back, how's that?" She stares at him. She hasn't even had her cup of coffee yet. "Couldn't you use some extra time at the office to help Gary?" He leads her like she's slow on the uptake.

"Yes, but—I thought you had—"

"I can move some things around." Her worst instincts try to parse out whether this is a trick, whether he's trying to win some kind of silent, unspoken argument between them, but no, that's just her who does that.

She focuses on her coffee mug and on the steaming brown liquid pouring into it. "Okay," she says, after a long moment. "Yes, thanks. That'd be great."

It's settled.

Nora makes it to her desk at a reasonable hour and fully caffeinated. So what? Hayden is acting strangely because he feels badly for bringing up the accident in yesterday's session. Of course. She's not picky. She'll take what she can get. And so she spends the entire day without the worry of a hard stop hanging over her head. How . . . novel.

Hayden's timing couldn't be better. Having made a sizeable dent in her projects owed to Gary, Nora is able to break free when at—what feels like—long last, Alexis returns her call. The women gather in Alexis's home—Cornelia, Penny, and Alexis. "Hi," "Hi," "Hi" and hugs all around. Nora is enveloped and experiences an unexpected wave of relief at having been reunited with them after only a short time, but still.

"Sorry it's taken us a few days." They lounge like old girlfriends across the sectional couch. "Some of us were on one of those couples retreats this past weekend. Really nice," says Alexis. Her knees poke through ripped jeans when she has her heels origami-folded underneath her like that. "You should come sometime." The chunky gold bracelets on her wrist jangle.

Penny sits quietly.

Cornelia sips at a glass of sparkling water. "It's something I offer to *some* of my patients." It's the "some" that makes Nora feel a dog-eat-dog twinge. She doesn't like the idea of being left out of something "really nice" that everyone else is participating in. "It's a chance to relax, reconnect, you know, all that good stuff. Maybe you and Hayden will be interested in joining us for one once you have a few more sessions under your belt. They're slightly more advanced, but very manageable."

"Oh my god, you'll love them. Great food, wine, solid internet connection, and so worth it." Alexis lifts her hands up like, *Praise God*.

Actually, getting away together is one thing that Nora and Hayden are pretty good at. In their early years of marriage they'd visited Thailand, Tokyo, Vietnam, Kenya, and Croatia, and after Liv, although the trips had been more domestic, they'd still happened. A two-day trip to Sedona. A long weekend in Jackson Hole. A quick getaway to Bar Harbor. They share a Pinterest board, always plotting their next trip. When it arrives, they find themselves at their best in a nice hotel, like kids with large coffee mugs and plush robes nestled beneath the covers. They have the exact same travel style—not everyone does—perfectly in sync, and Nora worries, for good reason, about these trips being put on hiatus when the baby arrives. "That does sound really nice," she says, more comforted than she should be not to be excluded completely.

Cornelia stretches her long neck. "Much needed given—given everything lately."

Nora looks at Penny when she says, "It's been a lot."

"I hope you know how grateful I am that you've taken so much of it on yourself," says Penny.

Nora takes a breath. She's more nervous than she thought she'd be. The question sounds far more ridiculous when put face-to-face. Maybe she should have asked over the phone. But it's too late for that. "About that. I do have a sort of random question for you. Alexis mainly. I hope you don't mind. *But*, does the Dynasty Ranch HOA prohibit stay-at-home mothers from purchasing homes here?" As soon as it's out, Nora expects them to laugh her out of the house.

"Jesus Christ. Did that journalist get to you?" Alexis doesn't sound on the verge of laughter. She sounds *really* annoyed. Though not at Nora, so there's that.

Still.

Sylvia *had* mentioned a journalist. Had one taken her more seriously than Sylvia thought? In which case, should Nora?

"I can't remember his name." Alexis thinks. "Kyle or Chris or something."

"No, it was Sylvia Lamb. I believe she tried to purchase the home"— Nora clears her throat—"the one on Majestic Grove."

Alexis and Cornelia share a look. Nora wonders if, like Nora, it's one Penny wants to be included in or if she's too consumed with her own concerns to care.

But they're interrupted by Alexis's eight-year-old son, Cruz. "Mom, I need a snack."

"I'm in the middle of something," she says in her mom voice.

Cruz proceeds to stand in front of the pantry. "Do we have mac 'n' cheese?" he asks. "Can you make me some?"

"We do have mac 'n' cheese," she replies, patiently. "Where's your father?"

Nora twitches. She has just experienced something. A perfect mix of surprise, recognition, and curiosity, because maybe Alexis has her own incredible vanishing man after all. However, the aftertaste that quickly follows, if she were to roll it around on her tongue for much longer, would be disappointment.

"He's upstairs putting Jax down in the crib."

Alexis checks her watch. The boy wears athletic shorts that cover his knees. "Oh, that's right."

But as if on cue, Max appears down the stairs, having not even been called—hollered at, more like, if this exchange were to take place in the Spangler household. "Can I make you a snack?" he says, and Cruz puts in his request for mac 'n' cheese. "It has to be something healthy," replies Max, ruffling Cruz's hair. "You can't just eat empty calories all day. You need *nutrients.* How about I slice up an apple for you?" Cruz grumbles his consent.

Nora watches out of the corner of her eye as Max peels an apple and slices it into spears. "Why didn't you mention her?"

Alexis's attention returns easily. "We were trying to be kind. We aren't in the habit of calling women 'crazy.' It's so loaded."

"But if the shoe fits," Penny says, though not unkindly.

"She said that her contract for that house"—*My house,* Nora thinks—"was terminated when she quit her job. The timing seems strange." She's walking a tightrope but presses on. Penny had told her, implored her really, that if she only knew what happened that night . . . and then Nora had promised to do her best to find out. She'd given her word.

Cornelia laces her fingers around her knee. "Do you really think we discriminate based on whether or not a woman has a career outside the home?" She studies Nora, who tries hard not to squirm.

"That's what I'm asking."

Alexis breaks the tension. "There are *several* women who live here in Dynasty Ranch that don't have a day job. Cheryl Ann, for instance. She's, like, super mom. Seriously, I bow down. She even runs one of those mommy blogs. It's really popular. And Danica. She used to be a nurse but left her career and does some volunteer work, fund-raising, that sort of thing, but she doesn't *work* work. You know what I mean. My point is that Sylvia's claims are ludicrous."

Nora sits back. That does make her feel better. "She mentioned some kind of roster, though."

It's because of the way that Alexis had mentioned, offhandedly, how they didn't have a lawyer yet that this tidbit burrowed its way into her brain. Nora had gotten the distinct impression that by "they" she'd been referring to Dynasty Ranch as a collective unit.

"You mean our neighborhood *directory*?" Alexis slaps her thigh. "Is that what Sylvia's calling a roster? Because I don't think there's anything particularly nefarious about a directory, do you?"

"Does it have residents' occupations in the directory?" Nora asks.

"It has people's office numbers, if they choose to provide them. I guess that may lead others to guess at their profession, but I'd hardly call it a roster."

A neighborhood directory. Her parents used to have one of those.

"That woman won't leave us alone," says Cornelia. "First it was the pathetic cease and desist letter from her lawyer. And then she tried to get that news story off the ground."

"She did seem to be holding a serious grudge." Nora softens.

"Penny was Sylvia's sponsor," says Cornelia.

"You were?" Nora had been the slightest bit hurt when Penny hadn't raised her hand to volunteer when it'd come to her own application. Maybe this could explain why.

"Only because she asked," Penny answers defensively.

"What does a sponsor do, anyhow?" Nora's now genuinely curious.

Alexis rolls her eyes. "We don't swap spit or anything, if that's what you're asking. Mainly, it's just our way of ensuring that every new neighbor comes in with a path to proper integration."

"Proper integration," Nora rolls the words over.

"It's not as fancy as it sounds," Alexis assures her. "We're just big on, like, human connection. Says the techie, I know, but that's exactly why. You always hear about a good corporate culture being a key to success. That's what we want our neighborhood to be, too—a success. We want everyone to be happy here. So a sponsor is someone who can vouch that we're not letting in, you know, a grouchy neighbor. Someone who's going to be yelling 'Get off my lawn' to the children, that kind of thing."

Nora does like the sound of that. "She mentioned that you two had become close," Nora says slowly.

"She'd read my book."

"That, for Penny," Cornelia says, "is apparently enough."

"I'm very vain." Penny shrugs, though she's not.

"Did you rescind your—your sponsorship?"

"I didn't think I had a choice."

"Like we said, not a good fit," Alexis hurries to add. "Not like you. But . . . I mean, well, you don't think—I don't even want to say it, but—you're not suggesting that you think *Sylvia* had anything to do with . . . the fire, are you?"

Cornelia sucks in a sharp breath, and for the first time today, Penny's interest seems vested. They all look to Nora.

"I think it's important to look at every possibility," she hedges.

"But, out of curiosity," Cornelia says, "What would happen if you found out the person to blame for the fire was an individual, like Sylvia?"

"What do you mean?" Nora asks.

"Like, would Penny still be compensated, financially?"

"Oh. Well, yeah. That part doesn't change, necessarily. There'd be a civil trial and we'd go after that individual personally as well as their insurance company. The police would reopen a criminal investigation if it were something purposeful like—like we're talking about. I'd work closely with the police."

"I've been saying all along," says Penny, "I don't know why the detectives called off so quickly. Don't you think that's weird? Why aren't they trying to figure out what happened?"

"Based on what I've heard from my fire expert, they don't have the right incentives to. Between us, cops are easy enough to pull one over on. It's the insurance companies that are relentless. They never give up. I know. It's frustrating. But don't worry, I'm going to reach out to the department first thing tomorrow and make sure that Sylvia's looked into properly. Once I have the results of the lab tests from our fire expert, then I can even see if the detectives will agree to share notes with me. I think if we gave them something to go on, they'd be more motivated. The only other real lead we have is the clicking noise that Penny mentioned. There's a paper trail on that with the appliance company, which is—"

"Clicking noise?" Cornelia looks to Nora, who goes quiet. She'd assumed that Penny told everything to the other women. But nobody tells anyone everything. Nora knows that.

It's almost as if her mind has sprung a leak lately. Memories of the moments leading up to the accident are finding opportunities to seep into her ordinary life. She understands that the reason is the baby. Probably for other second-time moms, reminiscing is a less fraught experience, one filled with nostalgia for pink gums and sweet breath, first smiles and warm weight asleep on chests, but for Nora there is that, but only underneath a layer of shame and guilt and also, *also* lies.

In the official version of events, Nora had stepped away for only a moment. It was a second of carelessness. It could have happened to anyone. In that rendition Nora had heard the sickening cracks, flown to her daughter like a good mother, smelled fresh blood. The revised story has come out much cleaner than the original. *Based on true events*, that's how Hollywood would characterize it. And until her most recent pregnancy she's made peace with close enough.

And so Penny, too, should get to choose, especially when it comes to what she tells her lawyer. She said Richard had been driven crazy. Maybe crazy isn't a mental image she's interested in her friends having of her late husband. Nora is sensing an undercurrent and wants to step out of its pull.

Cornelia turns to Penny. "Did you say Richard was hearing a clicking noise?"

"I mentioned he'd been hearing a noise, yes. It seemed relevant," says Penny. "I've been racking my brain."

"Like I said." Nora jumps in to help. "I'm investigating every possible avenue. No stone unturned. Sometimes it's the smallest detail that can become the linchpin in court."

"That's why we're so lucky to have you on our side." Nora takes Alexis's compliment to heart.

After that, there are a few minutes for chitchat, and in them, they devolve into relaxed chatter. There are updates about their jobs and kids, neighbors and recipes and celebrity gossip. It's normal and easy and doesn't feel rushed, the way Nora's lunches with girlfriends used to feel, so eager were they and she to download four months of their respective lives over forty-five minutes of salad. They aren't interrupted once by Cruz or Max. No one asks where the spare toilet paper rolls are or if it's okay to watch TV or if Alexis remembered to buy any more Chex Mix. And so the gathering dissipates naturally rather than by force. They all have places to go and people to see and things to do.

Cornelia walks out with Nora. "If it's okay with you, I'd like to talk to Penny, as her therapist, just briefly before you push forward with contacting the police department."

The outdoor heat is on Nora's face, cooking her pores. "Why?"

"I know the last thing she wants to do is go through any more questioning. They really put her through the wringer right when it happened."

"I think the not knowing is what's really getting to her," Nora says.

"I hear that a lot in my practice, but it isn't true very often. People think that it would be better if they knew everything, if they knew exactly what happened. But that's unrealistic. Nobody can know that. In which case, how much knowledge is enough knowledge? The knowing can actually make it worse, can't it?"

Improbably, it's Nora's father who springs to mind. When he told her that he'd left her mother for a woman he'd been sleeping with for over a year. *I didn't want you going crazy wondering why. I didn't want you blaming yourself.* Nora supposes that hadn't been better. Mainly because she'd never been in danger of blaming herself for the end of her parents' marriage. She would have blamed her father no matter what.

"Maybe I should just run back in to discuss it with her while I'm here," Nora suggests. She moves to enter, but Cornelia gracefully angles her body to block her passage.

"Maybe today's not the best day. I'm just saying to give me a second to prepare her, that's all."

"I understand," she says. "But getting to the bottom of this is why I'm here."

"Really? Because I think you're here for a lot more than just that."

Nora hesitates, no longer sure of what to do. She doesn't want to do the wrong thing here. But that's not necessarily the same as doing the right one.

Maybe Cornelia is correct. This had started with a desire to buy a house, and no doubt she's gotten a whole lot more than she bargained for. So yes, more. But what's most important to her at the end of the day? Is it solving Richard's case? Is it winning it? Or is it something else entirely?

"Speaking of," Cornelia says. "I meant to ask you: What are you doing for Mother's Day?"

Nora's thrown off. "Mother's Day? When is it again?"

"This Sunday. You should come. It's always fantastic. Around here, it goes Mother's Day, then Christmas, followed by Thanksgiving." Cornelia demonstrates the rankings, and Nora can't tell whether or not she's kidding. "And don't bring anything but yourself and your family. Consider it a taste of what your life would be like here in Dynasty Ranch. I think you're going to like it."

24

Nora resigns herself to the idea that the next best opportunity to speak with Penny will be at the Mother's Day celebration. She's already committed, having dashed off a short, but upbeat message to Andi—

> I know you're probably already tied up, getting ready for your flight and whatnot, so I won't bother you with a call, but did want to let you know I'll be a little late to our rendezvous. One prior engagement then I'm all yours. Lucky you. Xx

Nora had always understood "prior engagement" to mean plans that existed *prior* to being invited to take part in other ones, but that definition seems narrow and, frankly, inconvenient. For now, though, she'll try to forget about the weekend or the investigation or preschool, and focus on another matter entirely.

"I think we need to discuss this house situation." Which sounds a little too grown-up for her taste. "Have you seen any other listings that interest you?" Nora asks at home, knowing full well it's a trick question.

"Not really, no," is Hayden's predictable answer.

"I think it's a great house." She crunches into a pretzel crisp. Maybe it was her conversation with Cornelia that's spurred her to action. "It would be a nice neighborhood for Liv. We'd have room to grow. It's in our price range. And, okay, I know you didn't exactly hit it off with the other men there, but, you know, you don't have to be best friends with them. Just neighborly." She's relieved to hear that she sounds like Normal Nora now, not the one playing at adulthood.

He tilts his head, the corners of his mouth tugging. "I'm sure I liked them fine, Nor."

Nora takes another handful from the bag. "*You* called them *boring.*" She's teasing him, but only a little.

"I did?"

Is her husband going senile? They aren't even forty. "You most definitely did," she insists, though now she wonders if she'd taken it too seriously at the time. Obviously it hadn't been a lasting impression for Hayden. That's so Nora, giving even the smallest thing the weight of a ton of bricks. No wonder she's so tired.

"Well," he says, accepting the point.

"Well . . . I think it's time to make an offer." She uses the direct language suggested in the Women's Leadership Initiative. "It won't sit on the market forever and, in case you haven't noticed, I'm not getting any less pregnant."

There's something else, too. Nora wants to have her offer in and accepted sooner rather than later, so that if her findings regarding Richard March's death lead her down an unfavorable path, she can capitulate: come what may.

Hayden pushes himself up on the countertop and sits with his feet bumping up against the cabinet doors.

"And." She unspools a wad of paper towels and begins wiping down the surrounding kitchen counters with Windex purely out of force of nervous habit. "Remember we'll have the seven-day option period during which we can still back out. Ten, if we negotiate for it."

The lingering side effect of Cornelia's therapy appointments really is that they are both exceedingly polite to one another. "Do you love the house?" His fingers curl around the cold granite.

"I . . . see the promise in it. Yes." Inside, her heart feels like it's sitting on a ledge.

"Then . . ." he says.

"Then . . . ?" she says.

"We should make an offer."

"We should?" She pauses her wiping and looks up.

"Like you said, we can always back out."

"Wow, okay." She abandons her wet paper towel altogether and steps back with her wrist to her forehead. "I'm—I'm surprised," she admits. "I was expecting it to be more of an . . . *ordeal.*"

If the shoe were on the other foot and *she* were being pushed into a major life decision by *him,* she would absolutely make it a big deal.

But Hayden looks lovingly at his wife, starburst crinkles around the eyes, the little puff of wooly chest hair layered beneath his shirt, and stretches out his arms. Awkwardly, she goes to him and hugs him tightly around the waist while he murmurs gently in her ear. "You deserve it," he says. "Really, Nora. You work so hard."

◙

Later, Nora takes comfort in the order of the office, the way that here, there are always cold sodas in the refrigerator and coffee made and spare pens with ink and stapler refills. She can be alone without really being alone. She can ask her secretary to send her mail and charge it to her personal account. She can mark her emails as read. She can scroll through online shopping websites while on a phone call.

She checks off the email to the mortgage broker and reaches out to Isla Wong, who responds back quickly with a large quantity of exclamation points. All this is seemingly good news. Progress. A step or two in the right direction.

Although, she considers, something *is* definitely up with Hayden. He's being so . . . *nice.*

Too nice maybe. Is that possible? Is she crazy for even thinking it? Paranoid? But she does have to consider it. After all, what if he's done something bad? He could be having an affair. Shit, she hadn't thought of that. Men are extra accommodating when hiding something, she's sure she's heard that before. Who would her husband be having an affair with? Would she know?

She really doesn't think he would. Is that naive of her? It's just that, for all his faults, Hayden loves her, loves their family. That's the whole point.

But then again, it could be something financial. Are they having money problems and Nora is too in-her-head to know about them? Surely if that were the case, it would leave her husband more on edge than sweet. Right?

She opens up a fresh Google search bar and types in the acronym Cornelia had told them at the beginning of their sessions. "PACT couples therapy." She sounds it out aloud. She's relieved when the results yield immediately. Psychobiological Approach to Couples Therapy. But as she reads pages from *Psychology Today* and the PACT Institute and even the Mayo Clinic, nowhere does any author mention the sort of regimen that she and Hayden have been assigned. No treadmills, no polygraphs, no mild childhood traumas. When she attempts to locate Cornelia's purported mentor, Dr. Neha Vita, even less can be found. She has virtually no digital footprint whatsoever, just a small thumbnail picture on a hospital website where she has privileges.

Nora X's out of the windows on-screen.

Nice. Is that really what Nora's complaining about? When her husband acts as she's hoped he would, she resorts to questioning even that.

But there *is* precedent, in a way.

On a night that involved quite a few martinis, Nora once admitted the following to Andi: She's had premonitions. Three, to be exact. Not specific. Just a general feeling of foreboding, like she knew something bad was going to happen. The first occurred the morning before her brother, Tom, who was only three at the time, walked into a swimming pool without any of the grown-ups noticing. Seven-year-old Nora had dug him out sputtering and choking. He was completely fine, but Nora and her mother had cried for nearly an hour afterward. The second was the day her mother died during the half hour that Nora had finally relented and gone out for coffee. And the third, the *third* was the day that Nora found her daughter in a small toddler-size puddle of blood, broken. What's bothered Nora about each of these instances is that she might have prevented them altogether if she hadn't willfully ignored her intuition.

Andi, who is annoyingly rational for an artist, assured her that this was nonsense. Nora had never nor would ever have any psychic abilities of any sort. Either she'd picked up clues or Nora had simply added the memory of a funny feeling in the aftermath. There was nothing she could have done to stop it. That's the whole ball of wax. That's life.

And maybe she's right. Maybe it's nothing. Except the problem with that theory is that Nora *could* have stopped Liv from getting hurt. There's no question about that.

She just didn't.

And here it is again: a creeping sensation that crawls over her scalp, a sinking in her gut, a vibration in her bones telling her to watch out, something's not right and if only she pays attention, maybe this time she'll be able to stop it.

www.therealskinny.com

The Ultimate Mother's Day Shopping Guide
for Every Mom on Your List

BY CHESS ROBINSON

"Every mother and mother-figure deserves to be treated like a queen on this special day. Check out our complete list of no-fail gifts from the personal to the last-minute."

Read Comments

Lisa Yen

Ah, Mother's Day. My favorite part is being locked in my bedroom amid desperate cries of "don't come out here" while jonesing for a cup of coffee because I've been up for an hour already and my husband is trying to figure out whether we have the ingredients for pancakes.

Miranda Bachelis

Let's just skip to the part where I'm emailed my gift card that morning.

MommyDearest

This is going to sound kind of petty, but I feel like I spend the lead-up to Mother's Day totally stressed-out trying to make sure I have something planned for my own mom, my mother-in-law, my grandmother, and my grandmother-in-law. Then a month later when Father's Day rolls around, the whole thing repeats: my father, my father-in-law, and so on and so forth.

LS1986

Honestly, my husband does a really good job on Mother's Day. I love that he makes me feel special. He almost always gets me a massage and flowers, helps the kids make cards, and tells me to spend the day exactly how I want. Now if only a little more Mother's Day mojo could leak into the other 364 days . . .

Ali F

The key to a happy Mother's Day is simple: lower your expectations.

SamirDave

Honestly, as an adult son, I say this with nothing but the utmost respect but, moms, you guys are CRAZY when it comes to Mother's Day, okay?

25

Come Sunday morning, there's a system for depositing Liv with the other children. "Happy Mother's Day!" says the man at the address that Alexis provided Nora, just down the street from the community pool clubhouse, where she's told there will be some kind of celebration—no children. Alexis was clear on that point. "I'm Marcus and I've got Omar and James here on duty with me this morning and we've got everything totally under control."

"We'll just stop in for a minute," Nora had told Hayden. "To be polite."

The three of them had already eaten doughnuts in bed, Liv asking to lick the sticky glaze off Nora's fingers. She let her. Liv had made her a crown at school and Nora wore it atop her messy hair and Hayden took pictures, even though Nora was sure she had mascara smudged beneath her eyes. But it was all very nice. And there were lilies on the breakfast table and a card that Hayden had bought ahead of time. All in all, she's lucky.

She can remember a year where her own father had completely forgotten Mother's Day. Which meant that her mother had spent it screaming at them from behind a locked bathroom door. But then, her mother had known her father was going to forget and let him do it anyway. That was how it was, Nora's mom treating marriage like a test she wanted her husband to fail. Like when her mom said they didn't need to do anything big for their anniversary and later, she'd spent weeks holding a grudge because her father had indeed planned nothing big. When Nora got married she promised herself: no riddles, no trick questions, no ciphers. And she does try.

"It's nice of them to offer childcare," she says as she and Hayden walk hand in hand. It's a stunner of a day, robin's egg sky and soft sun. Behind the clubhouse the fairway grass looks to be in Technicolor. "Hey," she says, "have you ever noticed how there's never anyone actually golfing? Do you think it's closed?"

"It doesn't look closed," says Hayden.

"We'll go golfing, won't we?" she says. "I like the outfits." The idea makes her smile—a new start—as they make their way through the gates of the clubhouse.

Hayden whistles low, impressed. Though, really, perhaps floored is more like it.

"Oh my god, is this all for Mother's Day?" Nora whispers into her husband's shoulder.

"And I thought I did good with the flowers."

"I did, too." She pokes him playfully in the ribs. "But now . . ."

He pinches her behind and she yelps, checking quickly that nobody saw.

Right away, a black-clad caterer offers her a mimosa, which Nora is a teensy bit devastated to decline. "You better be cute," she warns her belly.

"We're at least pretty good at making those." Hayden pats her bump. "Cute kids."

As a consolation prize she receives fresh grapefruit juice in a champagne glass garnished with a raspberry. Also, her disappointment is forgotten entirely when she lays eyes on the buffet. The Mother of All Buffets, if you will. Across the banquet tables draped in white are an assortment of sweet breakfast favorites—beignets, made-to-order waffles, croissants, chocolate-covered strawberries, and cinnamon rolls—and more savory dishes—jalapeño mac 'n' cheese, spinach-and-gouda quiche, eggs Benedict, smoked salmon with capers, and home fries.

"Are those crab legs?" asks Hayden, leaning over one of the silver serving trays.

They are.

Nora salivates. It's as though she's scored the best brunch reservations in town and she won't even see the bill. She fills her plate to a level that is not-quite-embarrassing, making sure to insist that Hayden snag a few of her favorites so that she can share his plate. Then she finds Alexis.

"This is incredible," Nora says. "Did I see people giving *neck massages* out back?"

"And good ones." Alexis's eyes are wide behind her clear-framed glasses. "Also make sure you don't leave without one of the Sephora goodie bags—there are free consultations—and if you have time you can get one of the stylists to do a dry blowout. Not as good as the real thing but will still make your hair look fantastic for the day." She models her own.

"Who did all this? Did you, Alexis?" Hayden asks, scanning the room where men and women from the neighborhood mingle.

"Oh god no. I am *not* a party planner, trust me. Roman was in charge this year. Roman!" She waves at him as he passes by in a mint-green tie. "The guys take turns organizing each year. Isn't that sweet? The event is included in the HOA dues—well worth it, I think. I mean, sometimes what they say is true. If mama ain't happy, ain't nobody happy. But I'm happy." She gives a coy, one-shoulder shrug.

A petite woman who Nora instantly recognizes joins them and gives Alexis a warm hug. "Lucy! I don't think you've properly met Nora." Alexis stands back to make room.

"Hi." Nora shakes her hand and introduces Hayden.

"Nora is going to be moving into the neighborhood." Alexis beams.

"Well, not officially. We still have to get through the option period."

"Details." Alexis waves her hand, cavalier. A small thrill. Does this mean she's been approved? Is Nora supposed to ask her sponsor, Thea, about that?

Lucy gestures to a man in dark-wash jeans and a tucked-in button-down. "This is my husband, Eddie. Eddie, meet Nora, a potential new neighbor."

"Eddie," Nora repeats. *You mean the man who beat you?* The voice in Nora's head is harsh.

He puts his arm around Lucy and leans in to kiss the top of her head, and as he does, a turn of his head reveals that a large chunk of hair has been shaved off. A nasty, surgical cut with stitches curves over his skull.

"Nice to have an afternoon away from the kids, isn't it?" Eddie says. "Not that I mind them. But you know, for the two of us. Lucy works so hard."

Nora glances away from the wound and tries to focus her attention. Is that genuine adoration she detects in his voice? Not that it matters. Nora refuses to soften to an *abuser*. Though Eddie doesn't look like an abuser. *Christ, Nora, it's not like you can tell just by looking at him.*

"Lucy told me that you put together a really great home movie for her of this year's highlights. That's precious. I can't wait to see it." Alexis says this with such warmth that Nora doesn't see how she could possibly be holding a grudge. If a partner of Andi's hit her, Nora would hate her for life. This whole exchange is making Nora feel a tad bit wacko. She must be missing something and that bugs her.

Well, on Lucy's behalf, she hopes that whatever happened to that man's head hurt a lot.

She's plotting her exit from the conversation when she spots Francine White—wearing ripped black jeans and a worn V-neck completely inappropriate for the occasion—approach Penny.

"Nora?" Alexis's voice breaks through. "Did you hear—"

"Excuse me," Nora says, distracted. "I need to say hello to Penny."

But it's Francine she keeps her eyes on as she weaves her way through the neighborhood women, watching as the girl leans into Penny and murmurs something into her ear. Oh, how Nora wishes she were a fly on the make-your-own doughnut station.

The trip across the room is a minute, tops, but it's enough that by the time Nora arrives, Francine is pushing past Penny, having unmoored from where the two had clumped together. Nora feels a spike of anger claw its way out of her chest as she reads the mood lingering in the air like stale perfume.

"What did she say to you?" Nora's tone makes it clear whose side she's on.

Penny doesn't look up, not right away. Penny's chestnut hair falls loose over her shoulders and she's wearing a pretty A-line dress with yellow polka dots.

"Penny?" Nora leans in. "Penny, are you okay?" Penny's eyes are red and watery. "I'm sorry." Nora clenches her teeth. "But teenager or no, that girl is out of control. Do you want me to say something to Cornelia?" If she sounds like an old biddy, she doesn't care. What nerve, doing this to Penny. Her godmother. On today of all days.

Nora does a quick check over her shoulder to make sure Hayden's all right. He's pilfering the cheese spread. Nora lowers her voice. "Don't listen to her. She's just acting out. Testing boundaries." Her own therapy must be rubbing off on her. "Actually, I was hoping to get a moment alone. Francine—"

"Stop." Penny brings Nora up short. "I don't want to talk about Francine."

Nora pulls back, stung.

"Okay." Given the relationship with the White family, Nora does understand the level of sensitivity simply in raising the topic of the girl. But Francine *knows* something. She's *seen* something. Not to mention the matter of Cornelia and her request not to involve the police. "It might be better if we could talk more privately, though," she murmurs.

But before Penny answers, Thea locates them, bringing with her a man with a vaguely familiar face who stands very, very close to Penny. *Personal space*, is Nora's first thought and she tries to catch Penny's eye.

Nora reminds herself not to be offended by Penny's sharp tone. This is her first holiday without Richard. It's okay if she's not her best self.

"We were about to step out for a moment," Nora says to Thea.

"Stay. Roman's going to give a speech soon." Thea sticks her tongue through her teeth with excitement. "I heard him practicing it this morning."

Nora's eyes shift between Penny and the man. She's not usually good at this sort of thing, but she's reading something there. A *vibe*. He's quite a bit younger than Penny. A date? *No*. Surely not. Right? Do people bring dates to Mother's Day? Maybe if it's an extravaganza, she thinks. And this is an extravaganza. No denying that.

Oh god, she's thinking about Penny and dating and, yes, Richard, who Nora's never met and therefore has no real allegiance to, when she grasps that the man and Penny are staring back at her. Nora smiles too wide. "Hi!" She sounds manic. "I don't think we've met. Nora! Nora Spangler!"

"This is Trevor," says Thea, craning her neck to look for Roman. "I think you two met briefly when you came to my center. He's one of my neurology residents." Now she remembers. That's why he looks familiar. Nora eases. "Nora's a great lawyer. She's working on a matter for Penny, actually."

"About that . . ." Nora leads.

Penny gives a terse shake of her head. "Later."

Later? Nora stifles a groan. Better later than never, but—She checks the time on her phone. She shouldn't stay much longer. She can spare a few more minutes. If she has to. But that's it.

"Impressive." Trevor has very white, very straight teeth. "You must work really hard." He puts his arm around Penny. So, *that* vibe.

Un-clutch your pearls, Nora. Really, she shouldn't be alarmed. Grief is individual. "Did you two meet through Thea, then?" Here she is trying to be *okay* with Penny's love life. Very smooth.

"She set us up. Thinks I need to keep *busy*." Penny picks apart a doughnut.

"Are you still not writing?" Nora is gentle and also a little distracted because what's caught her attention is the sight of Francine passing by the outside of a window. There's a flick of nerves and Nora is deaf to whatever Penny's response may be. "Hold that thought," she says. "I'm so sorry. You know what? I'll just—I'll be right back."

Instinct takes over. Nora shoulder-presses her way through the door, past the catering staff and into the broad day where she catches the threads of gold-spun hair just as they disappear around the corner of the clubhouse. Nora follows, keeping her distance, watching, *spying* as Francine looks both ways and crosses the small parking lot, and out of the iron clubhouse gates. Nora pretends to take a call. Her phone has always been her best disguise.

She stays close to the hedges around the perimeter, watching as Francine White goes around to a car that's been idling. The hood of a gray Mustang is just out of view from up where the party is taking place.

The driver rolls the window down as Francine approaches and Nora can just make out the same baby-faced boy she met at the burn site. Only able to catch glimpses of him through the open window, she sees that he's dressed smartly in a pink polo shirt, like he's come straight from church. Maybe he has. Francine leans down and her body tenses, shoulders reddening as she makes a sharp, punchy gesture. It doesn't look like a couple *in* love. Bad body language. That's what a tabloid might say. As if Nora here is the paparazzi. She almost considers snapping a pic.

But then—god, she shudders to think what body language experts would say about her with Hayden sometimes. But *she* is cruising toward forty. *She* has a reason to be angry.

Words are exchanged and Nora can make out none of them until, without warning, Francine yanks open the car door and slams it shut, causing the boy inside to recoil.

That's the end of the conversation. Nora makes herself small and nonchalant, but Francine, occupied in her own head, isn't looking her way when she crosses the long way back across the small parking lot and around the clubhouse. Nora waits.

The car hasn't moved. But Nora does. Giving up on the imaginary call, she makes her way out of the gates as though she's just going for a short walk to stretch her legs. All told, she's sure it hasn't been five minutes since she left Thea and Penny, but she feels like she has no time to waste.

She approaches the car—an old, and not in a cool way, Mustang—with purpose, leaning her head into the window just as the boy looks up from the screen of his phone where he's tapped out part of a text message. He's reaching for the gearshift, but it's too late to pull away without the possibility of injuring her. "Devin?" she asks.

He doesn't deny it. He's stuck now. She's gotten him alone.

"You're the lawyer," he says. His Adam's apple, extra pointy due to puberty, leaps up.

Nora goes for nice. Motherly. "Did you get in an argument with Francine?" she says, sympathetically.

"It's nothing." His jaw flexes. His gold-green eyes travel to the windshield, where he stares out over the hood of his car.

"Devin, the reason I came over is that I felt like you wanted to tell me something the other night. Like you were holding something back. You did, didn't you?" Nora holds her breath. Maybe it's a long shot, but Nora believes that Francine knows something and is hiding it, she just doesn't know what or why.

He says nothing.

"I'm not trying to get anyone in trouble," she says. "I only care about the truth."

"That's what I told her."

"You did?" Nora keeps her hand on the door so that he doesn't get any ideas, but she squats down to give her thighs a rest. She should get in better shape after the baby. She probably should actually prioritize it. Fuck. "That's good, because the only way you're going to get in real trouble is by not telling the truth. Once a case like this goes to trial, everything will come out. It always does. Francine could have to testify under oath. Maybe even you if it comes down to it." She lets that sink in. "Did Francine tell you something, something about the fire?"

"She didn't tell me anything," Devin says.

"Are you sure?"

He nods.

"Devin." Nora's warning is gentle but unmistakable.

"She didn't see anything. She didn't hear anything. Because she was with me." Nora stays quiet. How much longer does she have until they're interrupted? A couple more minutes? Less? "I came over to Mrs. Ross's house after the kids went to sleep. We were together." Nora's knees are screaming at her. This is just perfect. All these days she's been worried that Francine White knew something when really they were just kids trying to hide from their parents the fact that they were fooling around. Mystery solved, Nora. There you are. "I told her that it wasn't a big deal, that we were better off being honest, but she said her mom would freak out. I snuck out the back and—" He breaks off.

Nora snaps to attention. "And what?"

He leans his head back against the rest and closes his eyes. "Nothing." He shrugs, returning to normal. "I snuck out."

Nora's heart beats faster. "Devin. I hope you know how serious this is. This isn't kid stuff. There's real money at stake. Real consequences." He shifts, but remains tight-lipped. "Okay." She taps the top of the door. "If you do think of anything, here's my card." She hands it to him. "Call me, email me, anytime."

"Wait, *wait*," he says, thumping the steering wheel with the heel of his hand. "Are you going to tell Francine's mom?"

Nora's knees pop as she stands up. She kneads her lower back. "I guess that depends. I'll think about it for a few days," she says. "How about we both agree to do that?"

⊞

Nora slips in the back to the sound of dull knives clinking glasses all around. *Ting ting ting!* and *Shhhhh!*

She scans the crowd for her husband as Roman takes the microphone.

"Happy Mother's Day." Roman's voice booms through the speaker system. "I know this day can be hard for so many." Nora wipes her palms on the skirt of her dress and takes a deep, shuddering breath. "People have lost mothers, people have struggled to become mothers, people have complicated relationships with their mothers," Roman is saying, and she tries hard to listen. "But today I'm so grateful to have the opportunity to celebrate the wonderful women who make motherhood look good here in our community." She snakes through the serving stations and around two caterers carrying between them a fresh batch of French toast. No sign of Hayden. "Each one of you has helped each of us to create beautiful partnerships and families. When I speak to the other husbands here, I hear the same things over and over. We don't just love our wives, we are deeply *in* love with them. Thank you for choosing to do life with us."

"We couldn't do it without you!" Thea hoots through cupped hands.

Roman raises his glass. "May every day feel like Mother's—"

His thought is cut short by a guttural yell.

"Oh my god." Alexis rushes past Nora, knocking a mimosa off a high table. The glass breaks and orange juice splashes out. "Penny. No. *No.* Penny!"

"Get off him, Penny." Cornelia is suddenly right there. "Pen-*ny*!"

There's a noticeable lag during which Nora can't quite process what she's seeing.

"Finally lost her mind." Thea draws back, taking a slow gulp of champagne and shaking her head. "Snapped. I told them."

Alexis embraces Penny from behind, capturing her arms. Trey—or was it Trevor?—tugs at his face.

"Ah, ah, ah, it burns, it stings. What the—?"

"Trevor." Cornelia gently takes his hands and pulls them down. "Let me have a look." Thin red lines crisscross his cheeks as though his skin's been thatched. "You're fine, you're fine. Shh, shh, shh. It's okay, Trevor. Listen to me. It's *okay*."

Trevor moans. Trickles of blood ooze down his face. Roman stands motionless in the background. Shouldn't the husbands be doing something?

Penny bucks against Alexis. She's shrieking. "I don't want Trevor! I don't want a fucking Trevor! I want my husband! You hear me? Richard! Richard was good." Alexis wrestles Penny, absorbing the brunt of her stifled elbow blows.

Thea cracks her neck. "I think that's my cue." She hands Nora her glass before joining Alexis.

Thea hugs Penny tightly, whispering close in her ear. Words that Nora can't make out. Until Penny eases. Nearly goes limp in their arms. And something drops from her hand. There's a ping on the floor.

Nora follows the flash of silver as it settles on tile. Registers it with the surprise and relief of a detective uncovering the murder weapon.

Out of Penny's hand has fallen a fork.

A civilized kind of chaos follows. Thea taking a cloth napkin to Trevor's face and determining that he doesn't need medical attention. Roman and Max ushering Trevor out to sit by the pool where Asher passes him a glass of champagne. Cornelia wrapping her arm around Penny and murmuring to her as she moans at intervals.

Nora has trailed them outside while nearly everyone else has remained in, eating and drinking as though nothing's happened.

It's the sound of the sirens. That's what changes things.

Cornelia perks up like a retriever. "Are those . . . are those coming for here?" she asks, incredulous.

"*No*," says Thea. "No, they couldn't be. We're fine. Everything's fine."

But the blare grows louder, more urgent, and then everyone is looking around at everyone else.

There's only a second or two between when Nora catches sight of Hayden emerging from the clubhouse—a look of relief on his face when he spots her—and when all eyes turn to him as he pockets his cell phone.

He squints in the sunlight. "I called the police," he says. His brow furrows. "Was I not supposed to?"

Cornelia smooths the tails of her crisp button-down. "It's fine, Hayden," Cornelia says. Obviously it's not.

Nora feels a protective instinct toward her husband, who she's sure was trying to do the right thing. A fork fight! At brunch! It's so unexpectedly terrible, Nora might guess she's being pranked. Or punked. Are kids still saying that—*punked*? Her mind does this, races off track when it ought to be focusing on the crisis at hand.

"He didn't know," Nora says to Alexis because she's the closest.

"Shhh, shhh, it's all right." Alexis clasps her forearm. "Cornelia can handle it."

Beyond the gates comes the sound of a slamming car door. The clomp of footsteps.

"Nora." Cornelia beckons. "You're Penny's lawyer. Why don't you come speak to the officers with me."

"Oh. Yes, sure." Nora obeys with a quick glance back to Hayden, who's been absorbed by the other husbands and tasked with encouraging Trevor to drink rather copious amounts of champagne.

Cornelia heads off the officer at the gate. "Officer." Her greeting is imperious. It says, *Pay attention because we are people with the full range of systemic protections at our disposal, so mind your p's and q's.* When Nora has a doctor's appointment, she often slips in that she's a lawyer for the same reason.

Officer Lorenzo, as his name tag indicates, holds his elbows out at sharp angles, thumbs hooked into his belt. "Ma'am, I received a call about a domestic disturbance. I understand a man was attacked."

Cornelia exhales. "A bit of an overstatement, I think. There was an altercation, but nothing serious." The bracelets on her wrists jangle. "A few scratches. Band-Aids will do the trick. Honestly."

Officer Lorenzo turns his rheumy eyes over to Nora. "Were you the perpetrator?"

"Me?" Nora's eyelids flutter. "No. *No.* I . . . I'm her lawyer." Though she doesn't look much like a lawyer now in a breezy maxi dress and sandals.

Lorenzo frowns. "Already has a lawyer? That's gotta be some kind of record."

"Nothing to do with this. Her husband died recently. In a fire. I'm representing her in a wrongful death lawsuit. I was here . . . socially. She's going through a lot, as you can imagine, so if you can take that into consideration."

"A fire, you said?" He rubs his earlobe. "Around here?"

"Yes, it was terrible. You can understand—"

"I heard about that one," Officer Lorenzo says, widening his stance even farther. "Does sound bad. But I still need to see the victim. And the culprit. Standard procedure. Make sure everyone's peachy keen."

"Officer—" Nora attempts to intervene, but Cornelia cuts in.

"Of course," Cornelia says. "Trevor? Trevor, can you come here?"

Trevor takes even steps, arriving with a calm, glazed expression. A good idea, that champagne. At the sight of him, the officer winces. "That's more than a scratch, I'd say, buddy."

"I'm not interested in pressing charges," says Trevor in reply.

"You might change your mind once you get a load of yourself in a mirror."

Nora digs deep, trying to remember her early criminal law courses. "You can't force him to press charges."

"That's right. But if the situation warrants, I may need to make an arrest. Now, Trevor, was it? It seems pretty clear to me that a person's nails didn't make those marks. That right?"

Trevor stands calmly and nearly motionless. "That's correct."

"'Kay. Think you can clue me in as to what kind of weapon was used?" Officer Lorenzo folds his arms.

"No weapon," Trevor says. "It was a fork."

"A fork. All right, well, that's a first, too. Listen." Officer Lorenzo speaks once again directly to Cornelia and Nora, like they're the two adults in charge at a keg party that's gotten out of hand. "I think it's in the parties' best interest for the perpetrator to be detained. For everyone's safety, *pending* charges."

Cornelia whisks her fingers through her hair and it fans back into place. "Can he do that?"

Nora thinks. "Yes. Yes, he can." It will be more difficult for the district attorney's office to prosecute without a victim pressing charges, but an officer of the law can make an arrest in the interest of public or others' safety.

Cornelia turns. "Officer. Penny's fragile right now. I should have mentioned this, but I'm a psychiatrist and I've worked with her in the past. Let me handle her. I'll even admit her. Right now. Admit her to a facility where I promise she'll receive the best care available under my personal supervision. It'll be the same outcome you're proposing. I just really don't think we need to get the law involved in all this."

Lorenzo leans back on his heels. "What hospital?"

"Saint David's. Just up the road. We'll evaluate her, assess the situation. You have to admit that would be a better outcome for everyone involved."

She watches Lorenzo decide which outcome scares him more—liability or paperwork. "Saint David's," he muses. "Well. Okay, then. I suppose. If you can go now, put an involuntary hold, then Saint David's it is. I'll wait."

"Nora, stay here for a minute while I get Penny. Trevor, I think you can go back inside, right?"

Officer Lorenzo agrees but steps within the threshold, the black bulk of his gun inches away from Nora. She takes an instinctive step backward, away from its gravitational pull. She's anxious until Cornelia reappears, holding Penny's hand, gently, like she's an invalid. Penny lifts her chin. Her lower lip quivers. "Good afternoon," she says.

Officer Lorenzo appraises Penny.

"Ma'am. Do you understand that you'll be admitted into a psychiatric facility?" he asks.

At this, her lips part. She looks to Cornelia, at the officer, at Nora, and back. Nora's heart aches.

"Penny, honey." Cornelia holds tight to her and Nora can no longer tell if it's to comfort her or hold her back. "He's giving you the choice between being arrested right here and now or agreeing to a short psychiatric hold," she explains in a tone that might suggest English is Penny's second language.

Penny swallows. Her eyes search. Frantic.

"You don't have to do anything you don't want to do," Nora says. "Though, I agree, it'd be best to avoid an arrest on your record for a variety of reasons." Nora still remembers her college roommate who'd missed out on attending her top choice law school because of a DUI arrest. She hadn't even been convicted.

Penny swallows. "I understand," she replies. "Yes."

"Okay. It's settled, then." Cornelia extracts keys from a Tory Burch purse that Nora hadn't noticed she'd retrieved. "Nora, we'll touch base later. I have my wallet. Happy Mother's Day to you."

That's that.

Afterward there is much milling around. The other women ask her questions. What happened? Where is Penny going? How did she seem? Nora's hands quiver.

What bothers her most is that Penny hadn't seemed crazy. Not even up to the moment that she'd freaked out. There's a thin line between sadness and lunacy and maybe, all this time, Nora hadn't realized how close Penny had been to it, teetering dangerously on top of it, waiting to fall one way or the other. But then again, there's another possibility, the possibility that Penny had already crossed it before. And if Penny is capable of this—really—what else might she have done?

26

F our hours after she's touched down in San Francisco, Andi Ogsby
deigns to answer Nora's calls.

"Are you giving me the silent treatment?" Nora demands.
"Can adults do that?" Yes, she missed Andi's layover, but she's had an
upset stomach about it ever since.

"No, I'm doing the cold shoulder. It's very different and age appro-
priate."

Nora paces in the small patch of grass that passes for her backyard.
Pollen has been falling for days, leaving a thick, spongy layer of puke-
colored fuzz that gets all over everything. "Look, I'm sorry."

"*Look?*" Andi erupts into a short burst of high-pitched laughter that
denotes the polar opposite of fun. "What kind of an apology starts with
look?"

Nora hasn't been in an argument with a friend since high school and
never ever with Andi. There have been instances of hurt feelings, but
usually those are swept under the rug until one party or preferably both
gives up being bothered. It's better that way. Less drama. These things
happen.

"I couldn't help it," she says, expecting Andi to understand.

"I beg to differ." She imagines Andi seated cross-legged on some
guestroom bed with a pretty duvet her mother picked out.

"You don't even know what happened."

"I know enough."

Nora still sees a possibility that they won't get into it. "Penny, my client, she sort of—well, there was an altercation and the police were called. Hayden called them, actually."

"You weren't supposed to be there in the first place."

"I told you—"

"Bullshit, Nor. There was no mention of this Mother's Day brunch thingamajig earlier. Also, I talked to Hayden and you know what? He didn't know the first thing about my layover."

The way she says it makes it sound odious when really Nora just wanted to avoid Hayden's attempt to talk her out of attending the brunch in Dynasty Ranch. It was *her* Mother's Day. And so, she planned on springing Andi's visit on him as more of a happy surprise.

Nora's heart kicks in her chest. "Why did you talk to Hayden?"

"Um, probably because *you* disappeared."

"I wish you wouldn't have done that."

Andi scoffs. "What is with you? Why are you acting so weird about Hayden? Are you two splitting up or something?"

"No, god, no."

"Then what? I know it's not me. I haven't done anything. I didn't forget your birthday, for instance."

"Andi! You can't expect me to drop everything. I'm not just on pause, you know. Your trip was really last-minute."

"I went out of my way to book a layover where you are. We *never* get to see each other."

"Exactly," Nora says, clipped.

"Don't give me that. We're the type of friends who can be separated for ages and as soon as we're back together, it's like nothing's changed."

"Except that things *do* change."

"Like what?" There's an edge to Andi's voice that Nora doesn't recognize.

"I have a kid. I'm pregnant. I have a stressful job."

"Oh, okay, so because I don't have a kid, I don't get it now? That's where we are? People without children don't have a clue. Lovely."

"No, I just need to make other friends who do understand that part of it. And who are here. Physically." There. At least Nora's said it.

She wants to lean her elbows on kitchen countertops and talk for too long over a cold glass of chardonnay. She wants to enter a friend's house without having to knock. She wants someone to have her spare key. She wants a friend who will hold her baby while she eats without asking, who will go for a walk with her if she fucks up at work, who will remember what it felt like to have stitches in her vagina and who will weigh in on potential new haircuts. And, in return, she will do the same.

"I want you to have other friends," Andi says. "But I would think they'd be friends with whom you felt comfortable enough around to say, 'Hey, sorry, can't make it this time, ladies. Other plans.'"

"I *can*. But it's early still."

"And so these new friends are, what, more important than me?"

Nora's done with obfuscating the truth. It's only causing trouble. "At the moment, I guess, yeah, maybe they are."

"Got it. Well," says Andi. "See you next time then. Or, you know, not."

"Andi—" But by the time Nora gets her name out, she's already saying it into dead air.

With she and Andi no longer on speaking terms for the time being, Nora finds all the distraction she needs in her casework. Perched behind her desk, Nora mentally does what she has been doing for weeks now. She

picks up each piece of her investigation into the March fire. The clicking noise. BURN BABY BURN. Francine. Devin. Richard's mental health.
Sylvia. Penny. Dave's V-pattern. And with each, she turns it over, feeling her brain fumble in the dark for another one that she knows must
be there because she's felt its edges as they slid past her fingers in the
dark.

True to her pledge not to contact the police department yet,
she spends her time checking in on the timing of her home inspection,
drafting interrogatories, and hounding Dave to hurry along the lab and
other test results. Better, she reasons, to be killed by the news itself than
the suspense.

There's an automatically generated message sitting in her in-box in-
forming her of a missed call from a local 512 number without a voicemail
attached. She picks up her handset and dutifully calls back the printed
numbers. She presses the phone to her ear as it rings.

"Who is this?" comes a woman's voice on the other end, muffled.
Young.

"This is Nora Spangler," she says, trying not to sound offended.
"From Greenberg Schwall. I'm returning a call from this number."

"You are?"

"Yes. Can I help you with something?" Nora asks.

"It was a wrong number," the young woman says at the same moment that Cameron Drummer materializes in her office.

"Are you busy?" Cameron grimaces, but Nora's already hanging up.
"What's up?"

"Help me out here. I took an extra week with Zara from Eleanor
because she's got the flu and I had no idea I was going to be in charge of
a class party for National Teachers Day. Since when is there a National
Teachers Day?" It's obvious from his tone that he thinks there doesn't
need to be. Nora thinks there should probably be seven or eight per year.
"Tell me what I need to do, with the caveat that it has to be something

that can get done in approximately"—he refers to his phone—"one hour."

"One hour?" She reads his expression. "Sorry. Right. Okay." This at least is a problem Nora has experience solving. "Whatever you bring is going to need to be gluten-free, peanut-free, and all that good stuff. Plus, since it's for the teachers, too, you need to try to get them something that looks homemade or at least kind of artisanal." Not helping. "Go to Swedish Hill and ask for their gluten-free brownies and make sure to tell them they're for a classroom. Have them tie a ribbon around a boxed pie for each of the teachers in your class. There are probably two. You can hit Randall's for paper plates, napkins, and cups on the way out. Grab a jug of lemonade and you're good."

He rubs his hand over the bit of closely shaved hair he keeps on his scalp. "And that'll look okay, you think? I don't want Zara's parent to be, like, the loser parent."

"It'll be fine. She'll be excited you're there." Nora doesn't have to worry about National Teachers Day today. Hayden made Rice Krispie treats. He read the back of the box.

"And I just, like, walk in with all this stuff and—what?"

"Is that a serious question?" Nora asks. "*Yes*. I mean, obviously. Put the plates and things down in front of each of the children. Pass out treats for the teachers. Clean up after. Don't let them lift a finger. That's the point of this whole exercise." Nora can tell that he wishes he'd been writing this down. Her phone rings. She checks the caller ID. It's the same 512 number that called earlier. The wrong number. She rolls her eyes. "It's nobody," she says.

"I can do this." When Cameron clenches his fist, she notes that he'd make a very handsome superhero. He moves to leave—time is of the essence when it comes to celebrating the nation's teachers—then stops. "Hey, that case," he says. "The one you've been working on. You haven't updated me in a while. How's it going?"

Nora peels the back off of the visitor name tag and sticks it on the spot over her heart. She brushes strands of hair out of the way and lifts her chin as she pats the sticker flat. She's never been any good with sick or old people. She doesn't know what to say. The closed doors. The quiet beeps. The sound of muted footsteps slipping in and out of rooms. If a person didn't come in crazy to begin with, Nora can understand how they'd wind up that way.

In the psych ward, she hovers outside of room 13 until a nurse passes. "Can I help you?" asks the nurse.

"I'm just visiting," Nora murmurs and then quickly slips inside.

It takes a moment to adjust to the murky gray light filtering in through the closed blinds. There's relief when she finds the room isn't padded. It reminds her of the hospital room in which she delivered Liv, crowded with machines that seem to serve no purpose.

The very normal hospital bed is center focus. That's where Penny is. A lump beneath standard-issue sheets. Nora should have thought to bring her a blanket or a nice pillowcase, something to make the setup less bleak.

"Penny?" she tests, approaching on tiptoe. "Penny, it's me, Nora. Nora Spangler." She cringes.

No response. Just the sound of even breathing.

She can't help but notice the leather restraints dangling unfastened from the bed. She'd imagined that those were a cliché, a movie prop, not a reality of mental illness.

Nora goes around to the visitor chair and carefully tucks her skirt underneath her thighs, not wanting to wake Penny. At least she's not in a straitjacket. So it's not impossible to imagine the whole setup as a forced vacation. No view, and, yes, probably as boring as watching paint dry, but Nora might consider it for the naps alone.

Nora tamps down this terrible thought.

She sits, figuring she'll wait a few minutes and then write a note to mention she dropped in. But then it's with a terrible start she realizes what's so unsettling.

Penny's awake.

She stares through Nora with shiny globular eyes, unblinking, like she's peering into the dark.

"Penny?" Nora whispers.

Penny's eyes roll in their sockets like Magic 8 Balls, floating around for the answer: *ask again later.*

"Penny, are you okay?"

The pupils dilate. At no point do Penny's eyelids lower. It's as though they're stitched back. Should Nora get someone? Is this normal?

A whiteboard chart hangs on the wall, Penny's name markered across its top. Down the left side, a list of medications and their time of administration. Haloperidol, chlorpromazine, fluoxetine, zolpidem, nitrazepam. Beside each one, the prescribing doctor; beside each one: *White.*

"Penny." Nora keeps using her name like it might *do* something. She moves her chair closer and clasps Penny's hand. "Can you hear me?" The little red call button is secured to the side of the hospital bed. She could call it. What's the worst that could happen, they tell her that Penny's acting exactly as any psych ward patient should? Yes, she might be over-reacting, but Nora doesn't really care. "I'm going to call the nurse, just to check, okay?"

She reaches into the bed, grazing the bone of Penny's knee with her knuckles. She pushes the call button and holds her breath. Penny's eyes seem to float again. Her breathing grows more ragged. Nora jiggles her own foot, waiting impatiently. She presses the button a second time.

Penny's chapped lips open. And then, without warning, her fingers clench around Nora's hand, and Nora stifles a yelp of surprise. And pain.

"Too much," Nora stammers, glancing at the door for the nurse. She'll be here any minute. It's fine.

"Richard was killed." Penny squeezes. The tips of Nora's fingers blanch. "He was killed."

"Wh—"

"What seems to be the problem?" A petite nurse with unflattering bangs marches her Crocs into the room.

"She was—" Nora looks down to see that Penny has released her hand. Her face returns to a blank canvas.

Meanwhile the heart rate monitor *blip-blip-blips*, the digital mountains on-screen passing with increased speed.

"Ma'am, are you immediate family?" asks the nurse.

"No, I—"

"Then I'm going to need you to give us some space." Nora doesn't want to tear herself away from Penny. "Please." The nurse repeats. "Go—outside." She's wheeling the monitors closer, adjusting cords. "*Now.*"

Nora gathers up her purse and backs toward the door. On the surface, there's no sign that Penny had been awake seconds earlier. Nothing of the frantic hiss of air through her teeth. Nothing of the words rasped, words that could mean anything or nothing, depending. Nora's hyperconscious of the ease with which women can be written off as crazy whenever they're saying something other people don't like. But this time's different. This time, the woman really is clinically nuts. And that's something to consider. Because if taken seriously, despite their messenger, Penny's words could suggest something sinister. They could mean murder.

⁂

Once ensconced safely back inside the blank, parchment paper walls of her office, Nora grapples with the only sane thing to do. She will have to press forward under theory of arson.

Meaning, she can't put off contacting the police any longer. She'll call Cornelia and offer the courtesy of letting her know that, sorry, their agreement to put the investigation on pause until she's been able to prep Penny is now null and void, effective immediately. Circumstances change, and after Penny's outburst, she feels a high degree of certainty that her client's wishes are to pursue an investigation into the possibility of an intentional setting of the fire that burned down her house and killed her husband. If there's a bright spot to be found it's that Nora feels more convinced than ever that Penny played no role in the burning of her house. She wants justice.

And so Nora will explain to Cornelia as best she can that while she hopes this doesn't impact their friendship, her hands are tied. She's duty bound. And besides, Alexis should be relatively impartial, and maybe even Thea—as well as, she hopes, Isla. With them, she'll maintain a strong foothold in the neighborhood if worst comes to worst. A path to proper integration.

She gathers her nerve.

The landline jingles in the handset cradle, completely ruining whatever cool she's managed to marshal up to this point. It's Dave's number on the caller ID. "Hello?" she answers, her tension clear in the short greeting.

"Good news, bad news," he says. "Which do you want first?"

She presses her hand in the space between her thighs to steady it. "The good news."

"Sorry, that was a trick question, it's the same either way." She doesn't even bother to muster a polite laugh for the occasion. She simply waits, stiff-backed, preparing for confirmation of her worst fears. "The fire," he continues, "it looks like a burning candle caught hold of something flammable, some spilled cleaning fluid, it seems. It's possible the gas on the stove top was turned on just prior and that was a contributing factor, hard to say, but the fire was an accident."

Suddenly, the air in her lungs feels too thick to breathe in or out. "You're sure?"

"I'm giving it to you straight. Heck, if I could nail a home builder, I would, but your client's still going to have access to the insurance money, I'd imagine, so it could be worse."

"A candle?"

"It was a hot burn but we've identified traces of the wax. Freak accident. I'll email the results to you soon as we hop off the phone, but wanted to get back to you soonest."

When the two hang up, Nora stares slack-jawed at the bookshelf standing sentinel across the room. She turns her cell phone over on her desk where Cornelia's contact information has already been pulled up, ready for her call. She clears the screen. She feels as though she's just gotten off the phone with the governor and been offered a stay of execution, and now she has to figure out what she's going to do with her life.

What was she thinking? Maybe she's the one who's crazy.

A few minutes later she reads over the report to the best of her ability, largely skipping past any words she can't pronounce. Under the list of substances she reads: *lint, dust, dirt, Lestoil, carpet threads, candle wax, insulation (cellulose, fiberglass, mineral-untampered), glycerol, polished wood, trace blood, saliva.* Each are marked on the corresponding map showing where the substances were found in the March home.

A freak accident, Nora repeats to herself. She's heard that before.

27

Hayden's not usually late." Nora sits on the stylish sofa in the empty waiting room of Cornelia's office, five minutes past the appointment time. She closes the issue of *Shape* magazine on her lap. She hadn't really cared what Carrie Underwood ate during her pregnancy anyway.

Cornelia takes a seat on the edge of one of the bookend armchairs. She's had a haircut since they last met, nothing different, but Nora can always tell. "He's already inside."

Nora blinks, surprised. "Should we should go in, then?"

Cornelia doesn't move. "In a minute."

"Okay." Nora looks down at the magazine cover, trying to decide if she should reopen it.

Cornelia misreads her restlessness. "There's no need to be nervous."

Nora can't find it within her to tell Cornelia about the conclusions of Dave's test results. Not yet. She knows how badly the women hope to provide for Penny and that a candle fire will mean a much smaller financial settlement, given that, without corporate negligence or personal malfeasance, only the insurance money remains at stake. It's not Nora's fault, but she knows how it can look to be the messenger. "I visited Penny yesterday," she blurts out instead.

Nora registers Cornelia's mild surprise. "Did you? That was thoughtful. I must have just missed you. I'm sure you noticed that she's a bit out of sorts still."

"How long will she be there?"

Cornelia bobs her head side to side. "The involuntary hold will last seventy-two hours and then after that we'll make some larger decisions for her continued treatment."

Three faint finger marks still linger on the back of Nora's hand where Penny had grabbed her. A day or two ago, Nora would have debated whether or not to tell Cornelia the details of that disturbing visit. But the lab results had let her off the hook, hadn't they? And, besides, she'd hate to say anything that might delay Penny's release.

"About the case," Cornelia says. "I don't think Penny's interested in pursuing it further."

Nora opens her mouth to speak, but Cornelia holds up her hand.

"She's still hopeful she'll get the insurance money. But digging into it hasn't been good for her mental health. As you can see." Cornelia takes a heavy breath. "I should have been more forthcoming. I take confidentiality very seriously. Really, I hope you do understand that. But this isn't really even about Penny, it's about Richard, and also you *are* Penny's attorney. So we're both on the same side of confidentiality, as I see it," Cornelia says. "A team, right?"

Nora finds herself nodding. *A team, yes.* But the tips of her fingers tingle. This is where she should jump in and tell her the fire was an accident. Insurance money is all there is. But she hesitates a beat too long.

"Penny and Richard were struggling over the last year or so. I should have done more. As her friend. But it's so difficult to know when to meddle and when to let well enough alone. It started with a bruise here and there," she says. "Oddly placed, back of her neck, her forearm, but I could believe, if I really wanted to—and I did—that Penny was clumsy. She's so fair-skinned. She bruises easily. The stories we tell ourselves, you know. But with time it was obvious that it was Richard and that he was getting more violent. A vase would get broken. A cut would appear. Penny was declining to socialize more and more. She was isolating herself. She stopped writing completely."

Nora's mind races to keep up with the facts being relayed to her. None of it is at all what she'd expected and so she can't think of how best to respond. First Lucy and Eddie, and now Cornelia is telling her that *Richard*, too, was abusive. Nora's stunned. Intellectually, she does know that it's more common than she thinks, but Hayden would never lift a finger. He'd never, in a million years, hurt anyone. That, she's sure of.

"Did she ever say anything to you directly?" Nora's never had a firm handle on how to respond to difficult news.

And to think of Penny, with her beautiful essays, enduring this underneath the surface. Well, maybe it makes perfect sense that she quit writing. It's got to be hard to offer advice when your own life is being ripped apart at the seams.

"A few weeks before the fire." Cornelia threads her gold pen through her fingers. "She told me she'd lost control of Richard. That was the phrase she'd used. I remember. She couldn't manage him anymore. I knew things were bad at that point. But then there was the fire and there didn't seem to be any point in excavating the memory of a dead man only to throw dirt back on it. But recently I've started to wonder what Richard was really doing."

"Cornelia—"

"I'm being realistic. Penny's insurance states that if either she or Richard destroyed the home, she'll get nothing. She'll be starting out without even a roof over her head. I started to think about what you'd said about an investigation and small details and working with the detectives. I made the mistake of broaching the subject with her before the Mother's Day celebration. I thought Trevor's presence would help. It was nice to see her with a man who was treating her so well. Trevor, I mean. I shouldn't have. And, before you ask, we're prepared to compensate you for the time you've already spent on the case. There will be plenty of other work, and now that you're so soon to be a neighbor, I have no doubt you'll quickly become the go-to. We can even do some kind of retainer, if it helps. I don't want this to affect your partnership bid. On the contrary, we want to do anything we can to help in that regard."

"Oh." Nora sees clearly the two ways this can play out. From the beginning, her value to the women has been, in some indefinable quantity, tied to her ability to successfully carry Penny's case to a favorable conclusion. That's why the categorization of the March fire as accidental was a boon, in that it precluded the need to confront the question of arson. On the other hand, a pure, stupid accident weakened her worth in this powerful circle. Here, she's being offered an out. It's being suggested to her, free of charge, that *she* could be doing them a *favor*. And that's worth something.

"That's—thank you. But," she demurs, "I do think I should still speak to Penny directly, when she's less medicated." She'll tell Penny the truth. When she's ready for it. Penny deserves to be told first, and if it's after Nora's finalized the process of her home purchase, then that wouldn't be the worst thing.

"In a strange way, I'm thankful. Because I think . . . I think Richard could have really hurt her." Cornelia studies her folded hands. "That's one of the reasons I'm such an advocate for couples therapy. I really want to help people. You guys are making such great progress." Like they're sharing a secret. "You feel it, too, I hope?"

Smoothness.

That's what Nora's begun to feel in her life. A texture she hasn't touched in years. "He's helping out more at home," is what she says. "And he doesn't seem put out by it. That's new."

"You know what you want out of it. And you trust the process. And that's what's so important. That you give yourself over to it. Just like you're doing."

They both look up at the click of the door to the session room opening. Unexpectedly, it's Thea who slips out to greet them.

Cornelia twists in her chair. "Ready for us?" she asks.

"All set." Thea says in a quiet voice.

Nora looks between the two women. "Is everything okay?"

"Thank you, Thea. We'll only be a minute."

"Take your time." Thea waves as if to say, *Don't let me bother you,* and makes a subtle exit.

"I nearly forgot." Cornelia stands, reaching into her blazer to extract an envelope. "This is for you."

"What is it?" Nora takes it up, peeling open the sealed envelope. Immediately, she recognizes the letterhead. It's from Liv's school. She scans the letter, devouring it whole. "But how?" She turns it over, as if she might discover the secret to a magic trick.

"I have a sympathetic friend on the board. I told her what happened and she wanted to help."

Nora's breathless. "Liv can keep going to her school? This is . . . this is too much."

"It's my pleasure," Cornelia says.

Nora stares, disbelieving. The truth—boiled down to its essence— flies out of her mouth: "I have no idea what I would do without you."

In Harm's Way:
The Damage Done When Mothers Aren't Supported

By Julia Shea

"Although every person in the human race has benefited in some way, shape, or form from mothering, the work of motherhood is often overlooked, to the emotional and often physical detriment of the women who bear the burden."

———————

Read Comments

———————

Rhonda Landay

Amen. People act like parenting is some kind of obscure luxury hobby. Whether or not YOU have kids, we still need PEOPLE to keep reproducing.

ZenAndTheArtofMomming

This is so true. Society doesn't seem to care about mothers and it's killing us. I've had severe back and pelvic pain for well over a year postpartum because of the diastasis recti that I developed during pregnancy, but insurance won't cover surgery to fix it because apparently knitting my abdomen back together is considered "cosmetic."

MomZilla

The person that suffers most from these oversights is always the mother because a good mother, when faced with a lack of support, will always rise to the occasion. And that's exactly why women are still in this predicament. Because motherhood is considered a women's issue and women's issues aren't taken seriously. That goes to the whole thing of why when women complain of migraines or back pain they're told it's anxiety or stress. If men can't see women's pain, then it doesn't exist. The work of motherhood is invisible and therefore it's not a real problem.

Terry D

I consistently feel like I'm on the verge of having an honest-to-god mental breakdown. It's the mental load that I'm carrying. It's not the laundry. Because, look, my family sees when the laundry is done. They register it on some level. It's the other stuff. I'm taking time out of what I need to do to listen to each of my teenagers' problems, my husband's work problems, his mother's requests for Sunday night dinner. I work hard to make sure we have friends as a couple, which let's face it, usually falls on the wives to organize. I work hard to make sure that we get together with extended family and I don't just mean my extended family. And that all means remembering schedules and birthdays and who needs to be where and when. About once a month I sit in my closet and cry so that nobody will see me. Maybe it's hormones. I don't know.

JP Liane

Thank you! All these influencers are so focused on this idea that mothers are made for more, that what mothers really need is to feel fulfilled. *Fulfilled?* Women are f*ing full. We hear over and over that we aren't enough. Not thin enough, not pretty enough, not stylish enough, and now we've added to it—not successful enough, not professional enough, not tough enough. So what's the natural reaction to hearing "not enough" over and over and over? Of course it's to take more. To shovel the "more" onto ourselves so that no one can accuse us of not being enough. "More" is so loaded, though. "More" is a clever innovation of a society that has always felt better when its women could be controlled. "More" is a distraction that keeps us from noticing. We "fulfill" ourselves to overflowing. We spill. We slip. Of course we do because taking on too much is a setup for failure. And when we do fall short—and we will—we're the ones who are going to feel bad about it because that's how it feels when you fail.

28

Buoyed by the news that Liv's year as a Giraffe at Trinity Fields has been saved, Nora enters the session room riding on an adrenal response similar to having escaped a near-death experience. She pulsates with gratitude. She is content to give herself over to the moment with Cornelia—*show me your ways*—hook, line, and sinker; ride the high; surf the wave. Nora Spangler will do anything that Cornelia asks her to do.

But when she sees Hayden, she falters. He's seated across from an empty chair, staring at the opposite wall. On his head is the brain-machine interface she'd been introduced to at Thea's neurology center.

"Why's he wearing that?" Nora asks sharply. She sits down heavily across from him.

"It's okay," says Hayden. "We've been over the whole protocol before you arrived. I feel very comfortable."

"It's been tested?" Nora asks.

"Of course. It's perfectly safe," says Cornelia, leaning against her desk.

"Then will I be wearing one, too?" She pats her head reflexively and thinks of the baby.

"Not today."

She speaks directly to her husband. "And you're sure?"

CHANDLER BAKER

"It feels like nothing at all," he says, lightly. It does seem fine, and Thea and Cornelia, for that matter, are doctors. If they prescribed her an antibiotic for an infection she would have no qualms about taking their advice. If Hayden's okay with it . . .

"Should we get started?" asks Cornelia.

Nora moves back into her chair. She is so close. She's come so far. And she sees no reason to stop now. She nods her assent. The pen snaps open and Cornelia studies the pair with the laser-focused observational interest of a scientist.

"Resentment." She pauses. "I believe that's where we left off last session."

Nora looks to Hayden, but at that moment her husband is as unreadable as a stranger.

"Resentment is insidious," says Cornelia. "It's like black mold growing in your home. If you allow it to fester, it will choke your relationship, keep it from breathing, it will suffocate you in your sleep."

A shiver of recognition runs down the length of Nora's spine.

"But if you remove it, if you pull it out at the root, treat and bleach it until it's gone, that's when you will find true, lasting change." For the first time since beginning these sessions, Cornelia sounds like a therapist. Soft, probing, intense. "Hayden." She leans forward. "I have one word written here in my notes. Do you recall what it is?"

Hayden's demeanor is overly formal. He looks uncomfortable, one hand on each thigh, both feet flat to the ground. Nora's sweat comes out cold.

She wishes that he would look at her before he says it, one moment of connection before the truth is cracked open.

"Accident," he says, looking straight into Cornelia.

Cornelia's eyes travel over to Nora. "Accident." She tries out the word as if she's learning it for the first time. "Are you surprised by his answer?"

"No." Nora shakes her head. "I'm not."

Cornelia's whole body settles. "Who wants to start? What happened?"

Nora swallows. There's only one right answer. Only one person who knows what happened, so only one person can tell it. *Her.*

Her own breathing plays so loudly in her ears that it drowns out all other signs of life and she finds herself with tunnel vision.

Unconsciously, she presses her hand to her belly. Every passing day of her pregnancy she has felt this, too, growing inside of her. An awareness that if they're ever going to make parenthood—let alone marriage—work going forward, Hayden has to understand what really happened that day. Why it happened. And that it can never, ever, happen again.

She feels like her stomach will heave if she tries to hold it in another second. But she still wants to. Part of her still prefers swimming in the nausea of her memory rather than letting it go.

Nora's voice is small and gravelly. "I was exhausted." It's the way she always starts the story, even in her head where it lives now, and mostly because it's the truth, but also, also it's less than the whole truth. "Our daughter, Liv, she was sixteen months. Perfect. She had the sweetest little indention between her hands and her forearms, like she was a doll someone had pieced together. I loved her so much. I think that's what hurt most after, after what happened. I felt that people—maybe Hayden, his mom—I think they thought I didn't totally love being a mother. Nobody would say it outright, but there were euphemisms bandied about. I got the implication. I heard my mother-in-law, Mary, I heard her whispering to Hayden, asking if I'd been seen about my postpartum depression. But I didn't *have* postpartum depression. It's the explanation everyone wanted. That way it wouldn't be completely my fault. People could label it. I think Hayden would have liked me to be some kind of poster child for postpartum depression and then he could feel like he stood by me through this Very Difficult Time. He wanted to feel progressive. Like an ally. And the postpartum thing, well, that was a diagnosis and therefore you could treat it. It would have an end date." She studies her husband. "You wanted to give me pills. I took them. For a while. But I knew that I wasn't ill. I loved Liv and I loved myself. I thought of myself as a good mom. I still do. Only now I don't really feel like I can say that to people. I have to walk around all the time feeling like there's a caveat. I have a footnote to my motherhood. Hayden doesn't. Hayden has no footnote to his abilities as a father. *His* record is squeaky clean."

There's the wordless energy present. If there's something happening underneath that cap contraption, Nora can't tell what. "What happened, Nora?" Cornelia asks. "In your words. Not anyone else's."

Nora drags a hand through her hair and gathers it at the back of her neck, conscious of the way her clammy hands are coating the strands. "Liv had been going through this terrible sleep regression. I felt like I'd been up for days. Sleep training and then giving up on sleep training and then trying to sleep train again." With this short description, she finds herself back there. The specifics have long been smeared, a fogged glass through which only impressions linger. Tangible snapshots. Eye sockets that ached through her sinuses. Clogged ears. Chin acne. Armpits that felt too sweaty even through their layers of deodorant.

The moment that Liv was born, Nora had lost her ability to sleep deeply, now waking at the sounds on the monitor, alone in the dead of night, the noise of Hayden's deep, even breaths beside her. Cornelia was right. Resentment had grown, exactly like mold, in the darkness, in moisture. It spread.

"Liv had gotten sick at school then. It was terrible timing. The sleep regression followed by Liv getting hand, foot and mouth disease." Nora had never heard of such a thing before having a kid. She wasn't even sure that it existed thirty years ago. Pustules formed in her baby's mouth and tongue, leaving pink streaks of blood on her crib sheets in the morning. It seemed like the bubonic plague had come to the Spangler household.

"It was . . . brutal. And then I thought I was going to have a break. I was counting on it. Hayden had promised to take over the night before, but then he remembered he had this big sales meeting in the morning and it seemed important enough for him—you know, for our family, I guess—that he be well rested and I figured I could take one more night. He was going to hurry back home as soon as he could, but he got tied up and it was already midafternoon. I was probably overtired by that point. We say that about kids sometimes, but grown-ups can be, too. I wasn't myself. I was in a bad mood. Snappy with Hayden . . . and with Liv, too." She flinches at the memory, at how Liv had been feeling miserable, but all Nora could stomach that day was to hand her a pack of graham crackers.

She pauses here. She can fast-forward the story, telling the parts that Hayden already knows: *I didn't feel well. I disappeared for a couple minutes to get myself some Advil. . . .*

But that's not everything. Not even half.

"I don't know exactly how to describe what I was thinking. Do you ever see those posts on Facebook and Instagram sort of—I don't know—bragging about being a bad mom? 'Mama needs her wine.' But it's actually gotten, like, a bit racier than that. Vape pens with pot in them. Women confessing that only vodka and iPads get them through the day. That kind of thing. It's self-deprecating and it's also started to be cool, you know? There were a couple movies around that time about being a bad mom, and the moms at Liv's school, they thought they were *hilarious.* You hear things like 'That's *so* me.' Women could relate. I couldn't, though. I'd never done any of that. I worked so much I didn't think I had time to be a flippantly 'bad' mom. I just couldn't. Except that day. I thought: *Nora, give yourself a break.* It seemed like all the messaging I was seeing was that moms needed to stop being so hard on themselves."

"Go on," Cornelia encourages.

She does. She feels compelled to, like she has a virus that her body has to expel.

"I decided to put Liv in front of a movie in the upstairs playroom so that I could nap in the guest room just down the hall. It seemed so innocent. I told myself, there are drug addicts that take care of children! There was no reason to feel guilty about *napping*. I poured myself a glass of wine. It was four o'clock. It wasn't like I was drinking in the morning. I could hear Liv watching *101 Dalmatians*. She *loves* puppies. But I couldn't fall asleep. I was so tired. I kept tossing and turning and all I wanted was an hour to close my eyes. I was sure if I could just get there, I'd feel better." Nora feels herself knocking up against the speed bump, wanting to go around. She's no longer trying to look to Hayden for encouragement, but she feels the weight of him anchoring the room, the heat off his body. Like gravity.

"I had a prescription bottle for Ambien," she continues. "That had been in my mother's effects after she passed. I'd saved it for no reason in particular at the time. She used to take them when she couldn't sleep. Even when we were kids. I remember her lying down and disappearing for a few hours while we played outside with the neighbors, poured ourselves cereal, watched cartoons, normal suburban kid stuff." Describing it now, Nora sees how she's romanticized it. Her mother had been lovely, especially before the divorce, after it, maybe less so, but still, her mother had been orange-slice mom, minivan mom, mom-jean and mom-haircut mom, and honestly, that was the kind of mom that felt right as a kid. You were safe with that brand of mother. It's a mom that, occasionally, Nora worries is going extinct. Moms can't just succumb to being moms anymore. They've got to sell patterned leggings or expensive skin creams out of their car trunks or be CEOs or be hot at fifty, but that's another issue entirely. Because even her own Mom-mom would check out every so often. She'd watch hours and hours of television before binge-watching was a trend. She'd nap. She would pour vodka into water glasses. But it was never a permanent status. Only as a grown-up did Nora really understand what was going on. It hadn't traumatized her. Her mother *had* felt better after those strange mental vacations. Her mother had always wanted to go to Bora Bora but had settled for a midday nap.

"I thought twice about it. I think that's the worst part. I did. But I checked on Liv and she was fine and I told myself I was being uptight, that I deserved to let go a little. What were the odds that something bad would happen?"

The inside of her throat thickens. She catches Hayden's eyes, his expression neutral, but a muscle in his jaw is flexing in and out, the way it does when he's angry. He doesn't look angry. She almost wants him to be, wants him to yell at her. He never did scream at her for what happened. She'd always thought, if he did, then she could tell him what she really thought. And this is what she's baiting, this is the reason she's spilling it all out now before the baby comes. She can't proactively blame him, but she's inviting his resentment at last because with it, she'll finally be free to tell him that what happened was his fault, too. He should have been there. He pushed her to this.

"I fell asleep. I don't know how long it took. I woke up when I heard the beep of the door opening. Hayden was home. I checked my phone. It was after six. I'd slept much longer than I meant to. I heard Hayden putting down his keys, taking off his shoes, and I went to get Liv. She wasn't there. That was when I saw that I'd forgotten to close the baby gate at the top of the stairs. It was like an out-of-body experience. I started screaming. I hadn't even seen her yet but I just knew." Her eyes fill. "There was blood. Her little body was crumpled down at the bottom of the stairs." She shuts her eyes, but that only makes the picture in her head clearer. "I thought she was dead. I flew down the stairs. She was breathing. She had tear stains dried onto her cheeks. She . . . she must have been crying for a while—I don't know how long—I didn't hear her." And this is the thing that haunts her, her daughter's cries that she never heard. Her imagination morphs them into horrible animal sounds, calling for a mother who doesn't come. Her nightmares are made of missed toddler sobs. "I was holding her and rocking, out of my mind when Hayden reached us. He . . . assumed it had just happened. That I wasn't watching her closely enough, that I got distracted cleaning or something. Everything happened so fast. I couldn't speak as it was. The ambulance arrived." Paramedics in her house leaving heavy rubber footprints on the hardwood that would last for weeks before she cleaned them. Liv's body too small for the stretcher, straps around her torso. A miniature neck brace. Her daughter's tiny fingers stretching out for her. "I was too afraid to tell the paramedics what really happened. I was too afraid to tell anyone."

"But you're telling someone now," says Cornelia. If Nora could put a name to the emotion she sees when Cornelia looks at her in that moment, she might call it something like love. Steady and maternal. "Hayden?" Cornelia's pitch changes. "What do we say when someone is hurt?"

Nora's husband doesn't blink. "I'm sorry."

"That's right. We say, 'I'm sorry.' Good job. You're so good at this, Hayden. A natural."

His jaw muscle flexes again.

Nora cracks two knuckles. She's seeing something, like a photograph taken too close up. She's trying to make out what it is. "Aren't . . . aren't you mad at me?" It's not a dare.

He cocks his head. "Of course not, honey," he says. "I should help you more. You work so hard."

She examines him, really examines her husband. But it's Cornelia she looks to for guidance. And she sees that it's not forgiveness she's being offered. It's more like Cornelia's heard both sides of the story and is handing down a full acquittal. Innocent of all wrongdoing.

But that can't be right. Liv had nearly died because of her. She'd suffered through months of painful rehab because of *her*.

"What's happening?" Nora asks. "Why is he—"

Cornelia gently lifts a finger. "You're processing," she says gently. "That's normal."

But Nora doesn't feel normal.

"You've had a breakthrough. It's a lot to take in. Try to relax. Breathe," she says. "I'm so sorry that happened to you. That sounds harrowing. Your daughter, she's—"

"She's fine. She has scars. She walks with a limp. But she's more or less fine." She looks to Hayden to chime in. She's waited a hundred years for some acknowledgment from Hayden that Liv's injuries weren't all her fault, and here it is.

"Lucky," says Cornelia. "Very lucky. I can't imagine how that must have felt. What it must have been like. Scary, I'm sure. Horrifying."

"Yes. I mean, of course it was. It was the worst experience of my life." Nora swipes at her lower lash line, her finger coming away damp. It's like someone has turned a fan on in her chest, high speed.

"That's right," Cornelia says. "Then I have another question for you, Nora. An important one. Are you ready?" Nora nods, like a child. Cornelia asks, "How far would you go to stop something like that from happening again?"

Nora stills. Her husband waits patiently. "As far as I could," she says. "I would do anything."

"That's what I thought."

29

For the first two hours following the therapy session, Nora has felt like she's sitting on a bomb—no sudden movements.

On the car ride home, she'd pinned her hands beneath her knees to hide the tremors. This was it. All her cards on the table, no going back.

But in the privacy of their very own home, where the walls are thick enough, the explosion has yet to come. "Do you want to talk about it?" Nora asks, the suspense too great. If they're going to have it out, then out with it. She can't stand to talk about a stupid TV show or an infuriating news article or Liv's poster project if their marriage is on the brink.

"I think that was healthy." Hayden stands in front of the open fridge, staring into it like it's the Oracle of Delphi.

"You . . . do." Nora puts her antennae up and tries to detect any hint of sarcasm, but the reading's turning up nothing.

"Absolutely."

She wonders if they should talk about it. Except isn't that what they'd just done? That's what therapy was, for God's sake. Maybe, just maybe, she had married a good person. Better even than she gave him credit for.

Okay then. She stares around aimlessly, not sure what to do in the absence of an explosion. Liv is singing to herself up in her room. She'll be down in minutes, Nora knows. Mostly, she feels like she's gotten a deep tissue massage—a little wobbly on her feet, a good soreness settling into her muscles, and she probably could use a drink of water. She sinks into the couch, spent and energized all at once. "That's great," she says. "Thanks."

The fluorescent light of the refrigerator is still shining on her husband's face. She counts down the seconds in her head until the moment when he's bound to make the inevitable observation: "We're out of milk." Or whatever.

But she doesn't even make it to zero before he starts taking things out. A head of garlic. Spinach. A carton of mushrooms. Arranging them on the countertop. Nora watches with passive interest. Liv comes down. *Here we go.* Nora wonders how long either of them will last this time before they give in and let her watch TV until her developing brain melts into goo.

Nora's phone rings and it's Gary's number on the caller ID. "Hayden," she says. "It's work, I better take this. I'll make it quick."

Liv runs to her daddy and stands on her tippy-toes, looking at the assortment of things collected on the counter. "No problem," he says. "No rush."

"My computer froze." Gary's frustration is a physical vibration delivered across the ether as she heads upstairs. "And everything's gone. Everything. I restarted and it disappeared."

"Had you hit SAVE?" Nora slides her computer out of her purse and sets it up on the corner of desk she's eked out for herself in the guest room.

"No," he says, as if daring her to make this his fault. "I wasn't finished."

"What were you working on?" She's afraid to ask.

"Those interrogatories. Goddammit." She hears a crash on his end. "I'd been working on those for three hours. *Three* hours. Gone!"

"Okay, okay. That's good to know." Her fingers hover over the keyboard. Panicking isn't going to do anyone any good. "Just. Gary, sit tight. Let me try a few things. Stay signed in. I'm going to take over your laptop screen for a second."

Nora uses the password given to her by IT for such occasions and with a few clicks she's able to view Gary's desktop screen as her own. She bites her tongue between her front teeth as she looks up a tutorial for recovering word documents. Meanwhile, Gary breathes into the phone like a serial killer.

"Hold on," she says. "Almost . . ." Yes. She locates the recovered documents in the not-at-all-easily-located unsaved documents folder and holds her breath until they reappear on Gary's screen like she's a freaking wizard.

"You did that? But, but it's not everything. There's—"

"The software only autosaves every so often, so this is what's recoverable. It's better than nothing."

"Thanks," he says, begrudgingly. "You know I'll have to redo the rest. What if we divide—" He clears his throat. "Never mind. You've got your daughter, don't you."

Her insides corkscrew and she feels twisted up.

"I . . . one second." Nora returns to the stairway and pads down. Dinnertime is always a hot mess and if she doesn't take control now it could be hours before Liv's in bed, sucking up any spare seconds of so-called me time Nora might have hoped for. She hits the MUTE button. "Hayden," she whispers unnecessarily. "Gary wants me to help out with an emergency, but I can tell him no."

Liv is sitting at the table in front of a plate of steamed broccoli, garlic bread, and sliced chicken. A napkin is beside her plate and she's even holding her fork correctly.

"I'll save you a plate to warm up," Hayden says as he sits down across from his daughter.

"You sure?" she says. Nobody likes to do bedtime alone.

But he is sure. It's a big year. Those are his words.

And so Nora spends two hours helping Gary rework his answers to his interrogatories and she isn't disturbed once.

When she's finished proofreading and sends over her track changes version of comments, Gary calls her again. "I couldn't have done that without you," he admits. "You do good work."

She has always done good work, of course. But it's taken a late night and a pinch-hit for him to notice and maybe that's not so uncommon really.

Liv's asleep by the time Nora is finished working for the night. Hayden watches TV. She's clawing through her dresser for sweatpants and an old Dartmouth T-shirt when a stray thought causes her to move her search up to the top drawer.

They're in the back. A pair of red underwear and a matching sheer bra. Her fingers graze the lace and she rummages around until she finds the garter belt that she hasn't laid eyes on since before Liv was born.

She used to try in the bedroom, you know. Nora likes sex. All of it. Even the kind with toys shipped to her in discreet boxes. She's never been afraid to try new things; it's just that new things take a certain level of imagination and there are some nights where even her nightstand seems very, very far away.

Anyway, it's not like she's the only one. It's hard to keep things exciting when you've been married to the same person for coming up on ten years. Except. *Except.*

Nora is slowly beginning to feel like she hasn't been married to the same person at all. She has a different husband. A new and improved version. She wonders if she should feel guilty. She'd vowed to love Hayden exactly as he was. But at the moment, probing this line of inquiry would require imagination, and as she slips into her best lingerie, Nora finds her imagination reserved for better things.

30

As anticipated, Penny's release comes at the end of the seventy-two hours and the group is eager to put the events of the past few days behind them with a celebratory welcome-home dinner. It's the opposite of pretending the whole thing never happened, which sounds healthy if more than a little awkward.

Hayden asks on the drive over, "Are you feeling okay?"

From the passenger seat, Nora bites her thumbnail, peering down at her phone. "I'm fine. I just—this number, it came up again on my work line." She cross-references it in her deleted emails. The local 512 number. She doesn't usually get spam to her work phone. It had been the wrong number. Over the last couple days, she's seen it pop up two more times under her missed calls. "Maybe I should try calling it back again. Do you mind?" She's sure there's a rule somewhere—*Cosmo*, probably—about no work calls on date night, and that she breaks it more often than Hayden. She calls the number back, tilting her head to free her hair from her ear as she listens. It rings and rings and rings. "No one's answering," she mutters to her husband, as if he's waiting for the play-by-play. She's about to hang up when the line clicks and it switches over to the voice mail greeting.

Hi, you've reached Devin Despanza. Sorry I missed your call. Leave a message.

Nora's eyes flit to Hayden and back to the road. "Um, hi, Devin." She's somehow caught off guard by the beep and hesitates. "This is Nora Spangler. The attorney. The, uh, one from Greenberg Schwall. I think you've been trying to get in touch with me. This is my cell number. Please feel free to give me a call back. Anytime."

She hangs up, staring at her dark screen. "That was weird," she says to Hayden.

"What was?"

They're pulling up to the restaurant now. She shakes her head slightly, a crease forming at the top of her nose. "Nothing. Well—it's too much to explain right now." And anyway, not important, she reminds herself. The case is closed. Settled. As good as done. "I'll tell you later."

She tucks her phone away and runs a hand over her wrap dress as Hayden helps her out of the car. He arranged for a babysitter and before leaving the house, made Liv dinner—spaghetti with meat sauce and broccoli secretly mixed in—then he laid out her pajamas, and suddenly, as if by epiphany, the phrase "it's the little things in life" had made sense.

Nora tries to put the call out of her mind and pull on her happy, fun, wife face for the evening. It's not so hard. There's a sea change going on in her life and Nora knows that it's probably only a matter of time before she gets her sea legs and adjusts fully. She might liken it to a religious experience. This occurs to her when she spots Cornelia at the table, a moment that's accompanied by a jittery flutter in Nora's stomach. *She knows my deepest, darkest secret.* Of course, as a therapist, Cornelia must know lots of people's deepest, darkest secrets. And besides, it doesn't exactly feel like she's subjected herself to blackmail. If anything, Nora feels like she's confessed her sins and come out on the other side redeemed. Born again. Her husband having at last taken up the cross of their shared life in earnest. Hallelujah.

The dinner takes place at a Tex-Mex restaurant on the west side of town, one with brightly painted murals and goblet-size margaritas and chips dumped into baskets via dustpan.

She bumps the table and makes a few waters slosh as she slides in next to Thea. "So sorry," she says, thrown.

Maybe it's got jack all to do with Devin's call. Maybe it's Penny. Nora hasn't been able to shake a low-grade hum of worry for her. And the backstory provided by Cornelia didn't help. Seeing her in person, in a better setting, that will help. Surely.

"I actually have good news to share," she says, once she's used spare napkins to help mop up the mess she's made. The waiter comes by to fill her water glass and the husbands greet one another with fist bumps (Max) and handshakes (everyone else).

Cornelia scans the large, laminated menu with its ragged leather piping. "Let's wait until Penny gets here. She'll want to be included."

"She's coming alone?" Nora asks.

"No, not alone," says Cornelia.

Nora bites into a tortilla chip, avoiding the salsa that promises to give her heartburn. Maybe Isla or another neighbor. Like Lucy. There are still plenty of women to meet, Nora realizes. But then the need for further explanation evaporates when Penny arrives accompanied by Dr. Trevor Washington.

Nora chokes on the chip she's just bitten into. Thea pats her on the back when she coughs. "Down the wrong pipe." Nora sips from her glass of water, her eyes streaming.

Hayden stands to shake Trevor's hand. "Good to see you again, buddy," she hears her husband say. The scratches on Trevor's face are thin scabs, hardly noticeable, but if you know where to look, impossible *not* to notice. He's as young as Nora thought—maybe not even thirty—none of the telltale crow's feet around his eyes. His forehead is still smooth. Penny looks lovely in a pink dress and espadrilles, though on closer inspection a few signs of her hospital visit linger. For starters, her cheeks, anemic and pallid.

"Oh, queso!" Penny rubs her hands together. "I never want to see another bowl of Jell-O as long as I live, thank you very much." At which everyone laughs with obvious relief and the tone is set.

"I'll be honest, I ate the quesadillas at the hospital when I had Jax," says Alexis, "and they really weren't bad. Did you try those?"

"No. I must have missed them. Shall I go back?" She half rises from her seat.

"Never." Alexis loops her arm around Penny's shoulder and squeezes their heads together. "You gave us such a scare, Penny March."

"Can I propose a toast?" says Thea, raising the salted rim of her margarita glass. "To Penny: You are our heart, and to the friendships old—and new—that, in the end, keep us sane. Cheers, y'all."

"Cheers," they agree.

"Now, Nora, you said you had good news to share? Don't leave us hanging." Cornelia presses a black napkin into her lap.

"You sound so hip, Cornelia," Thea teases.

"It's small," says Nora, self-conscious at having to follow the toast to Penny. "But the inspection report came back for the house on Majestic Grove and Isla said the sellers will agree to our amendments—just a couple little things. And the house appraised. So . . ."

"So you're going to move toward closing?" Alexis's eyes are wide.

"We haven't officially, *officially* discussed it yet, but we're excited, aren't we?" Nora squeezes Hayden's hand underneath the table.

"Thrilled," he says. "A new baby. A new home. It's going to be a whole new us." He leans in to kiss her on her cheek, and Nora's eyes meet Penny's. Nora swallows and looks down at her empty place setting, happy for the conversation to move on.

With the attention no longer on her, she checks her work email. No new missed calls. Same with her cell. What could Devin want now?

She shifts to watching Penny, trying to read her. Watches Penny ignore her drink, watches Penny eat her chips with the distant, medita-
tive quality of a cow chewing grass, watches Penny seem to participate
without actual participation, watches Penny with Trevor. And still she
doesn't know what exactly she's watching.

Around her the dialogue is free-ranging—what's to be done about
gun reform, what Alexis sees for the future of data security, the sheer
volume of inbound messages from parents at their children's respective
schools, a point that Max and Roman feel as passionately about as their
wives.

"I checked out that site you mentioned." She registers what Hayden
is saying to Roman. "Bless This Mess. You were right, man. You should
see our pantry."

"Wait, I haven't seen our pantry." Or rather she had, but the last time
had been the previous night when she'd gathered Liv's snacks for the day
and it had been its usual mess of plastic wrap, spare raisin boxes, piles
of individual Goldfish bags and almost-empty baking supplies with a
dusting of flour on the closest shelves. "When was this?"

"I found some time. A bunch of the guys at the office were knocking off early for happy hour so I took a rain check and came home to get
a few things done around the house."

"Thank you." She leans in close enough to smell his aftershave.

He rubs her back, but normal, not like he's performed a small miracle. A thought occurs to her, and it's a simple one. It's this: *Team Spangler*. Ra-ra-shish-boom-bah. The idea makes her smile. It makes her not
miss the margaritas too terribly much.

Thea is all—"I can't believe it's almost the end of the school year. I
say that every year, but it's the truth."

And Max—"I know, and I told myself I would plan ahead this year
with the teacher gifts. I don't want to be caught paying last-minute for
overnight shipping."

Roman—"What'd you get?"

"Kendra Scott earrings. I read in a guide that teachers love those. I had Cruz pick them out, so he feels like he's involved, you know?"

"I just got care packages sent to the girls," Asher says. "Just a bunch of junk food mainly, with some cleaning supplies. It's obviously a bribe to get them to call home more often, but let me tell you, it works."

Nora feels it again, that texture of smoothness, like she's just gotten onto a road that's been newly paved. Alexis and Asher migrate the discussion over to sports, something about an affair between a college coach and a player and everyone is lighting up a message board Nora's never heard of and it's somewhere in this mix that Nora realizes that she's no longer watching Penny, but that Penny is watching her.

She hears Roman ask Max, "You got camp registrations under control this year?"

"It's like a game of Tetris," Max replies, as if Camp Registration Tetris is a game he enjoys playing. It's all very normal, if it weren't all so very extraordinary.

Penny excuses herself to use the ladies' room. Her pink dress disappears among the bustling waiters balancing trays.

"You know," Nora says, scooting out of her chair, "I think I'll go, too. Pregnancy bladder." As if anyone had asked for an explanation.

Nora follows the sign for SEÑORITAS through a swing door and into a bathroom with terra-cotta floors and blue tile walls. There, she stands against the wall beside the hand dryer, tap-tap-tapping her toe silently until a minute later, she hears the lock to the farthest stall slide out of place.

"Hi," she says to Penny. A beat.

Penny crosses to the sink, her face appearing in the mirror. She turns on the faucet. "Hi," she says. It was only a few weeks ago when Penny had written her imaginary advice column for Nora. It seems like longer.

"I just—I wanted to get the chance to talk to you in private," Nora says. "How are you doing?"

The water from the faucet cascades over Penny's hands. She pumps the soap. "I'm fine. Don't I look fine?"

Nora pushes off the wall and stands at the other sink so that their eyes meet in the mirror. "Yes, but you're here with that man."

Penny pays special attention to the back of her hands, scrubbing them thoroughly. "Trevor's very nice, very helpful."

"I'm sure he is." Nora's testing, though she might as well cut to the chase.

Penny doesn't rush. She takes a moment to turn off the faucet and flick her wet fingers into the sink bowl.

"It was a candle," Nora says softly.

Penny moves for a paper towel. "I know."

"You do?" Nora blinks hard.

"Have you told anyone?" Penny asks.

"Not yet." Nora crosses her arms and leans heavily against the wall. "Life is hard to make sense of sometimes."

Penny tears off a sheet with an audible rip. As she crumples up the paper towel she finally looks at Nora face-to-face, no mirror in between them. "I'm sorry you went to so much trouble. I don't take that lightly."

"You lost your husband and your home."

"I know." Penny's smile is watery.

"I have to ask," Nora says. "What did Francine say to you? On Mother's Day?"

Penny sighs and glances at the ceiling. "She said she was sorry."

"Because she was with Devin that night when she wasn't supposed to be."

"She thought she might have done something if she hadn't been . . . preoccupied."

"I'm sorry. I misread the situation. I really thought there for a second that Francine—well, I don't know what I thought. Kids will be kids, I guess." And when she says it, she realizes that it's true. There is nothing that Devin could say that would change the evidence. Cornelia was right. It's been up to Nora to decide how much knowledge is enough knowledge, and now she has. Knowing more wouldn't make anything better; it wouldn't do anything at all.

So she says nothing more of it. "You're sure you're okay?" she asks, one more time, because *this*, this is the one thing she really must know. Because the answer could change everything.

"I'm sure I will be."

"Okay," she says, relenting.

"Okay."

"Okay." It's more than okay, really. Because now Nora can let it go. Let things be better. Not just better but *good*. And that, she reminds herself, is quite different from "too good to be true," which is not something she's ever been looking for. She's only been looking for good enough and here it is, exactly where she is.

No further questions, counselor.

31

After, Nora vows to enjoy all that her new-and-improved Hayden has to offer. It's not difficult. It just requires a certain letting go. A free fall onto a soft landing. And so she sets to work unhooking her claws from around the throat of her life.

There will be some adjustments.

Like the moment dinner is ready, her husband will no longer announce that he just has to take a quick shower. He will promptly change his nightstand lightbulb. When he texts that he's headed home from work—which he'll do every time now—he won't tell her that he'll be home in fifteen minutes and then get distracted and come home in an hour and a half instead. He'll help with the grocery shopping. He will wash sheets and towels. He'll organize playdates with parents he hardly knows. He'll pack the snacks. He will already have his shoes on when it's time to leave the house. He will problem solve.

There are moments throughout the day when Nora feels like she's in possession of a particularly juicy secret. She pictures whispering it to the woman on the other side of the bathroom stall. She imagines women in the dark masturbating to the things Nora's husband does. She nearly does so herself.

"One twenty over eighty," Dr. Perez had announced at her most recent OB-GYN appointment. "You've made huge improvements, Nora.

I'm very pleased. You're right back in the normal range. You must have made some pretty significant lifestyle changes to make such quick progress."

Nora sits obediently on the paper exam table, a small smile twisting the corner of her lips. "You could say that," she agrees.

And so when she pays Penny a visit to deliver the insurance claim form she must sign, Nora has mostly come to grips with the unsatisfying resolution of the March case. All is well. With the extra help from Hayden, Nora can devote her time to her partnership campaign at work. Everything happens for a reason. Nora used to think that was bullshit, but, hey, people change. Actually, she used to think that was bullshit, too. But then look at Hayden.

She finds Penny on the sofa, wearing a bright turquoise cardigan and cuffed jeans, her ankles crossed on the coffee table. Upon seeing Nora, Penny moves her laptop onto the table and greets her.

"You look nice," Nora says. Penny's hair is even shiny again.

"Do I?" Penny touches her face. "Thank you. Then again, it's probably because I'm not sedated up to the gills." She scoots up to the edge of the sofa cushions, lowering her feet to the ground.

Nora falters. "We don't have to do this now if you don't feel up to it," she says. "The insurance claim. I've gone over it extensively. I brought it for you to sign. It will still take some time for the check to come through, but my office will stay on top of it."

"It needs to be done." Penny's eyes trace the ceiling's seam.

"Is that your laptop?" Nora asks, pointing to the Apple icon glowing white.

"Yes."

"Were you writing?" Nora says.

"I might have been."

"That must explain the glow."

"Well, it's certainly not fucking Trevor."

Nora puffs air. "But you said—"

"I know what I said. And he's perfectly nice. He bought me a brace-let. And by the way, don't mention it to Thea or the others. They're hop-ing I'll fall in love."

Nora understands that the women have meant well. They want their friend to be happy, and while they might be trying to force the issue, their hearts are in the right place. It's so female, this desire to make ev-erything and to want everyone to be *okay*.

"You sound so much more like yourself." Even though the only self of Penny's with which Nora is familiar is the one that came into being post-Richard.

"Yes. Well. If I need to sign something, let me get my other pair of glasses. These are giving me a headache." She rubs her temples, rises slowly, and swishes into the bathroom.

Nora leans over the computer where a Word document sits open. She allows herself to steal a glance, plucking a line from the middle and scanning it.

There were three clues, each missed, until the morning of the confes-sion, the voluntary nature of which was thought to be, not a prerequisite for, but rather a guarantee of, amnesty for a violent act, "violent" being the operative word. The only word.

"That's better." Penny is putting on her reading glasses as Nora twists in the sofa cushion.

"I have a pen." Nora can envision the telltale red marks, resembling thumbprints, that creep along her neck when she's flustered. She fishes in her purse to hide the fact that she's snooped. "Here. It's a simple form, feel free to give it a read through. By executing the document, your claims will be limited solely to the destruction of property under the policy limits. It's all spelled out for you."

Penny gives her a long look. "I wanted to do the right thing. It just turns out it's really hard to do two right things at once." Nora waits for

Penny to explain. But in the next breath, Penny scrawls her name across the page and hands it back to Nora. For all intents and purposes, the life of Richard March was worth approximately nothing.

⬚

"Nora." Cornelia is kneeling beside a pot of geraniums wearing gardening gloves. "I didn't know you were here." She wipes her forehead with a bent wrist so as not to get dirt on her face. "You're signing the papers for your new home tomorrow, aren't you?"

It's finally happening. Tomorrow will officially end the option period and then getting out of the purchase of the home on Majestic Grove becomes expensive, just the way Nora wants it. She's already grilled Hayden. *Do you like the home or do you just like it because I like it? Do you want to keep looking? Are you sure? Speak now or forever hold your peace.* And now there's nothing more to do than to sign the papers and begin shopping online for furniture.

She doesn't know exactly how, but the women were right: Cornelia is a genius. And she has worked her magic.

"I had a form for Penny to sign, for the insurance money," Nora explains.

Cornelia scrapes dirt toward the center of the pot. "How did she seem?"

Nora glances over her shoulder to confirm that she closed the pool house door behind her. She inches closer. "Much better, actually. I didn't know she was writing again!"

"Writing?" Cornelia repeats. And Nora thrills at the turn of conversation, registering the change. She's on the inside now. Ever since the last therapy session. Something's shifted.

"Yes." Nora widens her eyes and enunciates. Gossip, sure, but the good kind. She has an intuition that maybe this is the flavor of all gossip within Dynasty Ranch. Did you hear that Charlotte was recognized in

Forbes? Did you know Elizabeth was promoted to chief operating officer?

Cornelia stands, dusting off her knees. "That's so encouraging. She told you this?"

"She more or less confirmed it," adds Nora quickly. She'd thought that maybe she would be the last to know, but here she is, offering brandnew information. "And I think it's a departure. I snuck a quick peek and it looked like maybe she was trying her hand at fiction."

"Penny? *Our* Penny?" Cornelia grins, mystified.

But Nora had already been thinking that maybe Penny isn't ready to give anyone advice, not yet. A novel. That could be her way back in, and Nora already knows, without a doubt, that the book will be a smashing success.

There's hope. Nora had *had* her foreboding premonition and the bad thing *had* happened, but things are back on track now. Penny's on the mend.

"She's a very good writer." Nora continues the thought that had begun in her head. "A murder mystery. Something in that vein." Cornelia's grin slips away. "I figured you'd be pleased," Nora says.

Cornelia blinks, and like an Etch A Sketch, the expression disappears. "I am. She's so talented. That's why I've always only wanted what's best for her."

It's when Nora leaves she thinks that Cornelia must have meant "*the* best." She wants the best for Penny. Because "*what's* best" would imply that Cornelia believes she somehow knows better than Penny. Wouldn't it?

32

"C an you keep a secret?" The question pops up between Nora and Cameron in the office kitchen. She checks the lower shelf for any overlooked coconut-flavored LaCroix, which is the only kind that won't give her a headache. The confidential information in question belongs to Nora. If she'd asked Gary, he might have pulled out one of the numerous nondisclosure agreement templates they kept on file. But Cameron Drummer just goes, "Hm."

"*Hm?*" She adds the punctuation on the end. "It requires *deliberation?*" She's never known anyone to turn down a secret.

She's been feeling carbonated since returning to the office today. Fizzy with what feels suspiciously like excitement, even hope.

Cameron uncaps the water bottle in his hand. The cuffs of his lavender shirt are rolled to the elbows, revealing muscular forearms. "Usually I just assume when people say, can you keep a secret, what they mean is, do you promise not to tell anyone that I know or who gives a shit about me this thing that I'm about to tell you? So if that's what you mean then yeah, I can do that."

It'd be lovely if her closest friend at the office were a woman, but she does appreciate Cameron. Anyway, it's not like this secret will keep forever. It's perishable. Though she's decided it's still best kept under her blouse, as it were, until after the partnership vote in another month. For now, she simply wants to turn the valve a notch, let off some pressure, keep herself from bubbling over.

"Yes. That's what I mean," she says with mock annoyance.

It occurs to her that she no longer has secrets from Hayden. She can once again say, *I tell my husband everything*, and it will be true.

"All right then." Cameron tips the bottle back. His Adam's apple bobs. He really is too good-looking to practice law.

"I'm pregnant," she says.

"You're . . . pregnant."

"We're having a boy." Hayden's right. It *is* fun to tell people.

Cameron leans against the stainless steel refrigerator and crosses his arms.

"What?" she says, because he's not doing the thing that everyone is supposed to do when someone announces a pregnancy. Even men. "Come on, it's not that shocking."

"Eleanor's pregnant, too."

As it turns out, Nora isn't quite fluent in the varying shakes of Cameron's head. She's going to need him to spell it out for her.

"I'm sorry, what now? Is she dating someone? Is she married?" Nora doesn't know how to take this news. He's not giving her the social cues. Is this good news or terrible? It has to be the latter, doesn't it? His ex-wife is starting another family. Nobody's that gracious.

He scrunches up his face, nodding slowly. He seems to be taking a keen interest in the to-go menus that have been stuck to the corkboard with multicolored pushpins. "Oh, she's seeing someone."

"Are you upset?" She doesn't even mind that his secret is clearly better. Nora never gets good gossip anymore unless you count reality TV. "That's a stupid question. Of course you're upset. Who is it?"

"Me." He delivers the pronoun with a sort of *huh* sense of wonder. Like: *Would you look at that.*

Nora's reaction is decidedly less coolheaded. "Eleanor is having *your* baby? Your *baby*?" She can't decide where the emphasis should land. "Are you back together? When did this happen? *How* did this happen?"

"I love Zara. I love that little girl so much." He shakes prayer hands at the ceiling. "But can I tell you, and you might think I'm an awful human being for saying this, but there is sometimes nothing *sexier* than dropping your kid off for the week. I know Eleanor feels that, too, because, well, she dropped her off and now we're having a baby. So."

"If you're an awful human being, then I'm a monster." Is she allowed to laugh? Would that be *completely* inappropriate given the circumstance? "But . . . what now, are you going to move in together? Get married again? Is it still a second marriage if it's to the same person? You're going to have to get rid of the Porsche," she says, a little too gleefully.

"No and no. And *no*. Eleanor was very clear on that point. We're going to keep on doing what we're doing. Shit. I'm going to have to read the baby books this time. I'm going to have to know what a sleep schedule is. And how to work those wrap slings. And when we're running low on diapers. I'm going to have to make a goddamn checklist just for all the shit I don't already have at my house." He runs his hand over his face, looking like a man who's seen war.

"That's so . . ."

"Crazy?" he asks.

"I was going to say modern."

The door to the break room swings open, interrupting their conversation. Nora's secretary pokes her head in. "Nora? Sorry. But there's a call on your line. Someone who says she really needs to reach you. I think she said Penny March."

❖

Penny's on the line when Nora returns to her desk. "Is everything okay?" she asks. "I haven't submitted the claim yet and I did warn you, the payout's going to take some time."

She notices Penny's breathing is heavy against the receiver. "I need to get away for a while."

Nora's ergonomic chair bobs beneath her sinking weight. "Like a vacation?"

"Like, away." She's speaking more quietly now. Nora smashes the phone into the side of her head, making the spot where her earlobe is pierced sore. "I've booked a red-eye to my brother's house in Washington tomorrow night. First flight I could get. Do you think you could take me to the airport?"

"I don't mind. But why not ask Cornelia or Asher or someone?"

"I'm not telling anyone in Dynasty Ranch. So, please don't mention it to them." *Secrets are having a bit of a day, aren't they?* Nora thinks.

"But why?"

"This isn't the place for me right now, that's all. I need some space. Also, I'm calling because I wanted to know, even though we're not pursuing Richard's wrongful death case, can I still count on attorney-client privilege?"

Nora can't imagine what's changed in the last few hours since she saw Penny.

"Yes." She keeps the response neutral, but half-wonders if she ought to call Cornelia. What if Penny is on the verge of another mental break? Cornelia could help, head things off.

Though Penny's just complicated matters by invoking confidentiality. Nora shifts uneasily.

"Do you keep files for former clients?" Penny is asking.

"Always."

"Okay, good, then tomorrow I'd like to give you some papers to keep on file. I don't need you to do anything with them yet, just hold on to them in case."

"In case of what?"

"In case of an emergency."

"Okay. I can do that. Are you sure everything is all right?" This time she infuses the question with more sympathy.

"I'll explain tomorrow." Penny's voice sounds farther away from the phone now. Nora holds still to listen. "Can you meet me at the entrance gate at eight P.M.?"

"Yes," Nora says, cupping the handset. "I'll be there."

"Right. Okay. See you then."

Hours later, Liv's breath is warm on Nora's nose, their faces side by side on her daughter's baby-blue pillows. "Can I get a dog at the new house?"

"Maybe after the baby's born and he's had a little time to settle in. You need to focus on being a big sister first."

Liv considers this. "If I get a dog, it'd give me more practice."

Nora hears the crackle of her own smile in the dark. Fatigue is finally catching up to her. She's like a ship taking on water. Tugging on Liv's comforter, she tucks it under her arm and sinks deeper into the mattress. "We'll talk about it. We have to move first." A different Nora would already be on her way to a panic attack at the thought of moving boxes, at the task of setting up utilities, at the prospect of all those closing documents, which must be reviewed.

"Will there be a pool?" Liv touches Nora's cheek.

"In the neighborhood. Not at our house."

"What if there was a waterslide?" Liv's toes wriggle on Nora's bare shins. The slightly medicinal and honeyed smell of her daughter's shampoo is baked into the sheets. "And I want my room to be black."

"Black?"

"Like outer *space*."

After another round of this, Nora tells Liv to go to sleep. She's only partially conscious to begin with, fighting the pull of her eyelids. Nora pushes the wisps of hair from Liv's forehead and rescues herself from falling asleep alongside her.

She comes downstairs to a clean kitchen. The plates cleared, the Crock-Pot stowed away, the dishwasher running. She answers emails and watches mindless television. She tells Hayden that Cameron and Eleanor are having another baby. She remembers to use her fancy eye cream.

Around 1:00 A.M., long after Nora turned off the last light and fell fast asleep, she's woken by Liv's knees jabbing into her thigh. A small but lethal elbow lands in her rib cage before the four-year-old tumbles into a pile in the middle of the bed.

"Do you want me to take her back upstairs?" Hayden murmurs.

"It's okay," she says. "I'm awake now." She's felt herself blink on.

Liv snores softly, nestled into the grown-up blankets. Nora considers depositing her back into her own bed herself, but she doesn't think that Liv is what's keeping her awake.

Now that her internal cursor's been jostled, thinking about nothing proves next to impossible. Andi's probably back in Berlin by now. Getting ready for the day. Nora turns over, pushing the thought aside.

She allows her mind to wander and the route it takes keeps leading her back to Penny.

At first, their exchange had read to her like Penny's decision to leave had been prompted by Richard's death or her subsequent breakdown. And that was completely understandable. But that idea had quickly been dislodged. Penny had said this wasn't the place for her anymore—or something to that effect—and by "place" Nora had understood Dynasty Ranch. Whatever has happened, whatever's prompting Penny to run, has something to do with that. Nora prods at the question, like her tongue pushing against the spot where a tooth had been.

She rolls over and checks the clock. It's after two. Careful not to wake Liv, she crawls down from the mattress and feels her way into the bathroom. By touch, she fumbles for the door to the medicine cabinet, where her eyes slowly begin to adjust. She noses in, still unable to find what she's looking for. She doesn't even know what she plans to do, whether or not she'll take one, only that she likes the comfort of knowing that she could. Sleep is within reach. Nora's fingers feel along the shelf. Frustrated, she pulls the bathroom door closed and switches on the light. It assaults her pupils.

She's looking for the familiar amber prescription bottle. The one with her mother's name printed across the label.

Nora's heart rate picks up. She dumps the entire contents of the medicine cabinet onto the bathroom countertop. She stares. There are no more sleeping pills. The bottle of Ambien has disappeared.

33

The next morning, Nora and Hayden drive to the appointment at Isla Wong's office separately so that afterward they can each veer off to work. Nora's exhaustion from the poor night's sleep seeps out of her pores like garlic or booze. So much for the fresh start that she'd envisioned, or at least so much for one that begins with clean hair.

"I've got it all laid out for you here." Isla shows them to the conference room table. Her office is very girly. There's a lot of pink going on, hints of gold, and pops of mint. Even her desk is a pale blush color. The whole place reminds Nora of those pink Cadillacs the top Mary Kay saleswomen used to drive around. "I've put *X*s in each spot that requires your signature. Do you need a pen?"

There's a pen in the pocket of Isla's gingham blazer, but she reaches for the pencil holder at the center of the table, extracting two blue push-tops.

"Thanks." Hayden sits right down in front of the small stack of papers and begins scribbling his name on the lines.

Hayden Spangler.

Hayden Spangler.

Hayden Spangler.

"Really jumping in with two feet there." Nora watches from above. It's her palms. They've started sweating terribly. She surreptitiously

wipes them on her skirt, but it hardly does any good against the verita-
ble fount of dampness springing forth from both her hands. Maybe it's
a side effect of pregnancy. There never seems to be a shortage of those.

"It looks in order to me." Her husband's face is perfectly content,
his eyes as trusting of her as a golden retriever's.

Nora makes a meal out of reading through the paperwork. There's
not much of it at this stage. The real heft will arrive at closing. If Isla
senses any hesitation on Nora's part, she's polite enough not to say so.

She's stalling. It's ridiculous to stall for no reason.

Not *no* reason, maybe, because there is the matter of Penny, but also
that's got nothing to do with her. So she's stalling for no *good* reason and
that's almost as bad.

Of course it feels like this. Buying a house is meant to feel like a mild
heart attack. The sums of money bandied about are astronomical, especially when she considers the number in one lump sum, like the listing
price typed neatly across the top of the contract, for instance.

Nora runs her sweaty hand along her belly. And the little thing inside her gives her fortitude. *I'm going to be a better mom*, she beams
to him. *Cross my heart.* And this is how. History will not repeat itself.
There will be no more footnotes to Nora's record as a mother. With four
more swoops of ink, she makes sure of it.

"Here." Isla smiles, holding out a gift bag blooming with bright yellow tissue paper. Isla is likely experiencing the reverse of Nora's sudden
onset of anxiety. The commission will soon be funneling into her bank
account. It's practically only a formality now. "A welcome gift on behalf
of the neighborhood. It's only a little something. And, Hayden, a few
of the guys in the neighborhood are getting together for beers tonight.
My husband made me promise to invite you."

Hayden says that he will talk it over with Nora, who of course really does think he should go because she's a cool wife. When given the
chance. Outside, she digs into the gift bag, first pulling out a stationery

card that reads, Howdy Neighbor! She checks her phone on the way to the car, the way she always does on the way to anywhere. Cocooned within the tissue paper, she finds a gold pen, nestled in a sleek crimson box. Like the one in Isla's shirt pocket. Pretty. There's a bulky cylinder at the bottom of the bag, too, and she carefully unwraps it to find an expensive-looking candle.

"Well, we did it." Hayden pulls her into a hug, pressing her nose to his shirt. She breathes deeply, easily for the first time in as long as she can remember.

"You smell nice." She sniffs. "Like a pine tree." Her pregnancy nose at it again.

"I spilled coffee on my shirt this morning. I used that stain remover that we talked about at Cornelia's house. Came right out. Magic."

She hesitates. "Stain remover." Something is trying to wriggle free from the back of her mind. "What was it called again?" Only ten more hours until she picks up Penny. She'll have to pass the time.

"It's called Lestoil."

www.themothership.com

A Group of Mothers Goes on Strike

By Sam Rainy

"On a quiet cul-de-sac in North Texas, a group of mothers went on a three-week strike, during which they refused to make snacks, prepare dinners, or find missing socks."

_____

Read Comments

_____

MotherBear4

You have no idea how many times I've been tempted to do this.

Anonymous

Cool, but, like, what changed?

Maria R

@Anonymous I think the point is that all the family members see how much the moms of the houses actually do because it's no longer getting done. They stop taking a refrigerator full of snacks and clean underwear for granted. They appreciate their mothers and wives more.

BowForTheQueen

@Anonymous @Maria R I get that and, don't get me wrong, appreciation is nice, but at this point, what I need is help. And before people comment with suggestions to hire someone or, as the upper-crust ladies around here like to say, "outsource it," I can't afford to.

Runner26.2

Raises hand I've tried this and I did not have the strength of spirit to make it three whole weeks. I don't think I made it three whole days. Stuff just did not get done. I'm very fortunate to have a nanny, but I can't let her show up to our house to a dirty work environment—dishes piled up, countertops not wiped down, the trash full. And my kids would have missed getting their projects done on time, their tutors paid, their permission slips sent back. Am I an enabler? Maybe. But I can't just sit back and watch my family fail.

Michelle Z.

Forget three weeks. Our house be like:

Me, leaving for a work trip: Here are three freezer meals, I grocery shopped last night, Martha will pick up from school both days, I've laid out kids' outfits in alphabetical orders, lunches are in Ziploc bags by day, I canceled this week's piano lessons so you don't have to worry about getting them there

Husband, leaving for work trip: *walks out door*

Husband, returning from work trip: I just need a few hours to wind down. I've been working, he says

Me, returning from work trip: Here are all six of our children, he says *walks out door*

34

At first, Penny is only five minutes late.

Then ten minutes.

Then fifteen, then twenty.

That's how time works.

After twenty, Nora quits counting by fives and her eyes never leave the clock on the dash. She keeps time in one-minute increments before she finally starts counting the seconds. *One, two, three.*

There are no missed calls from Penny. No missed texts. And she isn't answering her phone either. Nora tries reaching Hayden but feels bad interrupting his night out with new friends and, besides, he doesn't pick up.

Four, five, six.

She wishes she'd thought to ask where he was meeting the other husbands. But it's too late now. And if she doesn't reach a decision soon, Penny won't make her flight.

The engine's still on, humming through her seat. The lab reports sit on the passenger seat beside her, the one that's supposed to be occupied by Penny. She had thought the conversation would be better face-to-face. Because, for now, the pieces add up to nothing more than a suspicion, really. But in her gut, Nora believes Penny deserves to hear them.

Another three minutes pass, and Nora feels her spidey-senses begin to go haywire. She has to make a decision. Stay in the spot where they're meant to meet or go in search of Penny. She worries that if she leaves, they'll miss each other. Penny's phone might be dead or cracked open or dropped into a toilet. If you get lost, the advice is nearly always to stay put. But—for how *long*? Not forever. So.

A beat drums on in Nora's head. *So. So. So. So.*

Nora puts her lumbering SUV into drive. She won't be gone long. She'll just check the pool house, and if Penny is headed her way, they'll more than likely cross paths, so. *So. So. So.*

At nearly a quarter to nine, night is snuffing out the day like a candle. Straight ahead, the moon's electric. It could pass for full.

When she pulls up outside of Cornelia's house, the only signs of life come from the telltale fuzzy glow of lamps lit somewhere in its bowels. She disembarks from her car with extreme care, remembering Penny's request not to breathe a word of her impending departure to anyone else. *Calm down*, Nora remembers thinking. But now she tells herself the same.

She flips her cell to silent mode and slides it into her back pocket. The street's quiet. The ivy climbing up the walls of the White home whispers to her as she walks by. Nora opens the iron gate, steeling herself against a screech of metal that doesn't come. Once safely on the other side, she clicks it back into place. Traveling along the perimeter of the backyard, she sticks close to the topiaries and bushes. The moon's reflection bobs along the surface of the pool.

The detached pool house appears empty, the bathroom light on. Shadows consume the rest. She tries the door and finds it unlocked. Has Penny left without her? Is she on a plane at this very moment? The door opens with a *pop-swish* of the rubber weather seal.

Nora pokes around the room, using the flashlight on her phone to guide her. The book Penny had been reading—*The Invention of Wings*—is splayed like a fallen bird on the coffee table. In the corner, there's a stack of clothes folded neatly; in the bathroom, no evidence of Penny's makeup bag or toiletries. She slides open the shower curtain.

A tote bag leans in the basin of the white porcelain tub. Nora pulls the bag onto her lap and crouches on the tile. Inside, she uncovers Penny's wallet and ID, two granola bars, a pack of tissues, and a letter-size envelope marked *c/o Nora Spangler, Greenberg Schwall, Privileged Information* in Penny's looping handwriting. Nora fingers the stiff edges of the envelope, feeling the trifolded papers inside. She tucks it into the bottom of her purse alongside her keys.

She couldn't have boarded a plane without an ID. But then where is she?

Back outside, the night air is hot breath on every inch of her exposed skin. She eyes the main house and thinks: *At some point, I'll have to ask for help.*

Penny's still Penny. A recent widow. An even more recent psych ward patient. But for now, Nora intends to keep her word. At least unless and until she absolutely has no other choice but to break it.

Nora edges toward the large house. The interior shutters are flattened horizontally, so she can peer through the slats.

From this vantage, she can see straight through the lower floor—sitting room, fireplace, bookshelves, a part of the darkened kitchen, curling banister, front door, towering antique mirrors. Her breath leaves a white cloud of fog on the glass. No sign of Penny anywhere. Nora feels like a cat burglar.

So. Now what?

So. So. So. The internal beat thrums. Her baby gives a gentle kick in the vicinity of her ribs as if to change the *so* into *go. Go, Mom.*

She's about to leave when the beating inside her somehow becomes external. That's how it feels.

Thud. Thud. Thud.

Her stare is yanked back to the window. She either doesn't see it immediately or she does and it fails to register. She might have left, missing it entirely, but the dull pounding has turned her curious and once her brain has translated "that hand is a *hand*" into a language she can comprehend, she's rooted. Paralyzed.

She leans to the side for a better look. But a wall corner partially obscures her view. On the ground, on the slick hardwood, a hand stretches out by the bottom of the staircase, palm down. Reaching.

She must miss more than a handful of breaths because when her involuntary functions resume, her heart feels like thundering hooves. She coughs out: "Cornelia!"

Nora's at the back door. Locked. She yanks, trying to pry it free. Puts her foot on the house's side and wrenches with her full body weight.

"Asher!" She manages a deeper yell this time. "Cornelia!"

No response.

She can't tell if the hand on the ground has moved. But she confirms: It's still there. Someone has fallen. Or maybe collapsed. Someone needs help.

With sinking certainty, she believes she's found exactly who she's been looking for—Penny. Nora removes her phone from her pocket again. She taps the glass of the door, testing it several times. She takes a deep breath and tells herself not to think. Just do. She punches her phone through the tempered glass. It shatters in big, irregular shards, and she reaches through to flip the lock out of place.

"Penny?" Her voice is a scratch. She intends to barrel through the hall, but fear and apprehension turn her legs wooden. "Penny?" seems to be the only thing she can say. There's roaring inside her. A sea of white noise crashes against her borders.

Ohmygod. She probably doesn't say this out loud, though she definitely can't be sure. All gathered up in one clump, the letters that would form the words stick to the roof of her mouth.

Chestnut hair spews across the floor at the bottom of the staircase.

Familiar and unrecognizable. Penny is a foreign object. One leg still rests on the third stair from the bottom. It's like Nora's mind is taking snapshots and trying to make them animate into a sensible sequence.

Blood spatter coats the wall on the side that had been hidden from Nora's view when she was still outside. A pool of dark red seeps halolike from underneath Penny.

Nora thinks she's going to vomit as she experiences a disorienting bout of double vision. *It's not Liv*, she tells herself firmly. It is *not* Liv. But the reality is so visceral. Shockwaves course through her body.

"Cornelia!" Nora shrieks this time. "Cornelia! Asher! Somebody! Please. Come!" She doesn't even know whether they're home. She drops her purse beside her and bends down just as she hears footsteps. She pushes the hair from Penny's face. Her fingers come away bright crimson. "It's going to be okay." Nora's voice quakes. "We're going to get help."

Penny moves her lips. A clumsy, sucking motion, like a dental patient after Novocain.

"Don't move." Nora tries to marshal her own reserves. *Stay calm in case of emergency.* Her conscience is a flight attendant.

When Nora looks up, though, Cornelia is standing apart from them, her face stricken. "Oh my." She cups her hand over her mouth. "Oh my. Nora. Nora, it's okay." It's clear the sight has rattled Cornelia.

"I don't know what happened," says Nora. "I heard her fall. I was outside. We need to call an ambulance. Do you have any training?" Cornelia's at least a type of doctor, isn't she? She must have done basic ER training at some point.

"I'm so sorry." Cornelia presses her palms to her cheeks. She looks pale. Nora wonders if she's about to faint.

"She's still breathing," Nora says. "It can be okay."

Penny's brain could be bleeding. She could be hemorrhaging right now. Every second counts.

The clock in Cornelia's home *ticks, ticks, ticks*, taunting her.

"I really am." Cornelia shakes her head slowly. "This is devastating. The last thing I wanted was this. I can imagine how traumatizing this must be. I had no idea—Again, I'm sorry." Cornelia must be in shock.

"We need to do something." Should they perform CPR? Would that even work for a head injury?

When Cornelia speaks again she sounds much more calm and deliberate. "I don't want you to worry," she says, and Nora thinks, *good, she's taking over. Cornelia's in charge now.* "Penny's not feeling a thing. She's completely pain free."

Nora flinches. "How could you know that?"

"Cornelia?" Alexis appears with Thea following closely behind. Thea has a glass of wine in her hand. "Is everything okay?"

"Thea. Thank god," Nora says. "Please, she fell. She must have hit her head. I don't know if something happened before that. An aneurysm maybe. A heart attack. I found her like this." She's committed to giving Thea the facts. Thea's a surgeon. She can help.

"Oh god." Thea sucks in breath through her nostrils. It swells her chest. "I thought it would be over by now." She turns her face away.

Nora feels like a record skipping. "Is there anything we can do?"

"I'm going to be sick." Alexis closes her eyes and swallows.

"This was supposed to be quick." Thea skirts her eyes to the ceiling, as if willing Penny and even Nora to go away.

Cornelia speaks again. "Leave her," she says. "She's okay. She's moving purely by reflex. We've made this as humane as possible. Any of us would be lucky to go so blissfully unaware."

Nora hardens. At the sight of Penny in trouble, Nora's suspicions had blown away, but here, they click. Locking into place. "You mean, not like Richard." Nora's voice is low, and she's looking at Penny when she says it.

She feels Cornelia slacken, devolving into a less prim version of herself, the one Nora is accustomed to seeing. "I guess this really does crack open the egg. Yes. Richard was unfortunate. It's not usually this way. You have to understand. We've never had to do anything like that before. We had to be resourceful."

Still kneeling on the floor, Nora pushes her fingertips into the fleshy part of Penny's throat. The pulse is faint. "That's it. I'm calling nine-one-one."

They can deal with the question of Richard later.

"Wait." The word is a sharp command from Cornelia. "*Wait*. I only want what's best for you and I think it might be in your best interest to wait."

"If we wait any longer," Nora seethes, "Penny will die." Nora had gotten lucky once. Liv had survived. But she doesn't expect her luck to hold for a second time.

A tear slips onto Alexis's cheek. She presses her knuckle to the tip of her nose.

Cornelia removes something from the pocket of her cardigan. She tosses it to Nora. Nora misses it and it rolls against Penny's forearm. With trembling hands, Nora lifts an amber prescription bottle and reads her mother's name on the label. "How'd you get this?"

There's no Ambien left inside.

"Have I told you about how I grew up?" It's a deflection. And Nora gives Cornelia the satisfaction of reflexively shaking her head. "It was in the Family of Paradise Church. That's the proper name for it. Most people call folks like my parents 'Diceheads,' but I don't like that term."

There's an echo somewhere in the back of Nora's memory followed by visions of chanting and dancing and amphitheaters filled with people.

"My parents got married in one of the church's mass weddings. They'd been together quite a while by then—hippies for much of their lives. I was already ten when we joined The Family. To most, The Family of Paradise Church was, well, a cult. The media threw around a lot of scary, incendiary words like *brainwashing*. They weren't wrong." Beside them, Penny is still dying. Cornelia is talking. Penny is dying. Every passing second, Nora feels it. "But more academically, what they were doing was known as indoctrination. After the peak of the movement there was talk about deprogramming former members. My parents and I became estranged after I left the group as soon as I was old enough to fend for myself. I wanted to be someone. I wanted a career. I was ambitious and smart. I wasn't crazy for God. But I understood something about the church members. They wanted better." Cornelia's eyes burn bright and Nora finds herself too stunned to move, to speak, to break the spell of Cornelia's story. "That's the truth. They wanted to hear the good word and be changed. There's a concept in The Family known as 'indemnity.' Not like your legal indemnity. No. God's work to restore people to their ideal, unfallen state by having them fulfill indemnity conditions. That was what was known in the church as the Providence of Restoration through Indemnity. That made sense to me. I didn't—still don't—believe in God. It wasn't *God* creating those followers, it was the church leaders. I wish I would have made the connection myself, once I got married and tried having a career and children and a marriage. But it wasn't until I reconnected with a woman who'd once taught my Sunday school class at the church—Neha Vita—that I became involved in her work. I was a psychiatry resident then, doing research on certain aspects of the psychology of cults. I figured I had special expertise and I could really make a name for myself. At the same time, I'd gotten married and had a baby. I was so much like you, Nora." She squeezes her eyes shut and smiles, like she's recalling a sweet memory from one of her children's baby books. "I started looking up members of the church who had since left and that's how I found her."

"I don't understand. What does any of this have to do with Penny?" She feels stupid waiting, waiting for an answer, an explanation, for what? There has to be something, and that's what keeps her enrapt.

"Dr. Vita hadn't abandoned the teachings of the church, she'd been working to harness them. She saw the way toward indemnity." Something new comes over Cornelia. Fervor rises in her usually measured voice. Her face is alight with an inner force. "These roles that men and women so naturally fall into, the ones that make us crazy, the ones that keep us from becoming our best selves, those aren't nature, they're nurture. *Society* has performed the indoctrination and *we* are doing the hard work of *de*programming." She fans the heat from her cheeks.

It dawns on Nora that they've somehow moved off the subject of Penny entirely.

"We're inciting change. We're not just talking about it. We're not writing think pieces and going around and around in circles. We are making an actual difference."

"We?" Nora catches a glimpse of herself in one of the adorned mirrors. She looks like a wild thing caged. She looks crazed. No, *crazy*. Just like Penny had been.

But it's this, she realizes, that's kept her from calling 911: They think she's complicit. Complicit, though, in what?

"There are four different pocket communities around the globe like ours. Our community is especially exciting to Dr. Vita, given our recruitment of Thea, who has been working to further expand the reach of our procedures through her medical research and neuropathy. Otherwise, we employ many of the same tactics of The Family to help retrain our spouses to be better compatriots. You've, of course, witnessed much of this yourself. Love bombing. Physical stress. Thought reform. Channeling of guilt. Progression and harmony, it's a little different for everyone, and we use these tools to induce a sort of . . . let's call it suggestive long-form hypnosis."

Nora fights for calm. These are suburban women. That's all. Suburban women. Sub-urb-an wo-men. It becomes her mantra.

"But you didn't help Richard; you killed him," she says to Cornelia, hoping to shock the other two women into action. "You used Lestoil. I looked it up. It was found at the scene of the fire. Most cleaning products aren't flammable, but Lestoil is. Very. And the thing is, Penny never used it. Penny wouldn't have had it in her home at all." Who knew that her pregnancy nose would come in handy after all?

Nora waits for Alexis and Thea to freak out. That's what *she'd* do if someone told her that, say, Andi had killed someone. She would for sure have questions. Like a lot of questions. So many questions.

Why is nobody asking questions?

The answer is like a cement block tied to her feet. She sinks with it.

"You really are bright, Nora. You don't give yourself enough credit," says Alexis.

"Like I said." Cornelia's tone is gentle. "You remind me so much of myself at your age. You have *potential*." But Nora can't picture Cornelia with Cheerios in her hair and rewashing damp clothes forgotten in the dryer too long.

"I'm not like you," she says, wanting it to be true more than she's sure that it is.

The three other women look to each other like, *isn't she cute*?

Nora pulls back her shoulders, straightening her posture, which only makes her feel more pathetic—like a kid who's the last to learn what sex is and knows she's missing something, but can't figure out what. "Richard knew, didn't he? He started figuring it out. He was a good journalist. Which means he must have questioned things. And he—"

Cornelia holds up a palm, and despite herself, Nora hushes. "Yes. He was becoming less responsive. He was always the one who gave us the most trouble, but Penny loved him and he was her children's father, so we worked with what we had."

"You *had* a person. They could have, I don't know, gotten a divorce like normal people."

"And we could send him off to another unsuspecting woman and he would have thought that things would be different with her. And they would be for a time. Until the cycle repeated itself over again. Men want women to stay the same while women want men to change."

Thea takes a sip of her wine. "With my new surgical research, we're on track to make the changes permanent. We've already begun human trials. We can end the cycle. We're solving the problem of gender inequality. We are doing something. Isn't that thrilling?"

Nora's spit turns to putty in her throat. "You're a murderer," she says quietly, focusing on Cornelia.

"Now, now. You know this. Ask anyone. I was still at the gala when Richard died. With Penny."

It takes a second to soak in. Her heart pounds. She doesn't want to believe it. Doesn't want to admit how wrong she was about these women. Andi was right. Nora is experiencing a wave of vertigo. She's not sure whether she can remain standing. Her knees won't hold.

But . . .

Her ears ring. If it wasn't Cornelia. Nora's stare instinctively flits between Alexis and Thea, settling at last on Alexis. Not Cornelia. Now she remembers. That night at the dinner party. It wasn't Asher who had given the stain removal tip.

It was Max.

And it was Alexis who had left early to relieve Francine.

They are all in on it, for a penny and a pound, together. Nora begins to shake.

"Richard did set the fire. And he turned on the gas, which didn't help matters." Alexis looks every inch the tech CEO that she is, confident and capable, capable of anything.

"You brainwashed him. You hypnotized him. You told him to."

"All of our patients have free will when they consent to treatment. Including Hayden. You both did," Cornelia says, in a way that suggests she's growing weary of the conversation. "You wanted better. You came to me wanting to make your marriage work." She snaps her fingers. "Now it does. You should be thanking me."

Nora feels for Penny's pulse again. How much time has passed? She moves her fingers around, pressing, pressing, pressing. Until. She can't find it. She looks up at the women. "She's dead."

Thea crosses herself. "Hail Mary, full of grace," she murmurs.

"This is hard for us. We didn't want it to end this way," Cornelia says. "We wanted to help Penny. She came to us when Richard was out of control." Nora has a sudden flash of Lucy and her husband, Ed. They were the newest addition to the neighborhood. Alexis had said so herself. Not abusive. No. Fighting for consciousness. Fighting for autonomy. *Ed* is the victim. Not Lucy. Ed. And what had Thea said about her surgeries? Human trials have begun. "Richard was no longer an asset. He was too far gone. The plan was always to take care of the problem with Penny being none the wiser. We would never want to put her through that level of mental angst. We love Penny. Everything would have been fine. But she insisted on a lawyer and we had to go along with it. Anyway, in some ways, she was right. We agreed it would be best to do all the things normal people *do* in a tragedy. We had to act naturally so as to avoid any whiff of suspicion. So we searched for a lawyer who might come to see things our way, someone we could grow to trust, and found you. But the investigation—Francine, Sylvia—there were too many variables and Penny started wanting you to coordinate with the police again and it's obvious why we couldn't have that. We couldn't have a mess when it had all initially concluded so cleanly. So we told her the truth. Just before the Mother's Day celebration, as you've probably guessed. She didn't take it well. We figured she'd get over it. Eventually. But then you told me she was writing again."

Nora is hoarse. In her head, the ticker tape scrolls: *Penny is dead, Penny is dead, Penny is dead.* "It wasn't fiction."

"Most definitely not. It was insurance. Her account of what happens in Dynasty Ranch. Thanks to you, we've confiscated her laptop. We're grateful for that, truly."

And there it is. Nora betrayed Penny. She should have seen. She might *have* seen, but she didn't want to. Because there is a part of her—not just of her, but of every single woman—that is like them.

"She wouldn't have told." Nora's petition is obviously too little too late.

"Maybe not," says Alexis. "But also maybe. She was an ambitious writer. That's one of the reasons why we loved her. This would be a big story. And we can't have residents going back out in the world with no skin in the game, particularly when parting on terms that are less than amicable. With no significant other, she wouldn't have a need for us. Besides, Penny will be more famous than ever now. Artists who die young always are. People will know her work. Don't think we haven't thought this through. It's delicate, what we do here. Ever since Richard our balance has been . . ."

"Wobbly," Thea concludes, raising her wine to her lips again without taking a swig.

"Think of it this way: If you knew," Alexis says, "that one person would come up with the cure to, say, cancer, you would protect that person, wouldn't you? We have dozens of those persons right here in this community. And it's not just cancer."

Nora stands. When she runs her hands through her hair, she feels wetness hit her scalp. "I want you to fix my husband."

"You mean un-fix him," Cornelia says, and it could be Nora's imagination but she swears she bares her teeth. "You know what they say about those who live in glass houses."

Nora feels her face go red as Cornelia fishes in her pocket and pulls out her gold pen—*click, click, click.* There's movement at the top of the stairs. Something or someone shifts in the shadows. *Click, click, click.*

35

─ ─ ─

ora's legs go loose in the joints. Her husband descends Cornelia's stairs. "Nora, honey." His face lights up at the sight of her. Like she's the goddamn sun. "I thought you'd be in bed by now."

He is so open, so *sweet*. When had she forgotten how sweet he is? Deep laugh lines burst from the corners of his eyes, the lasting effect of a hundred floor tickles, a thousand airplane rides, a million light-saber duels, and countless hours of ridiculous couch commentaries.

She can't move. Can hardly even breathe. She's at their wedding day, on their honeymoon, with him beside her as they held Liv for the very first time, witnessing a miracle.

The memories pile.

And one by one by one, he steps down until this man, the one with whom she has built her entire life, is standing in front of her. She begins to splinter.

Red flecks dot the stubble of her husband's beard and spatter his nose like freckles. His hands are red-paint-bucket drenched. A nightmare. The horror is so surreal, she can't even scream.

"Hayden," she says as softly as if their heads were side-by-side on their pillows at night. "Hayden, what have you done?"

He has no idea. He reaches up to tuck a strand of hair behind her ear the way men do in the movies. And Penny's blood dabs against her cheekbone.

"I think we should all think about what the best course of action is." Cornelia's voice comes in as if from another frequency. "I figured you'd want all the facts before calling nine-one-one." Nora can't stop looking at Hayden. "Officially, as I see it, Penny was depressed. She took too many sleeping pills. She stumbled down the stairs and broke her neck. I'm her doctor. I might have even prescribed those sleeping pills, which might be useful, don't you think?"

"No," says Nora.

"Of course we could tell it a different way, but I'm not sure that way would go as well for you or your husband." Nora says nothing, which Cornelia takes as tacit permission to continue. "It had to be this way. If anyone was going to learn what happened, we figured it'd be you. Not that we don't trust you. We all have similar sensibilities and needs. That's why we *chose* you. But we can't leave anything more to chance. We'd hoped you would never need to know. Just like Penny. But just in case, now our motivations are better aligned." Her mother's Ambien bottle. Her husband. Her. They have roped her in, tied her to the crime, all for just in case.

"No," Nora repeats.

"Nora, this isn't self-serving. The world is a—pardon my language, but the world's a shit show right now. How many stupid Facebook posts have you seen about how things would be better if women ran the world? Think of all the contributions waiting to be made by an entire *half* of Earth's population. Do you realize the impossibility of materializing the potential of women's contributions to every industry, every facet of life, if all women are able to manage is survival?" Nora closes her eyes and tries to shut Cornelia out. "A child wouldn't grow if you kept her in a box, if you didn't give her food, room to exercise. If anyone saw that, they'd be horrified. Rightfully so. All around, I see women complaining about a time shortage. *Women*." Cornelia has to stop. It's too much. Nora plugs her ears but the words slip through. And what scares her the very most is that she hears herself agreeing. *Yes.* Her body says. *Yes.* "For far too long, it's been incumbent upon women to figure out how to scrap for enough hours in the day. So that's what we've done. We've figured it out. Men have been happily regulating our bodies for as long as anyone can remember. How is this any different?" Nora bends to the intoxicating lilt of Cornelia's pious speech. "None of it's trivial. It's not a game. Like Alexis said, we have a woman here who is literally helping children survive cancer. This is life or death."

Nora's fingers dig into her palms. Cornelia's right. It's never been a fair fight. The cards have always been stacked against women. And now that the idea's been planted, how can she possibly give it up? The answer is: She doesn't have to. She can give in. She can have a *life*. Her life. All of it. If you can't beat them, join these women, these powerful women who see potential in her, who want more for her without wanting her to *do* more.

Yes.

Yes, they may be right, but that doesn't mean what they're doing isn't wrong.

"You murdered two people." Nora won't say it. She will not lay the blame on Hayden. Her husband isn't a killer.

Cornelia's face darkens the moment Nora says "murder."

Nora backs away. Her mind is on a teacup ride.

Cornelia clicks the gold pen again. Again. Again. Soft footsteps from the living room into the foyer. Before she can turn. Something solid behind Nora now. She can't move. Hands on her shoulders. *Click, click, click.*

"Asher, honey, would you mind taking Nora out to the pool house while Alexis, Thea, and I talk?"

His fingers dig into Nora's biceps. She looks to her husband to do something, anything, but he does nothing but watch the scene play out with detached interest. She grits her teeth against the pain.

"Happy to help," Asher says. "I put tonight's leftovers in the fridge. Hayden's been such a big help." He smiles down at her. Actually *smiles*. "Great guy. Anything else you need right now?"

There is a strong instinct to maintain civility and Nora fights with every last fiber of her being to unhook herself from her manners and succumb to the tiny part of her lizard brain that's telling her to Get. Out. Now. She hikes her knee up and kicks directly into his shins. Then she does it again. "Richard . . . heard . . . clicking." She pants. She knows the trigger.

And again, turning on the third time to claw at a hand and sink teeth into his hand, catching a canine on his wedding ring.

The drag on her body goes slack.

Run, she thinks.

Without hesitation she sprints to the front door and tears it open, spilling back out into the night, gulping huge mouthfuls of air like a fish on land. Then—

Her keys. *Her keys.* She pats her jeans, her torso. She doesn't have her freaking keys. The purse is in the house. She looks back. *Not there.* She can't.

Nora takes off down the road. Feeling the moonlight on her, she juts off past one neighbor's house and into Alexis's yard, where she stops and rakes her hand through her hair. She's panting, her mind a jumble as she tries to think. Something. Anything.

Max. She looks up at the house, the sprawling, once mouthwateringly enticing house, uncertainly. He'd helped her with the tire. Would he—could he help her again? She's frozen with indecision when the door to Alexis's house cracks open. Gold light pours through onto the dark driveway.

Max?

"I thought I heard someone out here." Francine appears on the porch with baby Jax on her hip and Nora feels the chance and knows she has to take it.

"Francine." Nora's voice is pleading. "Francine. Please." She moves closer, and Francine recoils. Nora stretches out her hands to try to re-assure her but realizes too late she's probably frightening the girl. She stops in her tracks. Dead. "Francine." Her voice is shaky. "Francine, I get it. I get why you were hiding your relationship from your mother." She speaks quickly, her words slurring together. "Francine, I understand. You wanted to protect Devin. I can help you. Both of you. Please. I just need car keys. A car. Anything. I can help. We just need—" Nora keeps glancing back at the house, sure that at any moment one or all of them will come after her.

It's like she'd been looking at the image of Dynasty Ranch in a mir-ror and now that she's seeing it in real life, the entirety of the picture is reversed. Francine isn't just a teenage brat acting out. She's a young woman trying to do the right thing. Nora can help. Nora *will* help. She swears it.

"Francine!" She raises her voice, trying to startle the girl into action.

And then a shadow appears. Behind her. And Nora retreats two ner-vous steps before the shadow materializes into Devin. "Is everything okay?" he asks, kindly. He looks all of seventeen. A T-shirt slouched over the waist of his jeans.

"It's just that lawyer. Nora," says Francine, bouncing baby Jax, who claws at her hair until he's able to get a fistful of it into his gummy little mouth.

"Devin. Devin." Nora's eyes are saucer wide. "He was trying to call me. You were trying to tell me something. You knew. You *knew*, didn't you?"

Nora feels herself losing her footing, being washed away in a tsunami of new understanding, and she's left her husband back there. Alone.

Devin cocks his head. "Francine? What would you like me to do?" he asks.

"I'm the adult here," Nora tries. She has no authority. She's quaking. "And I believe you. You don't have to worry about anything. I know what you two have been dealing with and you two have been so mature and Devin—" She looks like a madwoman. She sees herself from their point of view. She probably looks drunk. Crazed.

"He's not going to tell you anything," Francine says.

Nora stays laser-focused on Devin. "This isn't her choice."

"He doesn't remember," Francine says.

Nora's eye contact with Devin falters. "Wha—What do you mean? He's been calling my work line, Francine. He can help us. I'm sure there was a reason."

Francine rolls her eyes. The baby is getting heavy and she tilts to one side. "Sure. There was. When he snuck out of the house that night, he overheard Alexis on the phone to my mom and what he heard spooked him. He got the idea that—that Richard's death wasn't an accident. I wanted to protect him from my mom, from—from all of it, really I did. I tried so hard. But, then you showed up and he started believing that he had to do the right thing. He had to tell what he knew."

"He's right." Nora nods fervently. "You are both right. I'm so proud of you. I know how much you love your father, Francine. I've seen it."

"I adore my father," Francine agrees. "I would do anything for him."

"Good. *Good.* Then, please, we need to hurry."

"I love him exactly how he is." A chill washes over Nora's scalp. "My dad is the best dad in the world." Nora is mouthing the word "no." *No. No. No.* "How's your relationship with your father?"

Francine had answered the phone. Francine had said it was the wrong number. But—

"Devin." Nora's begging now.

"I didn't want to choose between Devin and my family, but that's the choice I had to make," Francine says.

"Devin, come with me, honey. Bring your keys." Nora is backing down the driveway, twitching her open fingers for Devin like she's coaxing a cat toward her.

Devin watches her, unmoving. "I'm sorry, but I really can't tonight. Francine needs my help. She works so hard."

Francine offers Nora an apologetic smile. "You should come in. It's not so bad. I think you'll see that sometimes what they say is true. Mother really does know best."

Nora chokes on a scream. She clasps her hand over her mouth, and without another word, she pivots and runs back into the darkness, disappearing as she hears Francine say into a phone, "Mom?"

Nora crosses the street to another house. The ground is spinning under her feet as she crouches behind a row of bushes beneath the windowsill. Her lungs burn. The comforting lump of her cell phone presses against her from inside her pocket. She thinks of Hayden trapped in the house and as her mind puzzles through the options in rapid fire, she sees no other choice. She pulls it out. She has to try four different times before her thumbprint manages to unlock the screen. She steadies herself and hits the three numbers: 9–1–1.

"Hi, yes, operator? Someone's just died and I think—I think I'm in immediate danger." There's a high pitch to her whisper, as if she's accessed a brand-new register. "My husband, too, and can you please, please send someone quickly." She gives the operator her location. "Yes, I can stay on the line." All her neurons are actively bumping up against one another. Her knee shakes as she waits, watching Cornelia's house, waiting for someone to come after her.

Her breathing slows. She listens as the emergency operator relays soothing messages. Stay calm. Someone is on the way. They will be there any moment. It's going to be okay.

But she's wrong. Already it's not okay. The time for okay is long past. Now they are left with this. Irrevocably. Irretrievably. Inescapably.

Penny dead.

Hayden broke her neck, bashed her head in. The details are fuzzy, but there had been red. So much red. Remembering, Nora rubs her face, feels the blood coagulated there, tacky to the touch.

How many minutes?

No one is coming.

She's alone. She has to help Hayden. He would come for her if it were the other way around.

And then no siren but she sees flashing red and blue lights turn the corner, coming this way. A police car pulls into Cornelia's driveway, lurching when it's thrown into park.

"They're here," Nora says into the phone. "They're *here*." It comes out like a sob. Relief floods her as she hangs up and emerges from her hiding spot. She stumbles out from behind the bushes and once she's close enough she waves her arms overhead at the officer who's come to her rescue. "Over here," she says. "I'm the one who called. Me."

The officer is female, the angled, blue cap on her head, hair knotted neatly at the nape of her neck. She has wide brown eyes and cinnamon skin. She adjusts her holster as she gets out of the car and turns to meet Nora. "Ma'am." She looks at Nora with obvious concern. "Are you hurt?"

Nora checks herself and for the first time notices that her hand is bleeding from a long cut. She winces, thinking of her skin through the glass door. She tests it. Not deep. "Not badly, no. Just a scrape." She thinks of how to explain that she broke into Cornelia White's house. She'll stick with the truth. That's all she can do. The only way out of this mess.

"I'm Officer Aziz." She steps toward Nora, and Nora wants to run up and cling to her like a lost child. "I want you to take deep breaths.

You're safe now." She looks steadily at Nora and Nora nods to show that, yes, she's listening. "I'm here to help. Now, what seems to be the problem?"

Nora hears the creak of the door before she sees Cornelia appear on the front porch, regal and perfectly postured, in stark contrast to Nora, who is blood-streaked and wild-haired.

Nevertheless, Nora feels something like triumph standing next to the police officer. She's done it. *Screw you, Cornelia. You didn't think I'd really call the cops.*

"Responding to the call," Officer Aziz says.

"Maybe it's best if we all come inside so that we can talk this through," Cornelia says. She, too, is holding a cell phone in her hand. She drops that one to her side and beckons them in.

Nora looks at Officer Aziz uncertainly.

"That sounds sensible," says the officer. She offers Nora a comforting smile. *We've got this.* And so Nora follows her back into Cornelia's house. She almost expects the dead body to have been cleaned up. For Alexis and Thea to be on their knees scrubbing until the soapsuds turned pink. But Penny still lies where she has fallen—or was thrown—dead.

Nora's entire body shudders violently. The door clicks shut behind them. There's no Hayden, no Asher. No Thea or Alexis. The foyer's quiet. Two against one. Plus a corpse.

"I have information about the murder of Richard March." Nora speaks quickly. She won't give Cornelia the opportunity to speak first. "And now his widow, Penny. Richard died in a house fire a couple months ago here in this neighborhood. The fire was set by Alexis Foster-Ross. She's also a resident."

Static plays over the radio attached to the chest pocket of Officer Aziz's uniform. She unhooks it and holds it up to her mouth. "Yes, come in, copy. Officer Aziz reporting. I've responded to the call in Dynasty Ranch. Everything's under control. Over."

Under control? It hardly feels that way to Nora, but then maybe that's why she's not a police officer.

"Evelyn." Cornelia inhales. "Thanks again for coming. I know it's late."

"*Evelyn?*" Nora looks between the two women. Trying to compute is like trying to force two magnets of the same poles together.

Officer Aziz crosses the room and takes a seat on a chaise lounge. "Not a problem," she tells Cornelia. "Happy to help."

"You two *know* each other?"

Cornelia's lips flatten into a straight line. "Evelyn is a resident here and one of my favorite patients. Is Marcus well?"

"He is. Such a gift from god. I've been working late shifts and he has been such a help. I've hardly had to lift a finger at home. Praise the lord." She kisses her fingertips and lifts them gently to the sky.

"But—but *how?*" Such a small, inconsequential question from Nora.

"Alexis, of course," Cornelia answers. "As you've probably figured out, it's important to us to have women who offer a range of skills. Having a tech guru pays off. And Alexis is a great software coder, I'm sure she mentioned."

"You bugged my phone?"

"Only to keep tabs on the investigation and to make sure you were a good fit. Nothing to chance."

Nora's head hurts. Her cell phone had been chipped and so Cornelia was able to head off her call to the authorities by having Evelyn answer it. But Hayden's wasn't, which is why when he called 911 over the incident with Penny and Trevor, Cornelia had briefly lost control. She must have hated that. Even more than she'd let on.

Cornelia turns her attention away from Nora while Nora is still sorting through all that she's learned in the last hour. "Evelyn, I know I filled you in a bit over the phone on the way over."

Nora doesn't feel like she's getting oxygen. The edges of her vision blur. *What is happening, what is happening, what is happening.* Panic rises. The voices of the two women reach her as if she's underwater.

"Poor Penny," Evelyn is saying. "I'm sorry to hear it didn't work out. Such a talent."

"I agree."

Two against one plus a corpse. The game's flipped.

"And this is the new woman, then?" Evelyn tips her head, examining.

"Nora Spangler," Cornelia explains.

Nora feels her fate cupped in her hands. Fight or flight. Those are supposed to be her options. But she's already chosen the latter and failed. Could she fight? Can she do that if need be? She's out-armed. And assaulting a police officer—where would that land her? It would only make their job of burying her that much easier.

Instead, she feels unable to do anything but stand like a deer stuck in the crosshairs, waiting for the hunter to shoot.

"I think you've got the right idea of it." Evelyn Aziz pries herself from the cushion. She steps over to the crime scene and bends down to examine Penny's lifeless form. "Depressed. Too many pills. Accident. Maybe she even had something to do with the fire, if you need to cross off that angle. Guilt made her . . . ?"

"I'd considered that. If it comes down to it. Hopefully not," says Cornelia, in problem-solving mode.

"But that leaves Nora as a loose thread."

Nora spots her purse, a lump beside Penny's body. She gauges whether or not she could plow past the women. But then, Evelyn has a gun. A Taser. A club. So many things could happen to Nora in that short distance.

She suddenly thinks of Liv. Her daughter's face. The unborn child nested safely in her womb. A wave of emotion so strong it nearly collapses her crashes into Nora.

She has to get out of here.

"We'd hoped Nora would see eye to eye with us."

I do, Nora wants to say, but they'll never believe her. Not after she attempted an escape once. "Please," she says instead, because it's the word that feels most genuine.

"How would we eliminate her without raising suspicions?"

Nora's ears ring at full volume. Her blood is bass thumping inside her skull.

Convince them, her survival instinct shrieks at her. And she knows with sickening clarity that her very life, the future of her children, all depend on her ability not just to argue her case but also to fucking win it.

"It won't work." She fumbles the start, stammering, nearly incomprehensible with terror. Cornelia and Evelyn, her judge and jury, stare at her with the same interest that a well-trained dog might eye a steak.

She's never been any good in a courtroom. So she pictures herself at her desk. Head down. Crafting an argument. Prepared. Practiced. Her files and folders spread out before her. "In court, cases all come down to stories," she says. "People want a story that makes sense. Right now you have a cohesive narrative. A husband dies. His wife quickly follows. They're . . . connected. To anyone who might hear it, the story has an ending, and therefore people will swallow it. They can digest it. But getting rid of me creates a puzzle piece that doesn't fit. Someone will go searching for an ending."

"You don't have any real ties here," says Cornelia. It's Nora's cross-examination.

"That's not true. I put in an offer on a house here." She's steadied.

"With Isla," counters Cornelia, "who's one of our neighbors."

Nora's ready. "Sylvia Lamb knows, too. And you know she won't give it a rest. Even if I go missing. She's already tried to go to the news outlets once. I can help you with her. You'd be better off that way. I can make sure if she brings a lawsuit against you, that it goes away. I can represent you. But the second I'm gone, she'll smell something wrong. And what about Hayden? What about"—Nora can hardly say it, but she must, to prove her point—"my daughter? You'll never be able to catch up with the ripple effect unless you end it now. Think through the variables, as you put it. And you'll know that I'm right."

"You're still planning to move here, then?" Cornelia's look is incredulous.

"No. You make the seller let me out of the contract, free and clear. I want nothing to do with this." She won't think about what she's giving up. It's a no-brainer. Nora wants to quit these women.

"Then how can we be assured you won't give us . . . 'unwanted publicity'?" Cornelia uses air quotes.

"Hayden," Nora says.

"Your husband?" Evelyn asks. The woman who just described her own as a gift from god.

"He killed Penny, didn't he?"

Silence is all the answer Nora needs. It flips her stomach. The idea of her husband hitting a woman, pushing her—doing this to *Penny*, in particular—nearly sends her over the edge once more.

"He never deserved this." She sees now that she'd been naive to think that if she told the truth, she would have any more than a sliver of a chance of anyone believing her. They've tied her hands. They even used her mother's medication. The appearance of Evelyn as the officer in charge of the scene may just be her ticket through. She can erase Hayden from the night's events. She can do it as long as she cooperates. All Evelyn has to do is confirm in her report that, in her professional opinion, the scene appears to be the site of a terrible accident—too many pills, too many stairs. "The best way to make this work is if we all make it work."

This time Nora doesn't plead. She stands her ground. She lets the back of her knees sweat. She hides the tremors running up her thighs.

She hardly registers a single moment for the next five minutes. Only that she's won. Cornelia and Evelyn agree.

She is sure there are strings, but they are strings long enough to let her out of this beautiful house. Somehow, almost impossibly, she's awarded Hayden and her belongings. The air is fresh on her face. She's damp from head to toe.

Every home in Dynasty Ranch has neat lawns. Every home is sixty-three feet apart. Every home is a model home, perfect, a promise of domestic bliss. The American Dream. The white picket fence. She passes through the neighborhood one last time.

She will say nothing. She will wipe Hayden's stubble. She will burn his clothes.

When she relieves her in-laws from their watch over Liv, she won't be as polite as she should be, but they'll survive. It's only when she's undressing for the night that she'll remember Penny's envelope stashed in her purse: *c/o Nora Spangler.*

Cornelia doesn't know it exists. She breaks the seal and reads Penny's account of the precise events that led to her death, set down as only a writer like Penny could have done. Nora doesn't know how long she sits with the pages.

She's been given a gift. A hand from beyond the grave.

Penny's hand.

She knows what she has to do.

Nora lights the candle given to her by Alexis and dips the edge of Penny's final piece of prose into the flame. Penny drafted the piece for insurance. But in reality, it was always a liability. Nora smells lavender and vanilla as the words are kindled, scorched, and then, at last, devoured whole.

TWO YEARS LATER

Epilogue

There are wives everywhere. In yoga pants, in cutoff shorts, in mom jeans and power suits, high heels, gladiator sandals, orthopedics, and Toms, in ponytails, with curtain bangs, messy buns and dry shampoo caked to their scalps, with deodorant streaks and padded bras, leaky nipples and ample cleavage, with pregnancy weight and monogrammed water bottles and clothes that don't fit but never got returned, with tampons in their glove compartments, birth control waiting at the pharmacy and snacks in their purses as they push double strollers with ring fingers decked in round, cushion, emerald, and pear.

There they are, taking conference calls with China, teaching science, counting the minutes until bedtime, serving beers at halftime, skipping yoga, trying keto, neglecting recipe chain emails, texting babysitters, calling their best friends, remembering fourteen children's food allergies and all their moms' names. They are brides, the missus, nags, balls and chains, MILFs, girl bosses, total bitches, working moms or housewives, and tired as a mother.

And among them, Nora sits on a dining room chair that's been pulled up to a circle of like-minded women, each of them either having loved the book, hated it, never gotten around to starting it, or still trying to catch up on the one selected last month. Actually, Nora never has figured out how their minds are supposed to be alike, but it had sounded promising when the host, Katia, had invited her to join the neighborhood book club a year and a half earlier. Since then, Nora's slowly ticked her way through *The Underground Railroad*; *Educated*; *Normal People*; *Where the Crawdads Sing*; and a book about children who spontaneously combust.

Her chest is warm with the second glass of wine that had surely been purchased solely for its cute label and not its actual taste, which is fine by her.

"Okay, I know we're not supposed to *say* this," Jamila, a products manager at a local tech company, is saying. "But I just wanted the women to be *nicer* in the book." At forty, she's childless by choice but treats her two standard poodles like spoiled toddlers.

"Oh my god, you sound like my husband." Leah Malcolm rolls her sea-green eyes as she takes a slice of Brie from the charcuterie board. "This morning, he turned to me and says, 'I just think you could have been a little nicer to me this morning.' Nicer! I packed three lunches, brushed three heads of hair, made sure everyone went potty, did the dishes, put dinner in the Crock-Pot, put laundry away, and cut toast into quarters, and he thought what was missing was that I probably should have been *nicer*?"

Nora reminds herself that she ought to feel bad for Leah, though truth be told, Leah isn't very nice. Rose Bailey makes a face at Nora from across the circle, obviously thinking the same thing. Rose lives two doors down from the home that Nora and Hayden had purchased three months before the birth of their son, James, and the two had formed an unlikely alliance. According to her, Rose had fully intended to go back to work when her oldest started kindergarten, but had looked up to find that she was deep in the pursuit of raising good humans, and Nora loves her for it. Rose also believes very strongly that as a stay-at-home mom, she should only be expected to work business hours at mothering. The rest of the time, weekends for instance, should be evenly divided between her and her husband, Jerry. So far, as much as Nora can tell, Rose's principles on this matter seem rather bendy.

Jamila is a big hand-gesturer. She likes to emphasize her words. "I know, I *know*, I just get tired of how it's all *cutting* edge: Women can be *assholes* now! We *get* it. But what's so great about *assholes*? Does the world *really* need more of *those* right now?"

"I bleached my asshole." Nomi bites into a samosa and the women all laugh at different octaves because, here, at book club, they are fun. They're smart. They get to have nice things. They're naughty. They wonder aloud about the type of porn they find on their husbands' computers— why is lesbian porn so popular for men whereas gay porn hardly has a foothold among the heterosexual women they know? It's the big, important questions like these that warrant a night away, drinking wine and looking the other way as their husbands order pizza with loads of saturated fats to feed their starving children.

"Stop," says Maria. "Is that something we seriously have to think about now? I can't."

"I do it because it makes *me* feel good," Nomi deadpans.

"Well, I think that's nice," adds Rose.

As these monthly meetings have gone on, the amount of time spent discussing the book has grown shorter and shorter until now, as Nora begins her walk home with Rose, a little bit tipsy, she can't even recall if they'd gotten around to discussing the big twist ending.

Rose takes off her shoes and walks barefoot on the asphalt. They live in the sort of small, affordable subdivision where children play in sprinklers and neighbors issue citations for trash cans that remain on the curb too long. Nora likes it here. Life's good. Everything's fine.

"I feel like we should have another glass of wine," Rose says. "My buzz is already starting to go and I want more chocolate." A month or two ago, Nora introduced Rose to Andi, who now lives in Saint Moritz with a much older woman, and the pair got on famously. She and Andi never spoke again about the missed layover or the argument over the women in Dynasty Ranch. In the end, they didn't need to. Within weeks, the issue resolved itself and, for different reasons, they were both relieved to let it go.

And now she has Andi plus Rose. And Maria and Nomi and Katia. These are women who will never go to war together, but together they will text before 6:00 A.M. and offer thoughtful opinions about the mean boy at school, and at least one of their children will vomit in the lap of a woman who is not his mother and isn't that the same, really?

"I feel like if we do, I'll have a hangover for work tomorrow." Nora looks in at the mostly darkened windows, passing the blue glows of television screens inside. It's almost ten o'clock. A small dog yaps at them from one of the fenced backyards. Tomorrow, she has an oral hearing, an event that still sets her nerves on edge. She made partner narrowly, and then, a year ago, Gary suffered a fatal heart attack, making Nora the heir to all of his clients. "Do you remember when we used to not care about hangovers? Now, a night out is all well and good until a tiny hand is tapping you between the eyes at six in the morning." James, to her bereavement, is an early riser.

"You know, book club has taken on an almost mythic quality in my house," Rose says. "Alice saw the *Real Housewives of New York* and she said, 'Mommy, is that what you do at book club?' They were at a celebrity-chef restaurant. I've never even been to New York. Anyway, there's always a big fuss from Riggs about how fancy I look. I'm wearing jeans, Nora. It scares me to think what I must look like to them most of the time."

"You're doing manual labor in there. You've got to dress for the job."

"I do sweat a lot," Rose agrees.

They stop. Rose's house is the farther one. Another couple doors down.

"Well," Nora says, not really wanting the night to end either.

"I'm going to take a bath and finish the book we just talked about." Rose checks the time on her phone. Book club never ends at a respectable hour, everyone wanting to ensure that, for tonight, they miss the nighttime routine altogether.

"I'm going to bed." Nora yawns. "I almost skipped tonight. I haven't been sleeping well."

"You can't skip," says Rose.

"I know."

They say good night and Nora watches until Rose has unlocked her front door and slipped inside. Then Nora enters her own home. She hangs her purse—not her usual diaper bag—on the hook in the foyer.

"Mommy!" James comes barreling toward her, wearing only his Pull-Ups. She listens to the slap of his small feet.

"How was it?" asks Hayden, getting up from the couch and pocketing his phone.

"What's he doing awake?" The wine suddenly feels like a big mistake.

"He wouldn't go to sleep. I tried everything. He wanted you. He loves his mommy." Hayden says it like it's the best compliment in the world.

In the living room, *PAW Patrol* blares from the TV.

The house looks like a small tornado tore through it. There are fast-food bags on the table. Dishes piled in the sink. And, yes, her children are alive, but Liv's socks and underwear are on the floor and there's actual urine in James's baby potty and it's dried and now she's going to have to run it through its own cycle in the dishwasher.

It's amazing the lies that Nora tells herself. The willful amnesia. The belief that this time she can leave for a few hours and there won't be a price to pay for it upon her return. *Just once*, she will think. And then the next time she will get her just once. She'll come back and at least the kids will be in bed. But, really, she should have wished for just twice, just four times, just every single time. Because it's usually just the once and this, this disaster she's returned to, is the always.

Nora turns off the television.

Nora picks up James.

Nora carries him to his room.

Nora reads him a book.

Nora sings him a song.

Nora kisses his forehead. He's already fast asleep. And Nora tries to remember how lucky she is. Because hers is the beautiful family in the photographs mounted in the hallway, dressed in white, smiling from a sandy beach, and she is the woman at the center of them. A loving wife. A devoted mother of two. That's what her tombstone will say.

After doing a quick power pickup of the house, she changes for bed and slips her night guard over her teeth. Lying in bed, she does a thing she sometimes does: She imagines a place, a place where there are wives everywhere, yes, but instead of waking up in the morning already overwhelmed by the full weight of their household's duties, they do half and feel in control, they shop alone, they accept positions that require work travel, they talk to their sisters uninterrupted, they eat enough fruit, get their hair cut on weekdays and take baths without being barged in on, they come home to clean houses and to-do lists in their husbands' handwriting, they remember their great idea for that new marketing campaign, stay awake in meetings, score promotions, figure out the meaning of life.

Nora watches her husband, her sweet, sweet husband, with the kind eyes and the fading blue tattoo, wash his face and brush his teeth and she is so glad that she married him, so lucky to have the sort of family so lovely that if something tragic were to happen to them, they would make headline news.

Her heart beats. She rifles through her nightstand drawer, and in the back, she feels around for what she's looking for: a sleek rectangular box. With each birthday, Nora has found herself less willing to endure life's small discomforts, like thong underwear, a feeling she's noticed coincides perfectly with her increasing resistance to dealing with men's bullshit. It has been two years since she held it. But now, she flips open the box and takes out the gold pen nestled inside.

Honestly, whose fault is this really? How long did husbands think this arrangement could go on? Forever? Is that what they believe, that their wives will simply drudge for eternity? When, in history, has that ever been the case?

Nora turns the pen between her fingers. Hayden pads to their dresser and pulls on a fresh pair of boxers. She thumbs the top.

And clicks.

Author's Note

At *The Husbands*'s inception, I was seven months pregnant with my second child and starting to freak out about the recalibration of domestic chores that comes with a new baby. After the birth of my first child, a daughter, I seriously considered asking for a reduction in pay because I felt so overwhelmed with my competing worlds and guilty about failing both at home and at work. I was desperate to find a way to diminish that guilt, if only a little.* My husband and I went on to spend the last four and a half years slowly but surely getting into the groove of new parenthood and all of its shared responsibilities, an adjustment that came with no shortage of—to put it gently—growing pains.

Meanwhile, I was struggling to land on an idea for my next novel and struggling even more to figure out when and how I was actually going to write the thing with my due date (the baby, not the book) fast approaching. I'd recently had a long conversation with two of my best friends about the book *Fair Play* by Eve Rodsky and our efforts to implement its advice in our own homes. Honestly, I love that book and think it offers a helpful and practical framework to discuss the division of household labor with your spouse, but what sparked for me was the

---

* Thankfully, a well-timed read of *I Know How She Does It* by Laura Vanderkam convinced me not to.

way in which we talked (and talked and talked) about it. We were impassioned, yes, but also a bit befuddled. Nobody taught *us* to pack diaper bags. Do our husbands not *see* the clothes piled at the bottom of the stairs that need to be brought up? Why, when our husbands are in charge of making plans, are there so many missing details? Sure, they're happy to help when asked, but why do we have to be the ones asking? Especially when the very act of asking is so loaded that it tends to go by another name entirely—*nagging*.

It feels like women are such a critical component to our family's ability to function that we find it nearly impossible to unhook our minds completely and focus our undivided attention elsewhere. A benign example: We went on a weekend trip with another family. Both dads fell asleep for a midday nap and we, the moms, decided to let them sleep while we watched our collective four children. When the dads woke up, we mentioned our plan to get in a thirty-minute at-home workout and asked that they wrangle the kids during that time. Five minutes in, we were doing push-ups with toddlers on our backs, squats with kids hanging off our thighs, crunches with children sitting on our stomachs. And although the dads did attempt to shepherd the kids away, they surrendered with protests of, "We can't help it! They want to be with you!" And I thought: Wow, this is a perfect physical manifestation of how life feels right now. I'm out there trying to do all the things I'm supposed to—pursuing a career, negotiating for higher pay, practicing self-care, dating my spouse, exercising, keeping passably up-to-date on fashion trends—but I'm so loaded down.

And this isn't even a problem that affects only mothers. This affects all women. When I was a young associate, before kids or even marriage, I remember having to stay late for days on end, at last glancing up to realize I didn't have any clean clothes because I wasn't able to leave work before the dry cleaner closed. I didn't have any groceries either. I needed what a lot of the men in the office already had—a wife. I seriously worry that when men are out in the world taking for granted how cared-for they are, it can make the energy of overwhelmed women in their office read frazzled, or worse, incompetent.

Women spend almost twice as much time on unpaid work as their male counterparts, and strangely, even though younger people are becoming more open-minded about gender equality and the very notion of gender itself, younger couples aren't doing any better.[*] Where we *have* seen a shift is in parenting. As intensive parenting has become more in vogue, dads have gotten more hands-on with childcare, likely because it's more fulfilling than, say, doing the dishes.[†]

During the Industrial Revolution, men began leaving the family farms to work outside the home while women took over domestic life.[‡] This led into the nineteenth century, at which point men started to shape their idea of masculinity around two things: providing an income and avoiding anything considered "feminine," which came to include tasks viewed as "women's work."[§] While family dynamics have changed, the vestiges of this complex remain. This is all to say that what happens in our homes can feel incredibly personal, when, in fact, the issues are systemic.

As I wrote *The Husbands* I asked every woman I came across one question: In your fantasy world, what do you wish your spouse would do for you? The answers were varied and personal and deeply enlight-

---

[*] Donner, Francesca. "The Household Work Men and Women Do, and Why." *The New York Times,* February 12, 2020, https://www.nytimes.com/2020/02/12/us /the-household-work-men-and-women-do-and-why.html.

[†] *Ibid.*

[‡] Strauss, Elissa. "Getting Dads to Do More Around the House, Starting with a History Lesson." *CNN,* November 14, 2019, https://www.cnn.com/2019/10 /22/health/dad-father-equal-parenting-house-wellness-strauss/index.html?utm _content=2019–10–22T13%3A10%3A07&utm_term=link&utm_medium =social&utm_source=twCNN.

[§] *Ibid.*

ening. Drafting the book has been cathartic for both my husband and me, a way to externalize a specific battleground we often find ourselves marching onto. But criticism on an individual scale diverts focus from the critique of entrenched gender norms that still haunt our culture today. We can elbow and push all we want for every packed lunch, picked-up towel, put-away pan, and scheduled doctor's appointment, but until paternity leave is normalized, until schools call fathers about sick kids as often as they call mothers, until sons are given not just the same number of chores but the same types as daughters, until the helpless sitcom dad with a tool belt isn't quite so loveable, I'm skeptical of how much ground we're really gaining.

I happen to be loud about this issue, but I frequently find my heart heavy with the weight of women's quiet struggles. With their invisible efforts. With their impossible tradeoffs. And my hope is that this book makes mad women everywhere cackle with the possibilities put forth inside these covers, and just for a moment, that it feels like venting to a best friend, that it makes the unseen obvious. And that, like with my book *Whisper Network,* you'll tell me all about it.

Acknowledgements

Writing this book was a labor of love, but labor nonetheless, and I'm incredibly grateful that so many wonderful people stepped up to share in this project equally.

My deepest gratitude goes to my editor, Christine Kopprasch. There's nothing more valuable to me than having an editor who truly gets me. We've each survived a crazy year of working and giving birth to our second children and that will always make the memory of this process special—and fitting—to me. To that end, I'm especially fortunate to have had Caroline Bleeke step in with kind, smart, creative notes that improved my draft vastly while Christine was on maternity leave. This is my second book with Flatiron and it already feels like home. I'd heard wonderful things about Megan Lynch before she took the helm, and they've all proven to be true. Thank you, Megan, for your insight and care with my work.

The Husbands has brought another chance to work with an outstanding group of people who are taking the "second shift," as it were, in launching it. Thank you to Amelia Possanza, Nancy Trypuc, Katherine Turro, Maxine Charles, Samantha Zukergood, Katy Robitzski, Shelly Perron, and the rest of the team working behind the scenes. And an extra squeal of gratitude to one of my favorite narrators, Allyson Ryan, for agreeing to narrate the audiobook.

My agent, Dan Lazar, remains my most trusted ally. I need some-one with big thoughts, dreams, and ambitions like me to be on my side, so thank goodness I have you. A special thank-you also to Torie Doherty-Munro for helping me with all things big and small and book related. Maja Nikolic, Peggy Boulos Smith, and Jessica Berger, thank you for taking great care of my words across the globe.

Which brings me to Cath Burke and Rebecca Saunders. I feel like we are kindred spirits; you got my vision for this book right away and I'm lucky to be the beneficiary of your sharp guidance.

My film agent, Dana Spector, is another woman I am so fortunate to have on my team because she, too, gets it—motherhood is hard! I'm absolutely indebted to you for the work you've done on this book and others.

This story is a direct product of conversations with so many of my wise friends, both writers and nonwriters alike: Julia Jonas, Emily O'Brien, Kelley Flores, Jeff Langevin, Lori Goldstein, Charlotte Huang, Shana Silver, Amy Morehouse, Wendy Pursch, Lisa and Julia McQueen, and many others. But even before those conversations, the kernel of this idea was planted by the readers of *Whisper Network,* so many of whom expressed in book clubs, online, and in direct emails to me that their frustrations with work were also deeply rooted in their frustrations at home. Hearing from readers is already the best part of being a writer, and now these readers have helped spark something brand new.

But there is one person I would absolutely not have been able to write this book without, and that's Rob. To write *The Husbands,* I had to have a wonderful husband of my own, who knows my heart for women's issues and stands up for me and what I've set out to say—a true ally. We have two beautiful children, but drafting a book with a two-week-old is certainly a family activity and I'm so deeply moved that all three of you took it on with me and gifted me the space to work—thank you.